JOURNALS
OF A
MASTER

Also by John Preston

JOURNALS OF A MASTER

Two Classic Gay Erotic Novels:
Entertainment for a Master
The Love of a Master

John Preston

alyson
books

LOS ANGELES •NEW YORK

Manufactured in the United States of America.
Printed on acid-free paper.

This trade paperback original is published by Alyson Publications Inc.,
PO Box 4371, Los Angeles, California 90078-4371.
Distribution in the United Kingdom by Turnaround Publisher Services Ltd.,
Unit 3 Olympia Trading Estate, Coburg Road, Wood Green,
London N22 6TZ, England.

First edition: July 1997

01 00 99 98 97   10 9 8 7 6 5 4 3 2 1

ISBN 1-55583-401-9

Library of Congress Cataloging-in-Publication Data
Preston, John.
    [Entertainment for a master]
    Journals of a master : two classic gay erotic novels / John Preston. – 1st ed.
    Contents: Entertainment for a master – The love of a master.
    ISBN 1-55583-401-9 (acid-free paper)
    1. Gay men–Sexual behavior–Fiction. 2. Erotic stories, American.
  I. Preston, John. Love of a master. II. Title.
PS3566.R412E58 1997   97-11710 CIP
813'.54—DC21

Entertainment for a Master

To V. K. McCarty

The Ad

Volunteers Needed
For a very private, very elegant
S/M party for a discreet group
of ladies and gentlemen to be
held in San Francisco. Men
must be well-built and attractive, willing and able to perform servile tasks and endure
moderate to heavy pain. Only
the very willing and the experienced need apply.

The Reaction

The phone calls began the moment the advertisement appeared. Of course it hadn't mentioned my name or telephone; these were people who recognized the box number in the return address. These were not the new and unexplored ones I had hoped to hear from. Instead I was getting the reactions of people who already knew me.

The first, interestingly, was from the editor of a periodical in which the notice appeared. I thought perhaps I was being called to talk about an article. But he quickly brought me around to the real subject at hand. "What are you doing?"

I still hadn't a clue and made some inappropriate response about a project. "No, no," he said excitedly, "What are you doing at the party? Can I come? I want to be there."

I laughed at him. He was one of those terribly clean-cut young professionals who always disdain those certain elements of my sexuality they find socially unacceptable — at least they do in public or in print. But when there appeared even a small likelihood that I was holding a function where he could become a participant, then the other part of my life was glamorous — so long, I'm sure as no one would know of his involvement.

I waved the comments off. "No, no, it's a special event, only a very few people. And what, by the way, were you doing reading those classified ads? I didn't even think you were aware they existed."

That shut him up. The responsible image he tries to project isn't compatible with looking in prurient classifieds, even if they do pay his salary. He was seldom caught admitting that he did.

His call wasn't an isolated incident. Many people I knew had discovered the notice and decided that this event had sufficient potential that they would broach with me the subject of attending. Other authors, none who would dare write erotic literature, suddenly found my activities entrancing. The most obnoxious thought they could cover their reactions by joking about my party.

I wasn't in the mood for that to happen. I simply turned those off completely. To a few others, people I respected, I explained that the event was for Madame and Adrienne, and that Phil would be the only other man. It was set up only for the four of us.

Implicit was the statement that only the four of us would properly enjoy the entertainment that was planned. That was too harsh a judgment, but it had some reality to it. I had certainly hosted other events where many more guests had been in attendance and everything had gone on perfectly, but this party was a special performance.

It was my own reentrance into the life that I had left behind five years ago. I had moved to the country, bored by the city that had become more of a distraction to my work than a stimulation. In my rural home, the opportunities for the carnival sex life I had left were few and far between. I was more dependent on the visits of strangers and the kindness of friends who were willing to travel the long miles, at least in summer. Winter visitors in the north country are rare beasts indeed.

But now I'd be in San Francisco. Madame, my beloved if difficult friend, would be there at the same time. Phil lives across the bay in one of those industrial cities. Above all, there'd be Adrienne, the elegant author who had filled all our nights with fantasies.

The world the four of us shared was one of words and photographs and of appeals to higher planes of sexuality. Madame, Phil, and I had all aspired to it for years. We had learned its outline by living it in the sexual ghettoes of the modern urban world. There is still, in some ways, the smell of those places on us. We don't deny that. We nurture the memory of the odors fondly.

But Adrienne has joined us on her own. Her path has been less convoluted, her message more beautiful in a way. If her descriptions are less realistic, they are all the more precious for their eloquence.

Our circle is joined by separate lines. The distances between Madame's townhouse in New York, Adrienne's Victorian mansion in San Francisco, Phil's adored retreat in the East Bay and my own country home span thousands of miles.

We had each met in couples over the years, but never had there been a time when we four could sit in the same room and smoke cigarettes, enjoy conversation, simply be in one another's company.

Madame is ready to ritualize anything we can. It is her desire, her hope that she lend beauty to life with displays of courtly manners and appreciation of grace.

Phil had been so much a part of the sexual world that he could judge what were the most perfect sexual events. He could sit and watch any scenario I could develop and enjoy every element that I had worked to add to the piece. It follows, of course, that he could be my most severe critic. If my idea lacked authenticity, it was he who would pounce on me and actually be offended.

Adrienne would have her chance to see it all happening. She had been anxious in our conversations to know the details, to discover just how movements were made. Her fantasy life had reasons, she wouldn't want to participate in the few opportunities that other people could offer her.

I could do that. I could make this event happen for her. I could offer Madame a chance to see service in perfection. I could make this party an offering to Phil, a thank-you for the years of education he'd given me.

At a book convention? Where else? Why not? It was our chance to be together.

Other callers claimed I was doing this only for the sake of shocking the establishment around me. That wasn't my intention. But someone passed on the ad to the organization sponsoring the convention. Somehow the message had been garbled, and they were convinced that I planned a demonstration on the floor of the convention. I found the idea humorous and couldn't keep from laughing and wasn't able to hide the fact that publicity was the furthest thing from my mind.

My mind was on reentering the sexual world — with a vengeance. Why? That's one of the questions I've learned not to ask. My fantasies dictated it. My urges demanded it. It had been a long time since I had explored these things in reality. I had made my retirement from the scene for a period of time, and I intended to return to the country again. But now I wanted to make this one step.

I had lived my life, before leaving the cities, by merging fantasy with reality. I had gone out and done things that other people would whisper about. I had not been harmed, and harming others didn't interest me. I was interested in the beauty of sex and the possibilities of dreams coming true.

My current vision was accessible. I could achieve it with integrity. I could make a gift of an extraordinary evening to three important people in my life. I saw no reason not to attempt it.

One of my callers complained that to imbue my sexual activities with so much glamour was dangerous, it would make them more desirable to people who shouldn't be enticed into my particular sexual practices. I immediately rejected that argument. My sexual thoughts and actions are many things, but they are not hypocritical and they are not produced to do anything but give immense pleasure.

Who do I think I am? the caller asked me. What right do I have to take the private acts of sexuality and the fantasies of people and make them events, write about them, photograph them, lead them into being real?

I am the ringmaster of the circus. I direct the lights, and I coordinate the acts. That is my skill, my first love, my contribution to a world full of blandness and dreary morality.

I knew from the start that my party would be success.

The Thought

The idea of sexual service produces horror and strange anger in our society. It's sad. People find no problem with forcing teenagers to work in disgusting fast food shops, or with women being sent to the meaningless tasks in department stores, or about the kinds of jobs minority men are assigned to. But when the option of sexual labor is presented, there's an outcry.

The vehemence of the protest has little to do with reality. At least some prostitutes of both sexes continue to stand up and say they enjoy their work and receive adequate compensation, but they're never believed. Stars of pornographic movies can relate their intense personal enjoyment in the indulgence of their sexual exhibitionism, but the overseers of our morals demand that these people must be unhappy.

Even more stupid is the denial that we, as a culture, already drench ourselves in a sort of sexual slavery. So long as the words are never used we don't have to acknowledge the ways we honor and utilize sexual service. We deride pornography but grace the pages of our finest magazines with suggestive photographs of handsome men and women in their underwear. We send out young college men onto football fields where we demand they earn their educations by exhibiting intense physical sadomasochism for our enjoyment.

That example, college football, is one of the most amazing for me. I am a passionate fan of the sport, tending to follow those teams where the athletic directors seem to be at least unconsciously aware of their purpose and so dress the players in uniforms that are cut to reveal strong stomachs. While I sit and study the gridiron stars with my cock hard and my fantasies running rampant, I identify with my predecessors in ancient Rome.

These are our gladiators. These young men have turned themselves over to sadistic coaches who force them through appalling physical exercises. They've entered into a period of bound servitude much like that used in colonial America where free Europeans would sign over a period of their lives to a master in return for a future reward — citizenship, or perhaps land to settle upon that would be otherwise too expensive. In the same way these athletes give up their youth in hope of an education or some other prize.

For that future compensation these men will perform on the field, vying for my attention, experiencing untold tortures for my enjoyment, displaying their bodies in often obscene juxtaposition with other men's for my titillation. But, we're told, this is not sex. This is simple amateur sport. The farce becomes obvious when the season ends and the tallies of the universities' profits are made public.

I would much rather that the sexual reality of our lives and the desire of some of us for sexual service were open and honest. If I am to receive sexual pleasure from young men in return for my payment and my loyal following of their careers, then the world of sport could deliver that to me with much greater efficiency than it does now if only they would wipe away the moral hypocrisy that has infused our thinking.

What would my fantasy be?

Of course, there would be may options, but let me follow through with the example of athletics. We pay exorbitant amounts of money to enjoy the images of professional wrestlers making fools of themselves in staged and comic sport. We rob those men of their stature. I would rather see a situation where they're not deprived of their elegance. My view, of course, demands the acceptance by all of us that there is dignity in work. A job well-done and amply rewarded should be respected.

Here is the way I wish professional wrestling were set up:

There would be a public space, an amphitheater, where the ring would be surrounded by a limited number of seats. The cost would be high, but the entertainment value so immense that many of us would pay the admission. We would be seated in the round and wait for the wrestlers to arrive.

They would be handsome young men, well-trained and fed, given the best exercise programs and the most comfortable living arrangements to compensate for their hard labor. When two of them entered the ring, a hush would come over the crowd. There might be an occasional remark, a little joke, a pointed comment on the perfection of the bodies we were viewing, but nothing more.

The men would wear protective headgear and athletic supporters and boots. They would have on the wrestling singlets that are so highly sexual.

The rules would be strictly enforced by a referee. There would be no set-up here; the winner and loser have too much to lose or gain to even think of throwing the fight.

Imagine that there are two men now. Let's give them names and personal features. There's James. He's the younger, only twenty. He's smooth-skinned, blond, his hair is close-cropped and his eyes sparkle. They're that shade of blue that seems to lose its color in bright sunlight. He's anxious for the match to begin. He's waited for this moment when he could enter the ring for this big challenge of his.

His opponent is Roger. He's only slightly older, twenty-five, but he's a veteran of the ring by now. He's calmer, less enthused in a way. But he's hardly taking the event lightly. Another win will move him further forward in his life choices. Besides, while James is focused on the match, Roger is already interested in the outcome.

Roger is dark-haired. His head is covered with short, tight curls, and his chest has a full mat. His legs, too, are hirsute, and his arms as well. But there isn't such a covering that the firm, finely etched muscles aren't obvious to every one of us looking at him.

The match begins. The two men start in a traditional greco-roman position. They struggle as James finds an unexpected reservoir of strength and — almost too quickly — Roger is pinned. The younger blond man hears the official's announcement and jumps up, throwing his hands over his head in a victory stance. "Not so quick, youngster," someone from the audience jeers at him. "Don't think that fine butt of yours is safe yet!"

The expression of Roger's face has darkened. He hadn't thought the younger one could do it. But the veteran's polish is coming through now. There is a determination that underlines the impact of the other cries coming from the crowd. "What, Roger, are you so horny you're going to throw the fight?"

No. Not at all. The two men resume their positions. The official signals them to start. Just as quickly as his opponent had moved before, Roger now finds the right moves and acts at just the right times, and James finds himself flattened and helpless on the ring floor.

It's a tie. When the two men stand this time and face one another, the crowd goes wild. "Who gets it?" one woman screams from the far corner. "Save some for me, Roger," a man yells across the way.

The combatants are oblivious to the sounds now. Their moments of truth are coming closer. Again the official calls them to their positions. Again they take their stance. The signal is made, and they begin their final attempt.

The sweat has plastered Roger's body hair to his skin. The strain on his face shows his determination. There's just as much of the sweat and resolution on James. This match lasts much longer so long that James's youth shows. Tears flow from his eyes from the pain and the agony of the confrontation. Perhaps, too, he's in touch with his fear of what might follow if he loses. Maybe the full force of that hadn't struck him until now. After all, it's his first big match, and no matter how many private showings and practice sessions there might have been, nothing can prepare a wrestler for the crowd and its noises and its rough verbal demands.

They sneak and slip out of one another's embraces. There seems to be no end. The first two times were so quick, but now the audience is getting its money's worth as the gladiators vie for the win. It looks, for an exciting moment, as though Roger has done it, conquered the young upstart. But there's a quick movement, a lucky hold, and the audience cheers with delight as the older man is pinned, his shoulders immobile and his defeat obvious to everyone even before it's declared by the official.

Now comes the climatic scene, the reason for the crowd's delight. Waiters and waitresses rush through the stands to deliver beverages, knowing the guests will want refreshment.

Not that there's any break in the action on the stage. The official has, appropriately, moved on to the next part of the performance. He stands in his uniform and puts his fists on his waist.

James has been sent to his corner, but Roger remains in the center of the ring.

He lowers his eyes, refusing to answer the catcalls and whistles that have increased in their intensity. He unties his high boots while kneeling on the stage. He stands when the shoes and socks have been removed, and, following another order from the official, he pulls off first one and then the other shoulder of his singlet. The wrestling outfit falls to his waist.

The crowd roars. Roger is obviously humiliated. We don't care if it's by this or by the idea of having lost a match for the first time in months. He's not used to this role in the game, and it only increases our pleasure in viewing him.

The rest of the singlet comes down, and he's standing in only his supporter, his firm, hairy buttocks are now exposed to our view. Those of us who've not seen them before are able to get a good look at them as he is forced to slowly revolve on the stage.

Then he pulls off even the supporter. Again, the official commands him to display himself. Now, naked and his cock beginning to rise in the fear or anticipation of what will happen, Roger is forced to walk the perimeter of the entire ring. His pace must be slow, when he goes too fast the official correctly reprimands him and forces him to move backward to any place where the audience might have been cheated of a good opportunity to investigate his attractiveness.

Until this moment the match has been a totally legitimate sport. But now the game is the enjoyment of the crowd. They are here to view, and it's the official's job to make sure their pleasure is delivered. He doesn't mind that Roger is sulking as he goes through his humiliation. He knows that many of us enjoy that; we think of it as an additional element of authenticity that the young man should be having so much trouble fulfilling his obligations — at least we do so long as the obligations are, in fact, fulfilled.

Only when the official is satisfied that we have seen what we deserve to does he bring Roger back to the center of the ring. Now Roger kneels. Those of us who adore the details of the matches watch the little movements, those things we admire and treasure: We see that Roger has clenched his fists in anger and defeat, they move behind his back now, but don't relax. We focus in on his nipples, watching them rise up erect through the coating of his body hair and displaying their pink skin for us.

His stomach is heaving, the cuts of his abdominal muscles are clearly visible.

Everyone, of course, watches his cock. The wrestlers have been trained in sexuality. They may loathe defeat and its consequences, but a veteran like Roger would have found the pleasures as well. It's swelling. The official reaches over and pats Roger on the head. The defeated wrestler has executed his role well. His cock is getting hard and rising up in an arc whose angle increases. He also holds his body stiff. His head is lowered, he's still not going to look into the eyes of the crowd. But he'll follow through and give a good show.

Now, and only now, does the official wave in an anxious James. The blond youngster jumps across the stage and stands in front of his former adversary. He strips quickly and completely, not waiting for any orders and not lingering at any stage. He is not obligated to put on that show. Not now, at least.

Naked, his long pale cock is already hard, and the men and women in the audience make lewd jokes about the sexual abilities of youngsters. He plays with them, stroking himself and pointing his erection at one man in particular, obviously hoping he might earn some special favors from that audience member later in the day. He cups his balls and holds them up, rubbing the sweat off them. He's the victor, he's earned this right to be lordly, if only for a short time.

The official nods his head, and it's time to proceed.

He hands Roger a condom. The man unwraps it and carefully applies it to his victor's cock. The latex stretches glistening over the tight skin. Then Roger follows tradition and leans forward. He purses his lips and kisses the head of his conqueror's cock. It must be done slowly and softly and reverently. He must display a meaningful admission of his role now.

The official accepts his action. James says something we can't hear. The official barks the command that Roger should obey. His mouth opens and he leans forward, his clenched fists still behind his back. He takes in the entire length of the younger man's erection. The official makes another order, he's apparently unsatisfied. Closer, he must have seen some evidence that Roger was not doing well enough because now we see Roger's chest expanding and tighten. He's obviously choking. He must not have taken all of the young man in him before.

It is all up to James now. The audience shouts out suggestions to him. He laughs when someone says he should change position with Roger. He has no intention of doing that. Instead he crosses his arms over his chest. He moves his thighs, letting his hips guide his cock in and out of Roger's mouth. The inward thrusts cause the defeated gladiator great discomfort. Each one seems to produce a seizure of choking. That angers the crowd. They want more grace in these actions, much more.

If James wanted to, he could prolong Roger's anguish and probable later punishment. But no, that's not his desire. He is fixated on something else, just as a youngster would be. He withdraws his cock, then gives an order, and Roger immediately complies, knowing he has no choice and expecting this very thing in any event.

He swivels, still on his knees, until his back is to the younger man. Then he leans forward until his forehead touches the ground. His ass is left high in the air. James now kneels down as well. He playfully slaps one of the cheeks of Roger's ass and draws an appreciative round of applause from the audience.

The covered cock moves in to the dark cleft of Roger's buttocks, separating the hair. We all know that, as part of their preparation, both men were well-lubricated before the match. In fact, it would have been possible for us to watch that happening if we had chosen to pay a small premium. Many people find the image of the two wrestlers bending over and being probed by expert greased hands the most delightful of all events around the wrestling match.

In any case, James has no trouble entering Roger. He moves in with one long stroke that brings a rush of blood to Roger's face. Now the young blond man's body begins to thrust much more strongly than it did while his pleasure had been simply from Roger's mouth.

We can watch the buttocks clench and release with every entry and removal. "Show it, let us see it," screams a man across the way. James smiles. It will only add to Roger's experience of humiliation to have that happen, so the young man does just what is requested, each thrust removing his cock entirely from his victim's body and forcing Roger to experience the entry totally every time.

There's only so long this can continue. The official speaks to James, he should finish. The crowd wants the action to be complete, but they wanted it to be part of a quick-moving plot. There are more characters waiting in the wings for more struggles.

James picks up his speed and soon there's a vitality to his fucking that undeniably announces his approaching orgasm. Then a loud roar builds up from his belly into his chest, and the crowd begins to respond with even greater enthusiasm. James's belly contracts tightly, the red blush of his orgasm spreads up and out from the center, and his eyes clamp shut. He collapses on top of Roger, his chest sweat merging with the rivulets that run down the other man's back.

The crowd erupts into applause. It's been a good fight, a finer ending. James pulls out his cock and — as tradition decrees — unravels the condom. The latex is upended, and the white ooze of his seminal fluid pours onto the stage. Another round of applause, not only for him, but also in appreciation for the raging erection that Roger has no ability to hide.

His cock is sweeping away from his body, almost pointing straight into the air. Sometimes a wrestler will orgasm from being fucked in the ring. The audience always considers that a cheat. They want to see submission, and they might appreciate a display of perfect training in another context, but here in the ring — no — they want to see struggle and defiance. Roger's cock gives them that proof.

He's not allowed to touch it, of course, and so must let it painfully swing ahead of him while he follows James out of the ring. Those of us who come here often make a mental note to watch future wrestling notices. There will, inevitably, be a rematch, and we will certainly want to be here for it.

Now we have a choice. The wrestling will continue and another pair of gladiators is waiting. But, instead, let me take you through the rest of the compound that exists in my imagination. It is a rich place, full of particulars, and I want you to see as many of them as we can.

You see, this is not just a question of a wrestling match. The matches are only a part of the activities, the most public and the ones that most people will come to. There are many people who aren't interested in finer elements of the compound or else they have other means of reaching their sexual pleasures and don't use this exact outlet.

The men who are wrestlers are all here for a period of time. How long? Perhaps five years; some longer. How did they get here? Perhaps some have simply decided this is the way to earn their way through the same college education that our football players expect as their own payment. Others might have been petty criminals, young men who committed nonviolent crimes and who a judge decided needed the discipline that the wrestling camp can provide. Or they might be young men who wanted to have a larger nest egg to start their careers with than the mistakes of birth had given them. There are certainly those who simply wanted to be wrestlers. The society where these events are taking place, remember, doesn't degrade the men who have these experiences, in fact, we all think they develop character. There have been many young men who have listened to the appreciative comments of the crowds and the stories that are told and who have always aspired to join this troupe.

The men train constantly, and their workouts are outdoors. We can walk behind the stadium and find dozens of them developing their physiques with weights. They have on only the slightest garment, to give just enough support for their genitals that they don't harm themselves.

Otherwise, they are naked as they work with weights and various physique machines. The crowd cannot interfere with their concentration — some of these devices could be dangerous — but we are welcome to walk through their yard and come as close as we wish to them. We can study up close just how they are developing. Many onlookers have adopted them as their chests are expanded, or their buttocks tightened, or whatever.

There are some who adore the sight of the strain the men go through. While today's athletic directors might use threats or intimidations to force young men to work harder, this camp exists in a fantasy of sexual service. Here, instead, there are men and some women who stand by and watch as their favorite goes through a particularly grueling set of exercises and finally appears to give up in fatigue. Then the patron or patroness makes an offer: Do another set of the workout, and there'll be a special payment.

The young men will always do what they can to comply, going back to the machines or the weights and struggling with all their might and will to do whatever is necessary to earn the tip that's been offered. Some men have made astonishing progress with their physical development because of this little added touch.

Notice over there, the red-headed woman who's standing by one of the wrestlers doing gymnastics. He's just finished an appalling number of sit-ups. His stomach is so tight that we can trace all of his abdominal muscles. She's not satisfied, evidently. She leans over and whispers in his ear. The reward she's offering must be quite large. He sighs, almost in dread, but resumes his position and begins to do the exercises again. He strains, his stomach is rebelling against the torture she's demanded. But he continues while she counts each one of the sit-ups. They must have been enough. She smiles, tousles his hair and calls over the official to have the young man's reward entered into his book. If he's really attracted her affection in his workouts, the athlete will soon amass a large amount in his savings for his future.

Walk this way, past the place where the athletes shower. They, of course, have no privacy. They've given that up for the salaries they've contracted to earn. Some people even go to watch them sleep, finding the young male bodies in repose the most beautiful of their masculine positions. Others simply adore watching the common activities of daily life as they're carried out by nude men, as though the voyeurism can be more intense by being made ordinary.

But this is my favorite of those quiet moments of spying — the watching of the athletes while they shower. Stand here and look at them. Each has his own style, that one embarrassed because you see him soaping up the crevice of his buttocks and that other one exhibiting himself shamelessly, knowing full well that you're studying him while he lathers his genitals.

My friend Laurence talks of having lived in Berlin one summer. There is, he says, a nude gay beach in that city. He used to promenade there, fully clothed, holding his walking stick while he wandered around the littered naked bodies. The feeling he experienced he termed, "Olympian." That is just how I sense this sensation, this standing here watching a line of naked men, all of them aware — painfully or joyfully — that they are being observed by clothed and appreciative onlookers. This is a special joy, to be able to be so blatant about the pleasure and not have to play silly games about happening upon someone or else trying to catch random, unnoticeable views.

They should have a series of tables here. I've mentioned it to the officials. I, for one, would gladly spend an afternoon occasionally, sipping wine and watching the men as they move from the exercise area to the other, more…interesting arenas.

When the athletes need a break from their workout, they go to the food tent. They are, of course, well-fed and would never be allowed to actually go hungry or experience anything else that would truly harm them. But in this part of the compound the food and drink is only available to the customers. To be served, the young men must beg from a patron.

Besides, the young men are forbidden to have any cash. That's the purpose of the official carrying around the book. To allow the wrestlers to have money would give them the freedom to circumvent the customers too often; it would leave them with a false sense of their time here in the compound.

Don't worry, their compensation is carefully and honestly recorded. Their payments at the end of their service are often huge. They often return as customers. It's said the other wrestlers fear them most; they're the most demanding of all. There is no cheating going on here. But the idea of the penniless athlete who must come to the visitor and ask for even the smallest piece of fruit or something as simple as a glass of water is one of the appeals of the compound.

Cajoling words are seldom a pleasant enough attraction, though occasionally someone will reward a wrestler who's earned them good money from a bet. But more often a small service must be exchanged. Nothing too demanding. What then? Imagine that tall and slender brown-skinned wrestler you admire so much. He's entered the tent wearing only his supporting garment. He approaches you and smiles — he knows the games that go on here. He asks if you wouldn't please give him a glass of juice.

Not while he's wearing that piece of clothing, you say. He smirks, expecting this, and removes it. His long, thin cock swings free, you tell him how much you'd like to touch it. Make him move forward and stand on his toes to lift his cock and balls up until he can lay them on the palm of your outstretched hand.

Perhaps you'd rather he turned around and showed you how perfectly his buttocks are developing. Make him wiggle them for you, or else, bend over and separate them if you'd rather study how nicely his anus is placed.

The wrestlers can never join the customers at their tables, but are expected to stay close while they enjoy whatever's been bought for them. Your young man is given his juice by a waitress. He kneels appreciatively by your side, letting you catch the delicious aroma of his honestly earned sweat while you play with his hair and test the flesh of his shoulders. He will occasionally look up at you while you sip your own wine and answer your questions about the wrestling camp. He'll tell you how much he enjoys it.

Now is the time the young men show how much they understand the dynamics here. The naked youth tries to talk to you about the rest of your activities. He'll time his presence on the block if he thinks you're interested enough to offer a good enough price. Maybe, just to entice you more, he'll lean forward and rest his head against your crotch, rubbing gently to make your cock harden with passion.

Perhaps he pleases you enough with his conversation that you decide to reward him with a piece of fruit. No, don't just give it to him, have him eat it out of your palm. He'll do it carefully and thankfully, making sure to clean up your hand with his tongue.

This is all within the expected. Our fantasy society doesn't think in violent and extreme terms always. The natural grace and elegance of service is often a quiet pleasure, and there's really nothing quite so lovely as a well-developed, nude body in repose.

But after the refreshment, there's more. Much more.

The wrestling compound is highly disciplined. It must be. Controlling the activities and the energies of so many young men is difficult without a firm hand. Some of the patrons would, of course, love to be the ones who determined the extent of the punishment, but there'd be little chance the athletes would have the strength or energy to fulfill their other duties if they had to constantly act out the lusts of those customers. There's another way to accomplish the necessary goals.

The paid officials of the camp have a strict and highly structured list of punishments for each of a number of transgressions. Some call for extreme forms of humiliation, especially if the officials determine that the cause of the violation is a too-strong ego. Around the punishment area are naked, bound men, stretched out with their bodies curved over padded workhorses in a way that their asses are pulled apart and their cocks and balls left hanging. Little leather-covered paddles are near by. Patrons are able to pick them up and deliver blows while a careful official watches.

The cries of the men seem to fill the place with so much sound that one can barely hear the whack of the paddles against the tender flesh. But these are almost more painful mentally than physically. More serious crimes offer patrons more serious pleasures. Some men have been stood up against posts, their hands tied above their heads and their feet firmly secured to the bottom of the pole. Beside them are signs, each one detailing the punishment assigned to the athlete. For a set sum, the patron can buy the honor of delivering these chastisements if he chooses to pay the price.

The more knowledgeable wrestlers strain their necks and struggle to see who it is that is putting the coins in the official's hands. There are loud moans if the patron is recognized as one who knows how to use the long thin length of leather that will be handed to him.

There's Hugo, the wonderfully developed bodybuilder you've admired before. The price the official is demanding to deliver the five blows that have been decreed for Hugo isn't that much. Pay it. Enjoy giving the arrogant athlete his punishment.

The bound wrestler is yours to touch and feel in any way you choose. Go ahead, give him some preliminary slaps of the buttocks with your hand. Make his ass flesh jump, feel that strength. Now explore him sexually the way you've always wanted to. Don't be gentle. The man is being punished, after all. Grab his balls harshly and pull until you can hear that his pain is honest and that his pleas for relief are heartfelt. Pull the sac back and stretch it out until the testicles are pressed firmly against the skin.

Now he knows you're serious. Pinch his nipples hard, first one then the other. Watch how much he struggles to free himself even though he knows it's impossible. Aren't his enormous muscles gorgeous in this bondage? Don't his struggles make them seem even more beautiful and more desirable than ever before?

Now stand back. Remember, you're being carefully watched by the official. Take the long leather strap he holds out for you and swing it in the air to get the feel for it. Also, you want to let Hugo know you're going to use it with great competence. Now deliver the punishment with firm, carefully counted blows. The flesh of the buttocks rises in color, the pale curves of white skin take on sudden lines of red and flushes of pink with each application of the leather.

When it's over, Hugo is let down. But his punishment is not over. You have also bought the next step. Hugo, still sobbing from his ordeal, comes over to you and kneels in front of you. He reaches up, and your pants are carefully opened by the chastised wrestler. He reaches in and brings out your cock. He covers it with the omnipresent latex and then kisses its tip. Through the layer of reflecting protection, the young man sucks and licks, his tongue moving to try to nurture you. The faster he can achieve the patron's pleasure, the sooner he'll be released. And there's always the worry that you could claim dissatisfaction. That's to be avoided at all costs since it could lead to still further punishments.

I'll move away while you take your pleasure from Hugo's willing tongue and lips. Let me know when you're ready to move on...

There? Wasn't he worth waiting for and didn't the knowledge that you'd given him such a fine thrashing make it all the better?

In the next compound there's another crowd. Let's move over to it. It's even more obviously sexually excited than any other group has been before. The people stand around a raised platform, a small one, with room just enough for a single man to stand comfortably. This is the place where the wrestlers earn their real money.

At any time an athlete can stand in line to walk up the stage. It is a choice always open to him. Perhaps he found a man back at the restaurant who wanted much more than a slight kiss or an erotic exposure. Then they could agree to move here. Of course, they both run the risk that the patron will be outbid by others. but that seldom happens.

It's more common that a young man has completed the daily round of exercises and wants to relieve his own pressures and continue to build up his savings. He gets in line and waits, looking out at the crowd and wondering who will buy his services.

You're concerned about the idea of the wrestlers selling themselves? Clear your mind. Realize this: No man walks up onto that stage unless he wants to. He chooses the time. It's his desire to earn the money. Yes, of course, once the sale is complete he loses control over the events. But if he wants to retain control, he only has to decide not mount the stage.

Why is the idea of the sale so bothersome? The man has things about him that others desire. He chooses the time. It's his desire to earn the money. Yes, of course, once the sale is complete he loses control over the events. But if he wants to retain control, he only has to decide not to mount the stage.

Why is the idea of the sale so bothersome? The man has things about him that others desire. He'll not be irrevocably harmed by having them used; he'll receive just compensation; he understands what it is about and is informed. Love doesn't come from a slave auction, of course not. But just who is it that decreed love is a part of sexual pleasure?

Purchasing the services of a decent housekeeper or a fine secretary isn't frowned upon, why should you wonder about the gathering of a man's sexual abilities?

As each man is called up, an official stands beside him, right by the stage. His role is passive. He is only there to hear and record the financial transactions. It's up to the athlete to produce the bids. He must present himself at his best, offering with his body and his words the most possible in order to elicit the greatest offers.

Imagine that it's James on the platform, flush and cocky from his victory in the ring. He would know that some of the audience would rush here hoping he'd be smart enough to offer his victorious and well-displayed body. He's standing there, naked. His cock is softer now, but he's healthy and young, and he and the rest of us are confident he'll still be able to perform well for us.

He's smiling at the crowd. He runs a hand over his upper body, pinching each of his pink nipples. He licks his fingers and wets the two little pinpoints on his chest, making sure the liquid highlights the color.

Now he reaches down and cups his testicles, lifting them up to us. They're light-colored with the same blond hair on them as the rest of his body. They are young, held tightly to his torso. Over them is his cock. he reaches for it now, stroking it lovingly and coaxing it in hopes of an erection.

But these aren't the things that often interest the patrons and James knows that. He turns around and displays his ass. It's quite beautiful, hairless, round, standing up in smooth arches. He spreads his legs and then reaches both hands back to pull apart his buttocks. Roger had done this at the ring, but he'd been forced to, it had been sexually exciting, but not erotic in the same way. This young man now is displaying himself in hopes that you'll buy him for an hour's entertainment.

The image of James's small and naked hole sends a shiver through the crowd. He's achieved his hope. He'll get the highest bids today. When the figures are shouted through the air, he turns and smiles down on the crowd with obvious delight. He encourages each and every bidder to go higher. One man wants to know what he'd look like on his knees with his mouth open to receive a hard cock. Immediately, James takes the position. Another wants to know what James would have looked like if he had been the vanquished in the ring. It's not an insult. The young man spins around on the platform where he barely has room to lift up his ass and display himself.

Each of the actions is mischievously committed, always with a smile. There's a purpose to coming to the stand and offering oneself to the auction, and a bad attitude has no place here. Finally the sale is over, and the official makes a note in James's book to record his earnings.

James jumps down and walks to the winner. When he gets there the man grabs hold of his hair and yanks it. The smile goes from James's face. He falls to the ground and leans forward to find a hard cock waiting behind the patron's pants. Once the bidding is over, there is no limit to the ownership. The man pulls a short leash and collar from this pocket and wraps it around James's neck. They leave, the athlete who was so recently the victorious conqueror now scurrying on hands and knees to be taken to a private room where he will have no release until the patron is satisfied his money was well-spent.

But if this is the way it ends for the victor, what happened to the one he defeated? There's still another compound, and the cries and groans become louder as you approach it.

Here is the place a patron really finds the value of his money. All the losers are in service here for a day after their defeat. The rules don't allow for any great physical punishment in this area, but every one of the wrestlers here had a decidedly pink set of buttocks. Spanking with a hand is only their due in the place where the vanquished spend their time.

But that is the least of their concerns. All the young men are naked. They are running around the space trying to fill the commands that the rules say any patron can give. They have mouths that have been working on hard cocks for seemingly endless hours. Their anuses have been fucked often. At a quick snap of a finger, each one must bend over and receive a patron's cock.

That, though, isn't the worst. There, in the corner, is our Roger. He's being tied to a bench. It allows his feet to reach the ground, but in a way that spreads his muscled, well-haired legs. His hands are also tied tightly to the stand. His stomach and chest and, more important, his abdomen are all parallel now. The patron has reached down and is playing with Roger's cock, rubbing it into a new erection.

The patron is undressed. Once Roger is erect, the patron applies the latex condom and then straddles himself over Roger, impaling himself on the athlete's cock. Roger moans, actually in agony. This is already the third time he's had to perform since he was led out of the ring and already there's another man and a woman standing around him, playing with his nipples and assuring him that they, too, expect to get service from him.

For his whole time here, Roger's cock will be in agony, constantly forced to an undesired erection and fed into the mouths and anuses and vaginas of anyone who was able to pay the price of admission. If he can't get himself erect? He and all the others assigned this task are forced to work to make sure each and every one of them is taken to the utter limit of his abilities. While the patrons look on, they'll suck and lick one another. They'll be forced into exhibitions if that will please a patron. Their nipples will be weighted with little metal clamps and their testicles will be tied tightly with rawhide. Smoothly shaped dildos will be implanted in their asses and held in place by ropes. They'll get no rest from it. Everything possible will be done to arouse them.

The silly people in our society focus on those few tears, a minor number of welts from the necessary punishments and the pink remains of a few spankings. They won't listen to the realities. The tears and the welts and the blush of the buttocks could always be avoided by following the rules and trying harder in the ring. Some punishments in the world are deserved. The experience of them make better men, more understanding of their roles and more willing to learn to carry them out better.

Of course, there are always those men who choose to receive the punishments. There are those wrestlers who find the occasional way to slip in their training and force the officials to send them to the punishment posts. Most athletes would rather place themselves on the selling block to receive money for their futures, but the patrons are often heard to gripe that a few young men sometimes lose a match on purpose, just to find themselves in the area where their cocks and mouths and asses will be put to constant use.

The wrestling camp isn't perfect yet. Even the fantasy has its flaws. But that's part of its humanity, after all. The moralists forget they defy the gods — whatever gods they choose — when they attempt to be godlike in their perfection and forget to indulge in the vagaries of human existence. My wrestlers are not perfect, nor are my patrons. But they are aware that services well-rendered and well-received produce a tremendous amount of mutual respect.

I can't recreate my wrestling camp. Unfortunately, too many of the moralists have made too many of the potential participants uneasy with their needs and desires. But my party would give me a chance to come close, to see that the men who would answer my advertisement and my guests understood that the services being exchanged were highly valued and the people tremendously respected.

The First Interview

My plan of action was very simple. I had placed the ads, and I would soon be receiving answers. I would sift through the replies and decide which people to actually interview. It would be in San Francisco for a full week before the party; that would give me more than enough time to talk to the possible volunteers.

I continued to field the phone calls. I was honestly surprised by some of the people who tracked me down — these were all still people who had a means of knowing who had actually placed the classified and who could get hold of my phone numbers. There was a reporter for a newspaper who wanted to cover the event. There was another magazine editor who wanted to send a photographer to record it. These last ideas were unacceptable. The party was for the four of us, and all the attention of the volunteers had to be on us and our pleasure. To have them preening for cameras wouldn't have done it at all.

I had not expected the call from Martin.

It was the one I should have hoped for, but I had forgotten how possible it could have been. When I answered and heard his voice I was frozen with a kind of trance. This, truly, was my reentrance into the old existence I had loved so much and had been away from for so long.

His first sentence — without so much as "Hello" — proved that some things will never end, especially not those that are bonded by the fire and passion of sex. "I saw your ad. I had to call."

"Why not sooner?" I shot out my answer, but there wasn't any anger in it, nor any disappointment, it was just a genuine wonder that we had let it go for so long.

"Things." That was a typical response from him. There would be stories about his life that could entertain me and depress me for hours if I heard them. Martin is one of the pilgrims of the sexual life. There would be many adventures and just as many mishaps over the past few years. I would have to listen to them; they would tell me what had been going on while I had been in retirement.

"How are you?" I asked. "Are you well? Happy? Where are you, for that matter. I can never keep up with you. New York? Key West? Or is it Houston this season?"

"Los Angeles," he replied. "I've been here about a year now."

"Working?"

"On and off. A bartending job for a while. A couple stints as an extra on a big lot. A nice old man who just happened to have an unoccupied cottage on his estate, that kind of thing."

It was the existence Martin had always led. But he could afford to lead it. He was — after all these years — still only about twenty-eight. I had met him when he had lied about his age to enter the sex clubs in New York and the erotic conferences in San Francisco. I had known him when the strange millionaire was transporting him between Europe and North America for single nights of sex.

"I'm delighted to hear from you." It was true. I was, and I had a hard cock to prove it. There were memories of Martin that would always make me hard; they are my own private pornography, and their veracity was more potent than anyone else's fiction.

"It's because of your ad."

"That's the reason? Just for that?" I couldn't quite decide if it made me angry or not. A part of me wished he had simply wanted to call me. But then the rest of my mind recalled the other times we'd been together — the times that hadn't been so perfect and had showed another side of him.

"Isn't that enough? It sounds as though you'd want to hear from me if you're doing this. I could help. Besides, I belong there. Aren't I still your boy?"

Of course you are.

His voice was so roguish. He knew precisely what he was doing. He was responding to those small parts of one another that we had each captured. There had been an ad for an event he wanted to take part in. He probably would have done it with anyone, it didn't have to be me. But because it was me, he knew he could move in and take a central role.

He could, I decided. He most certainly could. "I'll need you for the entire weekend."

"I'm working…"

"Take it off. You always can arrange that. You have plenty of notice. I need you."

"We're spending the weekend together?" he asked, a little seduction in his voice.

"You're spending it with me. There'll be a lot of work to be done. Also, I'll be dealing with new volunteers, people I haven't met yet. I'll need to have someone around who can show them the ways things should be done. I've spent a lot of time working on you; if you haven't forgotten your lessons, you'll be a good example for the rest of them."

I spoke as harshly as I could. I didn't want any of this game playing with him. I wanted him. But I remembered now that there were only certain parts of him that I could have. I would simply take all of those elements I was able to and work them for as much as I could — it would be considerable. Very considerable.

He sucked in his breath, I could hear it whistle through his teeth. He knew exactly what I was saying to him. *Of course you're still my boy. I'll make sure you remember that as well as I do.*

"Fine. What are the details? When? Where? How?"

We went through the mechanics, and I made him read them back to me from the notes I had made him take. We would meet in San Francisco in a month. It would be a memorable reunion.

People who are appalled by intense sexuality — the kind that comes clothed in leather and chains and wears whips and handcuffs — usually are so agitated by it that they make many false assumptions. The worst is the idea that there are no emotions involved in it. Their vision of love is one that is filled with roses and gentle sea waves, breezes through pine trees on pristine mountain tops. When the acts they witness are really hurricanes carrying flaming winds, they can only think that they're seeing destruction. They can't perceive the truth — that it is often a more powerful event than anything they have ever imagined.

Martin and I are the proof of that.

Aren't I still your boy?

Forever.

I met him when he was a teenager. I hadn't known that. He was tremendously precocious and was dressed in his authentic Navy uniform. The pants were translucent and that first time I had been hypnotized by the outline of his white briefs underneath them. We had been at a party. It was one of those middle class gay affairs mimicking suburbia — a desecration of a desecration.

He was an extraordinarily handsome young man. At least six foot tall, with blond hair and blue eyes, clean shaven with a military haircut and a slightly drawling accent that spoke of a vaguely Southern background.

The men at the party were the type who attempt to make believe that gay men don't have sex at all. They wear suits that are as unsensual as armor and speak about their monogamy and make loud — too loud — judgments on the kind of man who would "betray the cause" by exposing the overtly sexual desires that they, themselves, were denying.

I was a strange person to have among them. But there were many occasions when I would join them for one reason or another. The invitations would come from a work colleague, and my agreement to attend would be grounded in a perverse desire to make them all terribly uncomfortable. The presence of a pornographer at one of their soirees was always disconcerting.

Martin's presence was easily explained. One or another of the middle-aged men would always have a presentable youth on hand. One never remarked on the obvious monetary foundation for the relationship, but it was understood. Martin was simply another of a long line. I never did quite understand who he was with. I hardly talked to him, I only studied his midsection and its white cotton bindings. The shape was promising — both front and rear. If his smile hadn't been quite so bright and his stance so easy and comfortable, I might never have let my eyes move above his waist.

I still didn't make my contact with him at the party. But I did find him later that night. I had gone home to change and went to one of the leather bars in vogue in New York that year. I was on the prowl, careful to limit my drinks and never using any other chemical because I was looking for something…major. I wanted something that would demand all of my abilities and faculties.

I hadn't expected Martin to come into the same bar, but he did. He was still dressed in his uniform. I thought that was dangerous at first; I had heard him emphasize that he really was a member of the service at the party. But, after a moment I realized that no one in that particular place was going to believe him anyway. It was a social setting predicated on false images, and the appearance of reality would go unnoticed.

That was ten years ago. I picked him up easily. But all the details of the night aren't still with me. Instead, I remember discrete moments.

I had a chamber in my apartment set aside for sex. It was well-equipped. Those were the days when the tools of sex impressed me, or at least interested me. I remember at one point:

Martin is crying, he's hanging down, utterly vulnerable. Wrist and ankle restraints were attached to chains that connected to the ceiling. A belt clamped to another chain supported his mid-section. There were pieces of metal attached to his nipples and his scrotum.

Later: I offered to let him go. He was free from the restraints and sitting on the floor, naked. He answered by reaching over in his hands and knees and kissing my foot.

I fucked him. He was flat on his stomach on the floor, I could lift up and see all of his back torso from the buttocks up. His ass cheeks were stripped red with new welts and so, too, were his shoulder blades. I was pounding into him. He was speaking rhythmically, as though chanting a mantra: "Yes, yes, yes, yes…"

Afterward: I was talking to him with the kind of sexual litany that I might use on any man, but I suddenly realized this one was listening and this one believed it. "I own you. I will have you again. You will come whenever I tell you to. You are mine."

I remember the morning. The sun had risen, and there were small rays that could sneak through the breaks in the curtains that were supposed to block the light from the chamber. Martin was crying. I had reached inside someplace and found something that he didn't want to give up, but he realized it was too late. He was sitting on my lap, suddenly a little boy and not the aggressive military male he had presented himself as. He was naked. I had some-how gotten my clothes on. I was rubbing his back. I held him tightly. It was so late; why wasn't I tired? But I don't remember that. I only remember his head on my shoulder and the thought that I never wanted it to be anywhere else, ever.

Even later: We had showered, and he was sitting on my lap again. Now he had on those briefs that had entranced me earlier. But that was all. I was once again dressed. This time we were kissing passionately. I reached into his shorts and found his cock hard and oozing from its tip. As though he were somehow someone even younger, I pulled it out, forcing the elastic band of the briefs down to let the whole length of it loose.

I began to pull and tug on the thick, long foreskin that covered it. He only kissed me more, as though that simple act of masturbation were the most intense sexual force he had ever felt. I remember him coming all over my hand, the stuff spilled over and drenched his shorts. I remember us laughing and having to have to shower again.

From that night ten years ago, Martin has been mine. Not always; there were long periods during which we were separated and only short times together. I don't claim him in those respects. He and I have never been lovers in any traditional sense. But, if I walk into a bar and he's there in whatever city, we never question whether we are going to have sex, only where and how soon. We never question what the roles are; who and what we are to one another is so well-established that neither of us ever wants to cross any of the lines we have defined.

Over the years, I have witnessed Martin as much as possessed him, though. We lived in the same sexual world. He had only begun to explore it when we met. It was clear to both of us that he had to make his experiments on his own. I was there as a source of support and a place he could come to talk through the experiences — genital or romantic. But he had to make the journey alone.

It was an exquisite one. He gave himself over to those people who actually train men. He lived once in a dungeon for six months, subjected willingly to every possible sensual torture and used by countless men, many of them masked and personless to him. He lived for a while on a farm that was ruled over by a former military man who insisted that the day-to-day life of the place replicate the most intense boot camp — only with hardons and fucking.

He would bring these experiences back to me and offer them to me, often as a gift. After his training in the dungeon he arrived at my door one night and came in, immediately stripping naked. He smiled as he fell to his knees. He spread his thighs far apart, leaving his testicles vulnerable and exposed. He lifted his head high, throwing out his chest and his prominent nipples. His hands were held behind his back. His hips were placed in way that his cock was thrust forward. All of those parts of his body that a man might try to protect, Martin offered to me. "Your slave…," was all he said. It was the start of a delicious week.

I met his boyfriends, sometimes they were men who were putting him through some new sexual encounter, but other times he would make his first attempts to be the leader. I even went on a vacation with him once, to Florida. He had been in a relationship, and it hadn't worked. For once, he didn't want me for the sexual frenzy, he needed someone to take care of him in the more gentle ways. When he requested that, I knew that there was no option. Of course I had to agree. That short trip was full of fine meals and good wines, soft talk, and only the softest sex. That time was healing. To be chosen to provide the restorative was an honor, and I accepted it as such.

Martin would be in San Francisco for my party. I had a month to savor that. I wondered what it would be like to have him in that public setting. He would adore it, and the audience would only intensify his pleasure. And I could be assured that at least one of the volunteers would perform perfectly, absolutely perfectly.

Should I have him serve the food and drink? Or should I recreate that torturous bondage that left him suspended from the ceiling? He would insist on surviving that; no force on earth would make him admit that he couldn't take the test I'd give him.

The last time I had met him he had begun a rigorous body-building program. He had always had a wonderful body, and by now it must be magnificent. I wondered if he shouldn't be simply tied to a piece of furniture so that my guests could enjoy the sight of naked perfection.

The Replies

It didn't take long for the letters to begin arriving. Their democracy astonished me. I had, of course, placed many ads over the years, but it had been a long time and I had forgotten just what a spectrum.

There were some scribbled on ruled paper. Others processed on computers. Some were insultingly xeroxed. A few were stupidly challenging. "If you're for real, prove it, and perhaps I'll consider your request." This was a response to an advertisement for slaves?

The only ones I considered seriously were those with photographs. A very few others were interesting enough that I did write back to request a picture, but only a couple of those complied.

I built up a folder of the answers. I sorted through them daily, conjuring up wonderful fantasies of just what each of them offered. I wasn't just after a collection of perfect men, I wanted a range of men. I wanted to show Adrienne how diverse the possibilities were, and I wanted impress Madame and Phil with my ability to gather in several distinct types.

I wanted my circus to have many rings.

One by one the choices made themselves obvious to me, and I made the calls. The respondents were all serious; that was my good fortune. I didn't need to deal with the fools who enjoy littering other people's mail with private fantasies that they never expected to be fulfilled.

During the phone calls, I made up my schedule for San Francisco. I had more than enough men from California to be assured of the necessary numbers. I got work schedules from each, told them where to meet me for interviews, and how to appear.

Everything went as planned, but there were two replies that were nagging me. Neither one was from California. That made me think that they weren't serious. But there was a sound of intent to them that I couldn't avoid. I decided they deserved attention.

One was from a businessman in Ohio who went so far as to write me on his office stationery, making it a point to declare it a proof of his conviction as well as his ability to afford the trip to the West Coast.

> Dear Sir:
>
> I been delirious since I read your ad. My fantasies are decidedly masochistic, but they are also very subtle. The basics of S/M are available in Chicago or New York, cities I visit regularly. I can wear a black leather jacket as well as any other man. My only problem in the bars and parties I go to is that I'm taken for a top more often than not.
>
> I'm six feet four inches, thirty-two years old, a conscientious weight lifter with a powerful build, as I hope you'll see from the enclosed photographs, which are very recent.
>
> But my sexuality isn't satisfied with those activities, especially not today with health concerns.
>
> I am aware that I am most attracted by the idea of being displayed. I love the attention that I get by exhibiting myself. I'm certain, to be honest, that that's the reason I work out as much as I do.
>
> Your party sounds like an extraordinary possibility for me to realize some of my most secret desires.
>
> I am self-employed and can arrange the time off to come to San Francisco for your pleasure. I would be happy to do anything to make your entertainment as complete and perfect as possible.
>
> Forgive me, sir, for admitting this, but my cock is hard, and I'm stopping and starting this letter over and over again just to jerk on it enough to keep up the tension that it takes for me to write all of this down.
>
> I've never committed these things to paper before. That's only one indication of how very much your adver-

tisement reached me. But there must be a time when every one of us says yes to a fantasy.

Being on display in full light, for men and women, with the possibility of being used and abused.... It's too much, sir. Please accept my humble application.

Your willing slave,

Christopher

The photographs were stunning. This Christopher was even more muscular than I expected Martin to be. The photos showed Christopher in classic bodybuilding poses, wearing one of those very skimpy pairs of briefs that are worn in competition. The artificiality of the posture couldn't hide the smooth bulk he'd built up. He had stopped short of being grotesque, but there was still so much there, so much of him, and the proportions were beautifully displayed.

I was, of course, as interested in the letterhead and his secret desires. This might be one of those men who need to have some balance in their lives. They were often so fascinating, so much in need of a moment of release. I decided I would try this one out. I had the time and the resources for a trip to Ohio on my way West.

I picked up the phone and impulsively dialed his office number. A receptionist answered and passed me on to a secretary. I was officiously told that he was very busy. I insisted that it was very important. With a grudge in her voice, she put me on hold. She came back in a moment and told me that he was unable to come to the phone, if I would like to try later...

Then there was a noise in the background, there was a disruption that obviously was setting the secretary aback. This was some kind of event she wasn't used to having to have to cope with. I knew instantly what had happened. Christopher hadn't remembered his letter. He had only registered a call from an unknown party in a far northern state where he wasn't used to doing business. He'd told the woman to get rid of me. But the connection between the source of the call and my initials — all I had identified myself with the ad — had come to him, and he had raced out to countermand his original order.

"He'll be right with you," the woman finally said.

"Yes," he answered not long after that. His voice was deep, almost too masculine to believe.

"I'm answering your letter, about the trip to California?"

"Yes,…sir." The sir was almost whispered, as though he still worried about the secretary hearing him. "I'm glad you called."

"Can you clear your schedule for the fifteenth? I'll come through your city and interview you."

"I would think you'd enjoy it." I smiled at his discomfort and began to look forward to this little visit.

"Is it honestly an interview? Is the party still on?"

"Yes, yes," I answered. "You should also be prepared to fly to San Francisco. I'll see you on the fifteenth. If you're…appropriate, we can make the other arrangements. The party is on Saturday night. You won't have to worry about missing too many days in your office if that's a concern."

"Hardly," he was laughing now. "I can't imagine why anyone would go all that distance for a single weekend. But I'm sure I can find some other ways to keep myself occupied out there — if it's necessary."

Ah, my Christopher was already looking for extra time and added activities.

"Are you sure that an interview is necessary, though? Didn't you see my pictures? Didn't you like them?" I wasn't surprised that any man as interested in his own body would be so confident that he would be admired and wanted. But that wouldn't be a proper way for us to proceed. We needed a more clear understanding of what was going on.

"As my ad stated looks aren't enough. I have to know that you're appropriate for my purposes. That can't be ascertained without an interview, a tryout if you like."

"Well,…" he was riffling through some papers, checking his schedule, "yes, the fifteenth would be fine."

"This is something that should happen on my grounds, not yours." I gave him the name of a downtown hotel where I'd been before.

"Of course I know it sir." I think he actually understood. "Can I ask…I would like to know what you look like. Do you mind telling me?"

"Yes, I do. In any event, it's my money that I'm spending coming to your city. If you are only after a certain type of person — rather than a type of experience — then you can always leave me. There'll be no hard feelings. But, for now, I think it's better for you simply to arrive, without warning and without the usual bottom fantasies. Just prepare yourself for the test. I am not, after all, calling in response to a dating service."

"I'm sorry, sir. I didn't mean…," he was backtracking after hearing the anger in my voice.

"Enough. I'll write you with my complete name and other instructions later. I'll expect you to follow them to the letter."

"Of course. Of course I will. This is very exciting, sir, I can't thank you…"

"Don't, not now." With that I hung up.

*   *   *

I was sitting in the hotel cocktail lounge when I did finally meet him. He was nervous, of course. I had told him to come directly from his office and he must have; he was still dressed in his three-piece suit and his wing-tip shoes. I guessed that the costume was one of the last that he would have chosen to wear to meet a sexual partner, but I was delighted by it.

He sat down across from me after I had motioned to him and signaled that, yes, I was the one. He had received a letter with a fair description of myself. I had learned to make the descriptions I send to someone I'm meeting through the personal ads for the first time as inauspicious as possible. I only describe myself in terms that will encourage them to show up, never in ways to make them have high expectations. That way they're invariably delighted with what they do find.

Christopher certainly was. The big smile on his face was full of delight and relief. He sat down across from me, and a waiter approached. "A martini, straight up," he ordered. But I countermanded it.

"No, I've already ordered a bottle of Chablis. It's on ice now. That will do." I turned to the waitress, a very appealing young woman with firm breasts that weren't being restrained by a bra. "You could pour it now."

"Of course." She went to got and get the wine.

Christopher understood immediately that the little exchange between the three of us was meaningful. It set the limits immediately. He sat back in the lounge chair, the grin was gone, but not the enjoyment.

We didn't speak until the wine was brought, opened, and poured. The waitress looked even better when she bent over to serve each of us. The management had forced her to wear one of those ridiculously short skirts and stockings with seams in them. I flashed on a fantasy of having both her and Christopher up to my room. They would make a fine couple together. But she left. I had him and certainly expected that he would be more than sufficiently engaging for this night at least.

He had dark hair, probably brown, but so deep that it could have been black. The lighting was so soft that I couldn't be sure. His muscles were developed enough that they were obvious even through the layers of clothes. His arms, especially, were so large at the biceps that they had presented the tailor with a special problem.

He was clean-shaven and actually had a small but noticeable cleft in his chin. His eyes were a dark shade — again the room's lighting didn't really let me see them, but I thought they were also probably brown. While he dressed and carried himself in ways that he obviously hoped would make him appear older, there was a boyish quality about him, a mischievous manner when he studied me over the top of his glass and an ease with his body that contradicted its size.

He lifted his wine and toasted me silently, but then stopped before he drank. He remembered the situation and — very enjoyably — waited for me to give a signal. I picked up my own glass and nodded, and we both took a swallow.

"Tell me about yourself," I said.

He put the glass back on the table and studied me for a moment. "I'm not used to that, you know — talking about my…real life." He wasn't challenging me, nor was he playing a game. I understood. But I also knew something else.

"If you hadn't wanted to talk about yourself, you wouldn't have written me on real letterhead and you wouldn't have been so calm about my coming to your hometown."

"Perhaps." That was all he'd own up to.

"My question stands: Tell me about yourself."

He took a deep breath. "You know my occupation. I'm fairly successful. I'm married." He took another drink, as though wanting to punctuate that last statement. He was studying me again, wondering how I was going to deal with his disclosure. I didn't react.

He continued, "I live here, president of the rotary, the youngest they've ever had. I am a member of the right church, Presbyterian in this town. I went to a local college, quarterback of the football team, president of my fraternity, ranked number one in graduate school…" He let his voice drop off and lifted his hands as if in defeat.

I knew the story. I'd heard it a million times. The man in charge, the one in control. He didn't have to tell me some of the details, I knew them by heart. He'd risen in his community by being everyone's ideal of the American male. He was decisive in business, a leader in small groups. His wife, without a doubt, was one of those totally dependent types, the ones who loathe feminism and run from its implications. She, like all the others, would have chosen this man just for those attributes.

And, for him, there was no escape. The dirty little secrets of his adolescence had terrified him and sent him scurrying into a deep and forbidden cave where they were made safe. All of his extraordinary activities were compensation for those concealed realities.

He would be one of the hungry ones. The ones who present themselves with amazing needs. "Are you gay?"

He shifted a little bit, his eyes avoided me. "Not really. That's not what's important — it being a man or a woman. What's important is…," but he stopped, he seemed to understand where he was and to think that the confession was inappropriate.

I understood that as well. I stared at him for a minute before continuing, "What's important is that someone — anyone — take charge. That's it, isn't it? You just need someone to relieve you of the pressure of all those decisions, all those responsibilities."

"Yes." He was staring back at me. I couldn't find the emotion he was feeling.

I reached into the pocket inside my jacket and brought out a small black paper bag. "This is for you. Go to the men's room and put it on. It will help us make sure we both understand what's happening here."

He looked at the parcel sitting on the table and seemed to be terrified of it. It was defiling his safe space. He scanned the room, as though he might find a fellow church member or a Rotarian witnessing his sacrilege. But — of course — he finally picked up the bag and did as I had told him to.

He walked away as though he were a busy man on a quick errand. He strode across the room and disappeared around a corner into the lobby. In only about five minutes he returned, but his walk was decidedly less jaunty and self-assured. I watched as he made his way across the cocktail lounge with careful steps.

When he sat down I told him, "Squeeze your hand into your lap, hard." I said it casually; no one looking at us could have seen anything strange about the way we were talking to one another.

As soon as he began to follow the single instruction, I added another one, "Put your legs together."

He was obviously obeying. He was struggling to keep the expression on his face from breaking into a grimace. The color had left his skin. There were a few beads of sweat gathering on his forehead.

"That's enough. Relax."

He couldn't hold back the comfort that came over him when he did. He opened his mouth wide, gulping for breath.

The package had contained a simple, but effective device. At first it appears to be just a cock ring, a small leather band with studs on it. But on the lining, the studs are not closed: The sharp protrusions are open. They are — at the least — terribly uncomfortable. When pressure's applied, they bite into the skin painfully. That pressure, of course, is what he had felt when his hand was in his lap and his legs were pushed shut.

It has always been a favorite of mine. Especially for men who chose to wear costumes like Christopher's suit. If they want to project that image for the world, fine let them, at least occasionally. But for me, just between the two of us, there should be something going on that is a constant and emphatic reminder of the roles we've chosen.

"May I?" He was reaching for his wine glass and picked it up after I'd said yes. He needed that drink and proved it by draining his glass. The waitress appeared almost immediately and refilled it.

"I've cleared my schedule, as you told me to. There are lots of reasons for me to be in California. Actually I go there — supposedly on business — at least four times a year. No one's suspicious."

"But we haven't agreed that you should."

The cock ring was serving its purpose now. I'm sure he would have made some quick reply before he'd put it on. But now he was more aware of the possibilities and the repercussions of what was going on. "I hope you'll let me."

It was a perfect answer. "Tell me more about why you want to do it — this particular event."

He thought for a while. "I told you I was an athlete in college for one thing. But working out and not having a real physical out-let like the athletic field makes me more…conscious of it.

"I spend my days aware of what I'm doing, developing my abdominals, expanding my chest, all of it. It has a strange reper-cussion I really hadn't expected. I had always liked having people watch me and like me and my body. But now, with the greater effort and the stronger focus on what things look like, I've discov-ered that desire is even stronger than I could ever have imagined.

"I want something more extreme. When I saw your ad and read the description, I knew that's what it was.

"You asked before what was important. I do — as I said — go to leather bars, and I do have nights with men. Yes, answering the ad was a risk. But the ad itself gave me the courage and the trust. It was so…elegant. I knew I wasn't dealing with any kind of street thug. It wasn't as though you were offering a gang rape. 'A private party for a very few invited ladies and gentlemen…' That's hardly an invitation to a cheap orgy.

"My private needs are almost completely segmented from my life. It allows me a great deal of freedom, actually. I can take the risk of your being here because I don't take any other risks. This is my hometown, of course, you're right about that. But I'm never found in the bars here.

"The homosexuality really isn't much of it at all. If I could find women who were as discreet as some of the men I know and if they knew how to fulfill my desires, I'm sure I'd be perfectly will-ing to do these things with them."

He had regained his composure and confidence with his speech. I quickly thought I should put him back in his place, but instead I was distracted with the idea of just how very much Madame would like to get her hands on this one. She would have a field day putting him through his paces. The thought of her plea-sure was enough to make me suspend my other criteria. Of course I'd have to have him at the party.

That didn't mean I couldn't have him now.

"Let's go to my room."

*   *   *

When we got there I took one of the two comfortable chairs by the picture window that overlooked the downtown area. I took out a cigarette and held it. It took him a moment to respond, but then he realized what I wanted and moved over to me. There were matches in the ashtray, and he took them and lighted the smoke for me.

"Undress."

There was a momentary hesitation. Of course, I realized, he would have preferred that I do it. But I wanted to make sure he had the experience of taking off his clothes to a passive observer. It was a lesson he'd have to learn.

He went to the nearby closet and opened it. He took off his suit jacket and vest and hung them up. Then he undid his shirt. He bent over and began to unlace his shoes. A sharp frown swept over his face, and I knew that the spikes in the ring had bitten into his balls. But he continued. He kicked the shoes into the closet. The shirt came off now and was also hung up. He seemed to hesitate again when it came time to unbuckle his belt. But the indecision was so fleeting that I didn't even have a chance to mention it. He stepped out of the trousers.

The socks and undershirt were next. Now he was standing there only in his tightly cut boxer shorts. He was already half erect; I could make out the lines of his cock through the fabric. Now he faced me. He pulled down the underpants and stood before me naked.

If was a fine sight. I realized, now that I was seeing him close up, that he shaved his body. There were only the slight hints of that — not a single hair outside a clearly defined triangle of his pubic region and under his arms. I knew that I would feel the stubble when I ran my hands over his chest.

He moved toward me. His cock was arcing out from his abdomen. It swung slightly as he moved, its base still entrapped by the black leather band. He moved until he was right in front of me. I reached up and circled my hand around the leather and applied enough pressure to make him wince. He loudly breathed in through his mouth, and his body stiffened from the sharp pain.

I stood up. "Put your hands behind your neck. Spread your legs apart as far as you can. Hold your head up. Eyes front, immobile."

He immediately went into the stance I'd dictated. I walked around him, running my hand along the expanse of his body. It was a work of art. He'd suffered for it. I could only imagine the hours of exertion.

His back was as wide as it had looked in the photographs. I could feel ridges and valleys in his flesh that I had never seen so sharply defined in other men. I reached down to his buttocks and felt them. Amazing. They were as solid as most other men's arms. I could squeeze them and feel the resistance of the well-developed flesh. His thighs were thick, and ropelike structures of muscle wrapped around them.

I came around to the front. I could feel the unnatural smoothness of his shaven chest as soon as my palm touched his pectorals. His nipples were developed as well, but I knew their exercises had nothing to do with gymnasiums. I pinched one a little — nothing severe, just enough to elicit a satisfying response from him. His balls, too, were shaven.

"How do you explain this to your wife?"

"She thinks all bodybuilders do things like this. Probably. If she notices at all. We don't have an…imaginative sex life."

His stomach was hard, with horizontal lines that displayed the sections as well as a textbook would. But, of course, the arms were the most appealing. The mass of his biceps was incredible.

The explorations I was making — and probably the distant manner with which I was making them — was turning him on incredibly. His erection had filled out as far as it could, the arc now lifted it straight up, as it appears in some of the ancient pictures of Pan, his cock pointing to the ceiling in a vertical bow.

The tip was circumcised — always a disappointment. But it was large, a thickly purple-colored and smooth-skinned prize on the end of a long and substantial shaft. I ran my fingers up and down its length, very gently. He closed his eyes when I did that, as though the very touch was a private and exquisite torture.

I moved away from him and took off my own clothes, simply draping them over my bed. When I was naked, I sat down on the chair again and spread my legs.

"Your knees."

He had been studying me and now stared, hesitating this time because he was trying to figure out the way I wanted him to arrange this maneuver. He did it correctly, keeping his hands behind his neck and his legs spread, he lowered himself into the space between my thighs.

He was going to move in to suck me at once. I put a hand on his forehead and stopped him. I reached for the small black pouch that I had earlier placed by the chair and pulled it up. I reached in and brought out a pair of rubber-tipped clamps. He knew what they were for, and his eyes dropped down, as though he was surrendering to them.

I opened one of the clamps and put it on one of his nipples. They were firm, but not viciously painful. They would begin to be, but later, and only if I chose to leave them on for a period of time. I repeated the effort with the second clamp.

He was used to this, I was sure of that. But he wasn't used to the next step. I took out two small bells from the pouch. Each one was attached to a tiny ring that matched a small hook on the end of the nipple clamps. I put them on him, a quick and surprisingly effective means of letting him know that I had tricks and expectations beyond the usual ones that he had been accustomed to in the bars.

As soon as I let go, the two little bells rang softly. His eyes were wide open with amazement as he studied them. His careful reserve was gone, and he was trying to understand that those sounds were being produced by his own body's movements.

Then he closed his eyes. His forehead tightened into a frown. His body actually seemed to shake slightly. Through clenched teeth he said, "I hate those — the bells."

I reached down and used my forefinger to tap one of them enough to create the sound again.

"You've spent all this time to create a body someone else would appreciate, and you get upset just because he does something to make you even more handsome?" My finger moved to the other side of his chest and rang the second small bell.

He seemed to relax quickly. I could watch the tension leave his shoulders and his chest as the muscles softened. He wanted this so badly — he thought he needed this so badly — that he was willing to put up with the new humiliation.

"Put your hands down," I told him.

He did, and at the same moment opened his eyes. He didn't look at me, though. Instead he studied the silver bells that hung from his chest. His arms rested by his sides. His cock was still hard. No matter how much he protested the bells, he was still being tremendously turned on.

I went back into the pouch and pulled out a collar. It was plain leather with no spikes inside this piece. I held it up in front of his face. "You are the kind of man who needs this — the symbol — aren't you?"

He studied the leather and nodded, "Yes, sir." His voice was barely a whisper; the person who occupied his office and dominated his wife while impressing his community wouldn't be able to loudly acknowledge the desire for a collar, of course.

"Bend your neck." He did, quite nicely. I reached over and pulled the collar around the broad stalk. After I'd secured the buckle that held it in place, I sat back again. My cock was hard, resting up against my body. This time, when he looked up, the bells made no difference, and the posture of submission wasn't so important. His eyes were focused only on my erection. He ran a tongue across his lips.

"What does that mean to you — the collar?" I asked. I was calmly stroking myself only inches from his face.

"That…that I have no control. That I have to do what you say. That you are my master, and I must follow your orders." He was speaking in that husky whisper again. The tone was nearly religious; he had undergone a spiritual transformation, and whoever he was outside this room was no longer important. He was only a naked man on his knees, a collar around his neck, his cock hard, his body available.

I pulled out a wrapped condom and handed it to him. He studied it for just a moment, then went to work. He carefully opened the foil and pulled out the latex. He looked at me, silently requesting permission to continue. I nodded. He reached up and put the unrolled condom on the tip of my cock. Then very slowly and very reverently, he pulled the thing down over my erection.

He worked at it carefully and methodically until the entire shaft was covered. Then he sat back on his haunches, still staring at my erection. The movement set the bells off again, but he didn't care at all; he hardly seemed to notice.

I reached down and took hold of the base of my cock. I milked it slightly until we could both make out the seeping precome as it was pressed up against latex. I pushed the erection away from me so it was pointed directly at him. "Suck it, carefully."

He moved very slowly toward his task. He opened his mouth inches before it was necessary. I was able to see the pink of the inside of his mouth. His teeth were white; hardly any evidence of correction could be seen. My adult athlete took in the head of my protected cock. But he was out to impress me. That, and he was out to savor the moment. He kept his jaw as open as possible, he had to have worked to relax his throat muscles. The whole length of me went inside him in the one, single movement he made.

The sounds were marvelous. I was looking down at him, engulfing my cock, and watching his attempts, no matter how vain, to give pleasure. I could have remained that way for hours. If my cock were at least as disciplined as he was, that is.

But he moved back after a few seconds, not letting my cock free, his mouth was now wrapped tightly around the head. Through the latex I could feel his tongue moving over the surface of my tip. It was a grand feeling, but now so dangerous to me that I was going to lose control from it the way I might have if he had been able to continue to capture my cock in the depths of his throat.

I regained myself, feeling as though some kind of chemical rush had just passed through me and I was only now getting back a sense of my actual self. I quickly collected some thoughts. I reached down, leaning over him while his head kept moving ever so slightly at its task. "Don't you dare let it slip out," I said softly. It was unnecessary in one sense: He obviously wasn't anxious to let my cock go. But it worked in another: It made it clear that he was still in his role.

I took both my hands and went to his chest. I found the little bells and began to move them both at once, letting them play a duet between themselves. The motions must have created some real discomfort, if not actual pain. He began to twist a slight bit from side to side and low groans escaped from his chest. The sounds and the physical reactions were too real to have come only from his hatred of the bells.

I kept one hand moving on a bell and moved another down to his crotch, having to move so close to him that now the thick hair on top of his head was brushing against my own naked chest. I found him still rock hard and now dripping fluid. I grabbed hold of the thick shaft and roughly twisted first one way and then another. More, louder, groans came from him.

But it wasn't until I moved to the metal-lined cock ring and grabbed it that he really began to display the effects of pain.

His mouth opened wide, and I felt a sudden draft of cool air where I had grown accustomed to the wet heat. He was gasping for strength and air. But he wouldn't move, I had to give him that credit. He stayed there, my rigid cock still in the center of his mouth. He overcame the pain and returned to his task, once again enveloping my erection in his throat. He wasn't going to give in quite so easily.

I released both my hold on his cock ring and on his bell and sat back. I studied him as he now returned to his task undistracted. His head was moving quickly, his tongue making its own its own movements to keep in sync with the thrusts he was creating. His hands were still at his side, but once he understood that I intended to remain passively enjoying the pleasures of his body, he moved them up to gently cup my testicles and hold them close to my torso.

The sight of his back was incredible. I saw all of the physical strength it contained. I could see his buttocks as they rested their meaty mounds on his heels. All of it was visually perfect. And all during it there was the sound of the small bells as they sent out the messages of his labor.

When I knew that his work was going to bring me to an orgasm soon, I pulled my cock from his mouth. He studied it, a lost look in his face while he saw it directly in front of his eyes. I had a hand on the back of his neck to hold him in place. Of course he could have used his power and freed himself from the embrace. But what he wanted, obviously, was to be free from the use of his power. That was his commonplace role — to be powerful. This was his fantasy — to be under some one else's control.

I guided his neck upward. He wasn't sure at first what I wanted. But soon he knew that I expected to feel that tongue on my nipples. When the recognition came, he leapt to the duty. Somehow he knew that it was important that I feel the opposite of what he was experiencing. Instead of his teeth nibbling and applying pressure that might possibly come close to pain the clamps were giving him, he worked my nipples with great and deliberate care.

He seemed to be timing himself to my movements. As I came closer and closer to my orgasm, his mouth only worked more intensely. His head crossed back and forth over my chest, taking care of both nipples as well as he could.

I could feel the boiling in my groin as I started to come with the vision of the muscled executive on his knees in front of me. I ripped off the condom. Pressure crept up from deep inside and when it erupted, so did my cock, shooting out pulses of fluid all over his chest.

I pushed him back while I was still coming, wanting to see the spurts fly onto his shaven body, once even hitting one of the silver bells. Without any hair to impede their movement, the strings of stuff rolled down over him quickly. When my belly was empty and I had regained at least some of my breath, I reached over and used my palm to smear the seminal fluid all over his chest.

I sat back, looking at him. There was no hint of the respected businessman left. As I saw him now with his knees spread apart his cock still erect, his torso showing the slightly white evidence of the rapidly drying come, he appeared to be just what he had presented himself as — a masochistic slave anxiously attempting to please his master.

"You do need this."

"Please, sir…," his voice trailed off as though he had been caught at something horribly embarrassing. He looked away from me. I leaned back over and grabbed his neck again.

"You do need this, don't you?"

He was there, collared and defenseless by his own choice. What could he say?

"Yes, sir." He hung his head back down.

"Come here, closer," I said, motioning him forward. He crawled the small space between us on his knees. I felt the contact with his still hard and now wet cock. I reached and again began to play with his bells. He closed his eyes again, the pain of the physical sensation and the humiliation were both merging. But the erection wasn't going away.

I moved my leg to the place between his thighs and ran my foot over the smooth skin. I lifted it up until I came into contact with his shaven scrotum. It was silky smooth; no other part of the body feels quite so perfect when shaved.

I rubbed my foot harder against him until it was again pressing the spiked cock ring into his flesh and eliciting the gasping sounds of his reaction.

"Put your hands back behind your head." He didn't hesitate to comply. "Now rub against me." I put my foot down on the floor as soon as I had said that.

He was puzzled. "Rub your cock against my leg until you come."

He lifted himself and pushed his erection against my shin, just below my knee. He began to move his hips to a silent cadence. I could feel the spongy flesh over the blood-filled shaft as the skin stretched and retracted with his motions.

His armpits were open to me. They were strangely pale in comparison to the otherwise tanned chest and arms. Seeing the few thin wisps of hair seemed to make him even more vulnerable.

"You enjoy that, don't you?"

"Please, sir, let me just beat off," he asked. I shook my head no. He didn't stop his movement. "Please, take off the clamps. Stop the bells." No again.

His scrotum was swinging now, and I could feel it bouncing against me every once in a while. The idea of masturbating against my leg was thrilling him and repulsing him. I knew that. But the thrill was dominating him. His cock was moving even more rapidly, and the actions caused the bells to continue to ring.

His breath was coming more rapidly, his face was beginning to flush. "This is just the way you should be, collared, your body adorned, your cock hard while you beg a master to let you come."

"Yes, sir," he said.

"You'll come to San Francisco for nothing more."

"Please, sir, when I'm there, please don't make me wear the bells." He was honestly begging me.

"The only thing I promise you is this: When you come to San Francisco and undress for me, the first thing that will happen is that I will put these same bells on your nipples and you will go around my party with them on, letting the others know you're approaching with the sound, announcing that they can do anything to your nipples that they choose…"

And with that, he came against my leg.

Teaching

I read the letter while sitting on the plane as it soared away from Ohio.

Dear Sir:

I've probably already made my first mistake. I mean, with the way I addressed this.

It's not that I'm inexperienced in S/M, but I do know I don't understand all the "right" ways to do things. If that makes any sense to you.

I'd better get to basics before I fuck this whole thing up. I'm twenty-two. I'm enclosing a couple recent snapshots of myself so you can see I'm not bad looking. I'm short, only about five feet six inches. I hope that doesn't bother you. I'm a student at a local university — studying to be an electrical engineer.

I come from Colorado. I grew up in a small town a distance from Denver. I've been gay as long as I can remember — and very active.

It started when I was young. As far back as I can remember, I was always trying to get the other kids to take off their pants. Most of it was the usual stuff. But I got into some things that you'd probably call S/M early on as well.

The other guys and I would play wild games. Our version of cowboys and Indians was a lot more authentic than what I hear other guys say they did when they were growing up, that's for sure.

We Coloradans know that the cowboys and the Indians tied one another up and tortured one another — all the time. I used to always try and figure out which side was the weakest so I could join it and have the best chance of being captured.

This went on until I left home to come to school here in Denver. By the end, a bunch of us had the game down to a science, and the science we were studying didn't end up with just a few rope tricks.

That was all just pretty hot teenage fun, though. I never was in any real S/M scene, just these really rough things with the kids back home.

I've always wanted to get back into it. There are some leather bars here, of course. But they don't do it for me. I don't understand all the lingo and the handkerchief codes and that. The discos I usually go to are just kiss and suck dating places.

I am planning a vacation in San Francisco. I was thinking that maybe the classified ads would give me a way to get into some new adventures. That's when I saw your ad. My problem is that I'll just be arriving in the city when your thing is going on. I can't get there any earlier. Is there any way to get an earlier interview? Or maybe we could just get together — you and me — after that's done with?

I began by saying I was sorry. I just don't know all the words, and I can tell from what I read that they're important. I don't mean to be disrespectful or stupid. But no one's taught me anything yet.

Well, not that kind of stuff, anyway. I remember being tied up by the guys at home, and I remember how much it turned me on. There's a lot going on inside my head about it. It's what I think about when I go on "nice" dates with "nice" guys and we play like we're never going to do anything like "that." If you know what I mean.

I suppose I'm just fresh to everything. I don't know if that bothers you very much. All I can say is I'll try very hard to do the right thing.

I'm so uneasy about it all because what you talked about in the ad is so…structured, I guess.

It sounds like you only want a pro who would be able to understand all of it. But, like I said, I'll try. And I want to try. It sounds like you're into some strange things, but they sound hot to me!

Your friend,

Keith

I folded the letter and put it back in my jacket pocket. I still held the photograph. I didn't have to worry about looking at it in front of my fellow passengers. If any happened to see the picture there was no possibility of them thinking there was anything nefarious about it.

It showed a very attractive young man. Actually, he looked cute. I seldom use that word, but it applied to Keith. He was standing in a pair of crisp, possibly ironed, jeans and a polo shirt. He was smiling directly into the camera. He was an icon of American clean-cut youth. And he wanted to be a servant at an S/M party.

One of the most ridiculous protests people make about those of us who explore erotic fantasies is the claim that our activities are products of the decadent city, as though they could only be produced by members of the urban subcultures.

My life in northern New England proved that was a sham. The men there are often like Keith. They might not know the precise meaning of the symbols that the urbanites have developed in order communicate with themselves, but they understand the lightning of harsh sexuality stripped of social pretensions.

Keith's letter resonated with the stories I had heard in other places. I would have been attracted to his open approach in any event, but the picture, with those wide and smiling eyes and the promising curves of his jeans, made him enough of a priority to justify a stop on my way to California.

I had talked to him on the phone a few times after receiving his letter. The openness, the sense of excitement and wonder — and certainly, the horniness — were all in his voice. There was no changing his schedule, college dictated that. But I could create this opportunity to spend a night in Denver. We could have our interview then.

The plane continued on, the steward served drinks. What a shame that they're forced to wear such formless clothes — not even room for a hint of chest hair to creep over the collars of their shirts. Their plastic smiles are so unmoving and so lacking in emotion.

I thought about the waste these stewards and their female counterparts stood for. They were forced to be automatons, deceived into thinking they were professionals because they had a union and rights and contracts. They were only servants, simply and purely. How much more pleasure we all would have gotten if they had been willing to assume that proper role. The flight from Ohio to Colorado was more than two hours long. There was more than enough time in there for some amusement with one or another of them if they weren't protected by their ideas of their places in society. Their airline would reap untold increases in profits and they could collect fine gratuities if they only understood better what their customers wanted and would be willing to spend for.

But the deceptions go on in many different arenas.

Christopher rankled me. That was part of it. The idea of him — his incredible body and his perfect masochism — were all intensely pleasurable. I wasn't going to complain about that nor deny it. I would have him at the party, and I would possibly have him to enjoy later on as well. But it would only be a masturbatory thrill. He would present only that body of his, there would be nothing else.

"Love?" No, I haven't used that term. I certainly wouldn't use it in relationship to Christopher. I didn't want anything like that from him. But there could have been more content, something to make the pleasure of that perfect body even more intense. There are so many sexual connections that can be made between men — between people — that can have so many benefits and include so many planes of experience, that accepting only the physical seems insufficient. Would I have accepted Christopher's limitations if he hadn't been so handsome? If his body hadn't been so perfect?

The segmentation he had constructed, and which he gave every indication he was going to hang on to, was the same that Keith was trying to avoid. Sex as revolution has its own appeals to me. I smiled as I thought of myself sitting in the first class compartment of the American Airlines jet and conceiving of myself as a revolutionary. But there were ways in which it was valid to think of that.

Adrienne says it is my duty to change the course of Western civilization. I! With my sexually ostentatious parties and my first-person paeans to males beauty? I don't think so. I certainly don't plan my life on it. But, as I looked at Keith's photograph still one more time, I decided it would be quite wonderful to change the course of his personal life history. My little Keith wouldn't be stuck in suburban discos with wistful memories of cowboys tying him to trees in preparation for exquisite tortures — not when I was done with him, at any rate.

*   *   *

I had Keith meet me in the hotel dining room. I purposely chose it because of its elegance. It is one of the finest in the West, known not only for the cuisine, but also for the extraordinary service.

He had told me that he'd never been here. In fact, it appeared he'd never been to a fine restaurant of any kind anywhere. His concept of a meal "out" was a steak house. I was appalled by that. There had been a time when the entrance into gay life had been a ticket to great social mobility. A young gay man who had been denied to social education could find many men, not all of them necessarily older, who would trade the appreciation of his body for the lessons in social conduct and knowledge that would allow him to move in the world.

Those were not mere hustlers — though I'm sorry to imply that male prostitutes should ever be described as "mere" anything at least by definition. They were young men whose birth had handed them the accident of membership in the lower classes — whose existence we are supposed to ignore. That we live in a democratic society is one of the great lies of America.

At least, once upon a time, being gay meant being freed from those restrictions. Now, with the superficial elements of "acceptance," our young men are sucked into the belief that they're like everyone else. Who ever told them that was desirable? To be like everyone else in America is to be ruled by television, to sublimate desire, to believe that a franchised steak house is the height of gastronomic delight.

If I gave Keith nothing else this trip, I would introduce him to the hotel dining room and let him have at least one experience with a waiter who saw his job as something more than a way station in life. Here, I knew, the staff would be delighted with their positions, honored to be a part of the traditions that existed in this hall.

I sat in the cocktail lounge and waited for him. He was a little early. I had warned him that there would be severe repercussions if he was late. I had refused to describe myself. He didn't know who he was meeting, and I enjoyed the few moments while he floundered, wondering whether or not to have a drink, hesitating twice as he moved toward the bar.

I finally stood and motioned for him to join me. His face lit up when he realized who I was. He seemed to bound across the room rather than simply walk. He had the energy and the enthusiasm of youth — a wonderful combination.

"Hello," he put out his hand. I purposely didn't take it, only looked down at it. "Oh," he said softly, "is that a mistake? Aren't I supposed to do that? I'm sorry."

But I did grab his hand and accepted his greeting. "I'm glad to meet you, Keith. Have a seat."

He was wearing a worn blue blazer. It was probably the same one he had purchased for his graduation party in high school. His slacks were old and scuffed, certainly not the height of fashion. But I could tell he'd tried hard to iron a crease into them, and the effort was more appealing than the vast majority of final products would have been. His shirt was also freshly ironed. The tie was knotted unevenly. His hair was slightly too long, not in terms of fashion, just in the fact it needed to be cut. He had done battle with a cowlick that had defeated him and which, probably without his knowing it, was sticking in the air at the back of his head.

All in all? A delightful picture.

I had made certain arrangements with the maître d', and we went directly into the dining area. Keith followed me as we were led through the well-dressed diners. I didn't even bother to ask what he thought of the extraordinarily high ceilings, the thick rug, the armies of waiters and busboys that moved so silently and efficiently through the room. If he had never been in such a place before, he was certain to be awed by it.

It took him a minute to realize that there was only one menu when we were seated at the table — mine. "I guess they forgot…"

"No, they didn't. I'll order for you."

"Fine," he said softly. He had the sense to sit silently while I read through the offerings. Water was poured, I ordered us wine, and then went over with the waiter the various foods that we'd eat, all the while refusing to speak to Keith. I simply chose for him what I, myself, was going to have.

I began the conversation over pâté. "This is, after all, an interview." Just keep to him off guard, I added, "It's cost me a great deal of money to arrange this for you. I would like to know what it is that you have to offer me that will make this worth my time and make it worth my time to include you in my party."

He was startled. "I...I sent you my pictures."

"A body isn't enough. A body can be had easily in many ways with many people. I want to know more about those attributes you have that make you think you're appropriate for my party."

"It doesn't seem like that's the question." There was a little insurrection brewing inside Keith, his back was stiffened and he spoke more loudly than he had before. "After all, you're the one who wants free labor for his party. I mean, come on, you expect... I don't know what you expect me to do. It doesn't seem like I'm the only one making the application."

"But you are," I smiled. I picked up my wine glass and sipped it. "I am the one who can offer you your fantasy. My fantasy is easily achieved. It isn't going to be difficult to hire a few professionals if I must. Obviously I could arrange that. But I am investigating letting you and a few others live out your dreams.

"I may not be playing cowboys and Indians like your childhood friends, Keith, but I certainly am arranging an event that will have more consequence than a night in your disco."

He let his head droop a bit. It was a very pleasant sight. "Tell me about it, please, the party, I mean. Tell me what it is you want. You've only talked around it. If I knew what was going on, maybe I could tell you why I'm the right one for it."

That was better, much better, I thought.

"The party will be private, as I said. There will only be four guests. In attendance will be an assortment of young men — all attractive. They will be the servants, obviously, some of them will be bringing on the food, pouring the drinks, that kind of thing. Naked. Of course. Then there will be others who will be the decoration. They will be assembled in various ways, bound, I suspect.

I haven't decided those details. But they will be a part of the atmosphere of the gathering.

"The only absolute thing — and I promise you this much — is the privacy of it. There will only be the four guests, and there will be no photographs, no intrusions, no surprises. Of course there'll be nothing that would in any way harm you over any period of time. No permanent marks, no injuries, no drugs that might produce psychosis, far from it. I doubt you'll have more than a glass of wine, if that.

"The party will be very low key. It will last only a couple hours on a Sunday afternoon. Then it will be over. All of it. You will have had your experience. I will have had your obedient participation. I'm offering you this trade — my ability to create a moment you will remember for the rest of your life in return for your being a part of the stage set I am creating. Is that clear enough?"

"But what are the requirements? I mean, how can I interview for something like that if you want more than my body?" He was puzzled, and I had no intention of not responding to his honesty.

"You can tell me what you have to offer. Why would you make a good servant? I'll examine your body later this evening to make sure it's all you claim and your photograph displays." He stiffened again; the idea that the interview would be sexual had only been implicit up to this point. "But your attitude is more important than anything else. Tell me about you. Why is it that those cowboy and Indian games reverberate through your memory?"

The arrival of our entree gave him a moment to collect his thoughts. He played with his food for a short while, studying it as a diversion. "I just liked it," was all he could come up with.

"There must be more to it than that."

"It made me feel...alive. That's all." He stared directly into my eyes now. "It just seems that sex should be more fun than it is with most of the guys I know. It should have more to it." He looked back down and blushed. "I'm a really horny guy. I used to think that I was sick or something, I jerk off all the time.

"I have this...appetite for sex. I want it whenever I can get it. I read the stuff about how it was before the health thing, and I know I'd be on the first bus to New York if it was still that way. Man, the idea that there are places where you could get it on two, three, four times a day!

"I do my work, go to school, keep everything in order, and that's all fine. But sex, man, sex is what makes life worth living.

"You know, I don't think it's that big a deal that what you're offering is S/M. That's one of the things I was hesitant about in answering your letter. I mean, it's fine, it's great, but I don't think I'm into it. I think I want to do it because it's sex. Anything that has to do with sex that I can do, I want it. I want it to be hot, and I want to know what it's like.

"I do think about the cowboy and Indian thing, that was no lie. But I think about circle jerks, and I think about the guys in the locker room, and I think about construction workers, and I think about.... . If it has a cock attached to it, I think about it."

He stopped his miraculous speech for a moment and seemed to soften as he looked at me now. "I think you understand. I used to think I was sick, you know, wanting to answer ads and wanting to go to parks and dreaming about cock all the time. No one else was talking about it, even in the bars. They were talking about all this other stuff — the love thing and all. But I think about it all the time.

"I'm not stupid. I know I'm not smart, but I'm not stupid. I did some reading. I forced some of the men I knew to talk to me. I discovered that I wasn't sick. I just had this overactive sex drive.

"So what am I going to do with it? I can't turn myself into a dream stud. I can't just add inches on to my height. I'm who I am. It's just that who I am is perpetually horny. That's why I'm going to San Francisco. I know, I know, I can't do it the way they used to, but I can see things, I can watch, I can be in places, and I can jerk off till the end of time.

"So there's your ad. It just told me that there was a sex thing that was going on that was different than anything else I could experience. Go for it, I decided. I answered your ad.

"Does that make you angry? That I'm not totally into the S/M thing?"

"Hardly. The...enthusiasm for sex overwhelms that. I'm delighted with what you've said. For one thing, you've indicated that you're not opposed to what you so drolly call 'the S/M thing.' So long as you respect it, how you use it in the rest of your life isn't of interest to me."

Keith started up again, "I don't want to be boring. That's the big thing. I mean, look at me, I've got blond hair and blue eyes. I'm short. No one ever notices me. I smile a lot in bars. I'm just like every other American kid. That bothers me. I want to do something exciting. Like you said, I want to have an experience that I'll remember for years after. Of course, I'll do everything you want. I promise that."

"We'll see, Keith, as soon as we finish our coffee."

*   *   *

When we got to my room I took him by the back of his neck and dragged his face to mine for a long kiss. He responded beautifully, wrapping his arms around my shoulders and using them to lift himself up to my greater height. He made no resistance when I began to undress him.

The skin on young men is so smooth, so perfectly wonderful to touch. I've always regretted the years of my own youth when I didn't realize what I had and thought the sleekness of my flesh was an ordinary event. That kept me from truly appreciating this sensation.

I lingered over it. My hands swept his back and played with the waistband of his pants for a long time. I moved my palms over to the front of him, still holding on to his neck and with my mouth now gnawing on the front part of it. I could feel the hard roundness of his chest. There wasn't any discernible nipple to my feel. I knew — and I would be proven correct — that there hadn't been nearly enough attention paid to that part of his anatomy. Until this evening, at least. The clothes dropped away until I had to let him go to take care of the pants caught around his ankles and the shoes and socks that are always so awkward.

I left him to the embarrassing tasks and sat on the edge of the bed to watch him. When he stood up he was still wearing his jockey shorts. He moved to take those off as well, but the sight was too precious to allow that to happen. "No. Leave them on. Come back here."

He had, I'm sure, expected some kind of violent and rapid action. He had probably fantasized about rape psychodrama — that's always the easiest thing to imagine in an assignation such as ours. But the circumstances were dictating my own response. Here was this small and adorable young man in his shorts, his hard cock poking a humorous bulge through the cotton fabric. His hair was already more tousled than it had been, and his face was red and looked even younger. I couldn't pass this up.

I pulled him harshly toward me. He was again on my lap. I kissed him more. My hands went to the seat of his shorts and felt the firm flesh underneath. He squirmed from it, and the little movements were beautiful indeed.

My hands moved under the crotch of the shorts and found his tight little balls captured in their sac. His cock was remarkably large in proportion to the rest of him; I could feel that from the base. I moved my hand around and grasped hold of it through the briefs. The tip had already wet the fabric.

He was moving wildly now, the very touch of my hand goading him on. He even began to moan a little bit. I moved my head down away from his mouth and neck and onto his chest. The nipples were, in fact, flat. They were barely pink colored, and there was no definition of the center at all. They were lovely. My tongue ran across them, and I discovered that even if they weren't well-trained, they were certainly very sensitive.

My teeth nibbled. Keith's reaction let me know that there was little pleasure in that. But he was in his place, he was acting as though he understood that this was the deal that had been chosen by him. He wouldn't fight it. I kept up my teething just long enough to let him know his protests weren't the reason for my finally stopping.

Then I pulled down the back of the shorts and exposed the ass. A slight blond down covered them. I was surprised that there was a thick line of hair in the crack of his buttocks. I let one of my fingers probe the crevice. He began to squirm with renewed vigor. I let my finger press harder at the ring of muscle in the center of his body, and there was a much louder and more emphatic sound coming from him than there had been before.

When my finger slipped past the protection and felt that perfect warmth of the inside of a male body, Keith began to really move. I forced the finger to continue moving deeper. My mouth was wandering pleasantly over his upper torso, just enough to keep all of his body in play.

Where was my mind? I was in such a state of utter enjoyment that I wanted to remember, but not enough to draw me away from it all. I conjured up a picture of a sultan with a young slave boy to play with. He was beautiful, all the slave boys would have been, and his cock was irrelevant. What was perfect was just this, just the simple fingering of his asshole and the wriggling he was involuntarily doing. It could only be that, he wouldn't dare attempt to escape. He wouldn't want to escape — being owned by this sultan would be the epitome of his dreams and desire. His only hope was to continue to make the sultan happy.

Keith was doing it, and he was doing it awfully well. I gently moved our bodies to place his face down on the bed, then I slipped out from underneath him and directed his face upward. My finger never left its sheath, and the picture with which I was eventually rewarded was unforgettably perfect.

Keith buried his head in the covers. His unflawed back was a wave of young muscles leading down to his waist. His ass appeared even more rounded and more pronounced than it had felt. The soft hair on it was so slight it could hardly be seen. My finger kept up its probing, and his wriggles increased with my motions, highlighting the curvature of his buttocks and producing occasional glimpses of dimples in the muscles.

Even the sight of the shorts gathered around his hips in wrinkles was perfect. He appeared only a young man being caught in something, and the mixture of his unwillingness and his submission was right there in the indelicate shape of the shorts.

"Please, I'm going to come," he whispered. I could barely hear him, his voice was muffled by the bed cover.

"Don't," I warned. But I couldn't imagine that the actions were too intense for him to be able to hold back. I didn't need to drive him to do something he couldn't control simply for an excuse to punish him. I already intended to do that. I slipped my finger out and left him sprawled out on the bed. I went into the bathroom to wash up and undress. When I returned I discovered that he'd turned down the lights. The room was subdued now.

Keith was on the bed, but this time he was face up. His hard cock was resting on his belly. His smaller balls were visible through the pubic hair; their excitement had lifted them up. His legs were spread apart to make sure I had a decent view. I wondered if he had consciously planned this exposure. He couldn't have done it any better if he had.

He smiled when he saw me and that I was naked. He lifted up his hands, as though expecting me to get on to the bed with him. Instead, I moved to the side and looked down at him. "Turn back over."

He did.

"Lift up your midsection."

He hesitated a bit, but then moved his legs up so his ass was raised to a better view.

"Spread your legs apart. I want to see in between them."

His thighs moved, and I could see directly into the crack. His small hole, where I'd just been doing my exploring, seemed too little to have accommodated even my finger. It was a sudden brown color after the paleness of his skin. His balls seemed bigger now that I could view the whole length of his sac. I love the line of hard flesh that dissects testicles and the way that it travels all the way from the anus around to the beginning of the cock. I reached between his legs and pulled the half-erect penis back. I tugged hard enough to make sure he had a sensation that it was being pulled for an inspection and not some little romantic ploy.

I released it and then ran a hand on the smooth back. His shoulders rested on the mattress, and his head was turned so he could look back at me. I could see an excitement in his view. Part of it was just the idea of being exhibited this way, I was sure of that. But part of it was the expectation as well.

I wasn't about to disappoint him. With my left hand, I reached down around his waist and took a firm hold of his cock and balls in one grasp. They would be my handle. My right hand was free. I lifted it up while he watched in silence and let it smack down on first one, and then the other of his cheeks.

He took the first few strikes quietly, as though the fact of them was so interesting that he didn't feel them. But after a half dozen or so, when the skin was beginning to take on a pinkness, he began the same squirming that had greeted my fingering of him before.

I had no intention of stopping this pleasure and only tightened the grip on his genitals. They were a perfect anchor. My hand flew back and forth, first one side, then the other. I would alter the order just enough to keep him from ever being able to know where it would land.

I could feel the tingle spread over my palm as the speed and force of the blows increased. He moved his head and his arms. He was fighting against the pain and the sensation. He had picked up the pillow at the top of the bed and buried his face in it. I heard louder sounds from him and then — after one particularly unexpected and hard slap — he reared up, his face freed from the pillow, and he yelled out.

Whatever he said was incomprehensible. It was just the physical response to what he was experiencing. I ignored it. I kept up the attack, watching the skin grow a deeper and deeper shade of pink until there were ovals of dark red occasionally. My hand was stinging now. I tried to ignore it. I thought of taking my belt out and using that instead but stopped myself. It wouldn't deliver the pleasure this was creating, and Keith might need to be brought slowly and carefully to that — the devices, no matter how simple, are always more frightening to the novice.

Then I stopped. I discovered that I was breathing with great difficulty. I had exerted myself immensely in the beating. My result was handsome. I still held Keith's cock and balls. There was no erection left. There was only the still upraised ass with its new rainbow of decorations. These are the moments I do want to have a camera, to capture the beauty of those marks. It would have been a momento worth having.

I released him carefully, letting his body slump onto the bed. His head was back in the pillow. I ran my hand up to the back of it and caressed him gently. I sat down now and both my arms went around his chest and pulled him up slowly. He'd been crying, his eyes were swollen and red, and his whole face was damp.

As soon as I had taken him away from the emotional guard of the pillow, Keith gave up his defenses. His arms swept up and wrapped themselves around my neck. I'm not sure what his emotions were. Was he relieved it was over? Was he embarrassed that he was crying? Was it that I'd broken some barrier and therefore, since I had taken something away, I had to be trusted? Or was he just appreciative of what had happened? Such answers aren't easy to get at in the moment of the event. I didn't try to explore them.

I returned the embrace. His smooth-skinned body against my own chest hair was a lush sensation. He finally lifted up and began to languidly kiss my cheeks, then my eyes. The movements were slow, deliberate, almost adoring. They were clearly an invitation to continue the lovemaking.

I reached down and discovered that his cock had resuscitated itself. Once again, it was a hard silky capsule. I held it tightly and began to stroke it. But this, I decided, wasn't the way I wanted to end. I moved him again, back onto the bed facing me. My own cock was hard as well, and it was just as needy as his.

I stood in front of him, forcing a place for myself between his knees so that his thighs were spread far apart. I began to stroke both of us. I did it so the motions were in harmony, both of our cocks building toward their orgasm. He laid there, his hands moving over his own body, gliding over his chest, down to his belly, cupping his balls, while my movements continued.

I felt the pressure build in me. My breathing was coming faster and deeper. His own rib cage was moving as well, swelling beautifully and then collapsing, making him appear older and his body more mature than it had ever before.

My balls began to move. They were pulsing with me now, the final announcement that an orgasm is really approaching. I stared intently into Keith's face. I heard him softly encouraging me on. I felt his cock stiffen even more, and then it seemed that every muscle in my body contracted for one split second. A wave of energy swept through me. Everything was suddenly focused in my balls. Everything stopped quickly and suddenly, and then, just as suddenly, it erupted out of me as the fluids all rushed downward and then out in pulsing waves.

I felt — just at the last moment — Keith's cock sharply rebel against my hand. Then, while I was still consumed with my own body's reactions, I barely began to understand that there was another source of wetness and warmth, that it was shooting out from him.

I collapsed on top of him while he was still coming, I could feel that hard young cock pumping stuff between us, and I was only aware of one slight sorrow — that it would cool and we would be finished with this moment much too soon.

The Place

I had chosen an old hotel near Nob Hill, neither in the seediness of Union Square nor the elegance of the summit. It had seen decidedly better days, but those days had been glorious. The rooms were much larger than the cubbyholes that the modern chains provide, thinking that a spare phone in a bathroom or a mint on a pillow case can make up for space.

In its days this place had been grand. You could still see that in the height of the ceilings in every room, from the lobby to the closets. The old rugs were still there, threadbare in many places, but in corners where there'd never been too much traffic, the rich reds and yellows of the design could be appreciated.

The lobby had an extravagant waste of space. Large columns cut up the huge room and the corridors were wide enough for a small army to march up and down in parade formation.

I had reserved the largest suite. The desk clerks weren't used to people coming to the hotel in style any longer, and I could see from their eyes that it had been ages since anyone had purposely taken the "Presidential Suite." Certainly the cheap hustlers and prostitutes who were loitering on the lobby furniture weren't any indication that people were spending large amounts of money to stay here. It was hardly a place that a traveling salesman would choose to impress his clients or a visiting starlet the press.

I had my reasons for staying here. The hotel — like so many others in dying downtowns — had decided that it could resurrect itself with gay business and conspicuously advertised itself in gay newspapers and magazines. The manager, staff, and — I was told — even the owners were gay and more likely to understand a variety of "special" needs.

The bellboy who carried my bags up to the room certainly seemed anxious to fulfill some of those needs. His tight rear was captured in pocketless trousers that accentuated his charms — both front and rear. He seemed to be Hispanic with olive skin, slick black hair, and brown eyes. He would normally not be of interest to me. There was no indication his willingness extended to my personal proclivities, but his beauty was beyond doubt and the flirtatious manner with which he carried himself was endearing.

I toyed with the idea of picking up on his not so subtle messages while he showed me through the suite. The sitting room was perfect. I was so pleased that I almost forgot he was there. It was made for my circus. I was stunned by it. The ceilings were easily fifteen feet high. There were large, nearly floor-to-ceiling windows looking out over the city. Small pillars, not unlike the larger ones in the lobby, guarded the entrance to the room. The furniture was in disrepair, but some was obviously the original stuff the old hotel had used.

The rug was just as threadbare as the one downstairs, but it was enormous, nearly covering all the floor and only occasionally showing bits of parqueted wood. There were three couches, one against each wall — the wall that contained the entrance was the one without. Two armchairs stood in the corners between the couches. There were utterly horrible but ornate fake paintings on the one wall that didn't contain either a window or the entrance. They were drab, but appropriately set off by the long dingy painted walls.

A large cocktail table, nearly six feet long, sat in the middle of the collection of other furniture. My mind took in the space, the perfectly oversized furniture and the hint of history in the suite, and I was overwhelmed by possibilities. Things had happened in this room that must have been extraordinary. The hotel had to have been built immediately after the earthquake and would by now have collected more than eighty years of stories.

And I would add another.

I was extraordinarily pleased.

"Don't you want to see the rest?" The bellboy had to break into my reverie to get my attention.

"Of course," I smiled to him and followed down the corridor.

"Sorry, the light's out here. I'll get someone up to fix it right away. It's not too dark, though. I mean, all the light from the other rooms is enough. But you should have lights. All this will get fixed soon enough. You know they're going to renovate. Man, this old place is going to be a lot different when they get done."

"Done? Who's going to do it?"

"One of the big companies, you know, with hotels all over the world. We're going to have to join a union, it's so big. But they're going to invest lots and lots of money into this place and make sure it's just as nice as the other ones around here. It's going to be something."

I was sure it was going to be another disgrace, another pile of little boxes for little businessmen and women to sit in while they did their little commerce in a society that was losing all of its sense of scale and majesty. I was having my party none too soon.

We went into the master bedroom next. This room was nearly as large as the other and was dominated by a large bed with tall and outlandishly decorative posts at all four corners. There were two more, smaller stuffed chairs. Again, a worn rug. The night tables that stood on either side of the bed didn't match. But the mirrors that stood at the head and across the room from the foot of the mattress were extraordinary. I studied them both and must have been smiling.

"Yeah, lots of guys, they like the mirrors. They can be pretty kinky." The young man was smiling lewdly as he watched me. The trousers weren't hiding anything; I could easily make out the lines of not only his cock but also his balls through the black cloth. He stood in the center of the room facing me and seemed to turn his head in a slight, seductive manner. Yes, of course he'd know how "kinky" those mirrors could be.

When I didn't respond, he seemed disappointed. His salary was probably minimum wage and the tips in a run-down hotel would-n't have earned him all that much more. He probably needed the extra money that a trick could bring him. But I wasn't about to squander myself on a bellboy when I had so very much waiting for me here is San Francisco.

He took the clue and went about his business of placing my bags on stands and then showing me into the bathroom. It was another treasure. It was tiled completely in white with only a very few black panels to create a pattern here and there. The toilet, the washstand, and the tub were all old porcelain. The tub and the washstand were much larger than expected in hotels these days. The floor was the same tiles as the wall. Everything was in perfect condition, as though the materials had been of such good quality when the place was built that they could easily withstand the neglect they'd received since then.

The only indication of the age and disrepair of the building, itself, was the heat. The steam pipes were noisy, they'd already actually banged a couple times in the few minutes I'd been in the suite. That seemed a minor problem in the midst of all this, and it did at least indicate that there would be heat. It was pleasant weather outside, and if the rooms became too hot I could simply open the windows and cool off that way.

"Sure you don't want anything else?" The bellboy's voice had a new tone in it. He actually sounded hurt, as though the rejection of his sexual services implied much more than I meant it to. I simply wasn't interested.

But he wouldn't leave, even when I hadn't responded. "I, uh, get off pretty soon. If you want anything, I can come back…"

"Not today. But I would like to have a special housekeeping done. I want it to be spotless. Can you arrange for a crew? I don't expect the staff to do the extra work on hotel time. I can see you're not paid for that. But I want this place in the best shape it's ever been. I'll pay for it."

I opened my wallet and took out a ten dollar bill as a sort of earnest money. He grabbed it quickly and studied it for a moment. "Sure, a couple maids, me and another guy to do the heavy stuff, it'll cost, a couple hundred bucks?"

"Fine."

His surprise showed that he had only been testing me. I could have gotten the job done for less. It certainly must have created the impression that I had unlimited wealth — which I don't. He warmed to me considerably.

"Hey, we'll have this place in great shape. We'll come in at ten in the morning, okay? Be done in a couple hours. You won't recognize it. We can get the best stuff out of the storeroom for you, make sure your towels are new and things like that. I'll tell my sister to take special care of you — she's a chambermaid. You'll see. You'll be glad you did this, man.

"What is it, you throwing a party? Or you got some big client coming here or something?"

"A party."

"Hey, you know, we can work it for you. We do that a lot. I can bartend, my sister can carry a tray of food, make it look like a real class act."

I tried to picture him and his sister naked at my party, with matching sets of metal earrings on their nipples. I smiled at the thought.

He mistook my humor. He thought he might have another chance now. "Hey, you interested in some…very special service?" he groped himself openly. His hand forced his cock and balls into a tight knot that bulged obscenely — and quite nicely — in those black slacks of his. He moved closer.

The idea was becoming more appealing, I have to admit. He had a wonderful, fresh odor about him. His hair, especially, smelt clean and attractive. He was only a few feet away when I shook my head, no.

"Sorry," he shrugged. "You know, most of the guys who stay here…"

"Oh, I know. And I certainly know you're attractive. I'm simply not in the mood."

"Sure," he smiled, a little unconvinced. "But keep me in mind if you do get…in the mood. My name's Joseph. You can ask for me at the desk if you want."

He began to leave. I felt a stirring in my crotch. I thought of a wonderful idea. "Wait."

He turned around. I had taken out my wallet again. "Just in case I do have the urge, I think I'd like to see what I'm going to buy." I handed him two more bills.

He took them and frowned. "Just to see?"

"Just to see," I assured him. I sat down in one of the chairs in a relaxed posture. "You needn't undress completely. Just drop your pants to your knees and lift up your shirt above your chest."

He hesitated for a moment, but then looked back down at the money I'd handed him. It was, I'm sure, as much as most men offered him for much more complex sex acts. He shrugged. After stuffing the bills in a shirt pocket, Joseph unbuckled his trousers and unzipped his fly. The slacks were so tight that he had to push firmly to get them down over his hips. He was wearing a pair of bright yellow underpants. There was no fly and their shape made his genitals appear much larger than I was sure they were.

He moved to push them down as well. His cock was half hard and arced out from his belly to point downward. It was darker than the rest of his skin, almost a chocolate brown. His testicles were large and had the same dark color. The pubic hair was a thick web against his white abdomen.

Then he took the bottom hem of his shirt and lifted it up. His body hair was sparse above the waist. His stomach was flat and hard looking. His navel had a protrudence of flesh, a little nub, that stuck out from it. His chest wasn't well-developed, but his very large nipples were the same dark color as his cock and balls.

"Seen enough?" he smiled.

"No," I said. "Stay there for a moment."

He didn't move. I imagined him as a proud mestizo in the Mexico of his ancestors. There was a warrior's pride about him, even in this humiliating stance. It made the sight much more interesting, much more delightful.

He was uncomfortable — something to add even more pleasure. He shifted from foot to foot and would alternately look away and then stare me in the eye, his face displaying a constantly moving series of emotions.

He moved to lower his shirt, and I stopped him. "No, keep it up there, I want to see your tits." He complied.

The event was turning him on. His cock was getting harder. I sat there, silently, and watched as the curve increased its length and pitch. It was uncircumcised, its wrinkled hood added a beauty to it. The small bit that showed through the foreskin became even more erotic.

He, himself, looked at it at one point, as though he were studying a foreign part of his own body. When he'd done that, the erection quickly increased. Soon it was fully stiff and standing out at a proud right angle to his belly.

"Good," I said as I stood up. "You have a fine body, a very interesting cock. I'll keep it in mind if the occasion warrants a call to you. Now, I have to make some phone calls. I'll see you soon, Joseph."

There was a moment where he seemed lost by my statement. Then he hurriedly put his clothing back in order. I was leafing through the phone book, ignoring him.

"You're as kinky as those mirrors," he said finally. "Man, maybe you better not call me." He seemed a bit hurt.

"Whatever. I do want you and the others to come at ten o'clock tomorrow, though. I have to have the place in perfect order."

"Sure, sure." He was buckling his belt back again. "I don't have a problem with that." He went toward the door, hesitated, then looked back. "I didn't mean that, about you being too kinky. I can get into it."

"For the money?"

He shrugged his shoulders. "It's sex, man. Yeah, I'll do just about any sex for money."

"I'll remember that, Joseph."

A Duet

While I enjoyed the anachronism of my hotel as a place to sleep and entertain, I was not prepared to eat my meals in its restaurant. Instead, eager to get into the mood of San Francisco, I walked up the steep slope of Nob Hill and treated myself to a fine dinner at one of the first class hotels there. I had an early evening appointment and my body was still on East Coast time, so I ate well before the rush and let the handsome staff wait on me. They were just as happy to pay me extra attention in the off hours of their shift as not. The boredom of standing and waiting for the night's rush of diners was obviously not their favorite activity.

I ate slowly and enjoyed every moment of it. I found the waiters intriguing. They were — to my studied eye — quite obviously gay. While their service was perfect, they were also taking great liberties with me. They had identified a kindred spirit and thought their jokes and asides would be welcome. I fell into the joviality of it all and bantered with them, even if it did erode the perfection of the experience.

Still, they were delightful young men, happy to be living in San Francisco and happy to have someone at one of their tables who would and could talk to them.

I had a second cup of coffee to waste a little extra time. I knew that it would be only a fifteen-minute cab ride to my destination and to be early would have completely spoiled the effect.

I sat and thought back over the answer to the ad that had produced the visit I was about to make. It was the most intriguing in its delicacy, the most appealing in what it could accomplish.

I was, after all, going to leave San Francisco after the party. Of course, I would walk away with new memories of Martin, and I wouldn't be at all surprised if some of the other men involved in Sunday's occasion wouldn't also become a part of my life.

Aren't I still your boy?

The words — as familiar as they were — hit me when they moved through my mind. The accumulation of adventures brings with it an accretion of people. They become part of my life, they linger with me, the emotional bond becomes a part of me, just as it becomes a part of them, I'm sure of it.

The Christophers of the world can erect the most formidable barriers against it, but even theirs can be destroyed, ripped open, never to be put back into place. I dismissed the idea of taking on Christopher directly. No, I didn't want to invest the energy, and there were too many other people involved who could be struck by the falling debris — his wife, the woman who had been lied to and emotionally cheated throughout his frolics, was certainly one of them. I wanted no responsibility for anything other than the overt sexual contract I had made with him. I would use him, and he would be used as he wanted to be in his dreams. It would stay a masturbatory fantasy, but he would never enter into those secret parts of my self. He would not be like Martin.

But there were others… The two I was about to see tonight were after something so specific and so easily and well-achieved by involving me in their lives that I could easily see myself performing a deed that one might call noble.

I smirked at that idea. The nobility of the sadist! What a fine ring that phrase had to it. But there was a slight bit of truth to it. They were in need. I held the means to meet that need. And I would leave, making the connection clean and clear and not presenting any tarrying complications. I would be a very good friend.

Finally, it was time to leave the restaurant. I paid my bill, leaving enough of a tip that the waiters would remember me fondly when I returned — and I knew I would return, for this was precisely the kind of grand hotel restaurant that Madame would enjoy. I went to catch a cab.

Phillip and Glen lived in a neighborhood that bordered the area south of Market. Their house was a Victorian, not really a very impressive building, but a solidly middle class two-story house that I was sure was worth quite a bit on the inflated real estate market. They had lived here for ten years, they'd told me. That meant, according to some quick mental calculations, that they had bought the house for a very small amount when it was little more than a shack and the area around it hardly the middle class enclave it had become.

The boys had done well. They'd described the hard work they'd put into the building, pioneers in those first waves of urban renewal. The structure looked sound, the paint on the outside was competent and attractive, the small yard was lovingly cared for.

I went to the front door and rang the bell. There was a sudden noise on the other side. I knew how very much tension can be built up by the expectation of a visit like this one. It had been arranged more than a month before, and the phone calls and the exchanged notes wouldn't have alleviated the worry and concern that they'd been feeling at all. In fact, each of our communications had produced an intensified reaction.

I'm not sure what it will mean to give up my role. The more I think about becoming a bottom, the more I worry what it will do to the way that Phillip looks at me. I worry about that. I worry about my need to be a bottom. It's not my only need, but it's a strong one. I still want to be who I've been to Phillip. I just want to be something else to someone else — *at least once in a while...*

Phillip answered the door. I recognized him from the photographs. His handsome skin was as impeccable as the pictures had made it look. He smiled; his tanned complexion seemed to dance with possibly natural highlights that actually seemed to convey a peach tone, and his teeth were as ideal as I had expected.

"Come in, please," he said, standing aside. As I walked by him I could sense the same kind of insecurity that Keith had shown — his hands seemed to move in midair for a split second. They didn't know if they were supposed to shake mine or stay out of the way. He bent his body slightly, perhaps in a half attempt to bow that was short-circuited by a realization that the melodrama of the action would be inappropriate.

I walked into the pleasant living area. Glen was waiting. He stood up and nodded. "Welcome."

I smiled, took a seat and accepted the offer of a glass of Scotch from Phillip. Glen sat back down on his own chair. He was obviously nervous. He was leaning forward with his elbows on his knees while his lover went about the host's duties in the other room. Glen's hands were clasped in front of him, and his fingers were rubbing the back of each of them. I let him sit in the silence. It would have been a sham to make any comment to relax the young man, given what I had planned.

Glen was quite as attractive as his lover. They were both brown haired, but Glen's appeared darker, and his clean-shaven beard was obviously heavier. He was wearing an athletic shirt, and I could see that his forearms were hirsute as well. I had seen a picture of him naked only from the waist up. From that I knew that his chest was as thickly covered as anyone would ever want it to be.

Phillip reappeared with my drink. He and Glen already had theirs, I saw. Too bad, it wasn't the best way to start. But their house had certain very distinct advantages over the hotel suite, and I had decided that the use of what they proudly claimed was a well-equipped playroom made up for the inconvenience and distraction of allowing them the luxury of having the action taking place in their own space.

"Is the party still on?" Phillip asked in a conversational tone.

I was stunned for a second. "Of course," I blurted out, not understanding why he would ever have doubted it. But of course, I realized, there are so many who talk about their plans so well and so loudly and then never, ever come through. "Everything's in quite good shape. I assume you're still prepared."

Glen began to fidget, moving more in his seat and acting very uncomfortable, so much that I wondered if he was going to say no at this late date. But that wasn't what was on his mind.

"We are. God, are we!" He laughed then; it had a good solid tone to it, and the smile that broke out on his face was full of good cheer and anticipation. He was finally looking at me. "We've been thinking about nothing else. We're a little scared, we told you that, especially me…"

Yes, they had told me that. This was a great experiment for them. A time of change in their lives and in their relationship. Not that its foundations were in doubt. I could tell that their protestations that they were committed to one another were true just by observing the look that passed between them now.

I sipped the Scotch and took in the sight. Phillip was not as large as Glen. He was probably five foot ten. He was well-built; obviously he attended a gymnasium regularly.

He was wearing the same type of athletic shirt as his lover. His arms rippled with rope-like muscles and sinew as he moved to reach his drink. His chest was expansive, and his waist was tight and compact. His nipples noticeably stuck out against the cloth. He had been, after all, the bottom in this relationship for quite a while, and his nipples would have received a great deal of attention.

Glen's, on the other hand, weren't at all obvious through his shirt. His jeans were as well-molded as Phillip's, the thigh muscles and the calves were obvious. I wondered how much experimentation he'd done before this one time. I thought now, as I had guessed earlier, that there hadn't been much. The authenticity in the way they had described their kinship and the length of time it had lasted didn't indicate that there would be a lot of lying or sneaking around between them.

I didn't speak. I let them sit with their thoughts. They had wanted this meeting to take place in a leather bar. That was so expected. I would have dressed in my uniform and they in theirs, and the roles would have been set with dramatic effect. I could have been the prop for their psychodrama, and that would have been so easy for them.

But I insisted the interview be in a social setting, not a sexual one. It is one of my most common conditions. They'd resisted, but then given up with the acknowledgment that they, themselves, were after more than the sexual. This encounter that I insisted upon would make them deal with their reality in a more concrete form. They acceded to my demands.

Now they were in their living room. The jeans, athletic shirts, and worn black leather boots they both sported were obviously their most comfortable clothes. These were boys who lived in the neighborhood, for whom the stuff of the leather culture was simply taken for granted. Their clean outfits — and the lack of keys on Glen's left side — were accommodations for my pleasure. I understood that.

The downstairs was directly below us. It would have been easy, also, if they had met me there, if we had gone right into the action—because the desire on all our parts was for action. The "interview" element in this visit was even less important than in the others.

These two men were making a trade with me.

Your party sounds like a wild time. It's not really what we would nor-mally get into. I don't mean to be disrespectful, but it seemed to me that we could trade with you. If you'll help us out, we'll return the favor.

Glen looked at me and spoke first. "We heard...about you. We have lot of friends in the leather world. They told us...you were the right person."

So that was the cause of their choice of me for this experiment. I hadn't investigated that before. It hadn't been of great concern to me. But, of course, I should have realized. The Network would be in effect. Many of the people who had recognized my advertise-ment would be talking.

People like Martin would have been building up the party for their own ego's sake: "I'm going to be a part of it." And people who knew me by reputation, the ones who could never quite believe that I had left this life and hadn't reentered in so long, would be taking a gossip's pleasure in reporting my activities.

He's coming back. He was supposed to leave, but he's in San Francisco. An ad, a personal, a few men...that Martin, do you remember the sailor he used to have...

The Network is the one part of the sexual world that makes all of its enemies right. The other dangers and warnings they spout are stupid, meaningless. But there is a network of men — and women — who do communicate. That their subjects are willing adults and that their contracts are all highly consensual doesn't take away from the impact of their reality.

The Network is a conspiracy, a group of like-minded people who have drawn together and who spread word through a hidden chain of information — all the most modern forms — computer modems, telephones, videotapes. Who are the actors and where are they playing? The word gets out.

I hadn't paid attention to it in years. I had no real reason to. I simply knew that it was functioning. I hadn't stopped to think that, yes, my reappearance on the scene would be announced.

"What did these...people tell you?"

"They weren't very coherent," Glen answered. "Some of them said, yes, he's the one. Others told us to watch out for you. But they couldn't — or wouldn't — explain why. If you'd been dan-gerous in any of the usual ways, I think I would have found out. I know a lot of people in the scene. But the warnings weren't that overt. They just said you were...pretty heavy."

Pretty heavy! What an archaic term.

"And that didn't concern you? That I had that reputation?"

"No," Glen said. "Who we are and what we're doing needs someone who understands. I think you do." He finally sat up in his chair. "This is all very difficult, for me at least. I don't know, Phillip says it's all fine. But the changes in our selves and our relationship are pretty drastic. I take all this very seriously."

I could see that. Glen was speaking with as much veracity as he could muster. I saw the way he was studying me, and I realized there was, indeed, danger here. There was ground being broken, and the manner in which it was done by whom would not go unnoticed. My expectation that this was going to be a totally clean dynamic was being challenged.

That, certainly, didn't mean I was gong to avoid what might happen. Hardly. I looked quickly back and forth between the two men and realized that this was certainly a remarkable find.

I had seen Phillip before in pornographic photographs and movies. When he had been much younger, before he met Glen, he'd acted in them. It was an expression of his masochism to let his body be viewed by as many people as possible. He claimed he'd never really needed the money, only desired the attention.

Now, like Glen, his looks had matured, and the maturation was very much in his favor. He was a handsome man, not just a pretty boy. The training he'd given his muscles had filled him out, made him all the more appealing.

Glen had been the stronger of the two for almost all of their time together. He'd taken the raw material of Phillip ten years ago and insisted that it be disciplined, that it be structured and made to function in a responsible and planned manner. They were not, Glen had decided, going to fall into the traps of the gay world.

If it would take actual physical and sexual correction to make Phillip understand the seriousness of Glen's intent, all well and good. Glen would give it. They had entered into a well-thought-out and articulated plan. They had saved the money for this house. In its basement they had constructed what they assured me was a complete stage set for their sexual needs.

Phillip had been led down the stairs as often as Glen thought he needed to be reminded and assured of his place in their lives together. Glen had gone and found older, more experienced men who explained to him the techniques, the methods and the finer points of the dominating sexuality that he wanted to deliver to his lover.

They had claimed that Glen became extremely proficient in his actions. The journeys to the cellar became more and more intense, the events more noteworthy, the ability he had to bring his lover to the peaks — and the depths — became more sophisticated.

It had worked for years. They had collected their leather and made the rounds of the parties, the bars, the weekend retreats, and they had done it all just by themselves.

But they were young, their proclivities hardly set in concrete. Glen needed room to maneuver, he discovered. The performance he gave for Phillip's benefit had changed in his mind. It wasn't enough.

I suspect he simply relaxed. His insistence on taking over and disciplining Phillip's life was a simple way for him to insist on structure in his own. When it was achieved and those base necessities — a relationship he trusted, a home they owned together, the beginnings of a real career — were accomplished, then he found himself floundering, and other personal needs began to surface.

Glen was fatigued. His role had been all for Phillip. People who aren't experienced in the scene seldom understand how much the bottom, the slave, is usually the focal point of all the activity. It's not at all strange that Phillip had desired to display his body in endless numbers of pornographic photographs. Most masochists are gluttons for attention. At least, the ones who play-act at it are. There are those I admire and covet so much who are willing and able to resign themselves to another man's pleasure.

They are most often the ones who have experienced both roles. They, like Glen, have seen the flow of energy and understand that the bottom is being given a gift by his master. *Attention* is the right word. Think of the most devastating S/M event you can imagine and realize just who it is that is the focus for all the action.

It is a perversity of the real meaning of S/M that I seldom allow. It is worth it to me when the figure I'm being given to work on is truly worth the sexual energy involved. And, I realize, isn't that precisely what is going on between myself and Christopher?

But, that's not the point here. The point here, right in front of my eyes, is this pair. Phillip, a well-trained and experienced masochist, had lived his adult life under the service of his lover/master Glen. And Glen had allowed his own desires to build and build until they approached the breaking point.

Glen wanted to change his role. Phillip, it was obvious to everyone, couldn't and wouldn't provide the opportunity. And it would have been a violation of their contract, if either had entered a separate relationship with another man. They'd told me in letters that they'd thought about doing just that. This was San Francisco, and it wasn't uncommon for people to have multiple relations. But there were the health concerns, of course. And there was the stickiness of the relationships.

Perhaps, they'd suggested, they could share the experiences of serving at the party. They would come and attend as servants together. There was danger involved. That was the issue Glen had written me separately about. What would happen to Phillip's vision of himself if he saw Glen in a servile role — and adoring it?

Of course it could work. Glen assured me that neither he nor Phillip wanted him to give up his role entirely. That was obviously going to have to be the dynamic between the two of them. But, if he could have his fantasies met, if he could enjoy the other side of the equation, if there were someone who wouldn't threaten their relationship... . And I, of course, lived far away. I could be that person.

I understood even more of it now. It was finally getting into my mind that there might be no end to what would happen tonight. I thought of Martin and the way he carried the image of me through his life, the phantom master who could always be turned to when needed, if only for a masturbatory moment.

I understood even more of it now. It was finally getting into my mind that there might be no end to what would happen tonight. I thought of Martin and the way he carried the image of me through his life, the phantom master who could always be turned to when needed, if only for a masturbatory moment.

I studied Glen and wondered if I would be that person for him as well. On those occasions when they were having sex and the role of the master was too tiring, too demanding, when he needed the attention and the release from responsibility, would he be thinking of me from now on?

Another one, another one to carry in my mind and to hold in my dreams and fantasies. Such a handsome one, too.

"I'm ready to go downstairs. Are you?" I stood up before they could answer. The two of them wavered for the shortest period, then got up together, as though their movements had been synchronized.

Glen led us to a doorway in the hall that I assumed went to the basement. He stopped when his hand had taken hold of the handle, and he turned to me. "We always make this our changing point," he explained in a way that let me know he meant that this was a major symbol in their lives. "From here on in, the language changes and the action begins immediately."

There *was* a boundary then.

Many men used the device, and it was a splendid one. Many men could not conceive of another who was a clerk during the day as someone who could, at a simple statement, change into the master. An effective means of dealing with it was to create a line — something as elementary as the entrance to the bedroom — past which the personalities changed. In the living room and the kitchen, the two men would be lovers, engaged in the mundane necessities of their existence. They could peel potatoes together, watch television, and argue as peers. But once they moved over that line, then the other parts of their personalities were in force.

This stairway was that line for Glen and Phillip. Their theater was more intense and more dramatic than most. They would need to have a clear signal that the curtain was going up; the doorway provided it.

I wanted to show them that I understood. I turned to Glen and took him very gently into my arms. At first he didn't understand, he must have thought that I was trying to begin some of the action. But when it was apparent that I was only going to embrace him and kiss him, his body melted into it, and he gracefully responded. I reached out a hand and brought Phillip in closer. His mouth was mine to kiss as well. The three of us stood there, our arms around all of our shoulders, and our faces pressing against each other. Glen sighed, delighted.

I went down the stairs first. When we had all reached the floor I could see the startling difference in the attitudes of the pair of them. They had entered their sacred space, and they were with the priest they had asked to reside over their services.

They moved slowly, but went about the tasks of creating the atmosphere for their rites. Candles were lighted in each of the four corners. They were all large and white, each sitting on one of a matched set of holders made of elaborately designed iron.

There were also the electric lights that we had turned on at the top of the stairs. They were all dim, the bulbs red-hued. But, with the candles, I could clearly see the details of the room.

In the very center was a table. The middle third of it was grounded on a stand, but I could see that the other parts of it were ingeniously constructed. They were hinged to the center piece. But their corners were attached to chains that were firmly attached to the floor and the ceiling. I understood immediately what effect they could have.

Another chain, even heavier, ran from the ceiling to a bolt in the floor. It stood like a sculpture beside the table. That, I knew, would prove to be interesting.

There was a shower stall, almost invisible behind a black rubber curtain that wouldn't have been noticed by an unsuspecting eye, and beside it a sink and a toilet. There was even a club refrigerator, probably stocked with beer and soda.

On one of the walls was an impressive display of implements. Whips, crops, leather straps, paddles, and canes were all in careful — even loving — place.

Another wall held just as extensive a collection of restraints, from simple handcuffs to antique-looking shackles. There were lengths of rawhide and rope, masks made of leather and rubber, even a straitjacket for total immobilization.

I take all this very seriously.

Glen certainly did. I could imagine how long it had taken them to accumulate the tools for this room.

Phillip had moved to the other side of the room where there was a stereo. The rich sounds of orchestral music suddenly filled the space. He turned down the volume and then stood there, waiting.

Glen was by the table. His arms were behind his back, his head was slightly lowered, just as it had been upstairs.

These males, those who had been used to having the role of master, had strict and uncompromising expectations that they had developed over their years with masochists. They understood the perfection of stance, reaction, submissiveness, and how very much it could be appreciated. They judged themselves very harshly, more willing and able to act for the master's pleasure than any other slave would be. Glen, with his pent-up frustrations, knew he was suddenly in a room with someone who would understand them exquisitely and would do anything to avoid a lack of grace; he knew how disconcerting that could be.

The music lent another level to the sense of the religious and theatrical air of the room. The boys had worked hard at this place. Another wall was a gallery of photographs. Purposely ignoring them, wanting them to enjoy these moments of disquiet anticipation, I went over to study the photographs.

Most of them were clipped from magazines. Here were the pornographic ideals that the two of them must have shared. The images were expected: the muscled young men in leather, the hard-looking bikers, the harsh military officers. There were also their own photographs, obviously the most cherished self images they had. Glen in his leather, with his forbidding cap covering the top of his face, but his cock stiff and hard in the opening of his chaps. Phillip standing naked and collared, his arms bound behind him, his body marked with scarlet stripes after a particularly hard session. The two of them on a motorcycle in the country, both in leather, but both smiling.

"I want you both naked." I said the words without turning to watch them. They were in their temple, and they understood that their clothing defiled it. Their skin would be more appropriate. I listened to the rustle as they both stripped quickly.

I turned and saw them both nude, awkwardly standing there, not quite sure what I had in mind for them next. There was a leather upholstered chair over by the fourth wall, a wall that was decorated only with a pair of large posters of drawings of men in leather. I went over and sat there.

Basement. What a strangely insufficient word to describe what this place must mean to the two of them. This was more intimate than their bedroom. It was the place where their secrets were shared and their risks were taken.

I sat in the chair and took in their bodies. Glen's body hair was as thick as I had expected, Phillip's as smooth. Their torsos were unflawed, the lines of their chests were perfectly matched fans, their thighs were thick and well-defined. Both their cocks had begun to rise.

Glen was again standing with his hands behind his back. I could sense the tension in his body, expectation was taking hold of him.

A small line of sweat was already making its way down the side of his stomach.

"You've never done this?" I asked.

"Never…*seriously, sir,*" Glen responded. They had told me only a few things, just hints really, about the times when they had attempted having sex with a third party and one of the three of them had given up. That had been one of their problems. Finding just the right person to do the thing correctly.

"And it's something you want to share?"

"Yes, sir," Phillip answered this time.

Other men would have found the repetition of these questions and answers unnecessary — we had gone over them in the letters and phone calls. But these two understood, as I knew they would, the ritual benefits of what was going on. They were making their confession before their communion. The words must be said and the honor must be done with the priest in attendance.

"Come here, Glen," I motioned him with my hand. He came forward, his head still bent. When he was only inches in front of me, he stopped, leaving his still-filling cock directly in front of my face. I could see the wrinkles of his scrotal sac, the veins in his penis, the purple of the glans skin covering. There was an odor about him, of excitement, perhaps fear. There was dampness on his pubic hair from the emotions.

I ran my hand up and down his right thigh, testing the firmness of the flesh. It was perfect. I wonder sometimes if my indulgence in this special world of sexuality has only to do with my desire to so minutely examine male bodies. I adore having them so obviously and openly available to me. I can't imagine being one of those people who talk about wanting to commune with the whole person, wanting to have just the merger of souls. Of course, I know that, and I honor that when it occurs, but this, male flesh, is a delight all of its own.

"Phillip." The other one moved over as soon as I spoke. He, too, was getting hard from the excitement of what was going to happen. I had them both in front of me. I reached out and in each hand cupped one of the sets of genitals. The soft feel of the feathery pubic hair of the testicles was perfect. I lifted up the two sets, as though weighing them. I applied no pressure, there was nothing to my touch that could possibly have created pain, but they both tensed, as though they expected it to come at any moment.

I let the two sacs fall back to their hanging position and took hold of their two cocks. Both were circumcised, both well-done. I pulled gently at the skin around the half-erect shafts and listened as the two men quickened their breath in response.

These were magnificent specimens. These were men I would be proud to own. I stood up in front of them, still holding on to their cocks. I moved them with those intimate handles to the center of the room. I let go and walked to the wall that held the restraints. Of course, my vassals stayed where I had left them.

I got what I needed and returned to them. I put the materials on the bench and calmly grabbed Glen's wrist. I quickly took up a pair of leather wrist restraints and attached them to his arms. He didn't resist at all, in fact he tried to be helpful and anticipate my movements. When the pair were securely fastened, I lifted his hands up in the air. I had taken small "D" clamps from the wall and used them to lock the restraints to the heavy chain at a point far above his head.

I went back to the bench and took hold of a large metal device. At either end of a three-foot section of iron were ankle restraints. They were locked into place with a turn key. I applied them to Glen's legs, and the iron rod forced his legs apart, ensuring that he couldn't use his body movements at all to evade anything I would choose to do to him.

Glen was utterly defenseless now. I stood back and looked at him. His cock was even stiffer, though still not fully erect. His balls hung down in the air, unable to touch his thighs now that those were forced apart by the bondage. His eyes were wild. I wasn't sure if it was desire — the realization that his dream was coming true — or the sudden rush of emotion that arrives when a slave is finally aware of the physical paralysis that bondage can produce.

He moved against the restraints, as though testing them, and the heavy chain moved ever so slightly, just enough to produce a metallic sound of rustling. But that was all. It wasn't going to give. I wondered if he had been the one to choose the bolts that made it so securely fastened to the floor and ceiling. If he had, I thought he might have been damning his handiwork right now. There was no way he would escape this position.

I turned to Phillip. He was staring at the sight of his lover, the man who had led his own way for so long. When he realized I was looking at him, he seemed to freeze and then he actually moved a half step away from me. Whoever could do this to the man who had controlled him for ten years must seem a particularly frightening figure to him now. "Does he look good?" I asked.

"He looks wonderful, sir."

I ran a hand on the stretched area of Glen's chest, just on the side, away from the nipples, where the lines of his rib cage were forced against his skin. "Does he look any less a man this way?"

"Of course not, sir."

"Get a condom."

Phillip sprang into action. He went to a cabinet and brought back a foil-wrapped container. I unwrapped it. It wasn't one of the usual types. It was dyed black and, while it was latex, it would have the appearance of black rubber.

"Get him hard."

Phillip immediately fell to his knees and began to mouth at Glen's balls. His tongue, tiny piece of pink, shot out and lapped at the hair-covered flesh. Glen began to struggle again, his hands tugged at the chain, and his feet worked against the iron. While it was futile, it also produced a kaleidoscope of visual poses that sent a shiver of ecstasy through me. One after another of his muscles would come into sharp focus from the exertion, then relax back into the rest of him as he labored to respond to the stimulations of Phillip's tongue.

In a very short time he was stiffly erect. I pulled on Phillip's hair to remove him. The boy was showing his passion; he unthinkingly resisted at first, his tongue still out even when I had him back on his haunches.

I took hold of Glen's cock and unraveled the condom onto it. The appearance of the black latex was wonderful, making it seem as though his erection was encased in a rubber trap.

I grabbed Phillip's hair again, harder this time. I twisted it in my fist until he opened his mouth in a silent scream. "Suck it." I threw his head forward so quickly and so hard that I was surprised he was able to manage getting the hard cock into his mouth. I crouched down beside him while he wildly went at his lover's cock.

"You love this, don't you? On your knees with that prick in your mouth? Naked, in front of your man, showing him how much you need his sex?"

Phillip didn't stop his abandoned sucking for an instant. He answered my questions with muffled sounds while he kept on going with such enthusiasm that spittle was flowing down the sides of his lips, running off over his chin.

I pulled him back again. He let out a sound like a wounded animal when he was removed from that object of desire. There was no doubt about how much he loved Glen's cock. His own was rock hard, standing up from his body at a sharp angle. I had watched—he hadn't had a chance to touch himself during any of this, his hands had been on Glen's hips. His excitement was just from the idea of being down there, worshiping his personal god.

"Get up."

I moved quickly and had wrist restraints on Phillip before he even understood what was happening. I lifted his arms up and attached them to the chain near the same point where Glen's wrists were locked. Then I put restraints on his ankles, clamping them to Glen's, forcing his legs just as far apart as his lover's.

Their faces were forced together as was most of the front surface of their bodies. I went to the wall and retrieved a long piece of rawhide. When I came back I found the two of them kissing each other, lovingly.

I took the rawhide and tied a section of it tightly around the base of Glen's balls, forcing the testicles to the furthest extreme of his sac and doing it so harshly that he couldn't help but moan in response to the pain. I took the rest and looped it just as tightly around Phillip's sac.

Their hips were forced to press even more closely to one another by the rawhide; I left no slack at all between their bodies. Their erections interfered with their desire to give some relief to the pressure on their balls, and the hard shafts of flesh squirmed between their bellies.

Now I brought back two sets of tit clamps. Both had moderate stress to them. These wouldn't be the easy stimulation that rubber tips could bring. The metal would bite into the flesh. I took one pair and put one of the clamps on Phillip's right nipple. He sucked in his breath when he felt the tight grip. The other end of the pair — they were joined together by a thin metal chain — went on Glen's own right nipple, crossing from one side of their chests to the other. I repeated the process with the other clamps, leaving an X of chain between them.

Their kiss before had been purely romantic eroticism. They had been reacting to the idea of their joint bondage. Now Phillip sought out Glen's mouth with a more desperate need, as the leather bindings of their balls and the biting pain of the nipple clamps became a shared ordeal that demanded their mutual support for it to be overcome.

I found a leather strap on the other wall. It was wider than a belt and had no buckle or metal studs to produce more pain than I wanted it to, certainly no damage. My twin captives were still kissing one another. But I wanted their attention. I stood behind Phillip and ran the leather across the wide muscular expanse of his back. He knew what it was — of course he did — and he knew it would be used. He drew back from Glen and stiffened, as though he could prepare and protect himself.

I moved up and down the lower half of his torso with the strap, hitting hard at one place, less so at another, and always doing it in ways that could never be anticipated.

I finally stopped. My own body was shaking from the work it had done and the leather hung from my hand. Phillip was sobbing, his chest wracked with contractions from the severity of the punishment. Glen was desperately trying to comfort him, raining kisses on forehead and neck and all over his face. I moved in close and put a hand on the hot surface of Phillip's ass. He jumped at the intent of my touch.

I moved my palm over the skin, calming him, assuring him that there was no anger behind the assault, only appreciation of his offering. His chest slowed down, his sobs turned into weeping and he began to return Glen's kisses. When I moved in even closer, he turned his attention to me, moving his lips over my face hungrily.

The clamps had stayed attached to their nipples, the rawhide was still in place. I reached in and tested the chain between their chests and they both reared up from the added pressure. I kept calming Phillip; he'd persevered splendidly and deserved the recognition. But I wasn't being comforting to Glen when I looked at him. Instead I smiled — I probably was closer to smirking.

"It was your decision."

He hadn't indicated any desire to pull back from the choice of being there, in the bondage, waiting for his turn with the leather strap, but I was making sure he realized that the resolution to have him witness his lover's trial was purposeful — it was meant to make him more conscious of what he, himself, was going to suffer.

I moved to the other side of them. There was Glen's unblemished back waiting for me. His ass wasn't the pale and uncovered flesh that Phillip's had been. Instead there was a coating of fine dark hair all over it. His back was as muscled, if more streamlined. His legs were just as clearly strong. I ran my hand over the whole of him, from the neck down to his calves. He shook from that slight contact.

When I stood back, my strap ready again, his body was shaking. Phillip was staring. I knew that he'd never been able to see this before — not just Glen, his lover, being whipped, but any other man being beaten at such close and intimate range.

When I brought the strap back for the first time, Phillip's eyes opened broadly, as though in wonder, as they watched the leather travel to deliver a sound blow on Glen's buttocks.

Glen was clearly less used to the strap. He yelled out in pain from the beginning. But he wanted the experience; he needed the experience. I only let myself soften the assault slightly. I went through the entire scenario with him. I began at his ass, I moved down the insides of his legs, to his calves, back up again, alternating the blows, watching the richness of the colors as they came out, luxuriating in the control of his flesh's response.

His screams were loud all through it, his tears more copious, his useless attempts at escape more frenzied. His reactions kept tugging at the nipple chains and the rawhide bonds, bringing Phillip greater continued sensations.

Again, at about the same point, I stopped and walked up to Glen. I put my hand on his softened skin just as I had Phillip. I calmed him down, wiping the sweat from his brow and running my palm over his face with soothing motions. He thought it was done. He thought he had suffered all there would be.

"Phillip's been put in his place. He's come to understand the lash, to understand that he needs it and that it brings him a kind of peace. You, though, are only learning. You think you retain a sort of control. You're wrong. A slave has to be introduced to his pain to understand that it is an ever-present possibility. Phillip only needed to know that I could do it. That I had the strength to inflict the punishment. He didn't need to know how far it could go. You do, Glen. You need so much more than Phillip does."

The words forced a new and stronger flood of tears. There was no doubt in his mind that I was going even further than I had with his lover.

I took my place. I looked at the beautiful results of the first half of Glen's torment, the decorations that lined his buttocks and legs. Then I studied the unmarred surface of his back. I lifted the strap and brought it down on his shoulders.

Now he lifted up in immediate pain. The leather sang out as it sped through the air and repeatedly found its mark on his back. The bone is so much closer there and the flesh so much harder that the sounds were different than the music of leather on ass. They're more masculine in a way, stronger, deeper. They are evidence of infinitely greater physical hurt and psychological humiliation.

A man might have his ass beaten by another; a true slave has his back whipped.

When I was done, the marks were evenly spread over Glen. Only the dangerously vulnerable area around his midsection was unscarred. I stepped back in and again wrapped my arms around the two of them. Again, I listened as Glen's cries turned into whimperings. Phillip barely noticed me for a while, so intent was he on seeing what his lover was going through. There was a sense of awe about it. He would always remember — as I had planned — that Glen had suffered more and hadn't cracked.

Tears? Sobs? They mean nothing. They are inevitable and only a foolishly proud man would deny them when he's being put through all of this. But there was not denial, there was no vain attempt to escape, to have the punishment lessened. Glen had accepted it, just as Phillip had. The lovers were obviously proud of one another, each in his own way.

"Do you understand now what it means to have me here?"

"Yes, sir," they both said at once.

"Do you understand that it never ends with me?"

Phillip nodded, only Glen answered out loud, "We're yours, sir."

"For What?"

"For anything."

"I'm going to make you prove that."

I went about releasing them. The clamps let an extraordinarily painful surge of blood into their nipples and both cried out when the pressure was released. The removal of the rawhide was less dramatic. They were only glad to have some comfort back.

The intensity of the whipping had frightened off their erections. But as I went about the untying of the rope that had joined their testicles and rubbed at the sensitive areas, both their cocks were coming back to life. I rubbed their genitals and licked lightly at their tits to help them. By the time I had moved to their arms and had let them down, they were both semierect and smiling from the pleasure.

When their restraints were released from the chain, I went to their collection and brought back two leather collars. They understood immediately. Both of them fell to their knees. I put the collars on. I thought that Glen seemed to be actually proud of his. Then I attached a lead to each of them. Again, I didn't have to speak. They went to their hands and knees. I walked them around the table. There was no resistance.

I led them to the chair and left them for a quick moment while I went to the refrigerator. I came back with bottles of beer and a glass bowl I had found. I opened two of the bottles, keeping one for myself and then pouring the other into the bowl.

The music was still going. While the strains of a baroque symphony filled the room, my two young men lapped at the beer in the bowl, thirsty from what had happened, knowing there was more to come. When they'd finished it they used their tongues to wash each other's face clean of the beverage that they'd spilt in their hurry. Then they looked up at me, anxious, smiling, and waiting. They were watching my crotch, staring at the length of my cock, knowing they were going to get that reward as well.

I looked over at a clock. It was only ten. I didn't leave the basement until six in the morning. I knew that there were to be two extraordinarily well-trained young me to serve at my party.

Preparations

Joseph arrived with his crew the next afternoon. I'd barely slept three hours but was refreshed, still exhilarated from my evening with Glen and Phillip. I showered and dressed while they began in the front room. Then I left them and went out to lunch.

A cab took me to Fisherman's Wharf, where I indulged in watching the tourists make fools of themselves while I ate a decent meal in one of the many restaurants there. The crowd of middle Americans pressed too hard for me, though, and I left right after I ate.

I walked for miles, it seemed, up and down the hills, watching the changing view of the Bay and fog as it kept trying to spill over the Twin Peaks in the distance — a sight I could catch at the top of each hill.

I eventually went to the Castro and sat in a bar with an open facade, a wall on the street that rolled up and left me with a clear vista of the march of gay men up and down the street.

This had long been one of my favorite neighborhoods, though not for any social or political reason. In fact, it offends my Eastern sensibilities in some ways. More and more it seems to be too much like the other tourist areas of the city. But the sheer mass of gay men in their tight jeans, all of them ready to strip off their shirts at the slightest hint of warm sunlight, is a hedonistic delight that I can't compare to many other urban landscapes.

I eventually made my way back to the hotel. The work had been done and the suite was immaculate, incomparable to the shape it had been in. The wood surfaces had been scrubbed, the drapes and rugs vacuumed, the windows polished. All of the dust was gone. Joseph had obviously raided more than the cleaning stores of the hotel. One table that had been scarred was replaced by a new one without any imperfections. The sheets on my bed, barely adequate, had been replaced with obviously new ones.

I was surprised that Joseph and another of the crew were still there. They walked me through an inspection tour. There was no doubt that they'd done their work well, and I paid the agreed sum and added a large tip. When Joseph didn't leave, I understood that there was another agenda here.

His friend was Robert. He was about twenty, blond, and appeared to be nicely built. I gathered from little pieces of conversation that he was new to San Francisco. He'd gotten a job here at the hotel as a houseman, doing the heavy cleaning — vacuuming the corridor rugs and moving furniture. He stood off to the side, his hands in his pocket, while Joseph did the talking.

"You know, that kinky stuff you like, what we did? I told him about it," he shook his head toward Robert. "He's up for it too. You know, for a little money?"

Joseph smiled and tried to speak in a *mano-a-mano* tone of voice. "He's pretty hot. I've fixed him up with some of the guys who stay here. Real hot. He'll do anything, man, he really needs the money."

Robert showed none of the enthusiasm for sex that Joseph had. With the first youth, one had a sense that it was a game to get paid for it. It was some kind of con that he was running. He left the distinct impression that he would have fallen into it by himself and given it away if he was sure that there was no possibility of monetary reward.

Robert didn't display any of that. He appeared sullen. Those hands were dug so far into his pockets and his shoulders were so slumped up with anger that there was only the sense that this was some last-ditch effort he was making.

"Are you that broke?" I asked him. He didn't move, didn't relax at all. He only shrugged. I turned back to Joseph, "And what's your cut?"

"Finder's fee," he smiled. "I gotta get something for putting you in touch with him. He's almost cherry, man. Never done it with a guy until a couple of months ago. You must like that. You don't find many males who are almost virgins in San Francisco these days, that's for sure. Here's your big chance."

Joseph was overdoing his salesman's rap. I wasn't at all pleased with the crudeness of the conversation. "I'm not interested, Joseph. Forget it." I spoke to Robert then. "You're very handsome. I don't mean to insult you, but I'm tired now. Thanks for all the work on the rooms. I really appreciate the good job you've done."

They left, sulky and dissatisfied. I decided to go back to bed to catch up on the sleep I'd lost.

I barely heard the knocks through the dreams I was having. I simply integrated the sound into whatever it was that occupied my sleeping thoughts. But they were so insistent that I had no choice but to abandon my slumber's adventures and wake up. I grabbed a robe and went to the door. It was Robert. He was in the same petulant mood as earlier.

"What is it?"

"I...um...really am up for it, what Joseph was saying? I mean, if you're looking for someone, I'll do it and cheaper than he said I would."

"Joseph never mentioned an actual sum."

"Well, he told me I'd get twenty if you fucked me. I really could use the money, you know."

"Come in." I stood aside and pointed his way to the sitting room. I turned on some lights before I sat down; it was well into the evening now. "What do you need this money for?"

"I want to go home." He was looking straight down to the floor. "I want to get out of this place. I just need a bus ticket. I got paid today, if I can get some more together, I'll make it."

"Where is home?"

"Pennsylvania, near Pittsburgh."

"How did you get here?"

"With this guy, a guy I knew at home. We were going to live together and everything. It was too hard back there, but we thought it would work here. I followed him, I guess. He's gone now. Found some big stud bartender and moved out on me."

He spoke all this without any passion, as though he deserved the pain and hurt that he was describing. There was no indication that he was fighting off any of the emotions. He was a passive sponge for the waves of bad luck. More, I realized he probably attracted them.

"Where do you live now?"

"Not far, over near Polk. I still have the room we got together, a furnished place."

"Is there anything there that you need? Anything to get you back to Pennsylvania?

"No."

Of course there wouldn't be. He hadn't any reason to accumulate memories of the city.

"I'm not interested in you sexually. I was being honest when I said that."

Robert stood immediately. He shoved his hands back into his pockets and started to walk to the door.

"Stop." He froze in place, but didn't turn to look at me. "I don't want you to drown in California, though. Are you going to do anything with yourself if you go back to Pennsylvania?"

"I want to go back to school. I never finished high school. That's why I took this lousy job, I couldn't get any other kind. And I'm no good at hustling. I'm just no good at a lot of things."

"It's probably a waste of time and money, but I'll send you back home. At least you won't have the luxury of blaming other people for your bad luck from now on. You're going to have to live up to the fact that someone did you a good turn."

Now he swiveled around and looked at me with disbelief. I went into the bedroom and quickly got dressed. "Let's go. I'm not giving you cash you can squander. But I'll buy your ticket."

An hour later I stood in the Greyhound station and watched the bus pull out. It would take him a few days to get to Pittsburgh, and I could only hope that the little money I gave him was spent well enough that he could eat.

What a waste. I walked back up to Market Street and was even more aware of the many poorly dressed, ill-fed people who were lingering hungrily around the bus terminal neighborhood. We throw away our children, starve them nearly to death, then wonder why they turn to petty crime.

The circle of poverty and ignorance is vicious, never ending, the one true sadistic fact of American society. I could never have taken a boy like Robert who would only offer himself out of desperate need and unhappiness. My wrestler fantasy demanded a freedom of choice. My reality said that I could pay Joseph for his humiliation because he was an entrepreneur, not a victim. The

Roberts of the world aren't a challenge for a man; they are the targets of vultures.

Collections of punks stood on street corners, probably to victimize the other poor people. They would rob the old ladies on social security, beat the women on welfare, rape the young men living on disability.

They disgusted me. There might be a nobility to the criminals in the worlds of Andre Gide and Jean Genet, and that was a nobility that attracted me. I feel a kinship with it. But these throwaway adolescents who feed on the walking wounded aren't that. They're volatile energy ready to land on anything that shows weakness. Such a waste of decent manhood.

I spied one of a group — handsome, well-muscled, black haired, and hard-looking with a cigarette dangling from the edge of his lips. We glared at one another. He began to follow me. I hoped he wasn't going to be foolish enough to try to start anything with me, certainly not in the bright lights of Market Street.

"Hey mister, want a smoke?" He was holding out a package of Marlboros. I stopped and wondered what he was up to. Out of perverse interest I stood long enough for him to catch up with me. I took one of his cigarettes and let him hold a match out.

"You interested? Huh?"

"Interested in what?"

"Me," he laughed, as though my question had been silly. "What do you think? I got a big one, and I know how to use it."

It was a warm summer night, and he was only wearing an undershirt. I could see a whole collection of crudely done tattoos on both his arms, the type of amateur effort usually done in prisons and juvenile detention homes.

"No. Thanks anyway. I'm not up to it."

I started to walk away, but he grabbed one of my arms. "Come on, man. I can throw you a wicked fuck. You'll like it."

This was, unquestionably, a perfect specimen of rough trade. I knew many men — many, many men — who would have adored it. They would have wallowed on their knees in front of him and eaten in his cock — big or small — and dreamed their fantasies of danger and real men, whatever that means.

"No." I repeated myself and took away my hand.

"Faggot," he snarled when he realized I wasn't going to play his game. I kept on going.

I went slowly up Market and then toward Union Square. The crowds only get larger, the waste of human life more obvious. I was burning with rage. Here was all the evidence of the unwillingness of society to deal with and care for its members.

Give them to me, I thought. I quickly envisioned myself at home; perhaps I'd need to buy a few more acres of land. I'd take the violent and anarchistic young males that terrorized the city streets, proving their "manhood" by being stupidly criminal. I'd turn my acres into a farm. They'd work their asses off. Naked in the summer, they'd pull the plows, their butts red from the strap. They'd sleep in dormitories, they'd eat wholesome food. They'd go to school in the morning — and no ridiculous social worker crap about modern theories.

They'd learn how to read and write and they'd study hard. No humanistic understanding about missing homework, only the well-applied strap. No worry about schedule, a series of overseers would make sure they were on time. No time for wasted analysis on why they'd gone wrong; they'd be too tired from work and study to lose sleep over the past and would only want to graduate to a future.

They wouldn't try to fool themselves about manhood being something you got because someone weaker was frightened of you. When they learned to take it up the ass and to receive honor by having an adult choose them for a sex partner they'd have something much more real to measure themselves against. The failing of the whole social services system could be overcome by a confederation of sadists. I thought of Madame taking in a street boy, her cane in hand, his face being scrubbed — hard — and his nails cleaned daily. After a year of it he'd walk away with his education, all right, and a skill. He'd be able to be one of the best waiters in the city, impeccably serving food in the finest restaurants. He'd have learned it quickly, and that swinging cane of hers would have embedded each lesson in his mind more efficiently than a horde of Berkeley graduates who would spend their time empathizing with him.

You think I'm wrong? Then realize this: The only effective therapy institution in the United States today, when it comes to dealing with young male criminals, is the Marine Corps. Talk to them, ask the young recruits why they're there. They'll tell you, as they've told me, that they needed the discipline. They were wild, dangerous, they saw their friends going to prison, caught at exactly the same activities that they were committing nightly. What was their option?

They self-medicated with a visit to the recruiting station and handed themselves over to the beast of a drill instructor who had them crawling on hands and knees and polishing boots and understanding that they needed it all within twenty-four hours.

My farm could do wonders for this scum that lined the city streets here and every other city in America. These wasted fools think they need "turf" to know where they belong in the world. I'd give them a sense of place with an engraved collar to remind them where it was. They whine about being denied opportunities that would make school worthwhile. I'd give them the motivation they needed to learn — a strap of leather they'd kiss every morning when they woke up, just to remind them that it was there. They cry that no one understands or cares for them. I'd show them the ultimate caring of S/M — the total observance of every minute detail of their minds and body by another being.

Reform school? *Hah!*

The Beginning

Madame arrived the next day. She called early in the afternoon, and we agreed to go to the convention floor with one another. As always, she insisted on staying in one of the most elegant hotels in the city. I went there and had to go through phalanxes of uninformed personnel to get to the elevator.

She answered my knock immediately. "How wonderful," she said sleepily, then offered me her cheek to kiss. "I've had coffee and croissants brought up." She vaguely floated a hand toward the set table.

The red hair she's so vain about was piled on top her head in a Victorian manner. A tight silk collar was wrapped around her throat and held in place by a small, elegant cameo. Her clothing, while chic and from the finest stores in New York and Paris, was all reminiscent of decades-old fashion with puffed sleeves and much longer skirts than one would ever see on the usual businesswomen on the streets.

We talked about little. She was, underneath her facade of relaxation, desperate for me to discuss the party. I wouldn't give her the satisfaction of my opening up the topic; I silently insisted that she ask me.

Finally she gave in, "Well, have your plans progressed at all?" One eyebrow arched in a schoolmarm mimic she so often affects. "Or am I simply taking you to your favorite restaurant again?" It was a challenge that she underlined by taking a particularly sharp bite out of a chocolate bun.

"Everything is progressing perfectly well," I defended myself. "You'll be pleased."

Pleased? She was going to be in heat with what I had planned. She made those little gestures she does so well to let me know we'd see about that.

"Is Adrienne coming to the convention today?" she asked, moving the conversation away from the dangerous area where we both might feel like competing.

"No. I spoke to her yesterday. She can't simply walk through it anymore. She'd be mobbed and can't deal with the idea of actually having the guards one of her publishers offered her."

"*Guards!*" Madame was suddenly transported into an obvious state of excitement.

"Yes, evidently they do it all the time for the big authors — Stephen King, Jackie Collins."

"In uniforms?" There was a new chocolate croissant stuck in midair as madame entered a dreamy state.

"I suppose." I should have been prepared for all this. Of course it would get to her, the idea of a woman moving through adoring crowds and having to have to be protected by her staff of strong hired men.

"Why isn't she doing it?" Now Madame was back down to earth. She was openly incredulous that anyone would pass up the splendid opportunity.

"It's not her style. Adrienne isn't like us. You know that. We live our private theaters; her life isn't so crowded with the details we insist on. She doesn't demand that the world conform to her fiction the way we do. She doesn't cross the lines between fantasy and reality so often and so easily.

"Not that she wouldn't like to do it, but it's not her life. She's married to her first husband. She's a mother. A distinguished novelist who cares about her literary reputation. She doesn't care about creating her life as we do; she's more intrigued with her books. Her words live for her so incredibly well that she doesn't need the actions to go with them as emphatically as we do."

"But the party? She wants this party as badly as I want it."

"She wants it because she trusts that I can do it as well as she could have written it. She wants to see her words. These are her fantasies. But they're all translated by someone else. They take on a new look and a different feel. It's amazing to witness it.

"Besides, she cares about the details so very much. You know how bitterly anxious she is that we discovered things in her books that weren't possible. Here is an opportunity for her to attend a…laboratory. She can witness the actual sight and feel and smell of it all."

"I don't believe you'll pull it off." There, she'd said what she'd been thinking. "I just can't believe that we'll sit in a San Francisco hotel suite with Adrienne and Phil and that it will all happen."

"Will you be disappointed if I do?"

"Hardly. I'll be astonished, and I promise I'll respect you even more than I do now." With that she stood up and walked over to place a kiss on the top of my head. "We should go to the convention now."

*   *   *

The floor of the convention center was packed with milling crowds. The meeting is the one large professional event of publishing. I stood on the escalator as it descended to the lower level and gazed at the incredibly long lines of booths.

Madame was beside me, doing her own reconnaissance. "Amazing, isn't it. Whenever I see this I cease to wonder about how people manage to be published and instead am amazed that anything ever goes unpublished."

We got to the main floor and began to stroll up and down the aisles. Every publisher was represented. There is a cartoon that was once given out by a major house. A character goes up to a clerk and asks for a book. What kind, he's asked. Cookbooks, diet books, cartoon books? No, the character says, I want a novel. The clerk is bored. That would be under antiques, he says.

So it seems here. There are extravagant exhibits for books on every possible inconsequential subject that one could imagine. There are displays for supposed novels on Hollywood, the Riviera, and other romantic locales. There are…there's a lot—and little of it is literature.

Especially not the literature that Madame and I create. But that doesn't keep us from being recognized by many of the editors whose displays we pass. There are some squeamish ones who've had sex with one or the other of us, and there are those who we enjoy socially. But more of them are business acquaintances.

Whatever else we are, Madame and I are known on this floor. Not for those selves that we've created, the sexual beings who constantly push against the lines between reality and fantasy, but because of the mundane earthiness of our lives. She is the editor of one of those magazines that everyone claims never to read, but which sells hundreds of thousands of copies a month to loyal readers. Those readers make her powerful in the eyes of even the most ostentatiously pretentious literary editors. There is no strength more valued on this convention floor than the ability to sell books.

I am…worthwhile. I can take the boring subjects that these people want to have in book form and create enough words with enough ability to justify a front and back cover. I am not so important that I am to be courted, I understand that. But I'm treated well. No one knows just when he or she might not need me.

We lingered at various places. Madame tried vainly to be excited by the image of a bodybuilder who was autographing books that featured photographs of his grotesquely over-developed torso. But she couldn't manage to make him a pornographic ideal. "He hardly has any meat at all," she said, dismissing him with that judgment of the small pouch that showed in his tight pants.

We moved along, stopping in one place to chat with one of Adrienne's editors. He was charming, shockingly handsome with his good looks, dressed in a three-piece suit. Of all the people we talked to, he was the one who would need us the least. His books were too refined to ever need coverage in Madame's sex magazine and little of my writing would ever be graced with the imprint of his house.

Perhaps that's why he was able to be so gracious, there was no need for anything but genteel discussion, and he was awfully good at that. He charmed Madame with flattering comments on her dress and spoke sternly to me about the elusive work that he and I had spent too many lunches dreaming about — the "serious" book he insisted I had in me.

When we walked away from him, I felt chastised by his questions. Madame felt the conversation gave her a free rein to jump on me. "There you have that great editor waiting for your masterpiece, and you flitter away your time with silly boys and your impossible life in the country. You should be ashamed of yourself."

"Would you want me to stop writing about sex?" I teased her.

"Never!" There was actually a little bit of hurt in her voice. The idea that I'd end my sexual fiction appalled her, as I knew it would.

"He will never publish it." I said.

"But he published Adrienne's!"

"Adrienne is a name, a proven talent, one of the great living novelists. Adrienne can be forgiven for writing about sex. A gay man who does it and doesn't accompany it with something they decide is literature doesn't find his works in hard cover with that imprint."

"They should. They should all publish you."

I had a quick fantasy of the miles of displays here at the convention, all of them with huge reproductions of my book covers with their graphic depictions of men in bondage and leather. I decided I should change the topic.

"Have I ever told you how Ken expects it would be to have him edit?"

"That handsome young editor? Why he would certainly be the pinnacle of professionalism." Madame insisted.

"Ken agrees, but thinks there'd be a different form of professionalism involved. He once submitted a manuscript to that man and spent two weeks in agony, hoping it would be rejected."

"He wanted it to be rejected?"

"Ken couldn't imagine ever saying the word 'No' to anyone who was that physically attractive. He spun out the details of how it would be to work with him.

"He envisioned the editor wearing nothing but a sparkling clean jock strap. Don't ask me why the jock had to be clean…"

"Of course it would have to be on that man!"

"Then you agree with Ken. The editor would be seated wearing that jock and a white athletic T-shirt . He'd have a leg swung over the arm of a chair, the full pouch visible in every detail to Ken who would be sitting naked on the floor.

"Every time there was a minor flaw in the manuscript, the editor would bash him one, forcing him to do something horribly humiliating as punishment. But, when he found Ken had produced a particularly well-turned phrase or created an especially powerful image, he would reward him with a pat on the head or an affectionate tousle of the hair."

Madame stopped short in the aisle and put a hand on her breast. "S/M editing," she whispered. "It's too perfect."

"He's too perfect," I answered and led her further away from the booth.

We found one of Phil's publishers later and looked over a large pile of his books. The publisher was pleasant but acted as though he didn't know quite what to do with us. Madame produces that reaction in people. They've heard all the stories about her and her magazine's reputation is no less than notorious. They expect, no doubt, that she should be cheap, slutty. They seldom are prepared for her well-groomed and well-attired presence and certainly are shocked by her highly cultivated voice.

I have to admit that I must create a similar problem for them. I, in their minds, should be clothed in full leather and probably should have a scarred face and a deep, gravely voice. I am often told that I should be even older than I am, probably alcoholic with a pot belly and vile cigars sticking from my mouth. That is the most popular vision of a pornographer. In fact, I look my Yankee heritage and almost all of my clothes are from L.L. Bean.

With my life and my writing. I feel little need for additional costuming.

"Where is the dear old man?" Madame asked after Phil.

The publisher's eyes raised in surprise. I doubt that many people have ever called Phil that, dear old man. "He's going to be here to sign his books on Saturday. I don't really expect him before then."

"Do we get him earlier?" she asked me.

"You can call and see if it's possible for the two of you to meet. I don't want to see him before Sunday. Nor Adrienne. I want the party to be the whole thing."

"Really," she replied with a slight humor in her voice, "you're going to pass up one of your marathon conversations with Adrienne? No afternoon with you and a bottle Scotch and her with her endless cups of coffee?"

"Monday," I answered, a little embarrassed to be caught in such an obvious manner. "We've set aside Monday for one another."

"I'm not surprised." She was leafing through another book. "Will you and I dine tonight?"

"I have business tonight, a publisher. Tomorrow?"

"Fine. That place you like. I'll call Phil later today and see if I can't get him to come across the Bay for me."

"You're only doing it to see if he thinks you're important enough for such an effort. It's selfish. He's an old man. Why don't you go to him?"

"I think a dinner at the Mark Hopkins is worth anyone making a little sacrifice, no matter how old."

"Go ahead, he'll probably agree. Though you should be ashamed of yourself."

"I always am," she answered.

Martin

Martin arrived on Friday night.

As soon as he walked into the suite, we began to kiss. Our hands roamed over one another in some undisciplined fashion, as though the need to assure ourselves that we were both there was more important than anything else. We broke off after a while, laughed, then sat down on a couch together.

We quickly caught up on more news than we had been able to on the phone. I listened to some of his stories; he heard some of my own. There was a little game playing, a few harsh words from me just to remind him of our roles, some jockeying for position on his part, but none of it undermined the essential emotion, the happiness to be together and the relief as well.

I took him to dinner at a French restaurant on one of the avenues south of Market. The place was wonderful, and it was a kind of food that he usually would enjoy, but he was unhappy over something, I could tell.

I got him to talk: "It's nothing wrong with this. I'm just unhappy about what used to be and isn't anymore. Don't you remember what a special place this neighborhood was? The way it used to be to come down here? And now it's a French restaurants and fancy nightclubs, leather bars turned into straight discos and warehouses renovated into loft condominiums..." His voice trailed off in disgust.

I didn't argue with him. So much had changed, of course it had. Not just in the types of businesses that were here and the erosion of the uniqueness of being first gay and then also a man in leather, but there was the cloud of decaying death here as well.

That I couldn't change. I could find a new bar, I could try a new club, I could find a new outlaw dress that hasn't made it into the pages of *Interview* magazine, but I can't deport a virus...

We dropped the subject. We both knew that we had each said too much about it at other times and there was nothing to be gained by going through it all again. The reality was part of our lives and we knew it.

The topics went on to my party and my plans. I described the men to him. He demanded details. I described Keith, Christopher, Glen, and Phillip to him. There were still others.

"Do I get to talk to them with you?"

"No. This is my creation. I want to do the interviewing myself. Besides, you have work to do."

"More interviews?"

"Hardly. You're going shopping."

He was furious; the blood came up to his face, and I thought he'd slam the table with his fist. "What the hell do you mean, *shopping*? I came all the way from Los Angeles..."

"To go shopping. There has to be food ordered, arrangements to have it delivered, a few other things."

"While you're out fucking?"

"Are you jealous?" I was laughing at him, making him only more angry.

"You know I'm not. That's not part of the deal. I just don't why I get to do that while you're off doing the rest."

"You get to do necessary tasks because I paid your airfare and you're staying in my hotel room. You're going to have more than enough enjoyment out of all this on Sunday. And tonight."

"And tonight?" That seemed to end the dispute immediately. "All right. I know I said I'd do the work for you. I will. What do you need?"

We finished dinner talking about the small details, the places each of us remembered where certain items could be gotten. Over coffee he seemed to begin to relish the idea of what was to come. He began to tease me with more coy little remarks. I was playing with him. He didn't realize that his fun tonight wasn't going to be with me.

"You don't understand," I finally said. "You have work to do tonight, but it's work that you're going to enjoy."

"Without you?"

"Yes. The one I told you about, the big bodybuilder, Christopher, he needs some special treatment. A visit to his hotel room by you would certainly give him that."

"You don't want me?" It almost wasn't a question. It carried with it a real sense of hurt. I felt sorry I'd even played with him a little bit.

Aren't I still your boy?

"Later, and I'll want you as badly as you expect I will. But there's more I have to do. This must be perfect, Martin. It must be something that the rest of them all remember. I have two more men to interview and decide just what to do with. And it is important that this Christopher gets what he needs. I would have thought you'd like to be able to try out all of your newfound master talents.

"And you'll have to come up with designs for Sunday as well."

"All right, then just explain what it is that I have to do with this man. If you insist that I take on some well-built hunk of a bodybuilder, I suppose I'll simply have to give in to it. You always have been such a demanding master." Back in the hotel room we changed clothes. I put on more casual attire. It was carefully chosen to fit my purposes later on in the evening. I knew from the letters I'd received from Carl that my appearance needed a certain flair to it. I wouldn't completely respond to his desires, but there was no need to fight them totally, at least not in the beginning.

I finished first. Martin had been talking excitedly. The image I painted of Christopher was turning him on. He loved the idea of the man who wanted to be used but who didn't want anything but his body to be involved. I sat on the bed and watched him changing.

It was so familiar, every line of it was exactly as I'd remembered it. The torso was hairless except for blond bursts under his arms and over his crotch. The smooth expanse was just as muscled as I had expected his working out to have created. But he was so tall that the impact of the muscles wasn't as strong as it would have been on another man or on one as over-developed as Christopher. One had to study the thickness of Martin's thighs to see how large they'd become. The arms were well-trained, to be sure, but on a man over six feet tall they just didn't appear to be as perfect as they would have on a shorter person.

But, then, there was his ass. He bent over to take off his briefs. I was sitting — without any plan — in the perfect position to see the freed buttocks as he angled his torso. They were perfect. They were large, like the rest of him, and there wasn't a mark on them. The pale skin simply bowed out, emphasized by his posture. He stood, reached into his bag and brought out a jock strap. He curled his body again. Now, when he stood up, the white ass was framed by an even whiter outline of the elastic straps.

He pulled on black leather pants over the jock. He'd decided to wear only a leather vest. It was still warm out. We both knew perfectly well that San Francisco weather wasn't at all predictable; it could easily become chilly later on. But Martin was going on an assignment in leather, and to do less than adorn himself perfectly would have perverted his art. This thinking — foolish though it might be in some ways — is only one of the reasons I love him so.

His boots came next. Then a leather cap. He put on reflector sunglasses, their mirrors replacing his eyes. As soon as he was finished, his smile disappeared. He turned to me, his thumbs hooked in his belt, his stomach sucked in, his chest expanded to its full width. He posed, perfectly, just for me.

I stood up and took him in my arms. He wouldn't relax into my embrace. His transformation had taken place. But I wasn't going to allow this. "Do I have to beat you?"

Then, slowly, his arms lifted up and surrounded my shoulders, and we kissed.

We took the elevator down to the lobby. As we walked through it, all eyes seemed to be glued on Martin's remarkable visage. He knew it, his steps were stronger, his stride longer. Joseph was there, just getting off duty I assumed — he wasn't wearing his uniform. He openly gaped at the two of us as we walked across the floor to the front door of the hotel.

I smiled and waved at him. Perhaps he would end up at my party after all.

A Military Presence

I wasn't at all surprised by Carl's attitude or his dress. "Sir." That was all of the greeting I got. But I expected that. He was wearing a pair of fatigue pants; from all indications they were authentic and probably from his own days in the service. He had on an olive-drab athletic shirt and a pair of brightly shined boots, again, probably authentic. The dark green colors set off the richly mahogany skin. His hair was close-cropped, but not so much that I couldn't see the tight natural curls of his African heritage. He was a proud and handsome man; some real indications of his warrior background were evident.

I wondered about that, as I had before. Is there something about some men that is bred into them by their ancestors — something that they spend their lives trying to discover in this modern, vanilla world? How do those men, who are by nature warriors, find their place in the world if the tight structures of modern society don't provide them?

Even his studio apartment took on the convincing air of a barracks. His bed was a simple metal cot. The wool blanket was stretched tautly and the sheet top evenly displayed over its top. There were only two chairs in the small apartment, both of them canvas director's chairs. Between them was a small, polished table with only about a one-foot square surface. The floor was as polished as his boots, the wax applied in many even coats. Not a thing was out of place. Even the kitchen was in military order.

The walls were either freshly painted or else laboriously washed. On them were only a very few decorations. I walked over to take a look. There were a few inexpensively framed photographs of a military camp. The males in the photographs were all young, surely only teenagers They were smiling boyishly into the camera. I could make out Carl in all of them.

I turned away and found him standing in perfect parade rest in the center of the room. His eyes were staring into space directly ahead. I moved toward him. He didn't move or flinch. I stood inches away. I listened to his breathing as it slowly but surely began to pick up speed. I began to study the rest of his body, letting my eyes travel downward.

When I got to his crotch I found a very expected bulge. Just having a man walk in here and allowing him the moment of his military presentation was turning him on.

"Have you read your orders?"

"Of course, *sir!*" He barked the last word.

"And you've followed them?"

"Of course, *sir!*"

"Have you any questions?"

"No, *sir!*"

"Proceed."

"Yes, *sir!*"

His face was flushed red. I took one of the folding chairs and waited. He swiveled so he was facing me. With great care — meticulous care — he began to mechanically remove each piece of his clothing. He folded the athletic shirt carefully and placed it neatly on the floor by his bed. Somehow he managed to retain his military posture while unlacing and removing his boots and pulling off his socks. The boots were stood side by side under the cot with the socks carefully placed inside them. Then came his pants. He couldn't have been more careful with their crease if they had been formal trousers. Standing now with only a cloth Army cap and his briefs on, he seemed to hesitate — only very briefly — but then took off the hat. Then — again, with the slightest hesitation, just enough to make this sexually fascinating — he pulled down his briefs.

Naked, he resumed his posture. The military truly has such a sexual component to it. Here was this man, standing just the way his drill instructors had taught him, and the result, once the offending clothes were taken off, couldn't have been better designed by a pornographic artist.

His chest was forced outward by the backward motion of his arms. His nipples seemed to be in a position of utter offering. His hips were jutting forward, carrying with them his cock and balls. His legs were slightly spread in a manner similar to any I could have a slave assume. I wouldn't have tolerated those thighs protecting his balls and neither would his drill instructor.

Carl was obviously transported by the experience. His cock was stiffening. His face was actually relaxing. He was, at last, back with a commander. That, he'd told me, was the one thing that was always necessary in his life. He had found it in the military. The Army had shown him how desperately he had wanted a sergeant to rule over him. But then, when he'd tried to express just how wonderfully important that was to him, it had ended. A dishonorable discharge and a nightmare of civilian life.

So, he decided, he would have to recreate his military existence. If the Army didn't want him as he was, he would discover people who did. The leather bars were his salvation. He had described his ecstasy when he'd walked into the first one. There were uniformed men. At least some of them were willing to command. With their discipline, he could structure the rest of his existence.

He'd become engulfed in the life it had offered. Suddenly no longer lost, he had a milieu that functioned for him. He had gotten a job. His needs were so minimal — as I could see in this apartment — that he was actually now, at the age of twenty-nine, fairly comfortable. He used his excess income to travel, always seeking more leather, more uniforms, more quasi-military events and situations.

I only wished that Martin's magic training camp still existed. Carl would have fit in, perfectly. It was made for his dreams of a military existence that had value for his hard cock and willing ass. But he was doing admirably well in reconstructing all of that for himself.

Discipline was the main goal in his sexual life. With it, he had enough for his other needs. But his demands had increased, not in terms of quantity, but of quality. There weren't many men who could carry out the fantasy with him in either of the ways he needed it: either to be perfectly aware of every detail of military life, or else, to be perfectly in command through other means.

I reached into the back rear pocket of my khaki pants and brought out a length of black leather about an inch and a half wide. This was the symbol of my command. He had expected it. My movement brought about the first visible distraction from his perfect carriage. His eyes darted to my leather strap. "Eyes front," I spat out.

I stood back a couple feet. His body was in fine shape. He had only a slight bit of chest hair. The kinky curls were small, dark swirls on his chocolate skin. His pubic hair was much more full. His cock and balls, a deeply dark color of mixed purple and brown, were in perfect proportion to the rest of his body.

I went back to my chair. "My understanding is this: You're prepared to serve at my party on Sunday and on this evening. You understand that your role is strictly that of a plebe. You will respond to every order with perfect discipline, and you understand that every failing is to be rewarded with the expected result."

"Yes, *sir!*"

"My standing orders were for your ass to be lubricated. Has that been done?"

"Yes, *sir!*"

"You don't look in very good shape, Carl. Have you been fucking off on your exercises."

He was trapped. That look of fear took over again. He searched madly through his mind to find an answer that wouldn't offend me.

"I thought so. Hit the floor. Fifty push-ups. *Now!*"

He dove for the floor. I sat and watched as he mechanically counted out the exercises. He had told me his workout regime. This wasn't going to be all that strenuous for him — unless he'd done them just before I'd arrived, hoping to impress me with his body. But, apparently not. He went through the movements with remarkable speed — and grace. Only toward the end, still counting off each repetition, did he begin to show the slightest strain that I could hear in his voice.

When he was finished, he stood up. His chest was expanding and contracting. He resumed his parade rest.

"Two more."

He started for a second. Before he got lost in his confusion, I went further.

"One to let you kiss each of my boots."

He moved quickly to comply. The two push-ups were done with even more grace then the others. With each dip down, his lips touched my boots and lingered there, just for enough time to let me know that he was performing the required actions with sufficient appreciation.

When he stood up this time his cock was in full erection. The strap was still in my hands. I lifted it up to head level and stretched it between my clenched fists. I brought the tightly pulled leather closer to him. He didn't move until it was touching his lips. "Kiss it."

Not losing his ramrod posture, he did. His pursed lips were sensual as they moved, in total contradiction to the military stance he had taken, to caress the leather. I moved the strap back and forth, letting a foot-long length rub against his lips sensually. He never stopped his attention. His eyes closed, almost in ecstasy.

I remembered that drill instructors almost always have their charges kiss some element of their uniform as part of their indoctrination. I must have discovered some deeply held fetish of Carl's, one so far into his mind that he hadn't even known to tell me about it.

He was being taken into some kind of sexual extreme, far, far, away from any I had thought I was taking him.

There was a sudden and tremendous shudder that tore through his body, forcing his shoulder and his chest to quiver and so powerfully gripping him that I expected him to fall over.

We both stood there silently. He opened his eyes. They were displaying obvious shock at what had happened. I reached down and felt the still warm discharge of his come on my pants. I scrapped it off with my palm and brought it up and smeared it on his face. He stood there and took it all.

"You'll pay for that." I said.

"Yes, *sir!*" he responded. I believed him. I believed him enough that I had to smile, and he did too.

"You're going to get fucked good and hard for that — coming without permission. And you're going to make one hell of a slave at my party."

"Sir, with all due respect, I don't have a moment's doubt that it's all true." His smile broadened. "Permission to proceed getting the officer's condom, *sir.*"

"Granted."

Questions

"How was your dinner with Phil?"

Madame looked up from her lunch and glared at me. "As though that's the most important topic of conversation! I'm much more interested in your news."

"I'll get to that soon enough. Come on, tell me about your dinner. Once I get started neither one of us will think to get back to it."

"It was delightful. We went to the Top of the Mark, as I had planned. I dressed for him, in my most formal gown. He was perfectly attired. We acted as though we were ancient lovers, recapturing some moment in the South of France from decades ago. We laughed and gossiped. We talked about everything.

"Some of the waiters recognized him and — of course — the service was even more exquisite than it would have been otherwise. They took wonderful care of us. Once they heard our conversation…Hah! The service could have been rivaled by Old Russia. Every bus boy in the place wanted to hear what outrageous story he or I would tell next. They hung on his gossip of writers and artists and the most *interesting* proclivities of theirs that he'd observed over the years.

"I, needless to say, had a few things to add of my own. At the end, they bought us a bottle of awfully fine champagne, as though we had performed just for them."

"Which you adored."

"Which I — of course — adored. It really was a splendid rendezvous."

"Did you get any of them to attend to your rooms?"

"No." I'd caught her in something. I could watch her decide whether or not to admit to her actions. "I had plans for later in the evening."

"Who?"

"What, is more like it," she smiled. She was finished with her crepe and sat back in her chair, carefully dabbing at her lips. "A fine young man from one of the more, shall we say, prestigious publishing houses. I got him on recommendation from a friend in London. He's English but working in New York now. I had to come to California to find him.

"His interests are very common among the English, especially the upper classes, and this one is certainly from there. I had brought my canes, as you'd imagine I would. I had him over my footstool with his shirttails up and his pants down and left all that near-porcelain skin the British have with some delightful red welts.

"I do think, sometimes, that none of them ever got over their experiences at public school. They seek to recreate them so often and with such…intensity."

We laughed over that, long and hard. It was true. We'd both seen it so often. While one wonders about the complex psychologies of American men and how they ever did get to the places that some of them have achieved, the English are so totally directed toward frequent and sound beatings that one can forget they ever do anything else. They love nothing more than a good, strong arm to take care of their backsides.

"I hope you got more than just the use of your canes," I said.

"Yes, but that wasn't really satisfactory. I would much rather be taking part in the roles of our fiction than simply fucking. That's all I could think of with this boy. He's thirty-five years old, but highly uncreative. I wanted to be some Amazon Queen, or one of your famous executive women who become natural dominatrices. Hell, I wanted to be my own creation, Madame. But, no. It was strictly tame.

"But, enough of this. I want the details of your activities. I'm so excited to think you might actually be making progress. It really is going to happen, isn't it?"

"Martin's here."

My comment made her freeze. She picked up her water glass as though she needed a prop to take in the news. "Martin," she whispered. She sighed then, "Are you taking him back to new England with you?"

"No, no. He's here for the party. He lives in Los Angeles now. Doing well enough. He's becoming a top."

"Martin!?" It wasn't just that she was shocked, she was angry as well. "What does that mean?" She slammed her glass down on the table.

"It means that he's moving on, at least with other men."

"You fucked him last night, I presume?"

"No."

"How could you have Martin here and not fuck him? Oh, my god." Her hand went to her chest as though she'd just thought a dreadful thought, "He didn't fuck *you*?"

"I'm not going to play at being a virgin after all these years," I said.

"When you were a child. Not while you've been such a man."

"This is beside the point. No. We didn't have sex — in the usual sense — last night. We each had an assignment. I was out interviewing someone for the party. Martin was applying some of his newfound skills as a disciplinarian to a particularly difficult recruit of ours, one of those who needs to get the humiliation and abuse he desires if he's going to be useful later on."

"How could you two go on as though it had never happened?"

"Because it did happen, and it exists for us. But, really, the chapter is over. Not the stuff that stays with me — and him. Not the most perfect parts of it, the knowledge that he's always there, always going to show up again and again and be as wonderful as the last time. But it wouldn't work to drag him away.

"We always use the term 'boy' in our conversations. We both know that has nothing to do with age. Your own, last night, was nearly as old as I am. Martin — if this helps you — is an adolescent. He needs to grow away from his parents. In a certain sense, that's the two of us. Like some nineteen-year-old going off to college, he needs to create his own networks, become independent of his family, learn his own lessons.

"It doesn't deny his patrimony to make those kinds of decisions and to take those routes. It only means he's growing up. When he's older, he might very well come back again, like so many other sons, and take up residence next door, renew his position.

"Martin needed things. He needed me at one point, and he needs not to have me now."

"But what will you do?"

"Madame, it is not the only love of my life. You care only because you saw it as something terribly special, which it is. Simply because it was the one S/M relationship that worked so well…"

"For so long," she insisted on adding.

"Yes, yes, it did work for a long time. But it was never fully traditional. We lived together for a very short time in there."

"But it was so beautiful."

"But there will be others, and in the meantime, Martin hasn't really left me. You must believe that."

"You should be settled down." She was becoming schoolmarmish on me again.

"I? Perhaps, someday, in a way. But the boys like Martin aren't what I necessarily want or need for that. I'm part of his network, his family. Much like you are for me. It all works for me, the sense of belonging and the sense of having others belong. That's my need now. I know he exists, and some of the others from his party will exist. Don't try to impose all the traditional structures on this existence. You and I are not here in this world to have church weddings in formal dress."

"I suppose not," she said.

The waiters came and cleared the empty plates from the table. We ordered coffee and made plans to return to the convention floor. It was all going to be tedious business. We tried to cheer ourselves up by daydreaming about certain personalities we knew at the party. The one editor who had been the subject of so many fantasies wasn't included in this conversation, as though we left him in a more honored space where it wouldn't be possible to joke about him. But there were many others we could imagine.

"That one stupid bitch who rejected your last book could use a bit of cane," Madame said.

"But, my dear, you're slipping. You know my thoughts in general, my philosophies as they've matured. This party's participants — in all their roles — should be there for good reasons. The need to serve, to display themselves, to enjoy the sensuous nature of bondage and the strap — those are the reasons they should have been chosen. To use this simply for punishment doesn't work. To squander all this art as though it was a way to get back at someone isn't appropriate at all."

"You can be such a purist," she said, but in a tone that conveyed appreciation, not rebuke. "You lose yourself so often in the world of your books — your own and Adrienne's. You two, wanting the fine world of masterful princes and their lovely charges…"

"A wonderful thought, to lift oneself up out of the gutter where this world insists that sex must be housed," I retorted. "It is a fine thought, to remove the ugly noises from sex and to find those jeweled places where it can exist."

"You would have had such a marvelous household in another time."

"Probably, my dear, only in the time of my fantasies."

"But you insist on creating them here, now, in this place as well." She stood up; it was time to leave. I joined her and took her arm. We walked out of the dining room and out of the hotel, moving toward the convention.

"It's like this gathering," I took up the conversation when we were out in the sunlight. "Everything around us is so defiled by corruption in one way or another. We're brought down to some low common denominator by it all, our sex is and so is our writing.

"Our finest moments, Madame, are in our minds and in our words. It's so seldom that we're able to translate them into our lives, no matter how much we try.

"You get upset about Martin, by my not keeping him forever and by his leaving. But, of course, I have my moment with Martin. He's like the finest paragraph I've ever written, my masterpiece. To go beyond him and the others with whom I've gotten that far is such an astonishing idea."

"Oh, but I remember when you thought you'd never write what you do. I remember when you and Martin lived in the far north together, creating an epic novel with your lives. That was taken from you — so sad, so tragic. But you began that epic. Someday, you know, you will try it again. I want to be there and see that happen."

"But you must remember," I said, "we didn't finish that one together, and when I do write the next one, it might not be Martin who's the collaborator."

"But the attempt, the simple fact of the attempt, will be awesome."

An Interruption

"You want to do what!?" I was incredulous. Martin was standing
in the hotel room with his arms defiantly crossed over his chest.

"You heard me. I want to make my own contribution."

"Your contribution is going to be getting your ass beaten to
a pulp!"

"Please, let me do this one thing. I know you've already made
plans for me for this fucking party of yours. All right, I know how
important it is that I perform well for you. I'll do it. I promise I'll
do anything you want there. But I want to bring my own slave to
the party."

"You don't even have one to bring! You don't know the men
in San Francisco any more. You think you're going to get dressed
in your show-off leather and waltz down to Folsom Street and
find someone who'd be perfect for my party? You're crazy."

"That muscle-bound closet case you got yourself tied up with
is hardly a catch."

"You know why I'm having him at the party."

"Yeah, sure, he's living beauty. You forgive that kind of man so
many things, a few muscles and a pretty face and you start relaxing those inflated standards of yours."

"The party's at least partially a visual event."

"Fine. I could have carried that off for you. I'm not exactly a
troll. You said this black guy was handsome; the blond kid from
Colorado's cute; the couple's hot. You didn't need to add
Christopher."

"Are you going to tell me that you didn't enjoy your little tryst with him last night?"

"I had a fine time. But it was one of those masturbatory things — the ones you told me about. There was nothing to it but the body. His mind is trapped in deepest Ohio..."

"The same state you happen to be from."

"And the one I left to live with you."

"Enough of this. Christopher is beautiful. We agree. He'll be getting precisely what he wants from the party, and he'll appear exquisite. The others will more than make up for him. But your street tricks..."

"I won't bring back a street trick."

"You sound like some puppy dog that wants to give his master a present and doesn't understand that the master isn't exactly delighted with a dead field mouse."

He threw his hands in the air. He tried once more. "*Please,* just let me try, for once."

I played back all of my conversation with Madame about him and finally shrugged a very resigned agreement. "Fine. If you have to prove something to me, then go ahead and do it. I'm not at all sure about this, but you know that."

"Yes, I do." He was jubilant. I realized suddenly that he hadn't really expected to win. I could have held out longer and won the argument. But it was done.

"You'll have hell to pay if you fail."

"It's Saturday night in San Francisco. How can I fail to find a perfect trick on Folsom Street?"

That made me laugh. I was remembering years ago and the far from perfect encounters I'd had. "Get out. You certainly have your work to do."

He was dressed in full leather, chaps over his leather pants; jacket, vest, shirt, all of them were leather; his boots were highly polished. He put on his cap. "And I do still know people here. Enough to find what we need."

"You have the rest of it all set up? The food's being delivered? All the tools you'll need? The bar..."

"All of it. I promise."

"Then, go on. I have my last appointed to keep."

He kissed me and bounded out the doorway.

*　　*　　*

My own activities were going to call for markedly different clothes than Martin's leather. I dressed carefully in a three-piece suit, the finest I owned. My best shoes and an especially well-designed silk tie were part of the outfit. So was the most extravagant set of jewelry — cuff links, tie stud — that I owned. My newest recruit would appreciate all of the details.

Francois's apartment wasn't far away, on the top of the hill, in one of the finer buildings. I arrived and my appearance met with the obvious approval of the observant doorman. He called up for me and then retrieved the elevator that took me to the appropriate floor.

Francois was waiting at his doorway. "Sir, a pleasure." He stood back, graciously holding the door open. While the other men I'd met had often been clumsy in their attempts to discover how they should greet my arrival, Francois knew exactly what the correct moves were. He bowed deeply at the waist as I passed by him.

I entered into an impeccably decorated apartment. It was small. I could see there wasn't even a bedroom. The upholstered couch had to fold out for a sleeping space. I took an offered chair and studied my surroundings. Every single item was superb. The china ashtrays I recognized as Limoges. The crystal was an assortment of the finest from Czechoslovakia and Belgium. The small tables were all covered in hand-worked leather.

"Would the _maître_ care for an aperitif?" Francois spoke flawless English. There was only a hint of an accent left in his voice. It made the use of his term for "Master" all the more impressive. He was standing in front of me. He was wearing a waiter's tuxedo, its creases sharp and the shirt crisply starched.

"Please."

He bowed again and seemed to be moving toward the small kitchen, whose entrance was only partially hidden by an antique folding screen of some oriental origin, probably Chinese. But he stopped just short of the door. He carefully took off his jacket and deliberately hung it over a large valet's stand.

In his shirt, he proceeded to go into the other room and quickly returned with a small glass of Byrrh in which floated a beautifully cut sliver of lemon peel. It was delivered to me on a small silver tray he held in the palm of his hand.

"If the *maître* will excuse me, I must see to his dinner's preparation."

I nodded my dismissal. While he quietly and efficiently moved through his tasks I watched the little glimpses of his body I could get from the space between the screen and the door frame.

He was a perfectly pleasant looking man. I had suspected he was thirty or so. I realized that he had taken such extremely good care of himself and his appearance that he could be older.

He had written to me saying that he was a steward on an international airline. He'd been living out that fantasy of mine concerning the perfect service that airline personnel could give if only our mores weren't so stupid. While he certainly hadn't gone about his duties in chains and hadn't — so far as he would admit — performed actual sexual acts on board, his dreams were fulfilled by the very role of being a servant to the travelers who were his charge.

I sipped the Byrrh, enjoying its plum flavor, and it seemed that he timed his reappearance precisely with the moment when I'd finished the drink.

"Your appetizer." He bowed less formally this time, but with now less meaning than he had before.

I went to the table and allowed him to pull out my chair for me. On the plate in front of me was a delicate duck paté, nicely formed and served with some fine crackers of a sort I'd never had before. While I began to taste the delicious morsel, Francois came in with a small split of white wine that he carefully poured into one of the array of glasses in front of me.

I only happened to notice that his shoes were gone. I was startled at first. Then with a smile I tried very hard to keep to myself, I understood his game. If he was going to be able to carry it off as well as he was accomplishing this meal, I wouldn't interfere.

A well-made, light soup followed, and with it, Francois's socks disappeared. His cummerbund went with the serving of a palate cleanser, a sharply flavored raspberry sorbet. He must have considered this an informal meal, there was no fish course. But the entree — a delectable small beefsteak that he'd sauteed perfectly and served with a delicate cognac sauce — meant that there was no longer a shirt either.

Like many French men, Francois's body hair didn't really extend up onto his chest. Instead it gathered in a rich swirl around his belly. His nipples were unprotected, dark colored pieces of hard flesh. They'd obviously seen a great deal of use, they stuck out with as much invitation as the tiny roasted potatoes that had come with my meat.

When the white wine had been cleared and he brought on the split of rich Lafite-Rothschild, Francois appeared wearing only his black bow tie and his small French-styled briefs. They were a bright yellow color, flyless, made of a particularly soft cotton that held his obviously enlarged cock and balls in a smooth pouch.

During the service, we both ignored his utterly perfect strip. Each article of clothing was carefully stored on its place on the valet. He appeared at my side for each service with all seriousness. If anything, his attention and sobriety increased as the clothing left.

He didn't bother me with the ridiculous banter of American waiters. The food was simply served and our conversation was that of a baron and his butler. "Was the *maître's* journey pleasant?"

"Will the *maître* care for more wine?" "May I take the *maître's* plate?" "Are the *maître's* plans progressing well?"

At least I was able to anticipate the final scene. My dessert, a chocolate mousse, arrived in the hands of my host who was now dressed only in his correctly attired bow tie. I'm sure that my ability to ignore his progression added to his excitement. Once his cock was free of even the briefs, it was half hard.

I finished and sat back in my chair, a hand on my stomach signaling my appreciation of what he'd prepared for me.

"Will the *maître* take his coffee in the sitting area?"

"Yes."

He pulled the chair back for me. I couldn't help but graze his cock as I moved past him. He sucked in his breath quickly and whispered, "I'm very sorry, *maître.*"

In my chair, I was served a cup of fine coffee. The tray was again silver, only larger. The cup, saucer, creamer, and sugar bowl were all of the same pattern.

"The *maître* must be very tired from all of the work involved with his party. Perhaps I could relax him."

It wasn't a question, more of a statement of intent. Francois knelt in front of me and carefully removed my shoes and socks. He began to massage my feet with a skill that could never have been anticipated. His fingers seemed to dance over my skin, never making a wrong move, always finding the tender areas that could use his careful ministrations.

This, obviously, was his desire. I thought of Phil's great and joyful fetish for men's feet. I would have to make sure that he and Francois had an opportunity to spend some time together to explore their mutual interests. Francois's metal-hard cock certainly was all the proof I needed that he was, indeed, in his private ecstasy. His heavy French foreskin still covered the head of his cock, giving it a smoother look than erections usually have.

"The *maître* is enough pleased to allow Francois to attend the party?"

"It appears that you have more than adequate skills to make that worthwhile."

He leaned over and elegantly kissed the tops of each of my feet. "I have a special love for food, *maître*. Is there, at this late date, some way I could help in that particular area?"

"The materials have been ordered. But, of course, you could be assigned that role, if you choose."

"I would be honored." His hands were still massaging me. "Your plate and silver service, the flatware..."

"From the hotel."

He froze, almost is horror. "Common commercial goods for your party? *Maître,* please, I have so much here, of the finest quality. I've dreamed of your party since I first heard of it. To have it be less than perfect is something I couldn't stand. Mightn't I please..."

"But the party is tomorrow afternoon. There's not enough time."

"If you'd allow me to perhaps visit your rooms tonight, I could take an inventory. I could come back with some help and get everything that could ever be needed here. I could review the food and drink and make sure that some slight thing that I could have provided from my own stores wouldn't be necessary. I..."

"Francois, yes. I can see that you not only have the knowledge but the...passion for this. Yes. come to my suite and see what's available. I'll have at least one boy there in the early morning who can help you. Now, put my shoes and socks back on. Get dressed. I know good talent when I see it."

"*Maître,*" he leaned forward one more time and kissed my feet again.

In his street clothes, Francois looked more like a French sailor than an elegant steward. He wore tight pants, but with an air of great masculinity. I had thought that he might have been somewhat effeminate in his day-to-day clothes, but while there was certainly a grace in his walk that reminded me of a ballet dancer, the image of his broad shoulders was intensified in his clinging short-sleeved shirt.

He was absorbed in his role. There was not a hint that he wanted to give up a single part of it. He opened the doors, always bowing his head. He never initiated a conversation. He walked a perfect half step behind me as we made our way to my hotel.

I had to unlock the door to let him in. It was late, the dinner had been long and leisurely. Martin had already returned. More than that, he had come back with his prey. Francois and I didn't wake them when we came into the suite. The two of them were sleeping on the couch; it had folded out to provide a double bed.

Martin was on his side with his back to us. His heavy arm was resting on a smaller body. I walked up, as quietly as possible, and looked over to see a nicely built young man asleep. There was an intricate rope harness wrapped around him. I could tell that it held him immobile. The bondage — I recognized it as a kind of art that the Japanese had been the most successful with — was complete. There was this young man, held at the same time by two forces: A man who had claimed him with lust and the rope the man had demanded.

Francois whispered in my ear: "Are they yours?"

"One used to be," I said, suddenly very sad.

We went to the bed room. Francois announced, "You're tired. The planning has been so much, making all these boys do the right thing! You must need a bath."

He immediately went to draw it. While it was pouring, he came back in and gently began to undress me, performing his valet's duties with the same dignity as he had everything else that night. I was tired. I let him go on and eventually lead me into the bathroom.

I sank into the water, which was at a perfect temperature.

Francois had brought a small pouch with him. I had assumed it was simply those things a man might have when he is to spend the night with another, and I hadn't paid it any attention. But now he brought it into the bathroom and emptied it out on the sink's shelf. He brought out some kind of salt, which he poured into the bath. The odor from it was solid, masculine and still very pleasant.

Then he took some kinds of tools I wasn't very familiar with at first. I recognized them but couldn't remember.... Of course, they were the implements necessary for a pedicure. My Francois was not about to stop with a minor indulgence in his foot fetish. This was an *Artiste!*

I actually slumbered off while his hands worked on my feet, seeming to find their own special pleasure in my toes. I hadn't had anyone pay so very much attention to those small parts of my anatomy in quite a while. I certainly hadn't had so very much expertise focused on them. I seemed to fall into a soft and welcome sleep.

I woke up with a bit of a start. It couldn't have been that long, my skin was still smooth. I had been roused by a strange smell. I looked down and saw that Francois, who had undressed during my nap, was applying the last touches of plain nail polish to my nails. My toes — such a woefully ignored part of one's body — seemed suddenly very beautiful. His work had been even better than I had thought it might.

He looked up at me while he replaced the top to the polish container. He was smiling, just as pleased as I was with the results. He went back to work, blowing gently to speed up the drying. When he was convinced that the job had been done, he stood up. His cock was again in its full erection.

I climbed out of the bath, trying not to be awkward as I kept my polished toes out of the water. He was waiting with a towel, and immediately went to work drying me. He knew precisely how to be gentle while still applying enough pressure that I understood that a man was doing the labor.

I felt wonderfully cared for. The meal, the wine and brandy, the bath, and the tingling on my feet were all combined in one totally self-indulgent sensation.

He led me casually into the bedroom. He pulled back the covers with great precision. I sat down on the edge. "If the *maître* will permit me to spend the night, I could perform my duties more adequately in the morning."

"Of course." I looked at him carefully. His head was bent far over, his eyes looking straight at the floor. His cock was rampant. "But you'll sleep at the foot of the bed, on the floor."

"Of course, *maître.*"

"Chained to the bed."

"If the *maître* wishes."

"After you've spent your time at my feet."

He looked up. I recognized the expression. It was almost a desperation. He was wondering if I really understood what he wanted. If I did, a dream could be fulfilled.

I stood up and went to my bags. I quickly found what I wanted. I told him to arrange the extra sheets and blankets on the floor by one of the legs of the bed. He did. I returned and placed a heavy metal collar around his neck. I took its attached chain and padlocked it to the bed. He was forced by the chain's short length to get on his hands and knees. He looked up at me, his mouth open, his eyes nearly tearing. He was so close to what he wanted.

"Flat on your stomach." I gave the order with a quiet authority, not the shouting I had used with Carl. Francois fell onto his belly. I moved closer. I forced on of my feet underneath his face. "Make love to me."

He actually cried out in some mixture of pain and delight. His two hands cradled my foot. His mouth opened and his tongue licked and sucked at me. The hands were moving and grasping and clutching and adoring all at once. His hips were moving rapidly against his makeshift bed. It took a very few seconds before his whole body was seized with a tremor. His ass, beautifully hairy as French asses so often are, quivered, his legs shook.

Then there was no more power in his hands. His head fell on my foot and rested there for a moment, only making the slightest movements to rub a little bit against me.

"Thank you, *maître*. Thank you, forever."

"Go to sleep. You have a lot of work to do in the morning."

The Morning

I woke up first. I was amazingly refreshed. It seemed my feet were the first part of me to become conscious. My soles, my ankles, my toes were all tingling with a special delight. Francois, of course. I smiled. I indulge in so many parts of my own and other men's bodies, but I hadn't remembered what special and lingering pleasure feet can be.

I stood up, stretched, and moved to the end of the bed. Francois was curled up there. I stood and looked at him, wondering what was the balance between the physical discomfort of his position and the metal joy? I nudged at his chest with a foot. He stirred, momentarily confused, but seemed to remember where he was quickly. He sat up so fast that he tugged at his chain. I had the key in my hand and reached down to unlock him.

He rubbed his neck where the metal must have chafed against it and then jumped to his feet. He had a healthy morning erection swinging in front of him. Typically, he ignored it.

"Your bath, *maître*."

He rushed past me and into the bathroom. I followed and in a short while was once again in the embrace of the warm water. He was moving quickly now, all business. He left me in the water and I could only vaguely hear him. I thought he was rummaging through the things in the front room that Martin had brought home.

"*Maître, it will not do!*"

I looked up at him standing over me with his hands on his waist.

"None of it is good enough. I need both of those boys this morning. We will have to go to my apartment at once and collect *everything*."

I sat there, stunned for a moment. "Fine, it's your responsibility. Wake them up after you've dried me off." I got out of the water, and Francois went about his duties to my body, much less gently than he had last night. But he wasn't going to shirk any of them. He had carefully gotten out what he must have decided to be the appropriate clothes for a master at leisure and dressed me. Only then did he storm out of the bedroom and into the front room.

I heard him clapping his hands loudly and yelling, "Up, up, there's work to do."

A barely awake Martin answered, "What the fuck…Who the fuck…"

"Our *maître's* party is in danger. Up!"

There was a highly articulate exchange of swear words then between the two of them, some sounds that must have been made by the other younger man who I hadn't met, and a rush of noises that told me Martin was getting dressed. Francois was winning his battle.

I had expected them to come into the bedroom and argue in front of me. But it didn't happen. In a few minutes the door to the room slammed shut and there was silence.

I wasn't about to leave the suite; I didn't want to miss a single thing that might happen next. I called the front desk and asked for Joseph. He called back in a few minutes. I gave him a short list of things to get me — just some rolls, juice, and coffee along with the Sunday newspapers. I had no intention of eating the hotel fare and gave him specific instructions on where to shop.

He arrived in a short while. He carried in the parcels and the paper and put them on the coffee table.

"Been having fun?"

The room was littered with some of the reminders of Martin and his friend. The leather was scattered all over the place. Obviously Martin had decided against wearing it out on a Sunday morning and must have had other clothes nearby. The long pieces of rope he had used to tie up his trick were thrown over the back of the couch.

I didn't say anything to him. I just opened the bags and began to pull out food.

"Leather. Real kinky. Like you said you were. What you going to do, man? Have your slaves all tied up, have little leather boys running around with their asses all beat and shit?" He was laughing. I didn't say a word or respond at all. His smile disappeared. "You are, aren't you? Jesus, man. You really are."

I opened up the newspaper. "Thanks for the errand, Joseph."

Before he could say anything more or leave, the door opened and Francois came in, leading the way for Martin and his companion. All three of them were burdened with boxes, and shopping bags dangled from their hands.

"Carefully, *carefully*," Francois was insisting as the others put down their loads.

He didn't stop to acknowledge me or Joseph. "You," he said to Martin, "Move that shit out of the way. Put it in some closet."

He was pointing to the things Joseph had gotten out of the hotel stores. "Hey, man, that's my responsibility," Joseph shouted.

"Then get it out of here. As soon as possible. It's unbearable that you would have brought that here for the party. Have you no sense of nobility when you're in it's presence? The *maître* can't be having his guests eating off that shit!"

Joseph was as dumbstruck as the rest of us. He was frozen in place for a moment and then, angry, began to move. He went to the telephone and called for some help. He spoke in Spanish and I could follow the conversation. "We'll get the stuff out of here. For Christ's sake, what kind of shit is this?"

"Joseph, here, for your trouble," I handed him another of the many bills he seemed to be collecting from me. It calmed him down considerably.

"Okay, okay. But I wish you'd made up your mind a lot earlier. Could have saved us a lot of trouble."

"It is not the *maître's* duty to attend to such things. Now, move it. Get this stuff out."

There was a knock on the door. When Joseph answered it there were two other young men there. He gave them some quick orders and a period of utter pandemonium broke out as his contingent went about one set of business and my own kept up its labor under Francois's sharp voice command.

I ate my breakfast rolls and drank my coffee.

* * *

"Where the hell did you find that one?" Martin demanded a couple hours later.

I only smiled at him.

"He's worse than you ever were."

"That's because I was only so demanding in sex, which you always enjoyed. Even the little things I'd make you do around the house were always in an erotic context. You never had to experience the reality of slave labor.

"If you had, you would have realized that the most vicious overseers have always been other slaves."

"Tell me." He collapsed on the bed, his arms and legs spread out. "How do you like Sean?"

"He looks fine."

"Is that all?"

"More than that." It was true. Martin's find was quite handsome. He was a perfect match for Keith, in fact. They were the same short height and had the same young and hard build. I was already playing with those possibilities in my mind.

"Your French bastard had us up and out of here by nine this morning. It's already noon. What time is everyone due here?"

"Three."

"Do you have it well-enough planned out?"

"Enough."

"The others? When do they arrive?"

"At one. You, your friend, and Francois had better start showering, shaving, getting ready. Christopher's the first one due. You're going to have to work on him."

"How? I thought my little session with him was enough to get him in the mood. It sure seemed to be."

"Yes, but his body needs to be shaved. Especially close. You'll have to prepare him."

Martin sat up at that idea. It obviously appealed to him. "What else?"

"You'd better get Sean in here. I suppose he and I should meet and get a number of things clear between us."

"You're going to play with *my* boy?"

"I'm going to inspect *my* slave."

Martin wasn't quite willing to give everything up that easily. He got Sean to come into the bedroom, but didn't give me the time to start giving the young man any of the orders that he knew were going to be coming. "Strip." He gave the command himself with a sharpness that even I admired.

The young man with the reddish hair and the pale skin I'd seen earlier in the day hesitated, then began to move, looking at me with a touch of apprehension.

He was wearing jeans, boots, a black T-shirt. A leather jacket was now in the back of the hallway closet, put there by Francois so its sight wouldn't offend my guests.

The boy was extremely attractive naked. He had a complexion on his torso that betrayed his Irish heritage. There were hints of freckles all over, especially on his shoulders and the whole length of his arms. His belly was flat and his chest was full, though they would have appeared even more extreme if there had been any body hair to emphasize their lines. Sean had only a pale red growth over his cock and balls. His legs, his arms, all of the rest of him below the waist seemed to be as naturally nude as Christopher was shaven.

He stood there while I looked him over.

"I hope Martin had the sense to explain this to you, to let you know that this wasn't a game. I'm doing something very important. I'm allowing him to include you as a special favor to him. I hope you'll live up to his expectations."

"I heard what he said," Sean answered. He seemed to have an air of defiance about him. But of course! That was what would attract Martin.

"Where did you two meet?" I asked.

There was a smile building on Martin's face and a scowl on Sean's. Martin answered: "There was a wrestling night at one of the gay bars."

"And you won." I answered my own question. "But before the match, you made him agree to do whatever you wanted him to?"

"That was the deal." *Aren't I still your boy?*

"And you agreed — and still do?" I asked Sean. "Yeah."

"No! That's not good enough."

"I keep my word." Sean was staring at me, real fury on his face. "I told him whoever won got the guy for the next day — no holds barred, safe sex the *only* limit. So he told me what it was. Okay? I'm here. I'm not gong to leave. I heard about you. Not just from him. Some other guys at the bar were talking about you and your party. I'm no amateur, you know. I get around.

"There's not many people that don't know what you're doing. So, you got me. I understand."

"But do you understand?"

"I understand I lost a match to a guy. I understand I made a bet. I understand I gotta pay up. I keep my promises. You got it."

"But I need more than a petulant loser. I need someone who's going to give me the kind of submission that will make this party the event it has to be."

"If I'm not as good as anyone else, you got me for another day. I don't hedge on my bets."

"You shouldn't have said that so quickly," Martin teased him. "You should think what 'another day' might mean."

"I'll do it right," Sean said, a little less passionately. "I promise you. I'll do it right."

*   *   *

Everyone seemed to want to do things right. The knocks on the door to the suite began sounding precisely at 1. Christopher was dressed in sports clothes. I was sure he realized nothing else was going to be necessary. He stood awkwardly and took in all the activity that was going on. I sent him off to the bathroom to be shaved.

"Martin," I called out as the two of them started walking out of the front room. "All of it. I don't want a single strand beneath his neck."

Christopher blushed. He was, I'm sure, humiliated by the very idea. That was just as well. It would help him create a more appropriate mind-set.

There was another knock on the door. I answered it. Glen and Phillip had arrived. They had a sheepish look on their faces. I slapped Glen's fine ass as he walked by. He yelped and turned quickly — too quickly. I stared at him until he shrugged and smiled. "Just a reminder, huh?"

"Only the first of many."

"Yes, sir." He said it with a nice mumble and nicer blush. Phillip didn't need any reminder. He was looking around the room at the disarray and was anxious enough to ask what he could do to help.

Before I could answer, there was another knock. It was Keith. He came into the suite with a long stride. He had no hint of hesitation. He kissed me when I had closed the door, something I wasn't quite expecting. "I'm real excited."

"We'll see about that," I replied. The details were getting out of hand. It was time to take some control. "Francois, what do you need done?"

"Everything. *Everything!*" He said in a Gallic temper fit. He was pawing through the groceries that I had had Martin shop for.

This was enough. I walked up to him and grabbed him by the shirt collar. "Strip. Now."

He froze and then seemed to move to begin arguing again. I yanked once more at his shirt collar. "Strip."

"*Maître,*" he said, bowing his head.

"You three, get out of your clothes as well." Keith, Glen, and Phillip joined Francois's undressing. Sean was over in the corner, vaguely playing with himself. "You get your hands off your cock. It's going to get more than enough attention today.

"Better, much better. Maybe you'll all get your minds back on what's happening here." Keith certainly was; his nice young cock was already swelling to an erection. "Now, get these clothes out of this room. There's a closet in the hallway. Francois, I'll ask you once more before I get out the strap, what needs to be done?"

"The table needs to be set. The dishes are all here now. I need to know who's going to be doing what, where everyone will be."

I explained my plan to him, being rewarded with his obvious esteem. "Beautiful, of course." Now he was satisfied that the plan was in hand. He went back to work in earnest.

In a few moments Carl arrived. I had him undress immediately. My entourage was complete. When Martin and a completely shorn Christopher entered the room, I checked the time and knew it was the moment to begin.

"Martin, I want him on his back over the cocktail table. His calves tied to one set of the table legs, his forearms to another. Not too tight. He'll be in that position for quite a while. Watch out for his circulation."

"Rope?"

"You'll find it in my black suitcase, as always."

Martin's years in the Navy had given him an intricate knowledge of knots. His ability with bondage is well-known. The rest of the boys watched as the huge bodybuilder was laid out over the table surface. He accepted his directions with an easy compliance. His muscles were not being strained. I could see that Martin was taking my orders seriously, but the position was allowing all of us to see the firmly etched development Christopher had achieved in his hours in the gymnasium.

Martin, knowing how important this was to me, did his work magnificently, using a long length of rope to achieve nothing less than a sculpture on Christopher's body, with some of the extra pieces crisscrossing his mammoth chest and emphasizing his pectorals. Christopher groaned, as though he understood this was a preamble to the bells, those wonderful hated bells that I had promised him.

"You," I turned to Glen and Phillip, "I want each of you standing with your backs to one of those pillars at the entrance of the sitting room. Put your arms behind you, behind the pillars, and your feet on either side of column."

I went into the bedroom and returned with four sets of leather restraints. "It's such a shame not to display those beautiful marks on your ass and back," I whispered to Glen as I went about my own work. "They look marvelous."

He didn't say anything at first, but then looked directly at me, "Thank you, sir."

"Don't you like them?" I asked as I placed the cuffs on each of his wrists and then joined them behind the column.

"Very much," he said, then smiled, "A lot."

"There'll be many more, I'm sure."

"I'm sure, too."

I bent down and put a matching set of cuffs on his ankles. I had placed hooks in the bottom on the pillars and used them now to attach his legs.

I repeated the process with Phillip. The actions I was performing and the sight of his lover only a few feet across from him had excited him. His cock was growing. I grabbed hold of it when I was done. "Save this, Phillip, you'll need to remember how much you're being turned on in a while."

He must have thought that the simple act of bondage was all I expected. There was a sudden panic on his face, "What else are you going to do?"

I kissed him and then said, "Anything I want to."

Carl was the easiest of the group. I had decided that to play to his military fantasy was the very easiest means of using him. He was naked now, but the only one with any piece of clothing at all on his handsome black body. A white metal military hat was on his head, a white belt around his waist. Tall military boots were on his feet. I didn't have to say a word to him. He had automatically assumed parade rest against the wall just inside the door to the suite. That was precisely where I wanted him.

Keith and Sean were next. Now that Martin had finished with Christopher I could put him to work on the two younger men. "A simple sculpture," I said. "Here, in front of the table. Have them kneeling, but absolutely immobilized, facing each other only a foot or so apart."

"You have some lengths of leather…"

"Whatever you choose. Create for me." I left him alone with his handiwork and went over to Francois who had been working at the food. In the other room there were hot plates to heat the water for tea as well as ice packs to cool the wine. I could see that Francois was working quickly with the basic ingredients we had on hand. The French genius was coming through. I tasted first one, then another of the things he had brought along and those he was making.

"Fine," I said. "This is going to do perfectly well."

$$* \quad * \quad *$$

It was done. It was all prepared. There were only the slightest touches left. I went back to my bags and brought out more implements. I went to Glen first. In my hand was a gag.

"You don't need that," he objected. There was no avoiding my intention.

"But I want it," I answered. I inserted the length of leather into his mouth. It was just large enough to fill him up, perhaps cause a little discomfort, but certainly not pain. More impressive was the intricate headband of leather straps that went with it. When I had finished my handiwork it was as though I had created a lattice around his head.

Phillip got precisely the same. I wanted them to be a perfectly matched pair. I stepped back and saw that they were.

Christopher got a similar, though simpler, gag. "You, at least, will need it." As soon as it was firmly attached I pulled out the despised tit clamps and their bells. He groaned, but through the gag the sound was just pleasant. As soon as the balls were attached I used my fingers to let play their little music for both my and his enjoyment.

Then I went further. His groans increased when he realized I had gone out and found more of the bells. I went quickly about the business of attaching two of them to his testicles and one of them to his cock. As though it was rebelling against his own desires, his erection stiffened at the humiliation and jerked upward, forcing the bell to sound.

Perfect.

Martin's decoration of Keith and Sean was exquisite. It was — I'm sure purposely — overdone. They had no need for all the leather bands and rope that he'd used. It was all for the sake of ornamentation. They were on their knees, as I'd told him to place them. They were separated by just enough space to allow their cocks to barely touch — a very pretty sight.

I put very loose clamps on their nipples — not tight enough to cause any real pain, at least not for a while, but they wouldn't fall off, either. They were actually earrings. Small eyedrop-shaped pieces of mother of pearl drooped from their chests.

Glen and Phillip got their own nipple decorations: matching sets of gold rings that I'd found that left the impression that they were pierced. Glen overreacted and started to protest through his gag as soon as I had put them on him. But he must have realized he was helpless and soon gave up.

When I reached for Carl's nipples he stiffened. "They still hurt from the other night?"

"Yes, sir."

"They'll feel even better tomorrow." I had found very plain metal decorations for his chest, masculine in a way that fit his bearing.

"Thank you, sir," he said. He was looking down at them, wondering, I think, what they were doing on his body. They were a silver-looking metal, brightly polished, and the small half-moon they formed under each of his tits made his chest look perfect.

"The rest of it," I said to Martin. "A glass of wine," I told Francois. I went and sat in my chair and waited for my guests to arrive, pleased beyond description at my handiwork.

Madame, of course, was first. She was wonderfully dressed. She had on a top made of some metallic fabric that clung to her breasts. Her makeup was flawless. I had once criticized her for her choices in powder and coloring and from that day on she's always spent hours on her face before showing herself to me at an occasion like this one.

I watched to see how my plan worked. At her knock, Martin had opened the door. He'd bowed. He motioned her into the room, not saying a word even though they knew one another. Carl stepped forward and took her coat for her. Martin then escorted her past Glen and Phillip to where I was standing waiting to greet her. In a moment Francois was beside us with a glass of white wine in a handsome crystal glass that he carried on a gold tray.

Madame sat down before she could respond. "Perfect."

I smiled and took my own seat back. The men were all naked. All of them were erect. I had sent Martin through them and had him place the black condoms on each one instructing him to suck the covered cocks hard if required — but that hadn't been necessary.

My orders were explicit: Each one of them had to be hard and Martin had to keep them hard with his mouth. He could use his hand only on himself. Christopher wouldn't be a problem; he was the only one with an unsheathed cock. I only had to put a finger on its extended length if I thought it was going to soften. I did that now, just to tease Madame.

But Christopher's cock wasn't the thing that was impressing her. What she was studying so deeply was the food arranged over his body. A pate was placed perfectly on his abdomen; a cheese preparation was on the shaved area where his pubic hair would have been; pieces of fruit surrounded the outlines of his pectorals; stalks of fresh vegetables rose up from beside his testicles and underarms.

He was the centerpiece to our banquet.

Then Phil arrived. I watched as he came and took in the scene. Now quite old, he still had all the handsome features on his face that had sent their messages into the minds and bodies of men and women in Europe, North America, all over the world, when he'd been a younger man.

I'd once seen a photograph taken when he'd been in his twenties, living in Paris between the wars and being kept by some of the most wealthy aristocrats who clustered to the French capital in those days. He was standing against an alley wall, wearing a kind of disreputable T-shirt that marked the Apache toughs, a cigarette dangling from the side of his mouth as he half-smiled, half-sneered at the camera.

That same expression was on his face now, decades later. It was proof of the perseverance of his sexual being that age hadn't defeated it at all. He was staring hardest at Carl. The combination of race and military artifacts would have touched him much more than the rest.

But, whatever else, Phil is a gentleman. He came across the room to greet Madame, trying not to appear to linger too long at the sight of the naked men tied to pillars or bound on their knees on the floor.

He kissed her hand elegantly, then stood and shook mine. He glanced down at Christopher and lost control of the leer that was bursting to get outside him. "You son of a bitch," he said to me. He ran a hand over Christopher's impressive torso and used a finger to lick a bit of pate from his belly. Then he laughed out loud. "You goddamn son of a bitch."

"Tea, Francois."

That caught Phil's attention. He watched as Francois walked back into the room carrying his tea on that same golden serving try. When the naked servant reached him he broke into a torrent of his fluent French that was too fast for either Madame or me to follow.

I could only hear that Francois was using "*maître*" to Phil as frequently as he did to me. I could also tell that there was something going on that appealed to both men. Certainly Francois's cock wasn't going down.

"Do you know him?" I finally asked.

"Think, think, of course we know of each other. I've wanted to meet him for quite some time. Evidently his specialty is so intense that he's not going to mind indulging an ancient man like myself…"

Of course! Phil adored feet as well. I could suddenly see that Francois would be willing to cross the Bay and give the old man some intense pleasure. I felt a new wave of pleasure, happy to have made any connection between the men. Just the idea of having the pleasure — the honor — of making a match between Phil and someone who would deliver sexual delight to him was wonderful.

And then, of course, Adrienne arrived.

I had been worried, so had Madame. But Adrienne entered the room with the same confidence and energy that she had when she did anything. There was, I think, a slight hesitation when the door was opened and my tall, muscular Martin was there, his erection standing straight out from his body. But she was not going to show that to us.

The boys went through their duties, carefully taking her coat, bringing her into the other guests. When she sat down and pulled out one of her omnipresent unfiltered cigarettes, Martin was on the spot with a light for her. She dragged in on it, leaned back in her chair, and exhaled a cloud of smoke with great melodrama. "Remarkable."

I looked at Martin and saw more than a little appreciation in his face as he studied her. He was never one to limit himself just to men, and the sight of the stately trim and blond Adrienne, so perfectly dressed, was something that he would admire.

I wouldn't have possibly cross-examined Adrienne on her reactions to the party and the men. It wouldn't have been right. She had understood perfectly well that this was, in it's way, a gift to her. Just the sight, just the experience of the naked men serving, was something that I knew she would admire for many years, forever.

And, I had to admit, they were wonderfully attractive and attentive. Martin wouldn't have let me down, as much for his won pride as anything else. His fat cock was dripping inside its sheath, we could all see the milky liquid building up inside it, a sharp contrast to the black latex.

Christopher was in agony. But the agony of his hugely muscled body was beautiful to see. He attempted to move around in the tight bounds, just trying to have some change in position. Each maneuver he made highlighted another set of muscles. We all made sure there was constant attention to him, I caught Madame and Phil both pinching and squeezing at his more vulnerable parts when they ostensibly were reaching for a piece of food.

Martin was going about his duties. With that kind of serious intent that he has about sex, he made the rounds of the tied-up slaves and sucked each of them, making their condoms glisten with sex those times that they didn't need to be made more erect. There was a constant sound of his slight sucking. But we all understood this was no simple sex show. The fact was that one man was mouthing the rest of them, not for our prurient desire, but because the males needed to be kept in their state. First, to be more beautiful and vulnerable with their erections swinging out from their bodies; second, because their erections left them so helpless, more subservient in a way that could never have been achieved otherwise.

The conversation was brilliant. We all discussed the various bodies in front of us. Madame thought Keith the most adorable and commented on his rounded ass and its blond coloring that would be made even more adorable if the crop were used on it. Phil was torn, unable to hide his attraction to Carl, unwilling to deny his excitement at Francois's personal proclivities.

Adrienne was more discreet, asking questions more than making comments. At one point Martin went around the men and removed the clamps and sucked on their tits. Each one of them reacted violently. "Why?"

"The clamps cut off circulation after a certain point," I explained. "To remove them forces a surge of blood into the flesh and a sharp pain. Then, after, they're much more sensitive. But, if he uses his tongue to massage them, they can take more of the agony, and he creates more pleasure for them."

Christopher, of course, was the one who reacted most strongly. That, I was sure, was because his audience was so close and so cold as much as anything else. We simply watched the actions that Martin made and the reactions in Christopher that he created.

"That young one," Madame said, referring to Keith, "is certainly darling. But this one has great potential." She took her long painted nails and used them to lightly scratch the underside of Christopher's testicles, lifting his sac up with the ends of her red claws.

"He is one who, shall we say, has many more realistic possibilities for you than any of the others."

"Oh." Her eyebrow arched, and her nails suddenly came together in a sharp scissor motion, and Christopher's midsection tried desperately to lift itself up off the table and away from her, something that couldn't be done because of Martin's handiwork.

Francois came around with more tea for Adrienne and Phil, more wine for Madame and me. The conversation continues, but moved on to the business of the convention. Phil and Adrienne were the two least acquainted of us and they found many people that they knew in common that they'd never had the chance to discuss before. Contracts were being negotiated on the floor of the association meeting. Editors were changing jobs. Each of us was a devoted fan of the others in the room and had to make appreciative comments on each other's work.

As though the commercial and literary discussions needed to be balanced, Martin went into his next stage. He brought out a handsome new leather strap I'd bought and vaguely wandered through the room. He delivered a substantial, but not violent, blow to the buttocks of each of the men. Keith and Sean followed him as best they could with their eyes, trying to prepare themselves. Francois sped up his service of food and drink, trying to avoid my overseer's lash. Glen and Phillip were wild in their total helplessness against the columns. Carl refused to display the least bit of concern.

This wasn't any kind of performance. Martin could have done that; I certainly knew he could. That was not the purpose here. This was simply part of the atmosphere. We four guests ignored it all, other than to make very occasional glances at his handiwork.

It went on for an hour and a half. Madame and I were — I knew — ecstatic. It was perfect. Adrienne was flushed with excitement, and, even if she would never be one of us, the sight of it and the invitation to be present was precisely the gift she'd wanted that I could produce. Phil was simply smiling. I thought he was probably remembering some party in Paris, or Berlin, perhaps London or Rome.

"I must go," he finally said. He stood.

Adrienne rose with him. "I must also. It's been astonishing."

"Would you like Francois's number?" I asked Phil.

"I'd like Francois," he joked back.

"Then, by all means. You shouldn't take public transportation across the Bay alone in any event." I gave Francois some orders, made some quick and simple arrangements for him to return to gather his things, then had him dress.

"You're giving him away?" Adrienne was standing there, her beautiful dress and her lighted cigarette couldn't keep her from giving the impression of being stunned.

"To Phil, for this one night…"

"Marvelous."

I realized then that the single act struck her more than any other.

They left. Madame and I went back to our couch, and I poured her more wine. The boys were utterly gorgeous now. The time in their bondage was beginning to tell on them. Their bodies were slick with sweat, their movements were more furious, and when Martin went through them this time to remove their clamps and suck their nipples, they were truly in agony.

The room was filed with a masculine odor from it all. Glen was crying now, so, too, was Keith.

"Marvelous." It was Madame who made the announcement this time. "I will go." It was over. This level of intensity couldn't be sustained and to move on to another one seemed to distress her, it would have made this one less perfect, I suspect.

Martin got her coat and saw her to the door. They kissed there, moving slowly back to the stuff of their long friendship.

"Shall I send this Christopher to you?" I called out.

She turned back. "Yes, and quickly." Then she left.

Martin and I went about the business of untying the men. I kept the discipline sharp. Glen and Phillip were ordered to kneel in their place by the pillars. Keith and Sean were unbound, but told not to move. Christopher was sent to the shower.

"You like very dominant women," I told him when he came out. "This is the chance for your ultimate." I held out a piece of paper with Madame's hotel name and address. "Do you want it?"

"I've done so much this weekend..." He said it in such a way I thought he was going to say no. But instead, "It wouldn't seem right to stop now." He rubbed his sore nipples and smiled at me. "What was it the old man said to you, 'You son of a bitch?' "

"Get out before you get the strap."

"Yes, sir." Then, in a move that surprised me, he kissed me.

I poured wine in to some glass bowls that Francois had brought with his things, and I put them on the floor in the center of the room. I took the strap that Martin had been using and stood there with it. "Come and join the party," I told my naked slaves.

They moved, with various degrees of tentativeness and eagerness, toward the bowls, anxious for the liquid, and suspicious of the strap. I stood there, letting the leather hang from my hand, and saw their buttocks, all of them striped to some extent or another, and simply enjoyed how beautiful men could be.

My party had begun...

The End

Two days later I was ready to leave. I called the front desk and had them send Joseph to my suite to carry down my bags.

I hadn't seen him since before the party. I hadn't really thought about him. But he was certainly enthusiastic enough when he arrived.

"You really leaving so soon?"

"Joseph, it's been a week."

"And we never did anything," he said with a petulant voice.

"That might be just as well."

"Yeah? I think that party of yours must've been pretty kinky, man. We were all talking about it."

"What did you know to talk about?"

"The studs you got coming up here all at once. And those two women. They were something, themselves. What were they doing there?"

"Enjoying themselves, that's all."

"The studs you got coming up here all at once. And those two women. They were something, themselves. What were they doing there?"

"Enjoying themselves, that's all."

"You shouldn't be so selfish. I could've enjoyed myself, too, you know."

"I doubt it, Joseph."

He carried my bags down the hallway to the elevator and through the lobby. He called a cab for me and opened the door. But he wouldn't let me simply enter the taxi.

"You worry about me enjoying your party, huh?" I wasn't at all sure what he meant.

He smiled and reached into his hip pocket. He brought out a

143

copy of one of Adrienne's most recent — and most intense — sexual fantasy books. Her picture was on the cover. He showed it to me. "You shouldn't underestimate people, man. I think I could have had a good time at your party."

With that, I laughed and got in the cab. It was a long journey home.

The Love of
a Master

To Anne,
and all the colors
of her many cloaks

A Reawakening

I had begun it all again. My party in San Francisco had been more of a reentry into the life of harsh and complete sexuality than I had ever expected. It was only supposed to have been a single affair, a gift I could give to my friends, an event to remember.

I had thought that my life in the county had been more than the most recent chapter in my life; I had thought it would be the last. But I was wrong, and now I knew it. A life is a series of cycles; there are no endings, only stages that have not yet been succeeded.

There was no reason to be upset by this. It was only a question of being surprised, of becoming aware that I was once more on the road to sexual adventure. How strange, I thought, that it would start all over again. Not, how unfortunate; not, how provident; simply, how strange.

The sight of the naked men and their beautiful bodies at my party, the enjoyment of my guests, the visceral pleasure I received from my role in making it all happen — these things combined, and there was no way that I could deny my desire to make them occur again. But even more dramatically, even more intensely, and much more for my own pleasure.

I spent the weeks after the party in San Francisco debating my options, looking around at the men who might be of interest to me, and making my renewed interest known to those people who might understand and who would share the passions I felt.

They were not all sympathetic. I received phone calls and letters that were nothing less than insulting with their implications that my "retirement" from the world of S/M had been a sham, or that my intentions weren't understandable. Those calls came from the people who thought that one had to make a pledge to the world of sexuality that was similar to the most draconian religious vows. I had broken mine by moving to the country, living a relatively quiet life, not maintaining the contacts, and not making the appearances that they felt were required.

Those were ridiculous rules and responses. There were other people who were much more understanding. They would call and talk about the pleasures and the learnings that were still to be had. These were people who understood that there are those of us who move in and out of the sexual world with some mobility, but never with a lessening of our dedication.

The people from The Network also contacted me. Of course they did. The conversations were pleasant, almost to the point of being mechanical. But while they were going on, small electric shots were being sent through my body. I wanted to be a part of it again. I was desperate for it. I wasn't about to have my reentry into the world of sex be something that happened just in chic leather bars or with uncommitted people who would only play occasional games. If I was going to do this all again, then let it be at that level: The Network's.

But perhaps not as a part of The Network. I'd have to think about that.

My passions aren't comfortably contained in other people's constructions. That doesn't mean I don't like them or that I can't appreciate the effort that other people put into their sexual work. Far from it. But there is a need to *create* that is best expressed by me when I am conceiving my own composition.

And so I began my reentry with travel. Madame, my friend and often companion, made contacts for me that I couldn't establish myself — at least not quickly enough. Certain other friends were more than willing to aid me. They made me welcome in their homes and made introductions to new people to whom I might be of use or who might be useful to me.

The experiences were exhilarating and terrifying. They were creating in me a compulsion that I hadn't expected. But they were undeniable in their attraction, and I would never be able to ignore the needs that were rising to the surface.

Telling Stories

"What was your trip like?"

Marc is one of the wonders of my hometown. A strikingly handsome young man of French-Canadian descent, he works in one of the many lumber mills. He has been able to create a sexual life for himself that would astonish most of those in New York or San Francisco who consider themselves to be sexual athletes. We had met nearly five years ago, when I had first moved to northern New England. There is a network of homosexually active men that is in its own way as rich a federation and as secret a fraternity as The Network. They had spotted me as soon as I'd arrived. Marc — then only nineteen — had been the only one in the group to interest me. He was too young and inexperienced for me to risk any sexual play — at least in the first years. But I'd been rewarded with the opportunity to watch him grow and mature. I could sense a verve in him that was at least as attractive as his tall, firm body and bright eyes. He would come to talk, to read my books, to ask his questions of someone who wasn't about to dismiss him. Young men really want only to be taken seriously.

I hadn't taken him seriously enough. I knew that now. He had actually been the one person up here who I most wanted. I had studied his body during the summer, played with seducing him at parties, sometimes even engaged in plain sex with him on winter nights when it seemed the need had been so strong in both of us that neither could deny it.

What would have attracted him to me if not my peculiar form of sexuality? But I had never explored that with him. True, when we had our vanilla sex, I was the one who would take the lead in all ways. But there had been no attempt to go further. Lately, he'd been seeing another young man. They'd recently moved in together, and I thought of them as lovers. But young men seldom know what it means to have a "lover." I had no reason to give their relationship so much respect — did I? There was a part of me that said it was the only ethical thing to do, to support young men when they attempt such things.

But Marc would always be here at the house. He'd take liberties with it, moving around the rooms whenever he wanted and coming by to swim whenever the whim struck. How much of that had been for my benefit and how many signals had I been missing, simply because I insisted on assuming that the men of the mountains weren't part of my sexual world?

Now he was sitting across the front porch of my house with me, a can of cold beer in his hand, his refreshment after a hard day's labor. I looked over at him and only shrugged. "It was fine." "*Fine!*" He shouted at me. "Come on, stop playing with me. What was it like? I can't believe it actually happened, that it exists, that you went, that—"

"It's all very, very true, Marc."

Like many other people who don't live in the major cities, Marc has no sense of their reality. On one hand, he thinks that he is somehow inadequate, lacking some training or experiences that he assumes everyone — or nearly everyone — in a place like New York does have. That's not true. I'd watched his development. He had already created more of a sexual circus here in New England than the vast majority of people I knew in Manhattan would ever believe. For one thing, he wasn't trapped into the belief that there were rules that had to be followed or that there was only one way that things could be done.

But, then, there was another side to Marc's perceptions. When he came up against something like The Network and could know someone involved in it like myself, the reality there was too surreal, much too extreme for him to ever believe it actually existed.

Not that he wanted to disbelieve. Hardly. The desire was obvious. His deeply tanned face showed all the excitement of a child hearing that his fairy tales might really be true. He was leaning forward on his chair with his elbows on his knees. I could see the firm muscles of his arms. His T-shirt — with its dark sweat stains under his arms and around his belly — couldn't hide the very obvious and tremendously appealing evidence of the rest of his muscles as they pressed against the fabric. I admired his body; my enjoyment of it was greatly enhanced because it was naturally his, earned at hard work and not in an artificial and ridiculously expensive gymnasium.

"Tell me about it. Please."

I sat back and took a sip of my own drink. I put my head back against my chair and looked out at the grand vista I have from my porch. In front of me I could see the tallest of the White Mountains. My house sits high on a hill of its own, separated from the peaks by a broad valley. I have almost complete privacy here. You would have to come two miles up a poorly marked drive to get to my home. That had been one of the attractions of the place when I had bought it.

But my mind wasn't here on the natural wonders and beauties of New England. My mind was exactly where Marc wanted it to be, back in New York and on the weekend I'd just spent there. It had been my first invitation to attend a function of The Network in years. I had accepted. It had been…awesome.

"You remember Madame, don't you?" I asked.

"The redhead? The one who's so beautiful? The one who wanted me to let her cane me?"

"Her." I laughed a little bit, remembering when my omnisexual Marc had met the omnisexual Madame — what a limiting word "bisexual" is when dealing with two people like them! She had been charming, as she always is with strangers. (Her dealings with those of us who know her well are often less than that.) He had thought that he was going to be able to have an encounter with a highly sophisticated New York editor/lady. She had in mind a most definite type of tryst and, once he understood her intentions, there had been some misunderstandings and some quick reevaluations between the two of them. It had all been very amusing.

Marc glowered a bit and took a violent swig of his beer, as though that little action could regain the masculinity he thought he had lost during that one interaction. "So?"

"She went to the party with me."

"Party? You call a slave auction a party?"

"Yes. It was that, at one level. You have to understand, Marc, these functions aren't some kind of coercive things that happen in your pornographic fantasies. This is a highly ritualized and actually ethical undertaking."

"It's a slave auction."

"It was, in fact, a slave auction. It took place in an exquisite penthouse on the Upper East Side. It is that kind of apartment that you read about and see photographs of and, somehow, can't really believe that it exists. But it does. "Madame and I arrived. The dress for us was formal. She had on one of her most stunning gowns. It's a floor length skirt of black velvet with a top that's made of a metallic fabric. It's a gold or brass colored, incredibly, almost indecently, suggestive. It drapes over her breasts, clinging to each of them. It comes as close to being shocking as anything else she ever wears.

"We were quite the hit when we arrived. There were a number of people I knew but hadn't seen in many years. The party of people — the customers, if you insist — gathered in the foyer of the penthouse. That was a room actually much larger than any room you ever expect to see in New York apartments. It was incredibly lavish.

"We were served cocktails and there were appetizers that were as delicious as any I'd ever seen. The food and drink were served by four slaves, two men and two women. The host is one of the most wealthy men in the world. You'd know his name if I told you. Everyone in America would. He can afford the luxury.

"The two men were naked except for a piece of white silk that was wrapped around their cock and balls and held in place by a strap. The effect was to make them seem more naked than they would have appeared if they had no clothing at all.

"Around each of their necks was a collar. Not made of the black leather that one expects with male slaves, but of another piece of white silk. It was tied in a knot which left a long length of fabric flowing down their backs. Still another piece of white silk was tied around their hair. They were gorgeous in those brief and probably humiliating uniforms. I expect that one of the better and more well-known designers had been commissioned to produce them.

"They were extremely well-trained. Their bodies were in marvelous shape, and you could see that every guest was staring at the bare and inviting nipples.

"The two female slaves were dressed in the same way, essentially. Their breasts were naked and remarkably firm.

"The four of them carried the trays and delivered drinks to the well-dressed crowd."

"You say that as though they were just any waiters…"

"Oh, no, Marc. These were far from that."

"Did you do anything with them?"

"Them? No. Nor did anyone else. They were there, and I'm sure their owner would have granted a guest's request for their use, but they had duties to attend to. It would have been very unthoughtful to keep them from their work."

"Didn't they want to run away? Weren't there guards or else chains to keep them there?"

"Of course not. I've told you before, your fantasies of these people who own and are owned have nothing to do with their reality. These are people who've chosen to take their places. Just as those on sale had."

"I don't believe you. I can't believe you."

"That's because you insist on looking at sex and slavery — separately and together — as though they had to involve a contest. Conquest is the only dynamic you accept as possible. These people wouldn't have understood that."

"Go on, tell me then, about the sale."

I could see that Marc was getting excited. He'd finished his beer and was moving the empty can around in his hands, denting it as he released the pressure that was building inside himself.

"At a certain point — actually, at exactly the announced hour — the male slaves went and opened the two large doors that provided an entrance into the living room.

"Madame and I followed the crowd into it. The room was spectacular. Its view of the city…"

"I don't care about the view of the city!" Marc smashed the can. "Tell me about the sale."

"The entire process is very formal, of course. We went in and those who were to be sold were on display. The servants brought the trays of food and drink into the room, and the party proceeded as it had in the foyer.

"Though, of course, now we could do our investigation of the slaves as well. There were four of them. The first two were each kneeling on top of separate mirrored tables. Their legs were spread far apart and were chained at the ankles to keep them that way. So, when you walked up to where they were, not only were their genitals forced forward by their posture, you could also see the reflections of their undersides on the glass.

"Each one had his wrists shackled to the back of his neck by an intricate gold chain that also produced a collar. They were totally naked. They'd have to be since the customers would all insist on seeing everything of any importance.

"The first male was dark in a Latin way. Italian, I suppose, or perhaps French like yourself." The allusion made Marc squirm. "He had a fine coat of hair on his chest, prominent and well-built pectorals. But the most amazing thing about him seemed to be his testicles. While they weren't in any way outsized, they were hanging loosely and not touching any other part of his body.

"Whenever a slave has the kind of noticeable attribute, it becomes the focus of much of the attention he's paid. It seemed that nearly every potential buyer who walked up to him felt a need to test them. They were slapped, tugged, pinched, pulled. He was in tears within minutes. I'm sure he must have been used to it, but, of course, testicles are simply too delicate to ever be built up in a way that would sustain someone when they're being tortured."

"So there was torture going on."

"Marc, listen to me, certainly they were playing with his testicles. But this was an elegant affair, a quiet one. The guests were all in black tie or formal gowns. They were simply testing his reactions. They would, after all, be spending a great deal of money to buy him and they had a right to investigate how he would respond.

"In any event, he seemed not too upset, actually. Yes, there were tears, but he was still able to look directly at the customers and even to smile once when one woman put a delicate and loving hand on his cheek. He was very handsome in the classic way of today's magazine models, I must admit that. A little older than most who are sold, I'd say at least thirty, but the fashion for youth is passing."

"Did you do it? I mean, were you one of the ones who tortured him?"

"I didn't *torture* him, Marc. But, yes, I couldn't help but feel him and test his body. That was one of the reasons I was there, after all. He was very smart, or his trainer was. Someone certainly knew what the attractions to his body were going to be and his sac had been carefully shaven, making the skin seem even smoother and more delicate. The balls themselves actually felt more vulnerable than they would have if his hair had been kept there.

"The next young man had a different attraction. He was blond, smooth skinned with hardly any body hair at all. He was wonderfully tanned. That was highly emphasized where his blond complexion had been covered by a small bathing suit. It left his very nice ass alabaster in contrast to the brown of his legs, stomach, and back.

"Just as our attention had been drawn to the other's testicles, this younger and blond man's buttocks drew everyone's attention. There was a strap on each table. Often the buyers want to see how a potential slave will react to a beating. It can be very upsetting to spend a great deal of money for a slave and then discover that he falls apart at the very appearance of a crop or a belt. It's important, some feel, to test out at least some of the reactions.

"The blond was in tears soon enough after a line of the customers had come up and commanded him to lean forward and put his head on the mirrored table so they could each deliver a series of hard blows to the white bottom that was quickly striped with angry red lines."

"So? Who were the other two?"

"They shared the same mirrored table together since they were to be sold as a couple. There was a man and a woman. I wondered about it, very much, but couldn't discover if they were lovers, friends, married, or what. They did almost look alike, and I had the fantasy that they were a brother and sister. That would have been so perfect that I refused to investigate to see if it was right or wrong. I wanted to make believe that they were, in fact, incestuous and both of them available.

"They received the most attention. That's almost surprising since usually those customers who are homosexually or heterosexually attracted wouldn't have been interested in a mixed couple like that. Or so you would have thought."

"What about you?"

"Me? I've never really limited myself only to men, though you know perfectly well that's my overwhelming desire. But these two, together, were astonishing. They were gorgeous. They both had dark hair, auburn, I think you'd call it. It was cut in nearly identical fashion. It left the man looking vaguely English, the woman slightly masculine. They had very white, pale skin. His body hair wasn't very thick, only a sprinkling on his chest and legs and a thick bunch of it over his cock.

"Their resemblance was accentuated by their kneeling posture. He was larger, but not much. They were perfect on the mirrored table. The contrast and the comparison of the reflections underneath them was amazing.

"They made themselves even more beautiful because they seemed to be in awe of the situation. It was almost as though they hadn't really been able to believe it was going to happen until they discovered themselves naked and on view in front of the guests.

"Their eyes were wide open. They were looking around, almost a little desperately, I thought. While the other two men were resigned to what was going on, these two didn't seem to be. They actually tugged at their chains on a couple occasions, but it was too late to do them any good. There was no escape. They had been given those opportunities before.

"As I said, there was something about the pair that made the two of them the most magnificent of the offerings. They inspired all the guests' imaginations."

"You?"

"Yes, me. It happened this way:

"Madame was entranced by them. She, of course, is much more honestly and equally attracted to both sexes. She had walked — almost glided — up and stood in front of them. They were studying her, looking at her arched eyebrows, that frightening red hair, her proud body. Then, to everyone's astonishment, she simply pulled at the top she was wearing.

"It fell open. She leaned, ever so slightly, toward the two slaves. She didn't have to say a word. Each one of them bent forward and took one of her nipples. They sucked beautifully. At first their eyes were closed, as though they were transported by the joint experience of serving this beautiful dominatrix.

"I moved behind them. His ass was gorgeous. It was very hard and firm. There were sharp lines in his buttocks and the muscles along his hips. The two halves were separated by the spread of his legs. I looked down on the mirror and could see the hairy growth that protected his anus. Her openings were almost as appealing.

"While they continued their labors with Madame, I reached down and inserted a finger in each of them. One of my hands rested on his ass and probed into the hot, tight hole of his. The other slipped into her vagina. While his had been liberally greased by someone, her lubrication was natural evidence of her own excitement.

"I was amazed by her wetness and the slippery warmth that I could feel. While they gnawed away at Madame, my ringers thrust into them, drawing out these wonderful moans and sighs and groans from the two of them.

"I had to stop finally, only because I was sure that the combination of my and Madame's attention was going to drive the both of them to orgasm. As soon as I did, one of the male slaves of the household was beside me carrying a gold bowl full of soapy warm water with a towel over his arm. The health concerns even move into the slave market, one sees.

"I washed carefully. I was hot, my cock was hard and I was staring at this beautifully near-naked house slave in front of me. While I was standing there, going about the mechanics of washing, he must have felt the intensity of my reactions. Inside his small pouch, he was getting stiff.

" 'Only a master can remove it,' he finally said. The tip of his cock was wet from his turn on and had soaked through the fabric, which was in danger of ripping. I thought that was too fine a possibility and chose not to respond to his ill-defined request."

"You just left him there with his hard-on in that silk thing?"

"Yes, I just thought it would be more amusing that way."

"You bastard. What happened then?"

"By then, Madame was finished. She had pulled away from the pair of them and was adjusting her top. They were studying her with a real sense of loss on their faces. When they saw me beside her, they had a surge of hope. I think that would be the best word to describe what they were going through.

"I think the two of them suddenly imagined themselves in the hands of a strong woman and a strong man. That would evidently have been the most desirable outcome for them. If they could have, I'm sure they would have begged to be bought by us. But that kind of behavior is strictly forbidden, and I know they would have been told so.

"We simply studied them. We hadn't discussed it, but I know that she and I were pulling off a remarkable event in the eyes of the two slaves. Our severity was certainly having an impact.

"Most often, the male slaves are always erect during one of the sales. If their cocks happen to go down, there's always a way to get them hard again. It wasn't surprising, then, that the male had a hard-on. His cock was very attractive. Not that it was particularly big in a pornographic sense, but it was especially thick, if not noticeably long. It was the kind that made a substantial handle and whose circumference was so great that one had the impression that it was even larger than it was.

"But the male had been more excited than simply that. His cock had begun to leak copiously. There was a long, translucent strand of precome that was seeping from the head in an unbroken line down to the mirrored tabletop, where a good deal of it had gathered in a puddle.

"I reached down and gathered some of it on the tip of each of my forefingers. Then I smeared it on his tits. He closed his eyes — I'll never, ever know if it was shame and distress or ecstacy and delight — the expressions so often appear to be the same in slaves. But I felt as though I had reached in and touched him at some extraordinary level."

"Did you try to buy him?"

"The sale started shortly after that. The four who were being auctioned off had all been examined and so had their papers."

"Papers?"

"Their contracts. I've explained this all to you before. Is it just that you don't believe that people can make these conscious choices? They do. These four people weren't dragged in off some street, they weren't kidnapped.

"They made contracts. Each one had to file a contract with the sponsors. The results were in folders that were attached to the table they were kneeling on. The couple, for instance, agreed to be sold only if they would not be separated. That is an acceptable limitation on them. Each one of them also defines a length of time for his or her slavery. It can be as little as one year. Some I've seen have been as long as ten. But that's allowed only for the experienced and most stable slaves.

"Too often people envision an exciting lifetime of slavery and they forget that there is a whip on the other hand of the master or mistress and that the whip stings. Only contracts that seem to be within the abilities of the slaves are accepted.

"There can be other limitations, but the slaves are clearly told that they risk reducing their value if they demand too many. Still it can be allowed."

"What? What kinds of agreements can a slave demand?"

"Well, for instance, a slave can announce his profession and have an agreement that he wouldn't be used or displayed to anyone who is a part of it, making sure that he could reenter his occupation after his contracted period. That can be very important. Or else, some smart and experienced slaves can object beforehand to certain things they feel will make them less valuable in the future: Piercing, for example, isn't considered a permanent mark. Those — permanent marks — aren't allowed under any contract that The Network assigns. But if the slave doesn't specify that piercings are a part of that, they can be performed as a transitory adornment of a slave's body for the duration of the contract."

"You really think that people who buy other people are going to honor these contracts?"

"Of course they are. There is an element of self-monitoring that's very important, for one thing. There's a tremendous screening process as well. Think, Marc, think of the potential scandal and think who some of the people involved are and realize that this must be taken care of internally very carefully and very well.

"I'm not saying that the people who are bought are going to have an easy time of it. They've said that there is a set amount of money that's involved. In exchange for this sum, each one will serve out his or her contract as a total slave to the buyer. They have given up all recourse to any sense of justice other than the master or mistress's pleasure. They certainly are not in control of the situation once they've signed their contracts. I wouldn't deny that at all."

"If these people have a contract that says that they're going to get a set amount of money, then why is there an auction?"

"Whoever brings them in — the trainer or the recruiter — receives all the money the auction brings above the contract sum."

"Other people are making money on these sales then? If slaves are trained by you, you get the profit, not them?"

"There's a great deal of expense involved in training someone. Look at someone like you and think about the time and energy I'd have to put into you to get you ready for the mirrored tables of the auction room."

"Fuck you!" he answered. I'd hit a sore point. He stood up and went into the house. He came back with a fresh beer, but I could see that the short break hadn't gotten rid of the erection that was fighting against the denim of his jeans.

"So these people — the slaves — they're on the block. What happens now?"

"Now the host comes forward and offers each one for sale. The contract's read out loud. The sums are quite substantial. The money to be made doing this — being a slave — is a great deal more than you make at your mill."

"Don't start," he said. I hadn't really wanted to do any more than prod him a bit and didn't pursue the subject.

"Then, the bids are made. They're done by a code, a simple wave of the hand. The slaves are never allowed to know the monetary sum that's finally agreed upon. It was discovered that they became too arrogant about those things. Better for them to concentrate on their contracted amount. The silent bidding leaves them in a great deal of confusion — it's never explained to them — and we all get to watch the delicious fear on their faces that comes from the terror or the humiliation that their asked-for sum won't be met. That's never happened. There *are* some other fools who say they will go in and be slaves for a year only if they're paid a ridiculously exorbitant amount of money, but they're screened out. It's all done very efficiently and quite fairly. The Network also won't let a slave undervalue himself or herself."

"So, what happened to these four?"

"The first man, the dark one, was sold to a very intriguing Chinese man. I've met him before. He lives in Hong Kong. He's fabulously wealthy from one of those mysterious Chinese banking fortunes. He maintains an incredible harem.

"The male slave actually will have one of the most interesting careers possible. His contract was only for two years. I'm sure he'll beg to be retained for much longer."

"Why? What goes on there? In Hong Kong?"

"The banker lives in a grand mansion. If you or I were to visit, we would see only the luxurious residence of a substantial businessman. But the house is huge. There is a half of it that only the most special guests are ever allowed to see.

"He maintains a household of at least twelve slaves at all times. He prides himself on the make-up; his slaves represent every race possible. There must have been an opening for a Caucasian; that would have been the reason for his visit. He must already have a blond; that would be why he chose his darker-haired man.

"The slaves are kept in utter luxury. They eat the finest food and have incredible facilities. In order to keep in shape, there's a large swimming pool and weight-lifting equipment. There are movies on recorders. There is fine music provided in very formal programs in the evening. If some slaves aren't educated, the others are encouraged to teach them.

"Their only purpose is to be beautiful — and sexual. They are dressed in sheer loose-fitting pants that are gathered beneath the navel and again at the ankles. You can clearly see every part of their bodies.

"They learn the arts of beauty, giving each other pedicures, manicures, and so forth, caring for each other's hair. They learn massage and have the most exquisite oils to enhance their odor and to highlight the appearance of their skin.

"They're all encouraged — actually, it's demanded — to have sex with one another as often as possible. The master enjoys watching them at their erotic play. He, of course, also expects that they'll perform any act on him that he ever desires.

"But the man has dedicated his life to beauty. What is most often demanded of his slaves is their exhibition for him. They're tied with silken ropes to the columns of his harem rooms. They wait on him, their nakedness obvious through those sheer clothes. They lay naked across his table while he eats. They are forced into remarkably obscene postures for his visual pleasure."

"No whips, no chains?"

"Whips and chains, of course. That's because there's nothing that makes a man look more beautiful than the struggle against real pain and real bondage. Theirs isn't a life without pain. But it's not the harsh life that others live and it's one that's full of pleasure as well. The few times that I've met one of his former slaves, they've always looked back on their years in that Hong Kong mansion as a pleasant dream.

"Any who've left have done so of their own accord. If one outlives his beauty, the master doesn't throw the slave out onto the street. He receives his contract money and then is given a good job in any one of a number of businesses. He inevitably becomes a dramatically loyal and willing employee.

"One of the leading bankers of San Francisco is a man who once spent ten years in Hong Kong. The first five were as a pleasure slave to this millionaire. But, then, the man was allowed to become a business apprentice as well and made the transition that allowed him to head his own company.

"I'm told, though, that he is prone to moods. I'm sure they occur whenever the master from Hong Kong is in the country and the San Franciscan has to remember what he gave up — all that pleasure, the sensuality, the luxury — for the sake of a transitory and not very attractive success in the world of commerce."

"The others? The blond guy?"

"He will have a much more difficult life. Very. He was purchased for a large sum — much larger than I expected — by someone whose true identity is very much hidden. I can only tell you this: He's one of the leading clerics of the country. He demands utter obedience, as the religious usually do. The boy will spend his years under the guise of being a chauffeur or some such thing. That's very common: many of these slaves masquerade in public as paid servants — pilots, nurses, drivers, butlers.

"But the cleric will, I'm sure, keep a devastatingly accurate list of all the slightest mistakes the young man makes every day. Each night he'll find himself under the lash for each one of them. His will be a term of agony. I only hope that that, perhaps, is what he was looking for and, remember, he had to know that this was a possibility."

"Your couple? Did you bid?"

"No. Only because I knew that the money would be much too rich for me. The sum was, in fact, astronomical. A Canadian oil man, a Texas land baron, and a woman who's made a fortune selling her own brand of cosmetics got into a bidding war that had heads spinning.

"When it was over, the Canadian had won. Then he put on a spectacle."

"A spectacle? After everything else you've described, what could possibly have gone on that you'd call it that?"

"As each slave is sold, he or she's delivered to the buyer. Most often, it's a very delicate and ritualistic event. The slave is brought down off the mirrored table. The hands are released from the neck chain, which is now attached to a leash, and he or she is led, on hands and knees, over to the master.

"The first slave, the dark-haired one, had done it brilliantly. He'd been taken over by the same household slave whose minor agony I'd provided. The Hong Kong banker simply took the leash, bowing gracefully to thank the auctioneer and even the household slave. He'd very delicately pulled on the leash to bring his new purchase in close between his legs. The man had done it very gracefully and was rewarded with a pat on the head. He'd responded by licking the hand of his new master.

"It was quite beautiful.

"The blond went through something similar, but without the affection. That — affection — was something the bishop was never going to give him in any event, and he might as well understand that from the beginning.

"But each buyer has the right to establish his or her self to the slave from the very beginning in any fashion. The Canadian evidently wanted the couple to understand their contracted lives well.

"He had two henchmen with him. When the couple were brought over to the Canadian, he didn't move. But each henchman took one of the leashes. The apartment, which appears to be so stylishly decorated, obviously has its secrets, and many of us know them.

"There is a chandelier very close to where the auction had taken place. From it dangle what appear to be ornamental metal ropes. They are, in fact, terrifically strong chains.

"The man and woman were dragged over to them. The men brought out wrist restraints and applied them to the two. In seconds, the male was on his toes, barely able to support his weight, and the woman was hanging from her wrists.

"They brought over a footstool for her. She foolishly thought it was for her relief. But quickly realized that it was just the right height to bring her vagina up to the level of the male's cock. The mystery and the tension had excited him. He was stiffly erect. The henchman slipped a condom over it and roughly shoved the hard cock up the woman's sex.

Then the two men took off their belts. While the two slaves were fucking, the belts began to fly. The henchmen walked around them in a circle, delivering constant blows to all parts of their midsections — their buttocks, their hips, their thighs.

"They were screaming in shock and agony, but they continued their sexual acts. They must have been true masochists. They kept thrusting at one another while the beating went on and on, bringing out bright red welts quickly and sharply.

"Suddenly, the beating stopped. The slaves were released and put back down on the floor. Their tears were ignored while their collars and leashes were reapplied. They weren't even allowed to move on their hands and knees. They had to crawl with their naked bellies on the floor back over to the Canadian who'd bought them.

"When they got there, they were forced to remove his shoes and socks and then to lick, kiss, and fondle his feet. Then the two hired men pulled out their cocks, slipped on condoms, and began fucking the slaves.

"One took the male's ass; the other the woman's vagina from the back. This was no easy fucking, let me assure you. This wasn't the sensual delight that the Hong Kong banker was going to be giving the new member of his harem. This was violent, unforgiving, and memorable.

"The Canadian was establishing the ground rules for the next five years."

"Five years," Marc whispered.

"That had been their contract. Five years of service.

"When the two had finished the fucking they yanked the long hair on the two slaves and brought them up to the owner's crotch. His cock was out. It was, quite frankly, enormous. It was one of those uncut *things* that some men have, with long, loose foreskin and very heavy balls underneath it. The two of them, still crying loudly and with tears falling down their faces, were put to work licking and stroking his balls with their mouths and masturbating him with their hands.

"The man came, not caring that his come spilt over his clothing. One of the household slaves was there immediately — his cock hard itself after what he'd witnessed — and went about washing up the Canadian's mess.

"The auctions usually revert to being social events after the actual sales are done. The new slaves are usually left kneeling with their masters and mistresses and are shown off while the food and drink continues, but the Canadian wanted none of that.

"His crying, bruised slaves were exhausted. They could barely move. The henchmen dressed them in nondescript loose clothing and literally carried the two of them out the door and down the elevator — evidently to a waiting car. The Canadian went about only the most essential social niceties, then he too left.

"As you can imagine, Madame and I were beside ourselves after that display. We left shortly. We decided to go to a small party we knew was happening. It had none of the elegance of The Network's affairs, but it provided us with what was — I promise you — *necessary* relief."

Marc was staring at me by the time I'd finished. My term — "necessary relief" — certainly appeared to fit him and his condition. He was so handsome, so wonderfully built, and so obviously receptive to my stories. He could be the answer to my question. I wondered if I needed The Network and its slick operatives and its perfectly trained slaves, or if I only had to think in terms of the raw material with which New England was presenting me.

Eating Conversation

I was only home for a few days. I had explained to Marc that I was going to the Maine coast for a visit. He wanted to get together again soon, and I agreed that we'd have a dinner when I returned. I wasn't terribly surprised when he asked if his roommate Tim could come along. We set a time and place to meet.

When I walked into the inn, I found the two young men already sitting at the table waiting for me. I greeted them and took my own chair. We made small talk while the waitress was filling our drink orders. I knew that they were wondering where I had been, but I played with them, deciding not to offer the information.

Instead, I asked after their own activities. I learned that both of them had decided to go back to college the coming fall term. They could only afford to attend the local state institution, but they'd correctly determined that any degree would be better than their continued existence as occasional workers. They would have to go to school part-time but were prepared to make the sacrifice.

"That's wonderful news!" I said. My pleasure was incredible. I couldn't believe what good luck this might be for me. It fit right into my plan. "I'm very proud of you." My congratulations were honestly heartfelt. No matter what happened to my own scheme, this was going to be an excellent move for the young men. They had been having a good life here in the mountains and had been willing to make do with the small earnings they received — Marc in the lumber mill and Tim at seasonal jobs that allowed him to indulge himself with skiing in winter and swimming in the summer. Being gay, they had no pressure to take care of or prepare for the family. They were genial roustabouts, but the flush of their youth would pass, and I had often mentioned to them my desire that they have some kind of credential that would allow them some mobility in their future.

Tim seemed to be happy to have my approval. He flushed slightly, looking down into his glass. His full head of hair and his thick mustache were a lighter brown than Marc's. His skin was also ruddier, it was already showing the wear of constant outdoor sports. I knew that the body under his clothes also displayed that conditioning. The times when the two younger men would come to my house and swim in my pond were fond, fond memories.

Marc, though, wasn't able to take praise so easily. "It's not anything big. We'll only go part-time. If it weren't for sharing rent, neither one of us would be able to afford it. We haven't saved anything at all. Big deal, so I'll get a few extra cents on my paycheck out of sitting in a school no one from out-of-state ever heard of."

He finished his drink and waved to the waitress to order another. I nodded when she arrived to indicate that she could bring us a whole round.

"Where have you been?" Marc asked. "To another of your slave auctions?"

Tim flushed again, as though the simple fact of verbalizing those parts of my activities embarrassed him. I stared at Marc for a moment, holding a slight smirk on my face until I was sure he understood that his adolescent behavior hadn't really gotten to me. I had no secrets about my life that these two couldn't know about. In fact, I was pleased that the subject had been brought up so explicitly. I had had every intention of talking to the two of them about it.

"It wasn't a sale at all," I said. I picked up the newly delivered drink. "I had met an old friend when I was at the auction in New York. He invited me to visit his summer home. We had decided it would be best for both of us if I could go this past week."

I studied the two young men. Tim was leaning toward me, his elbows on the table. Marc was sitting back in his chair, one of his arms arrogantly thrown over the back, as though he thought he could signal me that this was not going to be anything so exciting that he had to pay particular attention to it. I was amused by their postures; both of them were obviously more intensely interested than they were ready to admit.

I sipped my drink, savoring the story I was going to be telling them, not only for the reactions that I was sure they'd have, but also because the memory was so perfect.

"The visit was really very wonderful. My host was able to provide an extraordinary hospitality.

"His summer estate is on an island. I drove to the isolated area where he had told me I would be met. It was a deserted pier well off the main roads. I soon learned the reason for the privacy.

"At the appointed time, a long boat appeared. I had expected a powerlaunch, perhaps even a sailboat. But, instead, a rowboat came to the pier. It was a large one, the size of a lifeboat on a seagoing vessel, I would expect. It was powered by four men — obviously slaves he'd bought at auction, or so I had assumed.

"All four were handsome. They were wearing only the type of slim racing brief that I see the two of you wearing on the beach in summer."

Marc shifted on his seat in reaction to the idea that anything he did habitually could be similar to the behavior of a slave. Tim, I noticed, didn't appear to be bothered at all, simply intrigued.

"There was a pair on each of two wooden seats, each with one large oar in his hands. They used the implements very professionally. In the prow of the boat was a man much larger than the rest of them. He had the bulk of a professional weightlifter. The rest were obviously following his commands. But his size and the reactions of the four rowers weren't the only proof of his having a different status than they.

"His appearance and clothes were different. His hair was longer, much longer; theirs was very close-cropped. There was a wide leather sweatband around his head to hold back the thick locks. He was the only one who had a very full beard. Rather than a bathing suit, he had on a pair of white cotton slacks and a pullover shirt.

"The boat was expertly brought up to the dock. The largest one greeted me very formally, and I could hear that his voice was deep and masculine. He bowed slightly when he greeted me. This was also a slave, I realized, but one with a different purpose in the household than the four scantily clad males who ran on his orders to collect my luggage from my car.

"I was seated at the prow of the boat for the return trip. I was amused by the idea of what the vacationers who lived closely would think if they understood what went on in this private enclave.

"My comfortable seat allowed me to study the hard muscles in the slaves' backs as they struggled to follow the orders to 'Stroke!' the larger one yelled out to them. Their purpose was only to provide the propulsion for the craft; he controlled its direction with a rudder that he held firmly in his hands.

"The four men worked hard to fight against the sea. It took quite a while to get to the private island — I would say at least an hour. During that time they labored constantly. I felt Olympian sitting there and watching their tight, hard bodies struggling so hard to carry me to my destination."

The waitress returned to get our dinner orders. I broke off my story and read my choices from the menu, being careful not to allow a hint of discomfort with the interruption. I wanted the two young men who were with me to realize just how matter-of-factly I could relate this tale to them.

Marc had no such ease about them. He was overtly nervous. He seemed to have forgotten the menu was already in front of him and then answered the woman's questions about dressings and choice of potato with quick, almost sharp responses. Tim actually seemed to be calm. He was staring at me while Marc dealt with the waitress and then simply stated that he'd have the same dishes as I.

When she left, I continued:

"We got to the island and the five men and I walked onto the pier there. The muscled man came up to me and said that he would have to wash the others and change himself. I, of course, didn't really understand what he meant, but nodded my agreement to his real point: That I would have to wait just a moment before we went to the house.

"While I stood there, the four other men quickly got underneath a shower that was hooked up to the outside of the very small building that stood at the foot of the wharf. There was a shower outside it, in the open. The pipes must have been hooked up to a fresh water well. The water was certainly not heated. I could tell that by the way the four of them shivered under the spray. But they did wash thoroughly. It was almost a shame. I had been luxuriating in the odors of the sweat that I could smell coming from their labor even over the sea spray.

"I was also able to watch the transformation of the overseer. He had quickly taken off his full set of clothing and stood naked while he carefully put it away in a cabinet just inside the door of the closet-sized building.

"When he was nude, I could see why he wore clothing when he was off the island, even when he just went to the private pier to pick up guests. Both his nipples were pierced. There were also thick gold rings running through the head of his cock, at its base where it met his testicles, and then, again, in his perineum — that area between his scrotal sac and his anus."

The idea of the piercings broke through Marc's facade of nonchalance. He squirmed in his seat. "Why? Why would he have done that?"

"I didn't know that he had been the one to decide it. But, in any event, there are many reasons for the piercings. Many people find them highly erotic — on themselves or on others. They can be convenient on a slave, as you'll soon see."

"Convenient?" Tim spoke now. He was wide-eyed with fascination.

At that moment, our food arrived. When the waitress had left, I finally answered the question. "Let me go on with my story, and you'll understand their potential utility.

"What's even more interesting about him was the outfit he proceeded to put on. First, there were wide leather strips similar to his headband that went around his biceps, obviously they were used to emphasize his build. Then he put on a loin cloth. It was a band of the same leather, no more than four inches wide, gathered at his waist by a piece of rawhide. The flaps hung down at least a foot and a half in the front and in the back. Finally, he put on sandals with straps that wound up his calves.

"The whole impression was something close to barbaric, certainly primeval. The other four males were drying off by now, their shower had finished. I could see the way they studied the brute that the costume had the additional effect of making him seem quite frightening to them.

"He snapped his fingers, and they instantly responded by picking up my bags and starting up the hill. Many owners like to have pampered slaves. These men were not. I could tell by the quick and effortless way they walked up the hill over the rocky path in their bare feet. They were used to hard labor. I had also seen that in the way they had handled the oars in the boat.

"I followed them. In a short while we came to the house. It was large, and, if unexceptional, it had been meticulously maintained. It was a white clapboard affair. Around it, on the small plateau where the house sat, were handsome gardens. The lawn was a beautiful and even green. It had to be very difficult to keep it up on the island with the constant salt air."

"Amazing what you can do with slave labor," Marc said snidely.

"Isn't it?" I answered, smiling while I chewed on a morsel of veal.

I went on. "My host was waiting on his porch to greet me. I, of course, know who he is in the world. He holds one of the world's most prestigious chairs in philosophy at a major university. But his real fame, for me, comes from the solid and manly way he has maintained a household of males through the years.

"The academic calendar helps, obviously. He has the summer months for intense dedication to his slaves as well as a full month around the holidays when he transports them all to another island retreat, in the West Indies. The rest of the year he keeps them in various capacities in his home. He uses a vast array of false premises to cover their actual purposes.

"I mentioned that to the professor when we were sitting on the porch enjoying a cup of tea. Why, I wondered, hadn't he ever had any of them pass as his students?"

Again, the parallel to their own lives made both Marc and Tim move in their seats. They shot each other glances that almost seemed to carry abject fear in them. But, I thought, that was probably wishful thinking on my part.

"My question amused the professor and deeply upset the man who was waiting on us. I could see that in the way he became suddenly flustered and his body stiffened. I had watched this young man at the oars earlier. He was a fine specimen, tall with broad shoulders and noticeably firm thighs. His reddish hair had obviously been bleached nearly blond in the summer sun on his chest and legs as well as his head.

"The professor quickly explained that this young man was in fact one of his students. 'Not one, by the way, that was purchased at auction, rather one who understood the finest points of peda-gogy rather independently.' "

"Not purchased?" Marc said. "You mean, he was volunteering to do all this?"

"Yes, so the professor explained. They had been introduced when the young man had been an undergraduate. He had been a remarkable student and had risen to the top of his class with hard work and careful listening to his teachers. Still he had, so he told the professor, a hard time dealing with the structure of the university. That had surprised the educator. Students who do well sel-dom understand the flaws of institutions that seem to reward them with good grades.

"But the school was too liberal, too lacking in structure and limits. The student could discipline himself to study, and he had learned how to study — something you'll find important your-selves when you go back to school. But the whole of it wasn't sat-isfying to him.

"There were then a number of other meetings. In some of them, it became obvious that the student was gay. Then, through a mutual friend, the professor and his soon-to-be charge realized that they had a common interest in the more advanced areas of sexuality.

"Over a period of time, they came to an understanding. What the student wanted, really, was an opportunity to serve and to learn that part of himself as well. During the academic year he lived alone. Neither was willing to take the chance of merging their personal and professional lives, and since the young man went on to become a graduate student in the professor's department, they agreed that he would have to keep to that role during those months.

"But, when the professor transported his household to one of his island retreats, the student came along and transported himself into the new world of sexual service."

"Slavery," Marc said in a tone that conveyed his insistence on using the harsher word.

"Slavery," I agreed, finishing off my meal and refusing to be caught in his word games.

"A graduate student?" Tim seemed intrigued with that part of the story more than any other. "I thought they'd all just be...bums, people who couldn't make it any other way."

"Oh, no, don't think that. In fact, most masters would insist on an exceptionally intelligent slave. Only one who can understand the extreme complexities of that life can provide the master with the subtleties and the levels of understanding and experience that are needed.

"Another time — perhaps — I'll tell you about the types of men who end up on The Network's auction block. But, for now, let me tell you the rest of the story.

"It proved to be a perfect time for me to have humiliated the young man with my questions. The professor explained that he was being punished that night. It was not going to be a sexual event. There wouldn't be any of the enjoyable aspects of it to help him make his way through the penalty. The professor apologized, actually, saying that it was too bad he couldn't offer me the opportunity to explore the graduate student's many pleasures. But this was a serious event, a response to a number of incidents and worse, to the young man's attitude."

"What does that mean?" Tim asked.

"The young man had finished his class work for his doctorate. He has only to write his thesis to receive his degree. That will probably take him at least another two years since he's chosen a particularly difficult area to investigate. He was proud of his achievements — too proud. He evidently had arrived at the island and had rebelled at the role that was his once the party reached the retreat. The professor wasn't going to allow that.

"He told me that the graduate student seemed to go through this every summer, though this was the most serious time so far. The young man forgot his place; he'd argue with the muscled one who, I learned, the professor called his 'majordomo.' He'd also try to lord it over the other three men, thinking they were somehow inferior because they had been purchased in the block."

"Well, isn't he right? He at least had chosen to be with this old guy," Marc insisted.

"No. A slave may never forget that there is only one choice: to be a slave. When that's made, then all of them are the same, of equal status, except for any finer distinctions that the master might allow for one reason or another.

"Slaves are always forgetting themselves in that way. It's one reason that we've all learned never to let them understand how much money passes hands in their sales. They always try to establish a hierarchy by their value. Any man who had signed any contract had to understand that he is simply a slave and that only his master may determine whether he had any power over the others.

"The professor and I understood this. I also understood that the professor must have been facing a dilemma. If this rebellion was truly an annual event, it could be that the young man was only trying to provoke him into giving out the punishment. That's another common slave game that masters much watch out for."

"For someone to *provoke* punishment?!" Marc was incredulous. "Of course. Some are, after all, masochists for the most part and enjoy their punishments to some extent. There's also the fact that slaves enjoy the attention."

"Attention?" Marc asked. He was giving up his charade of indifference and had leaned his elbows on the table after our plates had been cleared.

"You must understand that slaves lust for attention, and they receive it. Think, *think* of every story I've told you and realize just how much the slave is the centerpiece of each one. He has the undivided consideration of all the others who are with him. He is on the table and being examined. In sex, his body is the one that is being stimulated the most. Yes, of course, they are the ones in the spotlight.

"And it's done in a manner far more overt than ever happens in the rest of society, certainly in terms of how society relates to males."

"Pierced tits are a hell of a price to pay for some attention," Marc said, trying to regain his stance of disinterest.

"Don't make me go too far. That comes later in the story.

"After we'd had our tea, I went to my room and showered and changed clothes for dinner. The professor is a gentleman of the old school and prefers his male guests to dress formally. My bags had been unpacked by some of the slaves, and my tuxedo had already been pressed for me. It was waiting on a standing valet in the room.

"I went down at the requested hour and had a fine meal with the old man. It was served by all four of the other men at one time or another. They clearly had their tasks divided equally."

"Naked?" Tim asked. "Were they naked?"

"No, no. They wore very, very slight coverings. They were, I suppose, the same G-strings that strippers wear, though I hate equating them with the vulgarity of the public stage. They're very utilitarian in many ways. They really serve the purpose of making the slave feel even more naked than he would if he were nude. The small, gripping piece of fabric around his genitals and the string that constantly rubs against his anus are constant reminders of his sexual purpose. Too, they make sure that a guest won't be bothered with the unwanted contact with the slave's cock.

"Though, of course, a guest could easily remove the cup if he wanted to."

"Did you?" Tim asked again.

"Not at dinner," I smiled when I answered him.

"There was, though, a tension. The man the professor called the majordomo was still in his leather trappings. He stood guard over the dining room, and when I looked up I could see that he was studying the graduate student. I soon learned why: The professor explained that the majordomo would be administering the punishment.

"That, of course, was to underline the purpose. If the professor had been wielding the whip, it might have been possible for the penitent to imagine the actions as something of personal value between himself and his master. That's another of the games the slaves use to undermine their masters' attempts to chastise them."

"You make it seem so difficult to be a master, what with all this work you have to do to outguess your subjects." Marc was trying to spar with me again.

I smiled just as easily as I had before: "Trust me, it is intellectually exhausting."

I let the two of them sit with that answer for a moment before I continued. "The punishment was to take place immediately after we had our coffee. The professor led me to the front lawn. There were chairs waiting there for us. Another of the slaves brought us brandy — I should say, a fine cognac. The professor would never serve mere brandy.

"There had been other preparations made as well. For one thing, there was a bonfire all set up, only waiting to be lighted. More ominous, a frame of heavy wood had been constructed. The majordomo had been busy while the professor and I had chatted and I had been dressing.

"He was waiting for us outdoors. As soon as we arrived, he started the kindling underneath the wood. Then the professor made some signal. The five slaves came out of the house. The three who were only going to witness this event — or so they thought — walked to one side of the area and sat down on the grass. The majordomo roughly grabbed the upper arm of the offender and dragged him over to where the two of us sat. He threw him forward, so harshly that the graduate student lost his footing and sprawled unceremoniously at our feet.

" 'You may leave, Daniel,' the professor said. This was the first time I had heard the slave's name.

"At first he thought he was being given an opportunity to simply escape his punishment. But he quickly understood that the professor meant that he could leave everything. He was free to depart the island and this entire life. When that realization hit, sheer panic swept over him. Daniel crawled forward on his belly and grabbed the older man's foot and began kissing it. He moaned, 'No, please, not that, no, let me stay with you...,'

" 'Then, accept my authority, both tonight with this punishment and in the future in every way I demand it.'

" 'Yes, please, of course...,'

"The professor motioned to the majordomo. He came and grabbed hold of Daniel again, then dragged him to the wooden frame. I looked over at the other three and knew that they dreaded the thing. There was such a strong reaction evident on their faces that I was sure they had all had their experiences with it in the past.

"The majordomo was quick and efficient as he tied Daniel's wrists and ankles to the extremities of the posts. He took up a thick piece of leather that had holes drilled through it at regular intervals. The professor obviously meant this to be an intense lesson. Those holes meant that each blow would leave a pattern of blisters wherever the bludgeon hit.

"The fire was roaring by now. It sent up utterly demonic lights around the while circle of us. The majordomo ripped the small covering off Daniel. When he did, even though our angle wasn't awfully good, I could see that the slave was erect, his cock speared out of his belly into the air. It was proof that the professor had been right to insist that his punishment be as harsh as possible. Daniel would, indeed, have turned it into a personal sexual event if he had been given the chance at all.

"The majordomo went to work without any of the easy preliminaries that one might use with a slave during a pleasurable scene. The piece of leather leapt through the air, the holes made whooshing sounds for those split seconds before it thudded into Daniel's skin.

"He howled from the first blow. I could only imagine the agony involved. The majordomo kept up the blows, carefully altering the target so he could inflict the major amount of pain without really damaging Daniel, or allowing the young graduate student to anticipate where the next attack would strike.

"I thought it had ended, realizing that it was over rather quickly since there had been no finesse involved in the punishment. Daniel's buttocks were a mass of red, there were deeply scarlet circles where the holes in the paddle had hit, the rest of his ass had less violent evidence of the torture. But I was wrong. The majordomo wasn't finished. Now he took out a cat-o'-nine-tails. He let the implement cut through the air before he turned it on the still crying slave.

"The cat was used on Daniel's back. It cut carefully designed stripes on those same broad shoulders that I had seen in the boat. It was, I knew, not as brutally painful as the other beating had been, but it was much more mentally devastating. It always is. Men are more able to suffer pain on their buttocks. Physically, there's more protection; psychologically, it's easier to take. But a whipping on the shoulders is more demeaning, more humiliating.

"The cat was also used elsewhere, and this time for pain. When he was satisfied that Daniel's back had suffered enough, the majordomo took the long lashes and attacked the back of the slave's legs. That's one of the most vulnerable parts of the human body. Only the truly knowledgeable master understands just what agony a slave receives from punishments that are inflicted there."

"All the secrets of the trade," Marc muttered.

I continued to play with him: "There are more. The soles of the feet, for instance, are even more tender, obviously the stomach is as well, though one must use optimal care not to do real damage there. I happen to prefer the insides of the thighs. There's always the added danger that the lash might wander a bit too high and hit the slave's balls. That fear in the slave, combined with the exquisite pain that's possible in that part of his anatomy, produces the maximal result in my opinion.

"In any event, the majordomo was finally finished with his

duties. He looked to the professor who nodded his permission to end the punishment.

"Daniel was released from the frame. The sweat that had collected on his body reflected the flames of the bonfire beautifully and made if actually increase the visual impression of the deep red evidence of his whipping. He fell to the ground, utterly exhausted The majordomo prodded him with his foot, thought, and wouldn't let him rest.

"Daniel was forced to crawl over to the professor. As soon as he arrived at his master's chair, he once again began to kiss his feet in a display of deep homage. The professor didn't even acknowledge the slave's obeisance. He reached into his coat pocket and brought out a handful of wrapped condoms. He threw them over. Daniel's head onto the lawn.

" 'Go and fetch one. Take it to Joseph,' the old man commanded. Daniel seemed to panic all over again. He stared up at his master as though silently begging him to avoid this one punishment. But there was no forgiveness in the professor's face, and there was the majordomo with the cat still in his hand standing close by.

"Daniel turned and crawled to the middle of the lawn where he found one of the condoms. He picked it up in his mouth and, still crawling, carried it that way to one of the other slaves.

"This, obviously, was Joseph. Daniel laid the packet down at the other slave's crossed feet. 'Use it any way that you desire,' the professor said. Joseph smiled broadly and grinned at the other two. He stood up and pulled aside his covering. He had a magnificent cock, one of those that is circumcised, but still shaped perfectly. The knob was in proportion to the already hardening shaft. His testicles were very handsome, two large eggs wrapped beautifully in dark hair.

"He was as well-built as Daniel and about the same age, twenty-five. Daniel followed his orders and removed the latex condom from its wrappings. He carefully unrolled it on Joseph's now stiff cock. Then, still following orders, Daniel began to suck on the tightly wrapped organ.

"The other slaves, of course, loved this. They crowded around the kneeling figure and began to yell at him, claiming he wasn't doing the job adequately, saying that he never would learn, would he? They took hold of his head and forced it further down on Joseph's cock until Daniel began to seriously gag on the large erection. Only then would they allow him to move backward for air and they sternly admonished him not let the head of Joseph's cock free."

"Great friends," Marc said with a sneer.

Tim didn't say anything, but I thought I saw a flicker of pain run over his face. Then I remembered Marc's stories about his friend. There had been experiences in Tim's past. I would have to find out more about them. They had seemed — from the little Marc had told me — to be simple enough. But his reactions tonight appeared to be so complex.

"Oh, everyone in this world understands that there is nothing more vicious than another slave," I continued. Tim actually grimaced when he heard me make that observation. "That was assuredly one reason that the professor had designated the large one his majordomo. A master's punishment might be feared — and usually with good cause — but even it would pale beside the image of one slave having power over another, especially if the one being punished had put on airs and claimed to be better than the others, which is precisely what Daniel had done.

"Finally, Joseph couldn't hold back his orgasm, and it grabbed hold of his entire body, sending spasms through his muscles and a flood of come into the latex.

"The professor ordered Daniel to return to the middle of the circle and retrieve still another condom in his mouth. The fire was still roaring, and now it caught the streams of tears that were flooding down the graduate student's cheeks. But, of course, he complied.

"This time Daniel took the packet to a slave they called Jose. He was clearly Hispanic with curly black hair and a silky smooth complexion. He was laughing with pleasure as he watched Daniel bring the present to him. He was intent on inflicting as much humiliation on Daniel as possible. He forced him to kneel with his back to him, then to put his forehead on the grass. Daniel followed his next order and reached behind himself and spread the substantial halves of his buttocks so that Jose was given a completely open target for a fucking that proved to be hard and harsh.

"The last slave was named Benjamin. He was a strikingly handsome blond man, the rare type who has a great deal of yellow body hair. He looked slightly older than the rest. I would say he might have been thirty. He wanted to humiliate Daniel as well. But he didn't choose to do it in the brutal fashion of the others. Instead, he stood over the kneeling Daniel and, not even using the offered condom — its protection wasn't going to be necessary — he had his fellow slave reach up with his tongue and use it to lick at his balls. He also ordered Daniel to lift his arms up and manipulated his tits. While he was receiving all this attention, the slave masturbated a very lovely cock, the largest in the group from what I could see.

"He sent his orgasm's fluid showering in thick waves onto Daniel's back. When he'd regained himself, he laughed and then rubbed his deposit into the graduate student's skin. The others joined him in thinking this was a fine joke. They took their condoms and emptied them onto Daniel.

"Then it was the majordomo's turn.

"Daniel was even more exhausted by now, though his erection was also back again. He crawled to the muscular behemoth and dropped the packet on the ground in front of him. The majordomo handed it back to Daniel. He waited patiently, with his enormous arms crossed over his chest, while the kneeling figure once again was forced to put on another man's condom.

"Then the giant slave had Daniel sprawl out on his back with his arms and legs extended. He took a position over the vulnerable, smaller slave similar to one that you'd use for sixty-nine. But he, of course, had no intention of taking Daniel's cock in this mouth. Nor was he going to be satisfied with a simple sucking by Daniel either.

"Instead, he began movements that can only be described as fucking Daniel's mouth. He used his ferocious hips to pile drive his cock down Daniel's throat. Daniel's posture had obviously been designed to give the majordomo the best angle for the deepest penetration.

"Taking the man's cock must have been excruciating. It was clear, for one thing, that Benjamin did not have the largest one of the group. The size of the majordomo's erection was proportionate to the rest of his muscles. But Daniel had no choice in the matter in any event. His body was trapped under the big man's bulk and he couldn't move at all. He had to take the constant thrusts that the other one forced down him.

"Mercifully, the majordomo didn't take too long to come. I'm not at all sure how long Daniel could have taken the attack. When it was over and the majordomo stood up over him and took off his condom, Daniel was left choking on the ground; his hands had flown to his throat as though he could protect it from the assault that was now already over with.

"He had certainly been more brutally used than he had been by any of the others."

The waitress came back and broke the spell that seemed to be weaving in Marc and Tim's minds. She offered us coffee and after-dinner drinks. I declined and instead offered to serve both back at my own house where we could avoid these interruptions.

Marc eyed me with a look of distrust, but Tim was clearly interested in anything that would let the tales continue.

Sven

We drove the short distance to my house in separate cars. I was pleased—even excited—by the reaction my stories were receiving from my two young friends. I cautioned myself to calm down and not rush any of the plans I had formulated on that island retreat with the professor.

They arrived shortly after me. I had put on the coffee and had lighted the fire that was already prepared in the hearth. They took chairs in the living room and stared at the flames. I wondered if they were being reminded about the bonfire on the island. I was.

"So, Daniel got his punishment." Marc finally broke the silence after I had brought in the coffee pot and cups and had then delivered a selection of liqueurs and glasses. I didn't respond until all three of us had gotten our beverages.

"Yes, he did. It was quite effective. At the end of the evening he was kneeling at the professor's feet with his head on the older man's lap. His body was covered with various bruises and his face was swollen from his tears. Eventually the majordomo took him away and it was obviously time for bed."

"After all this, you went to bed alone?" Tim asked.

"Of course not. The vision of Daniel kneeling at the feet of the blond man and licking his balls while playing with his nipples had seemed very enticing to me. I decided Benjamin should show me just how pleasurable an act it could be. I had been assured that any of the slaves were mine for the asking. They had obviously been told the same thing, and he didn't hesitate when I indicated that I wanted him showered and ready in my room at once.

"It was a pleasant night. He was extremely grateful that I didn't want anything more exotic, and he performed the simple acts I requested with a certain gusto. I had him spend the night with me so he could repeat them in the morning and then go fetch my coffee so I could enjoy it in bed."

"He was yours for the rest of the week?" Tim asked.

"No, no. I had my pick of them all. The four young men—the oarsmen—were there in those skimpy costumes whenever I wanted for whatever I wanted, and I did use them occasionally. But they were not the most intriguing option I had. I was much more interested in the majordomo.

"Over breakfast the next morning, the professor assured me that his offer of my pick of his slaves included the overseer. He was even a little taken aback that I had even asked, but I had thought it prudent since the man obviously had a special status in the household.

"I said I wanted to watch him work out. I correctly assumed he had to have a regular regime in order to have developed that awesome physique. It turned out that the majordomo was scheduled to be in his gymnasium at that very moment. Rather than interfere with my meal, the professor sent Joseph running to tell him to stop whatever he had done and wait for me to arrive.

"I learned a bit about him from the professor. The majordomo's name was Sven. His dark hair had misled me, I hadn't realized that he was Scandinavian. He had come to the professor via The Network at a very young age—so young it embarrassed the older man to admit that he had bought Sven the day he had turned eighteen. He had been waiting impatiently for his age of majority in order to mount The Network's stages and the organizers, admiring his persistence and drive, had even accommodated him by scheduling a sale on his birthday.

"Sven had a number of stipulations on his contract. They were hardly onerous to a master; in fact, they were quite appealing. One was that he be allowed to pursue his desire to be a competitive bodybuilder. Another, that he receive a college education; that's how I learned that Daniel wasn't the only one who fit into the role of student to the professor's mentor.

"Sven had gladly gone with the professor and had thrown himself into both his priorities. He had displayed a tremendous loyalty to the older man. When the degree had been earned and the physique title he had worked for had been won, Sven had come to his master and asked for a remarkable contract: a contact for the rest of his life.

"That was arranged and the sale money was put into a special account so that Sven would be quite a rich man when the professor passed on. As a symbol of that step in their relationship, Sven had begged the professor for the piercings that he wore now. Since he was no longer going to compete professionally, he could afford to have his body adorned in that way as a gift to his master. He got them, and he got the position of majordomo in the professor's household.

"I was surprised that Sven was only twenty-six. I would have thought him older. But it was a question of his size and his and the professor's desire that he have the image of a barbaric warrior with the clothing and the hair to go with it.

"I had that information when I went to the training room. Sven and I were left alone, and I was able to see something very handsome and appealing waiting for me. There was Sven, standing awkwardly and wearing only an athletic supporter. He was no longer the majordomo lording it over the others. He was now just another slave waiting for a master and wondering and worrying just what it was that the master would want from him.

"He bowed when I entered and kept his eyes lowered to the floor. I told him I would watch his workout. I asked if his routine was written down. He said it was and went and got a sheet of paper. I saw that it was written in the professor's hand and knew that it must have been something of the two of them had devised together.

"There was a whole set of different exercises and varying athletic events that Sven would do depending on the day of the week. I was pleased that I had chosen this evidently 'easy' day. While it would have been pleasurable to witness his struggle with the enormous free-weights that I saw neatly stacked in the corners, today's gymnastic rituals were more promising.

"He began doing a few stretching exercises. They were remarkably obscene, of course, with deep bends at the waist that exposed his anus.

"He did a few more aerobic actions to get himself ready and then started on his sit-ups. I sat and watched the huge bulk of his flesh as it began to puff up in response.

"You must understand: The other four slaves had great bodies. They obviously worked hard and they, too, probably worked out in this room. But their builds were those that we see in magazines: Sleek, hard, and lined. But Sven was of a different order. He looked the part of the barbarian as a Hollywood director would cast him. His body was enormous, and the muscles weren't the symmetrical visual delights of the others; each piece of his flesh was a component of a powerful machine.

"I walked over to him. I stood next to him and knelt down, just to be closer and to be able to smell the masculine odor of the sweat that was beginning to come out of his pores. His eyes darted to see where I was and what I was doing, but he continued his motions.

"I put out a hand and felt the surface of his skin as he worked. There was a slight stubble on his chest. Obviously he kept his body shaved. He was successful as he tried to keep his concentration while I touched him. He accepted the explorations I made on his body as my due while he continued working.

"He shifted after a time and began to do push-ups. I stopped him. He froze and looked at me, wondering what I could possibly want. I remembered that the professor was a great game fisherman. I told him to fetch the old man's box for me. He was puzzled, but ran to get what I had asked for.

"I rummaged through it. I found a handful of small lead weights. They're used to help sink a line. They have tiny hooks attached to them. I smiled and told Sven that I doubted he really needed the supporter to do such simple exercises. He didn't hesitate to take off the elastic garment.

"All of his piercings were exposed now. I walked over to him, and he sucked in his breath as he watched me attach two of the small weights to each of his nipple rings. Then I put two on each of his genital rings as well. They were heavy enough to tug at this flesh, though they couldn't tear it. When I was satisfied with my little body decorations I told him to resume his push-ups.

"It became a perfect scene. Each time Sven would lift his huge body up off the floor, the weights would drag at his cock, his balls and his nipples. He was in a sensual agony with the constant cycle of stress and relaxation that my devices caused, and soon his cock was fully erect.

"When he was done with the pull-ups I told him I wanted a glass of wine. He said that, of course, he would get it for me. But then he realized that I hadn't removed the weight that was still tied to his cock and balls. I had not intention of doing so. I stared at him until he realized that I was purposely leaving him with his metal burden. He knew enough to not even ask if it would be permissible to lift it up off the floor; I obviously meant for him to drag it.

"He walked from the weight room into the kitchen—a good distance—and returned presently with my drink. I sipped it while he stood there. I raised my leg and used my foot to stretch the wire taut. He squeezed his eyes shut with the sudden pain and then let the pressure I was applying direct him downward onto his knees in front of me."

"He must have hated you," Marc said. He had finished his drink and took a bottle to pour himself another.

"Hated me? Hardly. I think that was the moment when he fell in love with me."

"How could he?" Tim asked. His eyes were wide open, and he seemed almost frightened to know.

I left the question unanswered and went back to my story about Sven: "I let him up after a bit and finally removed the bondage around his cock and balls. I had thought of an interesting next step. I asked him if the list of that day's routine was all that he could do. He assured me it was simply a minimal requirement that the professor expected of him. That was what I had supposed.

"I told him I would like to see him work with some of the weights. He agreed readily, though he said it would be necessary for him to use his supporter again, and depending on what I expected of him, one of those thick leather belts that are used to protect a weightlifter's back. I told him to get himself ready while I went looking for something special.

"Jose was in the kitchen. He told me where I could find the sanitized dildos that the professor kept for his own and other people's amusement with the slaves. I was able to enjoy a few seconds of terror on his face. He thought I meant to use them on him. But I went to the closet and retrieved one that suited my purposes perfectly. It wasn't terribly thick, but it was quite long.

"I had Jose find me a hammer and nails. I took it all back to the training room. I hammered the base of the dildo onto a wooden stool I had seen there. It was only about a foot tall and was primarily for decorative appearances. I had also gotten a jar of lubricant and covered the dildo's rubber skin with grease. Sven realized at once what was happening. I placed my little piece of manufacture in the center of the weight area and resumed my seat. I poured myself another glass of wine and didn't have to say a word to him. He understood what I expected.

"He had put a number of the biggest weights on the bar. I think he was probably trying to impress me with his strength though I'm sure he regretted his little act of bravado at that moment. But he was resigned. He proceeded to do what they call squats. The weight-lifter holds a huge amount of weight behind his back and then bends his knees to lower his body as far as he can and then to once again lift up himself and the weights.

"But, of course, Sven had an added sensation. Every time he lowered himself, he impaled his ass on the waiting dildo. He had to fuck himself over and over again to do the exercises. It left him breathless and quite excited. He was stiff and there were wet spots on his supporter by the time he was finished.

"I was quite pleased with his performance. I told him that we could stop now. He should go and shower. He came back quickly; he hadn't even taken much time to towel off and his hair was still wet. He stood in front of me and waited for my next command. He was obviously interested in what it might be since his cock was hard. It was the kind that I like. It wasn't circumcised. I've said it was large, though bulk isn't always that important in a cock. I prefer that they look appealing more than anything else. I like to have a substantial knob on the head. I'm not one who desires extra layers of foreskin. On the contrary, I like it to be nicely molded to the knob, just a comfortable sheath. I like to see the veins on the shaft stand out, and not to have so much hair on it that you lose much of the image of a strong penis, especially when it's erect. Sven's cock was really exceptional, to my taste. It had all the right qualities.

"I got up and ran my hand over his body. I told him that I could see he needed it taken care of. If I could feel that stubble, it must be time for it to be shaved again. He nodded and went to get the razor and cream. He stood with his hands behind his neck and his legs spread while I applied the lotion to any part of his body where there might have been hair at one time or another."

"Didn't he have any?" Marc asked.

"Yes, actually, there had been a triangle left to crown the top of his cock and balls. But he had no good answer when I asked him if that was necessary, so I shaved that as well. When I was done he had only the thick beard and the long hair on the top of his head."

"You were trying to emasculate him, weren't you? I've read that, that shaving a man is like cutting off his cock." Marc made his declaration seriously. I waved his complaints away.

"How could people ever think such things? When I was standing there and enjoying the feel of his big cock, how do you think I was trying to cut it off, even symbolically? That's foolishness. I think the better way to understand the act is to conceive of my grooming a very valuable and very handsome thoroughbred. I was treating Sven just that way.

"He and I both knew that his body was remarkable. He had spent half his life making it that way. Of course he wanted it to be cared for and appreciated. I was helping do what he wanted. I was removing the hair that would hide the superb muscles he'd developed and those that nature had given him as well.

"There is a sense of danger that any slave must feel when he's being shaved. I know that. Sven was watching the long sharp straight-edge razor carefully, especially when it approached his nipples and his cock and balls. There is no denying the master's power at the moment like that. But I was talking to him the whole time, giving him deserved credit for the cords of muscle in his thighs and arms and buttocks. He was receiving a continuing line of praise from me.

"It firmly established many things between us. I moved on to make sure that there were even more levels of understanding. I was attracted to Sven; I also thought I knew things that he wanted, even needed."

"What an ego you have!" Marc said with a hint of challenge in his voice. He was agitated enough to pour himself yet another drink.

"Ego? I have certain knowledge that's been acquired, that's all."

"How?" Tim asked that question quickly. I ignored it and went on with my story.

"I told Sven that he could get me my lunch and that he should bring his own portion with him and join me on the lawn. He was delighted and started to put on his leather clothing. That, I informed him, wasn't what I desired. Didn't he have one of the small G-strings that the others wore? He did, though he blushed when he admitted it. I ordered him to wear it while he served my meal.

"The sun was bright and warm. There was a nice breeze off the ocean, but it wasn't chilly the way it can be off the Maine coast. I was in a chaise lounge and enjoying the sun when Sven came back out with a tray.

"I'd changed and was only wearing a pair of swimming trunks. No matter how beautiful his own body was, there was no doubt that Sven looked at me with undisguised lust. I was very taken aback by it, actually. I enjoyed it, of course, but I hadn't expected it.

"I had him set up the on the ground beside me. There were two plates. The food was essentially the same; only the more careful garnishments identified mine, while the larger portions distinguished Sven's. He must have had substantial dietary needs for his workouts.

"He watched as I began to eat and stared, immobile, since I hadn't given him permission. Our meal was made up of cold sausages, various salads, and a selection of fresh fruits that was so generous its size had to be at least partially for the visual effect.

"I ate the food with my fingers. Occasionally, I would take part of it and offer it to him. He would lean forward and eat from my hand, carefully licking it clean after every serving I gave him.

"I kept that up for a while and then altered my method. I put small piles of salads on parts of my body and would nod to him to give him permission to lick it up off my stomach, my chest or my thigh. The game had potential. There's no need for prudish behavior on such a private island. I eventually pushed down my trunks and had Sven carefully using his mouth to pull pieces of food out of my pubic hair.

"When we had both eaten as much as we wanted I indulged myself further. Sven took away our plates and brought me more wine. I sat there and had him do a series of poses for me, just those that a bodybuilder might use in a competition. It was…amusing."

"Didn't you ever just have sex with him?" Tim asked.

"Of course…that afternoon, in fact. After I was satisfied with my viewing, I had him go and get a condom for us. When he came back I had him put it on me. He was still well-lubricated from the dildo, and I had him squat on my cock just as he had done the rubber contraption. He seemed to appreciate it much more.

"From then on, Sven became my constant companion. The professor had witnessed some of my activities and that night, at dinner, suggested that I continue them for the duration of my stay. He had already ordered that Sven's dinner be delayed until I decided whether or not I wanted to feed him myself.

"The professor and I understood that Sven was getting something fairly rare out of my attentions, and we both knew that he would benefit from them."

"How can you say that?" Marc demanded.

"Sven is huge…"

"How big is he?" Tim asked.

"He is probably six feet and three inches tall. He weighs at least two hundred and fifty pounds. He has the hair and the demeanor of a warrior, as I said. That was for the benefit of the other slaves. But there are so many other masters that the professor and I knew who would have seen Sven and who wouldn't have been able to fight off the temptation of switching roles with him. Given that kind of build, they would…"

"They'd want to jump on his cock and make believe he was their master," Marc delivered his analysis with open contempt. I couldn't argue with his judgment.

"Yes. It's a problem that many, many large slaves have. It becomes difficult for them to find a master who can really take control of them and do it with any honest desire. The professor certainly wasn't one of those. But he had four other slaves to see to, and he was getting on in years. I, however, was there at that moment and delighting in giving Sven a lesson in his position."

"You probably rode him like a horse," Marc snorted.

"No. Unfortunately the island was too small, and there weren't any trails. It would have been very amusing to hitch him up to some kind of cart or carriage. I would have enjoyed it. But that wasn't possible. I did swim with him once though, and I did grab hold of his powerful shoulders and have him carry me through the water. It was a singular experience to feel the strength of him and to know that it was supporting me in that way.

"Actually, most of our activities were very quiet and not at all melodramatic. Just as there would have been masters who couldn't control their occasional desire to be a slave, at least in the sense of momentary sexual pleasure, there would be others who would have seen Sven and would have had the professor's permission to deliver very severe punishments to him. Sven didn't really need those.

"He needed more subtle things. He moved a sleeping pad into my room that night. For the rest of my stay he slept on the floor at the bottom of my bed. He'd jump up in the morning and bring me my coffee, wearing only the small piece of white fabric held in place by the strings. He'd wait cautiously until I'd give him some kind of indication that he might perform some other service for me.

"I would often have him slip a condom on my cock and then suck on it, carefully holding his mammoth body on the points of his hands and feet so he didn't disturb the rest of me. Sometimes I would fuck him instead. I would have him on his stomach and have him lift up his midsection to expose his now hairless anus. I would thrust in and find myself supported by the small mountain of muscle that was mine for this weeklong visit.

"I would sometimes allow him to orgasm as well, but seldom in the morning. It was much better to leave him in need during the day. When I did decide to allow him an orgasm in the evening, he'd truly appreciate my gift.

"Sven—big, powerful Sven—was able to display the deep yearnings he had for service. He wasn't at all ashamed to have changed from his leather; he seemed to grow quite fond of the G-string. He would see to my bath; he'd rub me dry with a huge towel afterward; he would deliver all my meals and wait obediently until I was ready to feed him."

"And then you let him fuck you."

I stared at Marc, "You think that I'm one of the masters who desired to change roles with Sven? Hardly, Marc, hardly. I usually would let him come to where I was sitting late at night, perhaps in the living room in front of the fire where we would be with the professor and the other slaves. The big chairs that the professor had would help me support Sven's weight. I'd have him sprawl across my lap, hanging his legs off one arm of the chair and resting his back against the other. As big men often are, Sven was aware of the burden of his size and compensated for it quite well.

"Then I would tease him. I'd play with his cock, fondle his balls, perhaps pinch his tits. The others seemed to enjoy it a lot.

I once had Benjamin come over, and I humiliated Sven tremendously by having the other slave tell me what he thought that Sven really liked.

"When he said that Sven's pierced nipples were the center of his sexual response, I had Benjamin suck on first one, then the other in succession. I had the slave keep it up until there was a thick ribbon of precome flowing from Sven's cockhead to prove his arousal.

"In that case, and most others, I would finally masturbate Sven myself, whispering into his ears and letting him nuzzle his bearded face against me while his enormous arms wrapped around my neck. While I was talking he would cover my face with his kisses, much like an adoring feline.

"The professor used to have the other slaves play at sex for his amusement in the evening. Often our nights in front of the fire were spent watching them as he had them masturbate themselves or one of the others. He would sometimes set up a card game where the winner would be able to perform any act of choice on one of the other players. When that particular game was played one night, I offered Sven as their prize. They played endless hands of cards, and I let them take Sven and put him in any position the winner chose, so long as they didn't orgasm. By the end of that evening all of them, Sven and the four others, were putty in our hands. When we finally told the four that they could come by rubbing against one another we were rewarded with the sight of a mass of handsome young male flesh squirming together, sending off the most powerful odors and finally ending up with a great sticky mess on the floor.

"I hadn't allowed Sven to join. Instead I took him to the bedroom and told him he might be given an orgasm only if he would plead earnestly enough. I'm not often turned on by the simple sound of another man's voice, but that night Sven was able to come up with some very erotic messages, indeed. And I allowed him to come eventually by having him put my cock inside his foreskin. I fucked the loose flesh and eventually drove him to his release by the rubbing together of our cockheads.

"I was pleased to see when I left that two of the professor's problem slaves had been well-taken care of. Daniel was as subservient as possible. He still had bruises from his punishment a week afterward. He had resumed his role as well-trained slave.

"When he had the other four row me to the mainland, Sven put on his long pants and his shirt once more. I had noticed that he had brought his leather outfit to the dock and left it there. After he returned he was going to go back to his former overseer self.

"He seemed sad as he called out the cadence to the oarsman. He looked at me whenever he could, whenever he dared. When the boat got to the pier and we had climbed out, we stood and stared at one another for a while. He cried and then, carefully telling me that the professor had allowed it, he gave me a few small gifts."

"How touching," Marc said disdainfully.

"Yes, it was. But, now, I'm afraid it's late and this will have to be the end of our storytelling. You two have had quite a bit to drink." I picked up the nearly empty bottle they had both been pouring from. "I don't think you should drive home. Stay here tonight."

"So you can sneak into our room and shackle us, take us off, and sell us to some Arabian sheik?"

"Marc, you know better than that. You've been coming to this house for years now, and you've never even had a pair of handcuffs put on you. It is late; you have been drinking; neither of you work tomorrow. Stay. Tomorrow you can swim in the pond and lay in the sun."

I think Marc might have argued about it; he was not in a very friendly mood. But when he stood up he stumbled and his tipsy condition was all too apparent. He shrugged, and Tim said, "Sure, you're right."

I put them in separate bedrooms and then went to my own suite. I undressed and climbed into the covers. Marc had actually been correct. I did have a motive in their staying the night in my house. This was perfect, I thought. The two of them wouldn't be able to escape the thoughts and dreams that I would have invoked with my tales. They would both be in bed now; remembering the descriptions and wondering what things had really been like. They were both probably masturbating on my clean sheets; they would have to be thinking that I was close by. When they woke up, the memory of these dreams would still be there, and they would find me waiting. They would have to deal with my reality. I drifted off with a smile on my face.

A Confession

Tim was the first one to come downstairs the next morning. His eyes were still sleepy, and his hair was mussed. He gratefully took a cup of coffee. I knew Tim was, actually, the more realistic possibility for my plans. At least he had more experience with my...areas of interest according to the stories I'd heard from Marc.

I realized that I had never heard of any of them from Tim's own mouth though. This morning conversation could be my opportunity for doing just that. I took my own coffee over to the table and sat down. I was trying to form the words to begin when Tim started himself.

"I know what you're doing," he said in a casual tone.

"And what, precisely, am I doing?"

"With these stories you're telling us all the time. You think that we're going to buy them, that you're going to be able to use them to get us into all that stuff."

"And just how do you know so much about all that stuff?' " I asked, intrigued by how far he might be willing to go.

My challenge obviously took him back a bit. He studied the coffee cup that was sitting in front of him on the table now. I wasn't about to let my advantage slip. "Marc's told me a few things about you and your biker friends."

My little statement had quite an effect. Tim's two hands gripped the cup. I could see the tension in his forearms as he clenched his muscles with anger. "He shouldn't have done that."

"He was only telling a friends something interesting about another friend. We lose control of words once they've been spoken to another. The ancients understood that. When you've begun to tell your tales to someone else, then they enter the mythology."

Tim wouldn't look up. He wouldn't even talk for a full minute. Finally, he lifted his eyes to meet mine. "That's how I know what you're doing and why. I know about you and your kind."

"I've already told you, Marc has only given me a few ideas of what happened to you. Certainly you don't seem the worse for wear. I would gamble that you're a better person for it all. How long ago was it? Two years."

"No. It was longer than that. I was just a kid."

"How old were you?"

"Eighteen, something like that."

"Seven years ago?"

"Yes. I'd just gotten out of high school then." He drank some more of his coffee and looked out the kitchen window to the lawn.

"So?" I was using all of my strength to keep my voice calm and not appear too anxious.

He finally began, and I leaned forward with anticipation.

"You know that big motorcycle run they always have over in Laconia? The national thing where all the clubs from all over the country come? There are thousands of them in that little resort town every year. There have been some raunchy times, then there were some other years where everything was so family-oriented it might as well have been a rotary convention."

"That was after they had to call in the National Guard because the bikers were tearing apart the place."

"Yeah, well, this was one of the last years that the thing was real — where it was a real biker thing and not all cleaned up for the sake of image and that kind of crap.

"I used to go over there every year to see what was going on. The bikers were sort of heroes to me; I used to think that I'd like grow up and be just like them, outlaws on the road.

"This one time — after I'd graduated from high school and thought I was a tough guy — I went over to Laconia. I was just standing there wearing a T-shirt and a pair of cut-offs. This one big biker came over to me and smiled. That's all he did at first, he just smiled. It was frightening when he did it. He was a lot taller than I was — a lot more than six feet — and he was wearing really filthy clothes: dirty jeans and leather jacket without a shirt. He wasn't really fat, but he was big and he had a belly on him. It looked like it was very firm — I know now that it was.

"He just waited for me to say something or move away or respond, and all he did was smile down at me. I should have been smart enough to understand that just trying to escape was the best idea. But I thought I could deal with him." Tim shook his head as he remembered that obviously foolish moment.

"So, I finally said, 'Hi.' As soon as I did, he reached over and put a hand on my shoulder. I thought that was really cool, I mean, here was this big biker, and he was acting as though I was a real pal, a buddy. He sort of rocked me back and forth with that hand.

"Then he said, 'You suck cock?' I couldn't believe it. I mean, yeah, I did. I'd been fooling around with the guys in school for years. But I was freaked that this guy could spot me in the middle of all these people and walk up and ask me if I...did it.

"I told him, 'Fuck no.' He just shrugged and took that big, warm hand of his off my shoulder. 'Too bad,' he said, 'you should learn how.'

"Then I did the most stupid thing of all." He had both hands back on his cup again. I waited, but he didn't seem to dare continue. A frown was building on his brow. I almost broke in and said something, but he began on his own:

"People talk about their big moments, the times when they make decisions that change everything, their whole lives. I made my own then. He was walking away from me, and I called out, 'Come back.'

"He turned around and that smile was on his face again. He walked over to me and put both hands on my shoulders this time. I was biting my lip, I remember that. Finally, I said, 'Yeah, I do.'

" 'You suck cock?' he said.

" 'Yeah.' That's all I could say. He put an arm around my shoulder — it was huge, mammoth — and started walking me away with him. I felt like my insides were going to explode with a weird mix of fear and excitement. I was just letting this biker take me away, and I didn't know where we were going.

"We finally got to where his big Harley was parked. He got on and I started to get on behind him. But he stopped me. 'My holes sit in front,' he said, and he patted the seat in front of him. I didn't really know what he meant by 'hole,' in fact, I thought I misunderstood the word. But I didn't want to look stupid, so I didn't say anything. I lifted up my leg and straddled the Harley. He put his arms around me to get to the handlebars. I was enveloped in this big mass of a man who had all these odors.

"Some of them were just disgusting. I knew there was old piss. Some were just from the machine — oil and gasoline that had gotten into his clothes. But a lot of them were wonderful — sweat and…stuff.

"We went on then, back to where they were staying, the club he belonged to. It was back in the hills above Laconia, on a small lake. It was really quiet, far from the crowds.

"Somehow they'd gotten this place that was a collection of cabins. There were four of them, I think. Like a compound of sorts. They were close to one another, but you couldn't see any other building anywhere close by. It was totally private. Just as well…there were lots of things that went on that other people shouldn't see, lots of things."

He was remembering more and more details. I could see it in his face. I didn't want this story to end. I wanted to give him time to remember as many things as possible. I got up and poured more coffee for both of us and then sat back down to wait.

"What else?" I finally asked.

"What else." He leaned back in his chair and looked away again. "Stuff you — people like you would really like. I bet you'd like my story just as much as you like your own.

"We got there on his bike. When he got off, I started to follow. But first he reached down, and he said, 'I don't like this shit.' Before I could do anything, he ripped off my shirt. He just put both hands on the back of my collar, and he tore it off my back. 'Better,' was all he said. Then he started to walk away.

"I was sitting there with just some rags hanging on to my waist. I got rid of them and jumped off the bike to follow him.

"There was a whole group of people sitting around and smoking dope and drinking beer near the shore of the lake. I couldn't believe them. There were at least fifty men and women. Lots of the men were dressed like this guy I had driven out with. I heard them call him Steamer, that was his name. They had on leather and denim and boots. A few others were either swimming — mainly in the nude — or else they just had on shorts. Almost all the women had their tits hanging out, they didn't wear any blouses.

"I didn't know what it all meant yet. I'd learn that soon enough. Steamer flopped down on the ground next to one of his pals and told me to go and get us both a can of beer from the ice-filled barrel that was on the edge of the group. I thought that was cool; my buddy had brought me back to meet his friends and then wanted us to have a beer together. I wasn't paying attention to the way he'd made me admit I was a cocksucker and the way he'd torn off my shirt.

"I just went and got it. 'Faster next time,' was the only thanks he gave me. I sat beside him and opened my own can. I figured he was just like me, that he was going to be really cool about being gay. These guys didn't seem that way, and I thought that Steamer and I would probably sneak off later and have fun, but that we'd have to act real butch in front of these others.

"But, instead, he put his arm around me and dragged me up close to him. His hands ran over my bare chest. No, I can't say that. They weren't hands. They were paws. These big paws were feeling up my chest.

" 'I got me a new hole,' he said to his friends who just laughed. 'Always had a weakness for boy-hole, don't you Steamer?' the other guy said. 'Sure do, sure do,' he answered. Then, in front of all those straight people, he reached down and put his hand on my pants over my cock and balls. I couldn't move. It was part being paralyzed by being scared of him and part that all these people were watching.

"But no one cared. I couldn't get over that. I was just sitting there, and he was feeling me up, and they just kept on drinking their beer. I liked it, all of a sudden, I just liked it. The biker with his smelly clothes and the touch of him holding me in public became more exciting and less frightening somehow.

"So I relaxed. I just decided to try to figure out who these strangers were. There were some of the women who were doing most of the work, I could tell that. They all were bare-breasted. They were getting the beers and some of them were starting to pile up wood at a spot where there'd obviously been a fire the night before. It was for food, I supposed.

"I didn't realize it then, but there were a couple men who were doing the same thing. It didn't sink in that they didn't have many clothes on either.

"All around were the club members, laughing and drinking and having a good time. There were lots of them who were feeling up women right in the open, just like Steamer was touching me. These guys would grab the women's tits and pull them onto their laps and suck on them, or else grab a chunk of ass or even their cunts.

"I got all excited watching it. Sex didn't happen this way where I grew up; that was for sure. Then this one woman who had long, long beautiful black hair was walking by a guy who reached up and got a hold of her leg and dragged her down beside him. She didn't seem to resist at all when he pulled down her jeans. There wasn't anything on underneath. He lifted her up in a funny way — with his arms under her ass — and then he leaned over and started to eat her out.

"She really got into it, yelling — not angry, turned on. The people around her just laughed more and talked to her and to the guy, egging them on. I got hard watching it all. Not because a woman would get me hard, but just seeing this sex in the outdoors without and restrictions.

"That's when I started to learn what a 'boy-hole' was. Steamer took the back of my neck and he pushed me — hard — down onto his smelly crotch. He used his other hand to pull out his erection, and then he shoved again. There wasn't any doubt what I was supposed to do. There was also no way I was going to escape that beefy hand on the back of my neck.

"I was all turned on again, just with the idea that these people were watching me. Someone yelled something to me, I never heard what it was, but it wasn't a real put-down, it was more like an encouragement.

"For some reason I decided I was going to be good at it — really good. I got it into my head that I wanted Steamer to be proud of me. I sucked that big smelly cock of his like it was the last lollipop on earth.

"I went at it for a long time, I lost track of how long. Then he lifted me up off it. I was…I felt like some kind of sex maniac, I guess. I had spit rolling down my chin and his cock was still standing up straight into the air. I dove down, to get it back again.

"That really made him happy, and he laughed at that, so did the guy beside him, but he wouldn't let me have it, 'No, little boy-hole, don't get greedy.'

"We just sat for a while and drank some beer. More and more people were starting to have sex. One other guy was going down on another man. That was the first time I happened to notice that he was one of the ones who wasn't wearing a shirt.

"Steamer had gone on and on, telling me how much he liked my body — this is before all my chest hair grew out." Tim reached down and absent-mindedly played with some of the thick growth that was on his forearm now, as though it was incongruous with the memory of his past that was flooding out of him. He stopped and went back to his story.

"He told this guy beside him that he liked boy-holes with no hair. That we were better fucks than women. 'Girl holes and boy-holes are all the same,' he said, 'except a boy-hole's brown and a girl-hole's pink. Of course, all you gotta do is slap the boy-hole's bottom around a little bit and it'll be pink, too.'

"They both thought that was really funny and laughed a lot about it. I was embarrassed, really embarrassed. But it was hardly the time to make protests, not after I'd sucked him off in front of everyone else.

"It kept on going like that for hours. Sex all around us and some of those bare-breasted women fixing a barbecue dinner over this enormous fire. Things got much more intense, but the buzz from the beer made it all seem okay. I wasn't used to drinking that much, and I couldn't hold it well.

"I just had these fuzzy memories of Steamer and me making out and him putting his hands down my pants and finally taking them off. When the food was ready and put out on a picnic table, Steamer told me to go and get a couple plates for us. I didn't mind; it didn't seem like a big deal; so I did it.

"Later on, he pulled out a joint, and we smoked it. I got really buzzed then. There were a lot of things that happened that night that I couldn't remember, even the next morning. I woke up in a sleeping bag with Steamer. His big body was all wrapped around mine. My nipples were very sore, I did remember that he'd chewed on them a lot. So was my ass where he'd fucked me — and slapped me around a bit.

"I was sort of dazed. I got up out of the sleeping bag and was going to go to the lake to swim and see if that would clear my head. My movements must of woken up Steamer. He grabbed me and pulled me back into the bag. I didn't want to get fucked again, not the way my ass felt. But I couldn't fight him at all, he was too big. He started to move his cock inside me, and I just cried and begged him to stop.

"It wasn't me that changed his mind. 'Why the hell are you dried up in there? Where's your grease?' I didn't know what to think. He got up and — with his hard cock standing straight in the air like some angry red battering ram — he went and got a bottle of lubricant.

"He brought it back to where I was still laying half in and half out of the sleeping bag. He threw it at me hard. I remember that it hurt a lot, and I knew at once that there'd be a bad bruise on my hip where it had landed.

" 'Grease up your hole,' he said. I was petrified. It had been one thing when he was trying to fuck me and I was sore; it was something else when he purposely hurt me with the bottle. Thank God I had enough sense not to fight him. I opened the bottle and put a smear of grease up my ass, trying to ignore the giggles from the people who were close enough to know what was going on.

"When he was done, he pulled out and rolled over. In a couple minutes he was snoring again. I did crawl out this time and pulled on my cut-offs. I was too shaky from the beer and dope to get it together to just leave; the idea of a swim in the lake was getting stronger. I walked to the shore and put my feet in the water. It felt wonderful. I got out of my shorts and dove in.

"When I came back to shore there was a guy waiting for me. He was very handsome. He was older than I was, I guess he was about twenty-five. He had dark hair and a great smile. He was only wearing a pair of cut-off jeans and boots. He had his hands on his waist and a big smile.

"He was as tall as Steamer, maybe, but much trimmer. That's only in relationship to Steamer's big belly, though. He was muscular compared to anyone else. And his chest was covered with hair. He looked really hot.

"He handed me a towel when I got out of the water. 'I haven't had a chance to say hello to you,' he said. He told me his name was Howie, and he was one of the club members. I immediately assumed that he was putting the make on me. I said something about it — about being scared that Steamer wouldn't like it — and he thought that was really funny.

" 'I'm a hole, too,' he said. Then I finally got it explained to me, the things about the club. I was pretty upset. That word — 'hole' — wasn't just something that Steamer was saying. It was a word they all used. They were all divided into two groups: holes and tops. Most of the holes were women, but not all; and the opposite with tops."

"There were female tops in the bike club?" I was sure that couldn't be.

"Oh, yes, there were. Most of them were lesbians. But I saw...some of the tops were women. Howie explained it all to me while we were sitting on the shore, letting the sun dry me off from my swim. I wanted to say that it was disgusting and leave, but I was naked and my cock was hard while he told me what the rules of the place were.

"Every hole was there for every top. You had a 'main top' most of the time, and so long as you were with that top, the rest of them would respect it and leave you alone. But when a top told you to do something, you did it. 'And fast,' Howie said.

"When I pressed him about it, he got strange and just said that the club didn't like it when holes got out of line. If you wanted to stay with the club, then you did what they said when they said it.

"I couldn't understand why this big stud was a hole. It was already assuming that it was a bad thing to be. I asked him about that. He just shrugged. He said, 'Let me tell you something. There are two kinds of people in this world that it's worth being: Tops and holes. You are what you are and if you're lucky enough to be one of them, you're thankful. Anything else is just too boring.'

"I told him I thought that was strange. I wasn't so sure about this stuff. To tell you the truth, if I hadn't been so uptight about being cool the way teenagers are, I think I would have broken down and cried. It was all too bizarre. Howie told me not to worry, to just go with it. He was like you." Tim looked at me closely, as though he wanted to make sure that I understood something. "He just thought you should do it well. And that you should take something like that as an opportunity to experience more than other people will ever know about.

"He gave me some pointers, though they weren't exactly encouraging, to me at least. I asked him how males could be holes. I was worried about that. He said I shouldn't be. Howie's explanation was simple: Males just had to work harder at it. Women were at an advantage because they had three places for a top to work on, a man only had two. We just had to learn to use the two we had — our mouths and our assholes — better than the females. It was like the female tops, he said, who had to become more creative since they only had their hands and their mouths while the men tops had cocks besides. He told me that women holes always got off on women tops because they had taught themselves so well how to use what they had. We had to do the same thing.

"He also said I should make sure that Steamer was happy with me in all ways, not just my mouth and ass, though those were very important. If Steamer was happy, then he'd keep me close by, and I wouldn't have to worry about the rest of them. How was I supposed to do that, I wondered. He told me his tricks, that I was always to try to crawl in between Steamer's legs, for one thing. 'Tops like it when there's a face near their crotches,' was his simple explanation.

"But whatever I did, he warned me, I had to follow every order and do it fast. 'Don't aggravate them, ever. If they want sex, give it to them. If they want a can of bear, run to get it. If you don't, you'll find out how mean this group can be.'

"We talked for maybe a half hour about all of this stuff, these ideas and roles that were so alien to me. Then Howie decided we should lighten it up. We went back into the water and fooled around a little bit. We sat back in the sun; this time both of us had to dry off.

"Howie told me about himself and his main top, a guy named Torch. I couldn't get over the story. They weren't always like this. There was a time when Howie thought he had to be a bad dude and he and Torch used to prowl the bars and alleys in Detroit, where they lived. They did all kinds of shit together as buddies. But Howie knew that he was in love with Torch all along. But the way he was in love didn't have anything to do with the way that Howie could see other people doing it. He certainly didn't see other men acting the way he felt, so he hid it.

"Then they met Steamer. It turns out that Steamer's really the founder of the club. It was just getting started back then. Steamer came and talked to Howie and Torch about it, he wanted them to join. He explained that there had to be certain firm rules about the way people acted. He was the one who demanded that men and women could switch roles, that they could be whatever their nature led them to be. And he was the one who said that the ones who were on the bottom — the ones they'd eventually call 'holes' — had to belong to everyone.

"By the time Steamer was done giving his pitch, Torch was all set to go. Howie was too, but he had to wait till later that night to explain to Torch just what that meant for him. They'd been together ever since.

"Somehow, Howie's story made me feel much better. I was able to focus on what had been exciting about Steamer and being in the camp and not on what was scaring me, that's the best way to put it. I felt like he understood and if a guy like him could get off on the things that I had seen and done, well, then it was okay.

"There was something else about Howie. No one had ever talked to me so honestly before. I'd responded and been truthful with him. We knew each other's secrets in just a few minutes, it seemed. It scared me, that someone knew things about me, but I was also really happy that I could tell him things and he wouldn't think I was weird. He accepted me. He kept touching me, not really sexually, but like he was letting me know that things were all right by putting a hand on my belly or on my head if he thought I needed a little support. In that short time, I think he became closer to me than any other man I'd ever known. And we shared something together besides. Even if it was just being holes, we were the same kind of person. That made me feel just great.

"We got ready to go back to the camp. We were taking this short path. There were some people not far from where we'd been sunning ourselves. Howie and I were still carrying our shorts and shoes. We were naked, which I could tell was okay in the club area and that it was especially all right for the holes. I was already thinking about myself that way: As one of the holes like Howie.

"We came on these two guys, tops. They were standing up with their pants down by their knees. In front of them were these two naked women. The women were having a real hard time of it. The men were yelling at them, calling them really filthy names. They were pawing the women's breasts in a way that was obviously causing them a lot of pain. The tops were saying that the women were lousy cocksuckers.

"These two girls were crying. I was back to being petrified, especially once the tops saw Howie and me. One of them pulled his woman's face away from his cock and threw her aside with this sneer. He had a stumpy cock, but it was fat, really wide and thick. He had big balls. He shook his cock, and he was staring at me. 'Boy-holes know about cock sucking.'

"I froze. But I felt Howie's hand on the small of my back, nudging me forward. He'd told me over and over again not to hesitate when one of them wanted something. So I moved ahead toward the guy and knelt down in front of him.

"Just as I did, I heard the other top saying that his pal was right. They shouldn't bother with women that didn't know how to use their mouths. I knew what he was doing. He was motioning to Howie to come over and suck him off. I already had the fat cock down my throat, and my face was stuck in the smelly pubic hair of the guy I was sucking. Then I could sense Howie beside me.

"It was the most intense moment in my life, having him doing that at the same time, especially when he reached over and took my hand. We sucked off the two tops together, and it was…magical. They didn't even exist for me, it was just me and Howie.

"When they were done — and they told us we really were better than the women — Howie and I were left alone again. I didn't have to say anything, we just embraced and rolled onto the grass. We just stayed there for a long time, with our arms around each other and our hard cocks pressing up against one another's bellies. I don't think I've ever had such a perfect moment with another human being, not ever."

"You haven't experienced that with Marc?"

He looked at me with complete disbelief, he must have understood what I was really saying, that he could try. I was surprised that he was willing to be honest with me. "No, I haven't had anything close to that with Marc."

I was even more pleased when he went on. He must have decided that so much had been said that there was no reason not to continue. There were few secrets left.

"I think I would have stayed just for Howie. So long as there was even a chance that I could have that moment with him again, I would have gambled anything to try. He was like a big brother, I suppose. He liked me a lot. He told me I was like him in many ways. He was happy for me, he said I was really getting into it, that he could tell I was, and that he liked seeing someone understand where he should be at an early age, not wait too long.

"We did all kinds of things. It was easy because Torch and Steamer were good buddies, and it was simple to arrange for the four of us to be near each other. It wasn't bad, not at all. Steamer thought it was wonderful that I was learning things so early, and he liked it the way that Howie would watch over me. Like, making sure that I greased up my ass. That was the one thing about men that Steamer didn't like, that you had to grease them up to fuck them. He thought that boy-holes should always be ready. It insulted him that the place he wanted to fuck was too dry.

"Torch was the same way. So he made Howie do it too. Every morning, first thing, Howie and I would take the lubricant and put it up our asses for the tops. It was as automatic as anything else. And when we'd be together during the day, we'd check each other, putting our fingers up our asses to make sure the tops could get in easy if they wanted to.

"There were other things that Steamer liked about me. I had taken Howie's lesson well and kept my face as close to Steamer's crotch as I could. I was always ready for him.

"One day, only the third or fourth that I was in the camp, Steamer took me to this guy who did leather work and had some stuff made for me. There was a pair of shorts that he wanted me to wear. They had zippers up the front, just like you'd expect, but there was also one up the rear so he could just pull the one tab and be able to get into me.

"Things went on. I thought this was the best place I'd ever been, with this biker who liked me and Howie, the best friend I'd ever known. It was pretty wonderful. But I couldn't escape the way there was so much possibility of violence in the camp. You could sense it, like it was a physical force all itself.

"And there were plenty of actual violent things that happened. All of a sudden there'd be a scream and you'd see some hole getting it from some top with a belt, or being kicked or something. No one ever, ever tried to stop it or cool the top down. There were other things too. I'd feel very good about Steamer and Howie and Torch, but there'd suddenly be some top who'd come along while I was walking to get a beer, or take a dip in the lake, and he'd just tell me to suck him, or else to fall on the ground and spread my legs.

"They wouldn't simply fuck you. There was more to it. You'd have to lift your ass up in the air with your knees spread far apart. Sometimes they'd want to slap your ass — they'd call that 'warming you up.' You were never safe from them, from the sudden interference of someone you had no right to talk back to or say no to. The vulnerability was total.

"There was one night that was the worst of all. The tops were mainly straight, like I said. They used to think that it was, well, cute that there were male holes — and they'd get blow jobs from us and stuff. But they really were the usual straight bikers you think about, and the way that guys like me and Howie were treated was different than they would have done it, themselves, at least for the most part. It was just because Steamer liked men and Torch loved Howie and they were in on the beginning of the club that it was so loose about sex things. Once that began to happen, then they also attracted some of these very scary women tops and a few other gay and bi guys who weren't welcome in most other clubs.

"This one night, the regular bikers and the women tops decided they'd have some fun with the women holes. They wanted to see them wrestle. They wanted it to be just like in the sleazy night-clubs — they wanted them to mud wrestle. Howie and I and a couple of the other male holes had to make a mud puddle for them.

"Everyone was pretty loaded on beer and dope and having a good time. These girls would get in the pit we'd dug, and they'd have to wrestle one another. It was…"

I couldn't believe that Tim stopped so suddenly. After all he'd said, this one memory was clearly the most horrible. I wondered about it for a moment, and then I understood. "It was the opposite of what you'd had with Howie."

"Yes, that was it. They were forcing the women to fight against one another when the only strength they had was from one another. It was terrifying — not just scary, but terrifying — to think that you'd have to be totally alone as a hole and have to fight another hole. I shivered, I actually shivered…

"My worst fear came true. Steamer was getting really rowdy. After we watched these obscene fights with the women holes pulling off each others' clothes and shoving one another's face into the mud, Steamer got it into his mind that some boy-holes should do the same thing. He shoved me forward and challenged any other top to send another boy-hole in with me for the big event.

"Thank god that Torch wasn't right there at the moment. I was looking at Howie, and we were both just horrified that maybe we'd have to fight each other. I couldn't have done that, I know I couldn't have…"

"Of course you would have," I said.

He grit his teeth with anger when he heard me saying that. "I don't know," he admitted. "But I didn't have to find out. It was bad enough as it was. There was a bi guy named Boot. He was a hole for a woman top named Elsa — they were one of the only such combinations in the camp. I had watched the two of them together, and I sure didn't envy him his place.

"I used to watch when they'd have sex. Almost always Elsa would have him eat her out. Every time you saw them it seemed like he was on his knees between her legs. But sometimes she wanted to fuck. He'd have to spread eagle on the ground just the way we did, but face up. He couldn't touch her, that was her rule. She straddle him, and he'd have to stay in that one position the whole time. She called it 'riding' him, and it was a pretty authentic description.

"It was incredible to watch the women tops, by the way. They seemed to want to make sure that they were tougher than the males; they didn't want to be underestimated. They were far more vicious to the women holes, and they were the worst to the boy-holes. Boot even had to have his nipples pierced for Elsa, and he had a permanent metal collar around his neck. He must have liked it — he never tried to leave — but it certainly looked like the worst existence in the camp.

"Anyway, Elsa pushed Boot out. He was much bigger than me, and older. Probably about twenty-seven or eight. He was laughing and high and having a good time. It didn't bother him and the crowd loved having the two of us in there together.

"Steamer thought having two males there called for a special touch. He didn't want us fighting in the mud. He brought out cans of motor oil. He had the two of us strip naked and then he poured the oil over our bodies, in our hair, gallons of it.

"I was stupid enough to think that Boot wouldn't really mean it. I thought he had to be like me and Howie and that he'd understand that we shouldn't do anything to each other." Tim shook his head as he recalled how very wrong he had been.

"We started in, with the crowds yelling at us. Boot and I couldn't get a hold on each other. The oil made our skin too slippery, and we'd fall every time we tried to make a move. But, after a while, Boot got me from behind. He got his arms underneath mine and reached both of them up until he could get a grip on my neck. That was it, I thought, he'd won.

"I hadn't really tried. I just wanted the humiliation to be over and to stop thinking about what it meant for us to be fighting one another. Maybe the crowd knew I hadn't fought well, maybe it was assumed all along…

"I could feel Boot's cock getting hard against the crack of my ass. Even if I hadn't greased myself up before, there was so much oil over all of us that it wouldn't have made any difference. Even while we were standing like that — with me immobile — he was able to throw me down.

"Everyone thought that was great, and there was all this applause and all these obscene things being said. I was crying — that only made them happier — and Boot got harder and fucked me harder in front of everyone. They especially liked it when I got hard myself. I couldn't help it.

"I was just mortified, I was more than embarrassed, and I was scared. I was really scared. This was the first time the violence of the place had honestly been directed at me.

"When Boot finally let me go, all I could do was think about Howie's advice that I should always stay between Steamer's knees so I would be protected. I didn't even stand up, still on all fours, I moved toward Steamer as fast as I could. I got him, and I opened his pants and brought out his cock. He loved it. He was laughing and carrying on about what a hungry boy-hole I was.

"Even so, the show had turned on another top. I could feel him moving up behind me. 'No.' I thought, 'you can't have me while I'm sucking Steamer's cock.' I believed it was some rule. But it wasn't. It had only been advice. Even while I was there, sucking on Steamer, another guy was poking my ass and then he put his cock up there. I was on my knees, cock at both ends, crying, covered with oil.

"It didn't help at all when I finally had a chance to look beside me and see that the same thing was happening to Howie with Torch and someone else. Actually it made it worse, because I knew that the display I'd put on had gotten the tops all excited and led them to this small orgy."

"It could be done then," I said, remembering the past with my usual nostalgic regret.

"Yeah, back then it was still all right from that point of view, at least.

"The night ended, and, I don't know how, but I got through it. Howie took me to the lake and helped me clean up. We talked a bit about things and how I felt. Then it was over.

"It really was all over about two weeks later. The club was going to move on. I hadn't even thought about plans. I wasn't living a real life, I was just there, immersed in the activities and the things I was learning about sex. But Steamer was a good guy. He was smart about a lot of things, I'd learn. He wasn't going to let me go with them. He told me I was too young and had to make too many decisions. I'd had the experience, that was enough.

"I was pretty upset. They were hardly going to write post cards or letters and there was no permanent address for them. I was losing them.

"One day, Steamer took me for a ride. We used to go out on his Harley a lot. That was one of the reasons for the rear zipper. What Steamer liked to do is sit me on the saddle in front of him and unzip the rear. Then he'd pull out his cock and stuff it up me. The engine of the big Harley would vibrate so much that we could just sit there and get off that way, it was as though I had an electric dildo up me, constantly shaking my insides.

"When he drove the bike over the roads, it felt like I was getting a really, really rough fucking. It was an incredible sensation. And, since we were so close and it was all happening just between the zippered openings, we could ride through the middle of a town and no one would know that we were having sex right in front of them.

"Steamer put me on the bike that day, and he undid the back of my pants. He got his cock out and shoved it up my hole, just the way he liked it. He took me to a place we'd been before. It was a smaller pond, a nice one, even more quiet than the one where the camp was. We both went swimming, which was very unusual. We both stripped down and dove in the water. We just played, like we were both kids. He even washed himself, I remember that, he brought soap, and he lathered up and even shampooed his hair.

"Afterward, we laid out in the sun. It was pleasant, nice. It was totally different than it usually was — he wasn't ordering me around, and he wasn't moving to try to fuck me. We just talked about things. I got very sad. I rolled over and put my head on his huge chest, and I felt this sense of loss like I'd never had before.

"That moment with Howie wasn't my only special time with the club, I realized. There were things with Steamer that were important to me too. And I was going to lose them all. I was going back to being a kid in a small town, and this was the end of it. I cried, and Steamer didn't get mad at me the way he might have before. He just hugged me.

"We both started to get hard, and I figured he'd fuck me now. But he didn't. He knelt between my legs, and he took both our cocks in his hands and began to rub them together. It felt incredible, especially because he was doing it. It was as though this man who'd been so rough with me was finally saying that I was grown up somehow.

"He talked to me, gently, while he manipulated our cocks. he told me I was too young for the road yet. That I had to learn things. He told me that someday I'd find out things about myself that he'd already seen in me. When the time was right, he said, then I'd find out about a group of people called The Network."

"What?" I wasn't prepared for that sudden revelation.

"Yes," Tim said, looking me squarely in the eye, "he told me that I'd find The Network when the time was right and if it was meant to be. He had been a part of it — I don't know how, I didn't know enough to ask him.

"Then he kept on masturbating us until we both came. We washed off in the lake and…and that was it. I went home that evening. Steamer drove me close to my parents' house. I went back to the camp later in the week, and they were gone. I never heard anything about them again. I'd just about stopped thinking about them and The Network until I met Marc and moved in with him. Then you. He told me about you and your strange stories. Now I've heard a lot of them. Now I remember what Steamer said about The Network, and I'm scared, I'm terrified that it's real."

An Accusation

Marc came downstairs. I got him coffee, and the three of us had an innocent conversation about the summer weather and the influx of tourists. It was obvious that they were going to avoid any serious discussion right now, at least as long as all three of us were sitting at the table together.

I had expected them to take up my offer to spend the day swimming in my pond. But they'd have none of it. A quick sense of discomfort settled in the kitchen when I mentioned it and they both stood and made excuses, claiming they'd each made other promises.

The rest of the day was consumed with the pleasant and easy tasks of living in the mountains in the summer. I made phone calls, did office work, and then wandered around the expansive property. It felt like a baron's domain, though, in fact, the cost of real estate in this part of the country is so minimal that I had been able to purchase this extravagant privacy for little.

But I had plans for it. I wandered the perimeter of the cleared section of lawn and thought once more about pushing the heavy brush back further and having a more professional job done on the lawn, which was too heavily composed of weeds.

I remembered Marc's comment about the wonders that could be achieved by slave labor. Yes, I smiled and told myself, it could be quite something. But I wasn't sure what the latest developments meant. They puzzled me. While it might seem that Tim's revelations about his time with the bikers and the top's prediction that he would eventually meet up with The Network would seem a very positive step, there was still the chance that things could go wrong.

I shouldn't have worried so much about that. Everything proceeded in a most remarkably beneficial manner. I heard a car come up my drive that night. I was sitting in my living room reading the latest in the remarkable Sleeping Beauty books and, as always, I was being swept away by the vision of elegant slavery that only A. N. Roquelaure can produce. There aren't that many people who would arrive at my house without forewarning, but it wasn't that strange, either, that a friend or neighbor would come by for some unannounced reason.

I went to the door and opened it just as Tim was about to ring my bell. "Come in."

"Thank you." He moved past me, almost slinking against the wall as though he wanted to avoid touching me. He went into the living room and stood in front of the fire I had lit to cut the evening chill. He put his hands out toward it, as though to warm them. I came back in the room after him and sat back in my chair.

I wouldn't speak. I refused to allow myself to ask why he had come to me. I wanted the confession to be given without any outside influence.

It took a while, but not too long, before he said anything. The beginning was just an awkward set of apologies, "I hope I'm not disturbing anything?"

"No, no. It's fine. I've done what work I had to finish today and was just entertaining myself with a book."

He tried to use that as an escape and came over to look at the cover. He picked the volume up off the table beside me. As soon as he read the full title — *Beauty's Punishment: The Further Erotic Adventures of Sleeping Beauty* — he dropped the volume as though it was a red-hot brick.

"You never leave it alone, do you? Everything about you is this."

"This? Sex? No, that's not true. There are many different books on the shelves in this room. Just take a look."

"I don't mean that. I mean…when you do anything with sex it's always this kind."

"Just about. Though I have been known to explore different experiences. And you?"

"Why are you asking me?" The tone of his voice was the answer to his own question. He was nervous, walking around on the balls of his feet, his head moving in quick jerks to scan the room as though he were afraid that someone might be listening in on this conversation.

"It interests me, that's all."

He moved back to the fire and stared at it again. It seemed to calm him down. His voice was more even when he spoke the next time. "Did you know Steamer? The guy I talked about? He said he had been in The Network — the same group you tell your stories about."

"No, at least I can't recognize him from your descriptions at all. You must remember that The Network — at least where I interact with it — is totally different than your biker club. Though I should have seen the similarities, and I should have been more prepared for your revelation."

"Just what similarities are you talking about?"

"The fact that the gender of the person didn't dictate the role he or she took in that world. The way that there was so little absolute ownership of the slaves — the holes as they called them. That, you realize, isn't really for the sake of the tops. They would have been happy in any case. That was for the slaves, to make sure they lived in their constant state of understanding. Also, the fact they sent you away. That's hardly the usual response of an outlaw group to a young, handsome initiate.

"But how your Steamer knew about The Network? I don't know."

"Do you think he was a slave?" The question seemed to fascinate Tim.

"Perhaps. Or he might have been one who chose to move on and leave behind the structured world of moneyed elegance. That happens, and quite often. More and more, the masters of The Network see money as something useless other than for its utility in procuring slaves-for-purchase. The rewards of corporate life or vocational advancement aren't really very appealing to them. They choose to leave it all behind. Though they usually do that with their households intact.

"Steamer might have been a recruited slave when he was young. Or else, he might have entered The Network when he was a highly driven businessman, thinking he needed to expand the area of his control and dominance to include even his sexual life. Once there, he would have learned that it wasn't so. The idea of being the creator of a sexual bike club could certainly have appealed tremendously to a man who had seen the shallow rewards of business success."

"It wouldn't bother me if he had been a slave. He would have done it well, I bet. And he wouldn't have been ashamed of it."

"I'm sure not. No one would ever try to make him feel that way."

"I wish he had told me, though. I wish I had known from him what it had been like."

"Why?"

"Because then I could have loved him even more, even as much as I loved Howie."

" 'Love' isn't the word I'd use to describe his feelings for you, not as you described them."

"Well, I told you a lot, but there were other things. When I was to sit with him for those few weeks and he was trying to train me, I learned that he wasn't doing it to be cruel. He was doing it to help me. He wanted me to be the best there was. I told you about that first time when I decided that I was going to suck his cock really, really well. He picked up on that. It was one reason I got to stay as long as I did. He knew I was trying."

"He wanted you to be beautiful."

"Yes, that's it. Is it what you want from me?" He turned away from the flames and looked at me.

"Is it what you want me to give you?"

"I don't know." Tim moved over and sat on the couch opposite from my chair. "I just remember those weeks with the biker club and I remember everything that's come, since and there's no comparison. None."

There was another car in the drive. "I wasn't expecting anyone," I said to Tim. I went back to the door. Of course, I should have expected it. Marc was storming up the walk. "Is he here?" He was speaking with barely controlled anger.

"Yes." There was no doubt who he meant, and I didn't intend to lie.

Marc walked past me, into the living room. "Why are you here? You said you were going to the inn."

"Why are *you* here? What right do you have to follow me?"

"I'm your lover."

The two of them stood in the living room. Marc's fists were clenched, and his arms were strained with muscles dancing up and down their length. He made it appear as though all his self-control was necessary to keep himself from starting to swing.

Tim was more relaxed. He turned his back on Marc and looked at the fire again. "Lover? We've never used that word before." His voice was soft, almost seductive.

"Words! Who cares about words."

"I do," Tim responded with the same soft voice. He knelt down and put another piece of wood on the fire. "I care a lot. I care about the words we whisper to each other in the night. Haven't you ever wondered about that? Why it is that we both use the same words at night?"

"I don't know what you mean." But something had gotten to Marc. The fight was gone from his voice.

"Come on, think about it. Think about how unattached we are. 'Lovers?' Be serious. We're a couple guys who decided to live together so we could have a safe piece of cock every once in a while and not have to worry too much about it. 'Lovers?' We share the rent, we talk about jobs and school. We're a little bit supportive on bad days, and we share a few of the good times. That's it. That's all.

"What's real is when we're in bed at night. What we say to each other under the covers. I can tell a lot from that. The way we each say the same things. And want the same things. Tell him about it."

Tim stood up now and looked directly into Marc's eyes as he continued. "Tell him how we are, when we're honest and the lights are out. Tell him how we get hard when we tell each other his stories and think about what he really wants from us. Tell him how, when you're getting ready to come, you beg me to bite your tits harder and harder. Or, how when you're jerking off and I have my arms around you, you ask me to grab hold of your balls and squeeze them. Or, how when you're getting close to coming you ask me to climb on top of you and straddle your belly so you can feel what it's like to have a man up there. Tell him."

"No." Marc's voice was almost hollow now. "No, I won't."

"Then I will. I'll tell him how every single honest expression of sexual desire that comes from us is bottom — hole — slave. That every time we're sincere, we let the words out about our fantasies.

But that's only in bed. And that's why we never talk about being 'lovers,' because we aren't. The rest of our life together is just housekeeping and daily chores and having someone, anyone. It might be better than being alone, but not it's not as good as being happy and honest."

"What are you trying to do?" Marc demanded. "Are you trying to say that you really want those things he's always talking about? How can you?"

"Because I do. I always have. You do. I know you want them as badly as I want them. It's in your dirty talk and your dreams. It's in the magazines you read the most carefully and the television shows you insist on seeing. It's in the movies, even the books. And you even hide them from me — or you think your do. Here, look, I've seen this one before."

Tim went over and picked up the Roquelaure. He shoved it toward Marc. "Deny it. Deny that there's a well-read copy of this in the glove compartment of your car. I dare you to. Even though you'll sit and tell me how weird his stories are when we go out to dinner and even when you tell me that the bikers I was with were sick, you're driving out on country roads and jerking off to this. You love it. You want it. Maybe even as much as I do."

Marc physically moved back to avoid the verbal attack that his friend was delivering. "But that book is a fantasy. It's a story. Just a piece of fiction about some other time and place. It can't be real."

"You know that's not true. You know he's telling you about real things. I've told you about real things. Those bikers and Steamer's demands were real. It's there if we'll take it."

"It's sick to take it."

"Sicker than just thinking it?"

"Yes," Marc said adamantly. "You don't have to do everything you think."

"Maybe not. Of course not," Tim said. "But you don't have to take things the expected way either. You can reach out for the different ways, the new experiences. Look at us, look at us being two little faggots living together and thinking it's hot shit when we go to Boston and walk into a leather bar.

"And just why do we always go to leather bars when we go to the city, Marc? Why is that?" Tim's voice was picking up a sarcastic edge now. "Is that a little game of chicken? Huh? Do we go and see if there's something there that can make us do the things we'd only think about otherwise? Are we hoping that's what will happen? Why are we so very chicken that we won't go for the real thing when it's in front of us? Tell me that?"

Marc was on the defensive. He moved over to the couch and sat down. "We can't do everything we want. We have to make plans. That's why we want to go to college. That's why we agreed to go together, so we'd have a future."

"I don't want to spend the rest of my life thinking that I could have done something, that I had a chance. I've already spent years regretting the bikers. Now I have another opportunity. I know one of two things are going on: Either this is happening because it was meant to — the bikers were really only a preparation for this — or else, this is probably a grand mistake, the last time I'll even know about this world happening.

"I'm not going to take the chance that it's going to pass me by again, Marc. I'm not."

"What do you mean?" Marc was frightened now.

Tim turned to me. "Will you train me for The Network?"

"No!" Marc stood up and moved over to Tim. He put an arm around his shoulder. "You can't do it. You can't go into that. What about me?"

"What about you? Why don't you join me? Maybe we can be like me and Howie were — really share something. Not just washing dishes and going to bars and wishing, but doing things together that could never be forgotten. We could stop lying, we could be honest about ourselves and see ourselves."

"Never," Marc stood back. His face was composed and his entire being had a look of resolute decision about it. "I'll never do it. If you do, I'll never speak to you again."

I had been quiet as the drama unfolded. I waited now, holding my breath and wondering at the way my plans were working themselves out.

The two of them wouldn't budge. They stood in the center of the room for a while, glaring, challenging. Then Tim turned to me again. "Will you?"

Marc stormed out of the house. I could hear his car engine starting and then the wheels speeding down the driveway.

Reality

We didn't see Marc again for three months.

I hadn't forgotten him — far from it — but it had been long enough that I stopped expecting him to appear.

Summer had ended. An early frost had begun changing the colors of the leaves on the trees. The evenings had a distinct chill to them. But most days were still very pleasant. I was sitting on the front porch of the house enjoying the fading sunlight as the day was ending when Marc drove up. He stopped and got out of the car. He leaned over the roof and seemed to wait for me to say something. I neither welcomed him nor gave any indication that I was displeased that he had shown up.

He came up the stairway onto the porch and sat down beside me. It was obviously a difficult moment, and it seemed as though he couldn't look me in the eye. I finally said, "It's been quite a while since you've been by."

"I've been busy," he answered. He was looking down at his hands dangling between his legs.

"College?"

"No. No." He spoke in a low voice, one that carried a tone of defeat more than anything else. But he sighed and seemed to have decided to go on with the conversation, "I never went. I didn't get there."

"What have you been doing?"

"Running."

I took a quick breath. He wouldn't have come to the house unless something was resolved, and this was the first indication I had that it might have been what I had hoped.

"Running?" I wanted to give him as much room to move as he needed.

"Yes, running. From you. From Tim. From everything. I nearly got married." He said that suddenly and sat up with a defiant posture, as though he thought I was going to hit him.

"But you didn't."

"No. I couldn't. I was ready to. There was a girl, and she wanted to, really badly. It seemed like a good way to handle things. I was blaming all the gay stuff for the confusion I was having. But I kept hearing Tim's voice talking to me about 'honesty,' and I couldn't follow through. I couldn't follow through with much — school never happened, I missed the registration deadline 'accidentally but on purpose' — you know what I mean. I kept on having fights at work, and I finally quit. I was going to move to Boston, but I never could come up with a decent reason why I should do that, except to get away. It's all been that. Running. Just running."

He wasn't able to go further, and I didn't press. "Is he still here? Tim, I mean, is he still with you?"

"Yes." I couldn't help smiling. Not at Marc. I was smiling with the pleasure I'd had over the past three months with Tim. "Yes, he's still here. He's out back, working." I looked at my watch. "It's just about time for him to stop for the day. Come on, we'll go get him and have a drink."

Marc stood up, but seemed to distrust what was going on. I wouldn't comment, but walked through the house. He finally followed me. When we walked out the back door he couldn't help but make this statement. "Jesus! What's been going on? Did Tim do all this?"

"He had some help."

My property had been transformed in those months. The brush had been cleared for tens of feet in all directions. Where there had been wild plants, there was now manicured lawn. Only a few very large, very thick-trunked hardwood trees were left standing. There was one long cleared path from the house all the way to the swimming pond. Along its edge were carefully trimmed bushes.

The lawn that had already existed was still noticeably lush, even after the frost. The weeds were gone and only carefully cut grass remained. I had been very pleased by the result, and I knew it must have looked even more dramatic to someone who hadn't been around for the transition.

I put my hands up to my mouth to form a horn and yelled out Tim's name, then I turned to Marc. "He'll be expecting me to call him about now. He'll come right in. Let's go down by the pond."

We walked along the newly cleared pathway toward the small body of water. It was a man-made improvement on an old beaver pond, about five or six times the size of a large artificial swimming pool. The stream that fed it a constant supply of spring water resumed its own way by spilling over a dam. The water was always clear and clean. It had been one of the main selling points of the house when I had first bought it.

As we were making our way toward the pond, Tim suddenly came into view, walking in the opposite direction. I wasn't worried about his seeing Marc. He must have always known that this encounter was coming and he must have prepared himself for it. Marc didn't say a word. When Tim got up to us, he stopped and looked at me. He didn't say a word. I only told him: "Drinks for two." He nodded and began to move quickly away from us.

Marc turned and watched him go. "God, he's changed that much in only three months! What have you been doing with him?"

"A lot of work; you've seen the grounds."

I took Marc's elbow and turned him back toward the pond. We got to a small collection of lawn furniture near the water and I indicated that he should take a seat beside me.

"He got that muscular in three months?"

"That muscular? Well, yes, he's been cutting down brush using an axe on trees and a power saw to make firewood. He's had to lug out the debris. All of that plus the weeding."

"You make sure you can see it, don't you?"

Marc was right. There was little question that Tim's body had developed awfully well in the past months. There had been a good frame and a fine head start when we'd begun; combined with the constant labor of the summer and early fall, the results had been stunning.

And, as he said, I'd made certain that those results could be seen. When he had passed us on his way to the house, Tim had been wearing only the simple racing brief that I allowed for him. He was carrying the heavy gloves that were a necessity for the rough labor he was doing, and he had been wearing his work boots, but that had been the limit of his wardrobe for virtually the whole time he'd been with me.

"Why do you even allow the briefs?" Marc asked. It seemed to be bought on by honest interest. He'd gotten beyond the tension of having come to the house and now there were questions that he wanted answers to only because there were things he hadn't expected.

"A number of reasons. The work is hard, and he probably needs to have some support. Also, the suit is made of that stretch fabric that makes his cock and balls look like such an attractive package. I have to admit, though, that a major consideration is simply that it leaves a broad band of white flesh on the midsection of his body. It makes him even more handsome when he's naked." I could have added that Marc would see for himself soon enough, but decided to let that happen naturally.

Just then, Tim came walking down the path with a tray in his hands. When he got to us, he offered each of us one of the two tall drinks he was carrying. I took mine. So did Marc. As soon as he did, he said, "Why haven't you said anything to me?"

Tim smiled, perhaps with a little superior manner, "I can't speak until spoken to, it's part of the training."

"Well, I just spoke," Marc said.

"How are you? I've worried about you."

"You've worried about me?"

But Tim wouldn't respond to the challenge. He put his tray down, and, after nodding to me with a small show of obeisance, he walked quickly down to the edge of the pond. There, he took off his boots and socks and then peeled off the tight elastic briefs. The outdoor work had left Tim with a dark tan and it had been so even that it seemed only the small shocking white part of his midsection wasn't brown.

As soon as he was naked, Tim dove into the pond. "It's become very much an evening ritual," I said to Marc. "I look forward to it, watching him bathe." Marc didn't say anything. Tim had a small cache of personal goods that he stored in a nearby waterproof container. He came back to the shore and got soap and shampoo out of it and went about cleaning himself. He would lather up and then dive in again to rinse off. There was one gorgeous moment when he was sudsing up his hair — it was quite long, I'd had him let it grow — and he was standing in just enough depth of the pond that his cock was barely able to float on the surface. His thick pubic hair was plastered against the white skin of his belly and the hard stomach muscles seemed to glide up and out to the expanse of his chest. It was a perfect erotic picture. I could feel my own cock stirring from the image and I knew that Marc had to be responding to it as well.

Then Tim went back to his pack and pulled out a razor. He used the soap to create more lather, but this time only on his crotch and in the crack of his ass. He carefully shaved his balls first, lifting them up in the palm of one hand while the other worked the razor. Then he reached behind himself and pulled apart his ass cheeks and shaved the deep and secret cleft there.

I wanted to explain to Marc how long it had taken Tim to learn how to do it and the reasons I had for insisting that he make this a part of his daily ritual. But the mystery about it that was so rich at this moment was too wonderful to violate with explanations. Whatever reaction Marc was having was more intense than any reasoning I could supply him in any event.

It also must have been very intense for Tim to be doing that now — in front of Marc — without any chance to know what his old roommate and sometime lover was thinking. I only considered it part of Tim's ongoing testing and graded him very well for his ability to continue with his duties in a difficult situation, though I understood that there might even be some pleasure involved for him. Many slaves, early in their education, love to tweak the noses of people who are different than they are.

The late afternoon air was still warm enough that Tim didn't need to towel off after his final swim. He simply shook his head — much as a playful dog might do after a swim — and then walked up the lawn to where we sat. He smiled at both of us, then sat down on the ground near me.

"I guess I can't just ask you how you've been, like I would other people," Marc finally said to Tim.

I put a hand on Tim's damp hair, partly in affection, partly to give him permission to answer.

"Sure you can. I've been fine. I've been happy. I've worked my butt off," he laughed and turned his head so that his face went into the hand I had left there. He nuzzled me, his warm breath on my palm was a delicious counter to the cool wetness of his skin.

"Well, at least you still got your butt," Marc said.

I didn't know if Tim was ignoring the attempt at a joke or if he was playing with Marc, but instead of just answering, he lifted himself up off the ground just enough to look at first the right, and then the left half of his buttocks. "Well, the bruises are gone at least, aren't they," he said very matter-of-factly.

I laughed out loud. Now I knew that Tim was teasing Marc. The blush on the other man's face showed he'd succeeded. He took a sip of his drink and tried to ignore the fun that was being had at his expense.

"I'm sorry," Tim said. He reached across and put a hand on Marc's knee. "I'm really fine. Thank you for wondering, for caring."

"Were there bruises?" Marc's question was serious now.

"Of course there were," I answered. I pulled Tim's head down onto one of my thighs. "There's been a lot to learn, and the lessons haven't always been enjoyable. There's been a lot of progress though, a great deal."

"Progress…" The word didn't sit well with Marc. "Tell me about it," he sat up, and his voice picked up some power. "Tell me about your progress. How did you achieve it?"

"Sven," Tim answered with a broad smile on his face. "You remember that big majordomo that Master was always talking about?"

Master. That was the first time Marc had heard the title applied to me, and he physically reacted to the sound with his posture.

"The one on the island?" Marc asked.

"Yes. Master brought him over to help me out." Tim moved his head and pushed it between my legs, an affectionate gesture that left his nostrils breathing warmly on my hardening cock.

"I had listened to all the things that had been said," I explained to Marc. "I knew that Tim wanted to share his experiences with someone and Sven seemed perfect. He was used to that role after all; as the majordomo on the island it'd been his responsibility to communicate as much as possible to the new arrivals. The professor was willing to lend him to me."

"What was he really like?" Marc asked Tim.

"You wouldn't have believed him. He was wonderful. He walked onto the property, and my knees went weak. I was petrified, for one thing. He looked twice as big as I expected him to be. He was also in love with Master. That didn't make him jealous of me — that I was going to stay here — but it made him damned insistent that everything was going to be done just right or else. And he let me know I was the one who was going to get the 'or else.'

"He worked me like some maniac. Nothing was right. Nothing I did was appropriate. He'd have me crying and feeling like shit…"

"Only in the very beginning," I said softly. "Things changed once you got over your fear of him."

"Yeah, they sure did. Marc, it was…wonderful. We got to be really close. He taught me lots of things, and we'd work together. I've lived in the mountains for a long time, but I didn't know a tenth as much about the forest as he did — that's what he'd studied in college, forestry. We'd get into boots and our briefs, and we'd walk for miles while we picked wild flowers for Master. He'd point out all the plants, and we found all kinds of streams and ponds I'd never know about.

"Back here, we just learned together, what Master wanted and how. We both knew that we were both trying very, very hard and it helped to understand that. We played, too. You should have seen it when we took our baths together. Sven used to show off a little bit when other people were here. We'd get in the pond, and we would always shave each other. That was something that Master had us do to learn to get along. I would have to soap up this giant and shave his chest and legs and even his underarms.

"But when he was in the mood, he'd just take me around the waist, as though I were a little kid, and lift me up with my ass turned this way. Then he'd tell me to spread my ass, and, while he was still holding me with one arm, he'd use the razor with the other one."

"Yes," I agreed, "that was amusing."

"*Amusing*," Marc said. He looked away from us. "So you were here playing slave games with your bodybuilder giant all this time? Working outdoors and having sex. That's all you've been doing."

"That's not the way I'd put it," Tim said. "I've been learning about myself and being happy. And getting excited. I'm working really hard at what I want to do, and I'm going to do it."

"What? What is there that you can decide to do here? You're just a plaything for your master."

"I'm going into The Network, Marc. This winter. I'm going to be sold."

"You can't be serious. You can't really mean you're going to follow through with that?"

"But I am serious. I'm very serious. It's been arranged." They stared at one another for a while. Then Tim said, quietly, in the most affectionate voice he'd used so far, "Wouldn't you like to do it with me?"

Marc didn't say a word — perhaps he couldn't. Finally, I pulled Tim back in between my legs. He must have felt my hard cock. He moved against it, and I could feel his jaws moving, the hard surfaces producing a pleasurable series of sensations, all of them intensified by his hot breath. Marc only watched. He didn't say anything to either of us.

"He's learned well," I explained, finally. "Once he's had even the slightest indication that a master wants him for any reason, then his own conversations and any distractions have to be dismissed."

Marc and I were staring at one another. I wondered if I'd gone too far with this particular performance and lost him again. But I hadn't, not at all.

"I wanted him to be unhappy. I wanted to come over and see him cringing with fear and being sorry that he ever stayed here that night. I wanted to see something that was even worse than what I had."

"What do you have, Marc?"

"Nothing. I have nothing. I used to have the two of you. But you've ganged up on me. You were my friend, and he was my companion. You two were just fine the way you used to be, the way things were. But you had to get together and change everything. You've locked me out."

"No we haven't. You walked out and never even tried to get back in," I said. "It might have been easier if you had stayed. You could have seen the transitions. This wouldn't seem so…extreme if you had watched the stages."

"You mean, if I had been part of them."

Tim had moved. He had been only leaning into me, but now he was kneeling directly in front of me. He wasn't reaching to press against my hard cock anymore; instead his face was easily moving around against it and my balls. I could look down and see his own balls and, above them, his hard cock. There was no way anyone could deny his sexual response to what was happening. There was a small sound just then. I had learned to recognize it. It came when he was being so excited that it began to be especially frustrating for him not to touch himself — something that he was strictly forbidden to do without permission. That little sound carried with it a load of erotic pleasure more obvious than almost any other I'd ever heard.

"I don't want to do it," Marc was whispering, I could barely hear him.

"You haven't even been asked to do anything," I said.

"I can't." He spoke as though he hadn't heard what I'd said. "I can't."

"What do you think you do want to do, Marc?"

"Run."

"You told me you'd already done that. Do you really want to start again?" I gently pushed Tim off me. "Go on in, start getting dinner ready. You might as well set another place."

Marc watched his old friend stand up with a stiff erection that had a small dampness around the tip. Tim didn't look at him, but at me. He appeared terribly unhappy, but only about being sent off, not about anything else, at least not at that moment.

When we were alone, I picked up my glass and took another drink. Marc mechanically did the same. "You want me to be like him, don't you?"

"Like him? I'm not sure. Do I want you? Yes. In this kind of sexuality? Yes. But perhaps in a different way. I haven't really thought about that, at least not in any detail."

"You want to sell me into The Network."

"No." I spoke adamantly now. "I don't want to do that. I could. Just as I'm doing it for Tim, because he's asked for it, he wants it. But it wouldn't be what I would want to have happen to you."

"Why not? There's the money..."

I waved that away. "I don't earn my income that way, and you know it. You've seen how I live. I have more than enough. I would never go out and seduce anyone for it, either. I never have. You've spent enough time at this house in the past few years that you'd know if it had been happening. It wasn't. I have never done that here. I don't recruit for the sake of income.

"I've taken on Tim because it was enjoyable — I won't deny that — I've enjoyed it a great deal. But he asked. You were there when it happened."

"But me?"

"I simply want you."

"To be your slave?"

"I want to live with you. I want to show you a way of life that I think you'd enjoy. I want to teach you things, and I want to give you a place to stand and be so you can stop the running, all of the running."

He put an arm on one of his knees and then bent his head down on his palm. I wondered if he was crying. Perhaps he was praying. Whatever was going on, it was a private moment, and I decided not to intrude on him. I hadn't been asked to open the door for him — yet.

Fellowship

Marc and I walked back to the house. I took him inside through the front door. I didn't want him to go through the kitchen even though that would have been our route in past times.

We sat in the living room and talked. We avoided the conversations about The Network and Tim. But at least we did talk about more real things than we might have resorted to — or, at least, he might have wanted to escape to.

We discussed his college plans — or rather, the lack of them. He confessed that he was becoming concerned with his life again. There might not be many options left. He discussed these topics as though they were irreversible mistakes, things that couldn't in any way be compensated for. That, I knew for sure, wasn't true.

There was a sense in which his problems were caused by the essential frivolity of his lifestyle: the money squandered on new and expensive cars, the constant vacations, the gifts he'd given to each of the succession of boyfriends he'd had over the years, and the gifts that others had given him that he hadn't saved.

There were also forces that he had had no control over — being gay, or at least bisexual, in the country, and not having the luxury of living in a community that would have encouraged him to go on to school or rewarded him on those few occasions when he'd done well academically. There had been limited chances in his developing years to even see the possibilities of advancement.

But there was also the truth that there were so many times when he hadn't grabbed hold of an opportunity. There were so many times when someone had made an offer.

The conversation seemed meaningless after a while. He was feeling his regrets earnestly, I didn't doubt that. But the main regret now had nothing to do with academics or career. It had everything to do with the sexual possibilities that were apparent as they flowed between us, no matter what topic we were discussing. Once dinner was served, they'd be even more obvious, and they'd have to be dealt with. That was going to be his own problem.

Marc was an alien force in our house, someone different from us. If he thought that the display he'd gotten at the pond was exotic, he was in for something far more that evening.

There's a danger when a stranger enters a fantasy that other people have created. There's the possibility that the beauty that's been produced out of people's imaginations will appear to be ludicrous and inelegant. The laughter of unkind people when they refuse to allow something foreign to them to have its own integrity can sometimes cause great disruption, even pain.

But Tim and I were beyond that. His time with me and the time Sven had spent as a part of the household had created a strong curtain around our existence; the possibility that someone could come in and cause him discomfort was gone — even if it were someone he had known in another life.

"Dinner."

I'd been waiting for the call. I stood up and so did Marc. But he'd been so involved in his own self that he hadn't noticed when Tim had walked into the room. He looked at his old friend now. Time had a smirk on his face. At another time I would have worked that superior looking expression off him quickly. But he had a right to this moment, I supposed.

"What…where did you get that?"

"Sven," Tim said. He lifted his arms up to give Marc a better view. "He trapped the animals and skinned them himself, right on this property. He designed it here, but it took too long to cure the leather and make the garments by hand, so he had to send it to me."

Tim had been ecstatic about his present and had begged to be allowed to wear it in the house rather than the briefs. The leather loincloth had been colored white; there were two others, one a light brown and the third burgundy. They weren't the barbarian's costumes that Sven himself wore. The Swede had declared Tim too civilized for those. The American needed something that would make him more sensual, not something to give him the appearance of power.

The front was a triangle of leather so wide that it was nearly as full as a pair of briefs, though it didn't extend quite all the way to the sides of Tim's waist. There was hardly any flap, just enough so the inch wide band of leather around his waist could grab hold. There was no back to it, only another band of leather that traveled up the crack of his ass to the same waistband.

Around one of Tim's biceps was a matching band of white leather. On the opposite leg there was a band that was tied at his thigh. Finally, there was a headband, actually necessary since I had wanted his hair to grow out. His carefully trimmed beard and mustache finished the outfit.

Sensual? Yes, it looked very sensual. Sven had done wonders with it all. But the most important thing — and Sven must have known this as well — was that Tim felt sensual when he put on this outfit. It was his sexual uniform. The outdoors work was sweaty; he'd be covered with grime when he finished every day. That bath was no little convenience of mine, it would be necessary. Afterward, when he came indoors, Tim would leave the elastic briefs outside, and he'd go through that special transformation that only clothes can produce, much like the banker who deposits his three-piece suit in a closet and alters his appearance and his self-image when he puts on a pair of jeans and a tight T-shirt before he begins to start his private life.

Marc was stunned. There was no other way to describe it. I wasn't sure why this would have more impact than the image of his friend shaving his ass at the pond, but perhaps the idea of the costume was even more astonishing somehow. And we were inside the house; there was no overlooking the clear purpose of this clothing. He might have been able to ignore the actions at the pond. They were, perhaps, something he could understand or interpret in terms of watching someone wash or shower. He had seen something more intimate than he should have. But he didn't have to think that it had been something that was structured to present an erotic response. These clothes were.

I went into the dining room; Marc followed. A salad was waiting at our place. When we were done, Tim appeared and cleared the plates. Then he brought in the main course on a platter. As I served it, Tim opened and poured wine for us. When he wasn't actually involved in any task, Tim would stand behind me, waiting for a signal for any other request I'd have.

He's learned to stand with his legs spread apart. His arms were behind his back and his eyes were looking straight forward. Marc would constantly steal glances at him. I knew that Tim wasn't responding. It had been one thing for them to have a conversation at the pond in front of me, but Tim wouldn't have dared to interrupt the meal.

When it was over, I poured out the rest of the bottle of wine and had Marc join me in the dining room. "When does he eat?" That mundane question seemed the most pressing at the moment, at least it was the one that Marc dared to ask.

"Various times," I said. "Sometimes I feed him myself at the table. Now, I assume, he'll quickly eat something while the coffee is brewing."

"Does he always dress like that? Is this a show you're putting on for me?"

"Oh, it's not a show for you, believe that. We didn't know you'd be here, remember. That's his unusual clothing, if he wears any."

"Sometimes you don't let him?"

"He's very proud of those outfits that Sven gave him. It can be a subtle, but very effective, means of punishment to deny them to him."

"Was he really bruised?"

"You're still on that? Yes, of course he was."

"Just because you wanted him to be?"

"Marc, we've been through these issues many times. It's no different simply because you know who it is. Just because this isn't one of my stories doesn't change anything. There are times when I find it beautiful to put him through an…endurance. There are other times when he needs correction. Either of those—and perhaps still other circumstances—could lead to punishment.

"But I'm tired of this. I want to know about you."

"Me? What about me?"

"What do you want? Really, Marc, what is it that you want? What made you come back here? You didn't have to. You could have just phoned if you were concerned with Tim's well-being. There was no need for you to actually visit."

Tim came in then. He was carrying a tray. He poured and delivered the full cups of coffee to us. Then he sat at my feet. Marc stared at him. "You want me there. I know you want me there."

"I think you might want to be there, Marc." That's all I said. I could see Tim studying his old friend carefully.

"What do you think?" Marc suddenly asked Tim. "Do you think I want to be there?"

"I think you should find out if you like it. You've dreamed it. I know you have. Why don't you find out if this is right?"

"Are you sure it's right for you?" Marc asked.

"I'm more sure now than ever." Tim put his head against my knee. "I want this."

Marc stood up and went to a window. He wasn't looking toward us when he finally spoke. "I can't say I'll do it forever."

"A night," I answered. "Just take it seriously for one night. Join us. See if you can handle it."

"If I can handle it?" he spun around. "I can handle it."

"Then what's your problem?" I asked.

"I'm not sure. I'm frightened of it all."

"You can try it. I would normally never say that one night would be enough. But this is a unique situation. I know it must have been difficult for you to get here. I also know that Tim will be leaving in a few months. You were close once. I'm willing to show you more than you've been able to see so far about what's involved. If you'll enter into this one night understanding that Tim and I mean it to be in earnest."

Then Marc looked at Tim. "Will you help me?" I thought for a moment that Marc would cry. He had made some move he had been struggling against for years.

Tim stood up and went over and put his arms around his friend. "Of course, of course."

I had my glass of wine left. The two of them left to get Marc prepared. I sipped at the burgundy and threw my head back against the chair. I was going to have them both after all! I was going to have them both.

*   *   *

I was in bed, nude, waiting for them when they were done. Who knows what secrets they told each other? No master ever really knows what goes on in those private conversations. There must be talk about fear and envy, about anticipation and attempts to manipulate situations. Who knows what games they play? Some must have sex of some sort, if only foreplay with one another. Others must argue and fight. Getting rid of the discordance that a master would never allow to interfere with his pleasure. Those weren't my concerns at all.

The room was dimly lit. There was still another fireplace here and its flame provided most of the light. I was on the sheets of a king-sized poster bed I'd had constructed on commission. There was plenty of room here for anything that might take place.

But this wasn't really a night for theatrics. This wasn't one of the nights to create a circus. It was to be easy, I had decided. This would be Marc's lesson, his introduction that could lead to other, more intense occasions later on.

Marc seemed strangely shy when they finally walked into the bedroom. They were both naked. "Go to the other side and crawl in," Tim said softly.

They walked to opposite sides of the bed. When Tim was in place Marc put both knees on the surface and moved toward me. "Just follow my lead," Tim was whispering now that they were so close to me and to each other. "Just do what I do or tell you to."

He crawled over to me; Marc did the same. They both put their heads on my belly, just above my crotch. I felt first one, then another hand reach down and fondle my balls. "You have to remember that everything that can cause you pain can cause him pleasure," I could barely hear Tim talking now, his voice was so low. "Handle these carefully, they are something very important."

"Treat them well because he can make ours hurt?"

"Stop it, Marc, just let it happen, don't think everything through right away. Things will come. Just give him pleasure now. It's not something you're used to. None of us are really used to turning ourselves over to creating someone else's pleasure, especially not men. That's why we can be so special, we can overcome it all and do it."

Those were Sven's words. I had heard them when the Swede had been giving Tim his first lessons. I soon could feel the benefits of that education. Tim must have leaned further down first; the mouth that followed must have been Marc's. Both of them were licking my balls soon. Their hands were moving as well. It was as though it were a slightly out of tune duet. One part of one body would do something, and then, in a matter of seconds, the other body's same part would mimic the action.

I spread my legs for them as their hands explored underneath me and their fingers probed into the cleft of my ass. Then the mouths moved up along the sides of my inner thighs, and my hard cock was trapped between their faces. I could feel the hardness of their noses one minute and then the soft flesh of their cheeks the next.

Two warm, wet tongues now were moving very, very slowly up my stomach. "However fast you want to go, it's too fast," Tim whispered, speaking quickly so his tongue wasn't away from the surface of my body for any longer than necessary.

They moved further. There were two palms that were back on my balls now. Soon, any moment, there would be two hot mouths on my nipples. Tim wouldn't have dared tell Marc why they were taking so long. He could only have hazarded a hope that they were creating an erotic response in me. But there were age-old lessons in what Sven had taught him. They were more delicate and secret than the harsh rules of Tim's biker camp.

No, a slave couldn't always have protection from everything when he had his face between his master's legs. But the slave could please the master and be allowed to stay in the bed. There were always much less desirable activities a master could come up with if the sex play wasn't satisfactory. And there was always the possibility that he could find another favorite. These were time-honored lessons of every sexual slave. Tim knew them.

Then their soft mouths were on my nipples. I reached my hands out. Tim must have given Marc one of the most important lessons. On either side of me I found the matched sets of balls. The legs were spread far apart to make sure nothing could keep me from enjoying the feel of them. As soon as I reached them I found my first pleasant surprise: Marc's were shaven as smoothly as Tim's. That had been one reason their preparations had taken so long. I reached further to see if his anus had been shaven as well; it was. I could feel the tightly gathered skin of his hole, and I could sense his shivers as I ran a finger up and down the cleft to create the incomparable sensations that a slave receives when his nude hole is touched.

If this had been any night with any two men, I might have let that play go on for hours. It was utterly enjoyable to have them in my hands and to have their mouths working so erotically on my body. But this night had to be significant. I put my hands on their faces and pulled them off my chest, lifting them up to my own. We all kissed at once. Tim's posture was so much more learned, even after his short training. He had so naturally understood the reasons for so many things that many lessons had come intuitively. His kisses to me were on my cheek, my forehead, small little gestures that carried with them a whole vocabulary of submission.

Marc's were much less studied, and much more passionate. We kissed each other on the mouth; while Tim was moving around so quickly. Marc and I were exploring each other more intimately, perhaps as lovers would. But that was one possibility, that this was our chance to fall in love, and we both understood it.

Then I pushed them aside. Marc was immediately disoriented. His cock had leaked precome on my cover. I didn't care, but he seemed embarrassed as he looked at it. Then he made a movement that he instantly knew was ridiculous; he tried to cover his hard-on, the source of the dampness and the proof of his excitement. I gestured to Tim, and he slid off the side of the bed onto his feet.

I moved to get off the mattress. Tim quickly made way for me and was standing on the floor beside the bed. I waved to Marc to follow. By the time he'd gotten to the space between the fire and the bed where I'd gone, I was already opening the doors of a cabinet there. Tim stiffened when he saw me doing this. At another time it would have meant that he had failed to arouse me in the more gentle arena and it was his own fault that I was turning to this alternative.

Marc, of course, couldn't have known any of those intricacies. I found what I wanted and turned to Tim. "Show yourself."

He went into position at once. "This," I said for Marc's benefit, "is the way a slave displays himself to his master. His arms are behind his neck, leaving his chest and underarms open, exposed, vulnerable. His legs are spread far apart, he wants his cock, balls and anus to be easily accessible to the master. His head faces straight forward. He has no need to watch what's being done to him because he knows he will accept it in any event."

I moved toward Tim and reached up to his chest. I had a pair of clamps in my hand. I attached one to each of his nipples. They were extremely harsh, so painful I had usually kept them only for special punishment duty. But this would be a good lesson for

Marc. Tim's face grimaced when each of the two metal contraptions were attached. I quickly applied a small band of leather around the base of his balls after that. It was tight enough that it forced his testicles to strain against the very bottom of his sac.

"Look at him now. See how he's kept his position and how the slightest piece of chain and leather make him so much more attractive." I ran a hand across Tim's belly. He was already sweating from the exertion. There was a strong odor coming from under his arms, and his stomach was damp with perspiration.

"Look how much better he looks than you do." I swiveled to face Marc. "You're standing there awkwardly, your arms dangling at your sides, you don't know where to put your hands, your hard-on is embarrassing you. Why don't you copy him? Come on, Marc. Display yourself."

His movements were much slower than Tim's instant compliance, but he did it. He stared at me—not into the distance as he should have—but I appreciated the fear and excitement on his face so very much I didn't reprimand him.

When he was in position, with his fine arms over his head and so nicely stretched to show off his own muscles, I complimented him, "Don't you feel better now? More graceful? You are. You look much more handsome that way with all of your best features open for view. It's such a shame that men are always hiding those very things that would make them so appealing to others—their cocks, balls, the recess of their asses. And even their legs are so often covered that we can't appreciate them nearly as much as they deserve to be."

I walked up to him and ran the same hand over his body. His cock was still stiff and erect. I let my hand fall to his genitals and hold his newly shaven balls once more. Then I reached up and my finger traced the line of a thick blue vein from the base of his cock all the way down the shaft until it disappeared into the thick purple skin of the cockhead.

"Are you really ready?"

He nodded, his brow a mass of wrinkles. He seemed amazed he was here and allowing this to happen. It might have been too much to demand that he say yes out loud. I had another pair of tit clamps in my free hand. I applied them to his erect nipples. They were much less severe than Tim's had. But, after all, he hadn't had Tim's training. The very idea of being in front of two other men and seeing his naked body adorned in that fashion was more than enough of a trial for him—at least for now. He sucked in his breath as each of the rubber-tipped machines bit into him. I also wrapped a band of leather around his balls.

Then I stood back. In the firelight they were extraordinarily handsome. Actual rivulets of sweat were running down Tim's sides now. Those clamps were very harsh and the physical response was all I had hoped from him. I loved watching him in all of his tests of endurance. When Sven had been here and he had entered into a full-blown case of hero-worship of the big Swede, Tim had vowed to never say no and to never plea for escape. Sven hadn't; he wouldn't. Now, the fact that Marc was here and witnessing him reproduced the same pride in him.

"I never asked," I finally began, "when you two were together, who fucked whom?"

They were both taken back by the question. Marc finally answered, "Tim usually did it to me, but not always."

"Then we should have a new start, don't you think?"

Neither one of them spoke; they didn't dare. I moved back to the cabinet and pulled out a few more things. I moved over to Marc, and, after I put down a bottle of lubricant on a nearby surface where I'd be able to reach it easily, I opened the condom wrapper that I had retrieved. I started to talk to Tim. "This will be good, don't you think? To show him how well you've learned to be fucked? You didn't do it very handsomely when you first came here, not at all. But Sven helped, didn't he?"

"Yes…, sir."

"Tell him."

I started to unravel the condom over the length of Marc's cock while Tim's voice struggled to tell the story. "Sven would be beside me while I was getting fucked by Master. He would talk to me, whisper in my ear all the secrets of how to do it the right way. I'd follow all of his instructions."

"Just the way you did when he told you how to suck cock?"

"Yes, sir."

"And other things he told you?"

"All the other things he told me. He would be beside me while Master did…whatever he wanted and he would show me how to give Master the most pleasure possible while they were happening."

The condom was covering Marc's erection now. "You get to see the benefits of all that education. Follow me, keep your hands up high and your legs spread. I'll do the work for you."

I led the one naked man over to a position where he was standing behind the first. I put my hand on Tim's neck and guided it downward. "Look how beautiful a slave can be. His legs are so far apart and now he's leaning over at his waist. There's nothing that could possibly interfere with anyone who wanted to have a good fuck from him."

I ran a hand over Tim's ass and could feel the way the skin was stretched tautly by the unusual but graceful position. "He is more muscular now, isn't he? He must have gained at least fifteen pounds in these few months, all of it hard and well-proportioned."

I took hold of Marc's sheathed cock and pulled him the few inches forward until the tip made contact with the bunched brown skin of Tim's anus. Then I reached and got the lubricant. I poured some of the grease over the condom and then used the residue to slip into the tight, hot pocket of Tim's ass.

"You'll be amazed by how well he's learned this," I said to Marc. Then I pushed him forward until his cock was gripped by the heated muscles. "He's taking hold of you," I explained. "He's been taught not to fight you, but to let you in and then to clamp down to make sure you have the most intense sensation. Now, pull back, just a little." Marc did as I told him to.

"Stand still. He's been trained to do the fucking if you want, haven't you, Tim?"

"Yes, sir." His voice was strained from the sex and the tension of leaning over. But he began to move back and forth, letting his anus hold on to Marc's cock just at the head and then pushing backward to have the whole length of it slide in until Marc's pubic hair was pushing against the shaven area right around his hole.

"Slowly, Tim, slowly, let Marc understand what it must be like."

Tim groaned, I wasn't sure if it was frustration or agony. But he made his motions even more languid. I looked at Marc. "Don't change a thing," I said. "Don't grab hold of him or try to make it go faster. Don't do anything but enjoy what's happening. Then try to think of yourself on the other end. Think what it would be like to be bending over on command and having some other man's condom-covered cock up your ass. But don't think of it in terms of pain or humiliation, think of how you could make it better for him."

I moved around until I was standing in front of Tim. His hips were still moving back and forth with exquisite slowness. I took another condom and rolled it out onto my erection. Without needing to be told, Tim opened his mouth. "He's trained not to do anything but be ready," I explained to Marc. "It's not his place to decide to suck it; it's only his purpose to prepare himself in case I want him to."

Then I lunged forward, and the length of my cock went down Tim's willing mouth. "This is his reward," I said as I allowed Tim's motions move his head up and down my cock as his hips moved back and forth to take Marc's shaft. "He's waited for this since the moment he saw you walking onto the lawn."

I felt my orgasm approaching, but I didn't want it so soon. I pulled my latex-covered cock out of Tim's mouth. He moaned again. A part of it must have been simply from the exertion, but it was just as much the hurt of having my body taken away from him.

I moved over to Marc and gently put my hands on his waist. I pulled him back until he understood that I wanted him to stop fucking. He looked at me with a confused and regretful expression, but complied.

"Get back in position, both of you." They did. Now with the activity stopped, Tim was left only with the tight and torturous bite of the clamps on his nipples. He looked down at them, helpless and clearly in pain. I reached over and lifted up the chain that connected the two metal devices. The simple act of removing even a slight amount of the tension created a wave of agony so great that his knees actually seemed to buckle slightly and the groan that roared out of his chest was certainly honest.

His hands involuntarily jerked off the back of his neck and would have moved to stop me if he hadn't stopped himself quickly. He was embarrassed, ashamed that he'd cracked even slightly. The arms were securely positioned again without my having to have to say anything. We stared at one another. I watched his resolve take a firm hold once more.

I put a hand on his cheek, and he reached down to run his tongue over the surface of my palm. He closed his eyes. His own imagination was transforming the actions back into the romance that he so fervently wanted.

I turned to Marc. For the first time he seemed to want to offer something. It seemed that he lifted up his chest. He expected me to play with his nipples as well, and he was telling me that he was prepared.

I went behind him and ran a hand over the firm ass. Unlike Tim, whose body hair included a cover over his buttocks, Marc's rear was smooth, almost silky to my touch. He tried too hard. Thinking my touch was a command, he bent over as though he assumed he was the next one to get fucked.

"No, no," I said softly, drawing him back up to a standing position. "I want to show you more of what Tim's learned."

I kissed him on the side of his face and raked my fingers through his hair. Then I returned to Tim.

There were tears forming at the corners of his eyes. The sensations on his nipples must have come close to unbearable by now. "Please," he whispered.

"Do you think this is all that might happen to you in The Network?" I mocked. "You want to be sold, to live in that world, and you're concerned about a little pressure on your tits? Perhaps you're not as ready as I had thought."

"I am." He drew upon whatever strength he still had.

"You just want me to make it easier and shackle you, so you don't have to use your own resources to maintain your posture. That's so easy for all of you, to have bondage remove your options, to have your hands and feet tied so you can believe things are being done to you without your complicity."

He blushed. He wouldn't have known this shame three months ago, but he did now. The lessons had taken hold wonderfully. This particular one was done. There was no need to continue with it. I took hold of each of the two clamps and removed them at once.

Tim couldn't restrain himself now. He doubled over with the sudden rush of blood into the restricted flesh. He cried out in pain. I listened while he struggled to regain control of his breathing. As soon as he had, he began to straighten out, but, in the middle of the motion, he kissed the side of my neck—a small and beautiful gesture to ask my forgiveness.

"Go to Marc, show him your abilities with your tongue."

I didn't have to be explicit. He knew I was encouraging some creativity now. He moved over to where the other man still stood with only the easier clamps and the leather strap on his body. Tim knelt with a fine grace. He moved to the floor in one fluid gesture. As he'd been taught, he left his legs wide apart. He bent over even further, and I could see his lips touch the top of Marc's feet.

Then the small pink tongue came out and began to wash the surface of the skin. Slowly, he moved up Marc's legs. He came to the two testicles that were drawn up tightly against Marc's underbelly after minutes of careful progress. Then he lifted first one, then the other up with his tongue, washing each of them with long laps that left a covering of his spit on the sac.

Marc was responding to the attention. His cock was rampant again. Small drops of liquid oozed from the slit. I put a finger there and gathered some up, feeling the viscous stuff.

"You could be down there," I said quietly. "If you stay, you'll be down there for a long, long time. Just as he has been." I played with Marc's nipples then, teasing the clamps with slightly more pressure, lifting their chain, tugging at them slightly. It was all I did, just that. It was all Marc was feeling along with Tim's tongue on his balls. But it was enough.

Marc shot pulsing waves of come out of his cock and onto Tim's hair. The white ooze sank into my kneeling slave's long locks and darkened them where it had landed.

I stood back and looked directly into Marc's eyes. "You weren't given permission to do that."

I will always treasure the memory of Marc's face. It was swept up into an orgy of fear and anticipation. It was the most handsome moment of his life.

An Idea Takes Hold

I was vaguely aware of Tim's movements the next morning as he slipped out from under the covers. He left the room to go downstairs to begin his day. But this time I wasn't left alone. There was still Marc.

I reached over and wrapped one arm over the top of the young man. He initially tried to push me away. He must have still been deep in sleep. But he seemed to suddenly remember where he was and what had happened last night. His stiffened body relaxed suddenly, letting my arm pull him close to me.

I slipped my other arm underneath him to make my hold on him even more secure. He didn't resist. In fact, he moved closer to me. I was facing his back, and now I could feel the whole of its broad expanse against my front. His hard, round buttocks pushed against my crotch and let my erection nest in the cleft of his ass.

My fingers moved and found his nipples. They were raw from the night before. I only had to graze them to get a quick response. But, as he'd proven last night, Marc was not going to quit. He melted back into my arms, refusing to let the physical discomfort of his nipples keep him from my body.

I only had to remember the red stripes that would still be there on his ass to have my cock go from enjoying itself to needing release. I let it slip and slide up and down the crack of Marc's ass. The smooth, shaved skin was satin-soft. I could feel the natural hairlessness of Marc's chest and the results of last night's play on his scabbed nipples, and I was driven on toward orgasm.

Driven. That's the only word I could possibly use. I rolled my hips back and forth to use my cock's foreskin to let me glide over his ass and then, in a short time, I shot a load of come onto the crevice. I sank onto my back, slowly extricating my arms from his body.

He turned over on his side to face me. He had a hurt look on his face. Before he could say anything, Tim appeared in the doorway with a single cup of coffee in his hand. He put it on the stand by the bed.

He was still naked. His cock was hard as well. I could see the puffed flesh of his chest where those clamps had so viciously bitten him last night. I could also see the stripes on his hips and thighs where the lash had attacked.

I smiled as I thought all that: *...those clamps had so viciously bitten him, ...the lash had attacked.* No, no, they hadn't. Those were inadequate descriptions. I had done it. *I had made love to him last night?* No, that didn't work well either. The language was simply too limited to be able to express the reality.

I stopped worrying and took the cup. While I sipped it, I used my other hand to draw Marc in close to me. I directed his head to the closer of my own nipples, and he obediently began to suck. Tim was looking down at the scene, his cock still erect. He obviously wanted something to help him relieve that pressure. Marc too evidently wanted something: His cock was stiff now as it pressed against my thigh.

I pushed Marc away and took more of the coffee. "You'll learn to live with that." He didn't understand, I could see it in his eyes. "The burden of the slave is his erection; the thing that makes his master all the more awesome is the control he has over it. You'll learn that your sexual pleasure is the least of my concerns, other than in its usefulness as a means of rewarding — or punishing — you."

I sat up and my movements pushed the covers down further. Marc looked down at his hard cock as though it was something foreign now. He was studying it, but also understanding that he could do nothing to it — if he wanted to stay. But that hadn't been decided.

I gestured for Tim to get back into the bed with us. He approached cautiously. He knew after last night that Marc's presence didn't mean that there would be any lessening of discipline in the house. In fact, he had good reason to suspect that I was enforcing it even more as an example to his old roommate.

But he did climb on top of the sheets and moved quickly up against me. I sat there with both of them and their hard cocks pressing on my flesh. This was my moment, more, in its own way, than last night had been.

I finished the coffee and put the empty cup down. I ruffled both their heads, messing their hair and embracing them even more. We laid there silently for a moment while I luxuriated in the feel of it all.

"What will we do today?" I finally asked. Marc didn't speak or move. Tim nuzzled closer, his face burrowed in the space between my arm and chest.

"What do you usually do now?" Marc asked.

"Tim would make breakfast. Then, perhaps, we'd play a bit, try out a new toy, maybe I'd want to have sex again." Tim's body reacted to the simple statement: ...*try out a new toy* had nothing to do with innocent recreation. I was sure Marc understood that.

"Then, there'd be work to do. The house, the yard, whatever, while I went about the business I needed to attend to. Lunch would follow. A nap — usually together." Tim actually relaxed when I spoke now. Those naps were always among the most gentle times for him. When, for whatever reason, they hadn't been shared between us, they were something that he and Sven could have together.

"There might be shopping in the afternoon, or more work. There'd be dinner to prepare, then eat. Finally reading, perhaps a movie on the video machine. In there, as often as not, there'd be another opportunity to have sex, of some kind."

" 'Of some kind,' " Marc said, lifting his head up and looking back and forth between Tim and myself. I think that was the first moment that he had actually noticed the marks on Tim's buttocks. He reached over and ran his fingers over the skin.

"What do you think of them?" I asked.

He pursed his lips, and then he reached across my body and put a series of small kisses on the red welts. He placed the side of his head on one of Tim's firm asscheeks. "I don't know how you can do it. Just this way."

The three of us were now all touching one another. I had the warm weight of Marc leaning over the middle of my body, his cock was caught pressing against my side. Tim was facing me. "I think that's a very silly question given the circumstances. This is possibly the most enjoyable way to do it I can imagine."

"But it's so ordinary," Marc whispered. "It's not theatrical, it's not anything unusual."

"What do you mean?"

"If…if we were in the city, at one of the leather bars that Tim and I used to go to, and you were in leather…if it was a trip, a night, a trick…that I can understand. But this is so complete. There's no relief from this.

"Last night…" He faltered even more now than he did when he had been struggling to get the words out just before, and there was an excruciating moment while he tried to get his speech back. "Last night was all those things that you read about. There was the excitement and the sense that it could happen because it was going to end. I was going to wake up this morning, and I'd just be able to put on my clothes and leave.

"Maybe we'd have something to eat together. And, like the other times, we wouldn't talk about anything, we'd make believe it didn't really happen the night before, not that way."

" 'Like the other times?' " I asked the question, but Tim had lifted his head up sharply when he heard that.

"I told you I've been running. But not always in one direction. I've been to New York, trying to see what this was all about, what it was that Tim would leave everything so as to have it. And what it was that it would make me so crazy, having dreams about it.

"I did it the other way — with handsome men in uniforms and leather costumes. They weren't like this. It was never the same waking up the way it was this morning, with you just taking it all up again and Tim never leaving the role. It was always different. I could handle it so much more easily.

"It was as though I was an actor in a play. No one really expected me to continue the role when the curtain came down. Sometimes that meant that I had to follow through or play along until I left the physical apartment. There were some people — couples mostly — where they'd be a little bit like you and Tim in the morning. But I would already know that it was either a scene being strung out for my benefit or else just a longer trick than usual. Some men would do it for a night, some for a weekend. That all made sense to me."

"Why?" I asked.

"Because it made the sex better, more. It made everything so intense." He moved up, off of Tim, and laid his body onto mine. His arms went around my shoulders, and his head rested on my chest now. "But I was only having sex with their roles. Never them. You want me to do it with you and then wake up and discover that going to work, making a meal, even watching television is a continuation of it.

"I don't think I can do this."

Tim reached up and put his arm around Marc's middle. I could see him squeeze slightly to give his old friend a fraternal show of confidence. Marc looked over at him. Then he remembered something. He turned to me." Can I ask him some questions?"

I nodded, almost amused that he was taking rules so seriously in the middle of his unsure place.

"Why do you want to go to The Network instead of staying here? What's the difference?"

Tim thought for a moment, "I want the adventure of it. I don't have any better answer than that. I might end up in a household just like this one, I know that. I might end up doing nothing more than I do now. But it will be with a different person, and I know it will mean I'll learn something different just for that reason. It'll mean I'll have taken a greater risk. And it means that I can't retreat into the familiarity of this place.

"There's always the fact that this is near my home. This is the place I grew up. I want to stretch something in my life."

"You see, that's one of the problems. It was so hard to come here yesterday because this is all so familiar. It's where I live too. Last night, with the fireplace going and the strange light and the careful way you two did everything, I could suspend everything and make believe I was in one of those tricks' 'dungeons' in New York. But now it's morning, and out there is the pond where I used to go swimming every day. I don't know if I can just change everything so much that I can forget that."

"You want a curtain?" I asked Marc seriously. "You want a way to make a transition?" He nodded. "But you've been doing this exploration in the cities. Wasn't that enough?"

"No. It was with strangers, and they aren't the same as you two. Even now, I'm going to have to go through watching Tim again this morning doing all those things in those ways. It's more…it's more everything — dangerous, frightening, strange… ."

"Do you want a curtain to help you with the two of us or do you want it so you don't have to face it — really face it?"

"'It?'" he asked. "I'm not even sure what 'it' is when you talk that way."

"Tim's going to leave. You and I will stay here. You could stay with me alone. There are so many ways that you make it sound as though you want to. I want it as well. We could, if you're willing, construct our own contract. I could put you through college. You want it; I can provide it."

"And I could become like Sven?" His voice was so distant sounding that I couldn't decipher the cause. Was he picturing a dream or was he having flashes of a nightmare?

"Sven didn't know what he was going to do when he started, at least he claims he didn't. Tim doesn't know what he'll choose to do after his contract with The Network is done, either. I don't need to know what your next decision will be when we might be done."

"Oh, that's not true." Marc burrowed his face into my flesh again, then rested it on my shoulder. "You want me to stay here for a long, long time. You'll do everything you can to keep me here. Tim is a project. You're like me, actually. The theatrics are easy for you, and you enjoy your little trips with your friends in The Network a lot. You've had a great time with Tim here, doing the training and all the structuring and having the bodybuilder come. But you want something different from me, I can tell that.

"Not just that you want me to stay. But you're going to want…more. What is that?"

I didn't want to talk about these things now. Nor did I want to lose Marc. I'd waited too long to reenter this world, and I'd overlooked his potential for too many years. But there was a way.

"I'll give you a chance to have your ritual, your curtain. We'll give you a transition. It can be quite easy. I'd already thought about going away soon. You haven't any commitments, you've said that clearly enough. You've lost your job, and you never registered for school. Then you can't have any reason to stay here.

"We'll go somewhere else. Not to the cities you've already been to where the way you did things was to 'trick,' as you put it. I loathe that word, the way it demeans the sexual exchanges that

men have with one another. I don't want to simply transpose us
on to that. But we'll go away. You can try it on with an audience
— that will scare you, but at least the audience will be made up
of strangers and you can deal with the eyes looking at you without needing to face ones you already know — at least this time."

"A trial?" Marc asked.

"Not in any usual sense," I responded. "A 'transition,' that's a
much better way to put it, I think. A way to begin."

"But I told you that I don't think I can do this," he complained.
"I really don't know…"

"I know that if we stay here and think about it, you'll never be
able to. But if we go to a different place, then you can see your
strengths and you can test your desires. It's the best way."

He didn't argue anymore. He and Tim were quiet now, their
hard cocks were both leaking onto my skin and both of them —
not possibly knowing that each was doing it — began to rock
their bodies against mine. The idea had taken hold.

Moving Into the Arena

Any comparison between the art of modern sexual slavery and the institutions of slavery in history is dangerous. Those ancient forms carry with them implications that do damage to the facile creativity engaged in by the people of the sexual underground.

But there are moments when a parallel asserts itself and can inform and entertain us. One of those occurred to me as the three of us were walking down a crowded street in the Southern beach resort two days later.

I imagined a vanquished barbarian giving his allegiance to a Greek conqueror in ancient times. It probably had been something very difficult for him to do; it may well be beyond our ability to comprehend the humiliation he suffered. His life had been spared on the battlefield. He must have thought that he was the one who was to blame for the fact that he lived. He hadn't fought hard enough to join his comrades in whatever heaven they believed in.

So, he had no choice but to give himself to his new lord as a slave. There was bitter defeat in the act of bowing to his new master. But it was his fate. There, on his knees before an arrogant Greek, he might even have thought that this was his due. His tribe had been bested by other warriors. It must be that their gods wanted this new power to rise over them.

There could have been a certain nobility in all that. His master was the better on the battlefield. And, to the ancients, that meant he was a better man. The chains that the newly enslaved barbarian wore were made — in his mind — of the same metal as his lord's sword. *So be it,* he might have thought.

I had not conquered Tim and Marc. I had simply allowed them to enter a certain world. But in our mountain retreat they had seen only the slavery that existed between myself and them. They had only seen their Greek lord in his armor.

But the barbarian slave, after his moments of grace in defeat, would eventually have to be taken to market. He would have to walk through the crowds of housewives and peasants who would gawk at him and make jokes. No longer only submitting before a military hero, he would find that he was possibly going to be sold to a lowly merchant and would find his slavery not the payment of his debt to his physical better, but a cruel twist of fate that made him into a shackled clerk.

I envisioned that as Marc and Tim's predicament as we made our way through the crowds. This was the bazaar where the warriors were displayed to the soft and unworthy civilians. My two slaves in their finery, with their handsome uniforms, were only two more males who were available to anyone who wanted to look at them.

Marc had wanted this transition, and I was giving it to him. I only hoped he'd see how tawdry this alternative was and, instead, learn to love the intensity that could be created with a certain elegance in our mountain retreat.

I had decided to underscore the dramatics of it all to the two young men as soon as we had arrived. After we had checked into our guest house, I had taken them immediately to one of the leather stores that line the main street. Here the office workers from cold Northern cities and the timid souls from the Midwest towns who would never dream of entering the world of sexual creativity went on a vacation binge and bought themselves outfits that they would never have worn at home.

It had been perfect for my purposes. Instead of the exquisite loincloths that Sven had made for him, I had Tim dressed in a factory-made costume. The same for Marc who, as a result of his own request, was now wearing the uniform of the urban male on the quest for the perfect trick. That phrase was a contradiction in terms. But that would never be understood by someone who didn't realize that spontaneous moments can never equal the results of years of learning and the accretion of years of another man's mastery.

They had on typical black leather boots, the ones that people suppose bikers wear. I imagined that Tim was able to remember back and realize that not one of his old friends would ever have had anything on his feet that had the polish his had at this moment. They also had shiny black leather chaps to cover their old blue jeans. The chaps did have a purpose: They outlined the crotches in front and the asses in back, forcing the eye to recognize the superb bunches of flesh in both places.

Of course, when I saw those gathered and displayed sections of a male's body, I understood the possibilities they held in a different way than most other people. I could see the men who watched my handsome young charges walk down the street. Those faces had all the marks of desperate desire—but desire to suck the fat cocks that Marc and Tim displayed or to touch the firm asses. The more...subtle options of the lash and tight rawhide bindings weren't so obvious to others.

I led them into one of the many gay bars. It had advertised itself as "leather." As soon as we walked in, the early afternoon crowd paid immediate attention. Before they even were aware of the young men's attractiveness, they saw their T-shirts. I had bought them at the same store as their chaps. The shirts were black. In bold print across their chests was white block lettering that spelled out: SLAVE.

The ancient barbarian would have had to carry some public identification of his status — his chains or his collar would have made his humiliating slavery obvious in the crowded bazaar. Why should these two have any less obvious display of their status?

If they noticed the stares, Marc and Tim didn't give any indication of it. I sent Marc off to buy us cold drinks. As he went I was certainly aware that both of them were humbled. But not just by this situation. The time in the shop had scared them so much more that they hadn't overcome it yet.

There had been the two clerks, first of all. They'd been large, muscular men who gave off an extremely strong odor — the mixture of their own perspiration and the smell of the leather that had been sticking to their flesh for the whole warm and humid day. They'd eyed Marc and Tim openly, sizing up their bodies and their sexual potential.

As soon as I began to give the orders and make the judgments, the two brawny clerks caught on to what was happening and spent the rest of the time they waited on us rubbing in the degradation I encouraged. They'd felt up the two younger men's bodies, openly grabbing their cocks and balls and slapping their asses. They would make the most debasing comments when clothes were tried on — T-shirts since they claimed the normal size wouldn't let anyone get a good look at the sharp points of the slaves' tits. Those two men knew perfectly well how those nipples had been developed.

Marc and Tim had been so shaken by the rough manner of the two other men that I wondered just how I was going to arrange a situation where they would have to submit to even more from them. The lessons were certainly valuable for both. They weren't used to seeing just how vulnerable their status made them. They had gotten over their inhibitions about my studying them, and they had learned to expect me to comment on even the most intimate details of their bodies and clothing. But to have a stranger make an evaluation of the curves of their asses or the adequacy of their cock size was a sudden shock to both.

When Marc had brought back our drinks, the three of us stood against a wall and surveyed the crowd. "If I were to give you away, which one here would you want to have fuck you?" I asked Marc.

He was startled at first. "Give me away?"

"I certainly will have that right, you know."

He looked around the group and finally pointed to one man about his own age who was obviously looking back. "Him."

"Why?"

"Because…" He had no good reason.

"You're only picking out the one who's the most attractive in the most usual sense," I said. "You shouldn't settle for that." I made my own quick evaluation. "Him over there in the corner, the one with the jeans with the holes in them, that's the one you should have chosen."

"Yes," Tim agreed.

I was amused by that. "And just why?"

"Look at his balls, they're hanging far down his left thigh. And the keys, there's a bunch of them hanging on his left. He has a belly — there's no denying that. But those balls have been through things, you can tell. And the keys may not mean he'll be like you, but at least he knows what he wants, and what he wants is just the thing that I'd probably want to give him."

"Good answer." The man had the appearance of someone who had, in fact, been around a good deal. His face was older than mine, and his hair wasn't very well-taken care of. But there was also bulk in his arms; the stomach that protruded over his belt line would be solid and firm. There was also a look about him. It was one that said he was hungry, so hungry that I was quite sure I would have had the best luck with him, not either one of my keeps. But I wouldn't destroy their illusion so quickly. They would learn soon enough that it was difficult to find someone who was naturally inclined to be on top.

Various men would come up to us and talk. I'd banter with them, but Marc and Tim were under strict discipline. They knew better than to speak without my permission. Eventually, each of the visitors would pick up the intensity of what was passing between us and would retreat, almost as if burned by us. There would be an occasional rude comment about us, or about me. That always was a simple display of jealousy, and I reacted to it as such.

I was ready to go back to the guest house when the two men from the leather shop came in. I nodded to them and smiled. They came over and joined us after stopping at the bar. They had extra drinks for us in their hands. "This is what Mike told us you were drinking," one of them said as he handed the glasses around.

"Thank you." I was the only one who spoke. That brought a smirk from the first clerk, the one who had carried the drinks.

"I'm Sam; this is Joseph," he said. I shook their hands. They had picked up enough to realize that they shouldn't exchange the greeting with the other two. Marc and Tim simply became more uncomfortable and shifted nervously on their feet.

We passed small talk that gave Sam and Joseph enough time to continue the minute examination of the two SLAVE-shirted males beside me. Joseph seemed to understand the most. While we talked he would run a hand across one or another of the two in a casual manner, simply testing their flesh.

I liked the two of them. They turned out to own the store together. They had another one in a different resort where the season was complementary to here. They made their lives traveling between one of the tourist spots and the other.

They were older than Marc and Tim. I guessed them to be more than thirty. They were taller as well, each of them at least my own six feet. Sam had balding hair that looked attractive on him, especially with the thick black mustache over his mouth. He was wearing a worn leather vest over an athletic T-shirt. There was a piece of rawhide gathered on his left side and tied to one of his belt loops. Another was tied across his firm left biceps. His jeans were even more worn than the vest. While there was no rip, yet, the crotch was worn nearly white and the seat of his pants showed bare threads.

Joseph was blond. He, too, wore a mustache. His skin was a dark tan from the constant sun his seasonal travels allowed him to indulge in. His muscles were even more developed than Sam's; Joseph had put more time into his body and had been rewarded with larger results. His clothing was essentially the same as Sam's, though the jeans were less worn and the vest newer. The shirt was light enough that I could make out small rings decorating his pierced tits. He also had the length of rawhide on his right biceps. Since the arm was bigger, the effect was even more impressive. I felt myself respond to him.

I enjoyed talking to the two new people. I enjoyed the effect they had on Marc and Tim even more. They had reacted so strongly to Sam and Joseph in the store that they had probably been relieved when I had brought them to the bar. To find their tormentors standing here, as well, created major anxiety. They moved from foot to foot and their eyes darted crazily as they tried to gauge if there was any danger here — was I going to create a scene that they'd have to endure?

I decided to play on it. I told Marc and Tim to go back to the guest house. I would meet them there later. I wanted to go to lunch at another bar and invited Sam and Joseph to come with me as my guests.

The two young men who moved quickly to follow my directions were very nervous—so nervous that deep and loud masculine laughs from the leather storekeepers followed them out the door.

They were waiting in the room when I returned after my meal. They were naked, as they had been told to be once they were inside the closed door. They looked at me with apparent dread. They were still concerned with Sam and Joseph and what we might have planned. At least now they had reason to be.

"I want to show you off at the pool. Put on your briefs." They jumped up and got their swimming suits. They had pulled them on and were waiting for me while I was still undressing. I pulled on my own suit and then turned to look at them. "No, that's not enough of a display."

Neither one spoke. Marc put his arms around his chest; even though it was very hot in the nearly tropical climate, he looked as though he was shivering. I went to my suitcase and pulled out two rawhide strings. I sat on the edge of the bed and waved them over to me.

When they were standing in front of me, I pulled down both their briefs. They both were getting the start of an erection in response to the rude nudity of having their swimming suits caught on their knees.

I took one of the pieces of rawhide and weaved an extravagant web around Marc's cock and balls. It not only separated each testicle from the other, it wrapped around to create another separation between the cock and balls. The package trapped the blood that had flowed to his cock, leaving him with a partial hard-on that wasn't going to go away for a long time.

I repeated my handiwork on Tim. When I was done, I insisted on pulling up their briefs myself, not even allowing them the self-sufficiency of doing it themselves. The result was a much larger and more prominent bulge in the cup of the suits. Both their cocks were forced up and to a side, the half-engorged heads were easily seen through the stretch fabric. Anyone whose eye was at all trained would also be able to see the evidence of the rawhide around the clearly discernible balls as well.

Now, I told them, we were ready for their public. That phrase hung in the air as we went downstairs and found a place on the patio around the guest house pool. I took a long chaise lounge and Tim and Marc found inflatable cushions they could bring over and spread on the stone surface nearby.

When I had Tim go and get drinks from the poolside bar, he used the errand as an excuse to pose a question. "What did you mean, 'ready for our public?' "

"Well, since you are going to give a performance tomorrow evening, I thought it was only right that you should get used to the idea of being on more intimate display than you have been."

"Please," Tim was being very careful to word this correctly, "what do you mean when you say we're going to give a performance?"

"There's a very special AIDS benefit tomorrow evening at the leather bar. Sam and Joseph told me about it. It seems that what they call the leather community here has come up with a particular form of public service that will raise money."

"What is it?" Tim couldn't stand it when I stopped talking and had to ask more.

"A slave auction." I let that sink in while I sipped my drink. "It seems that the men of the community offered themselves up for bids. The money goes to the charity, and the high bidder is able to indulge in the services of the purchased man for the evening. It is an admirable thing — to raise money for the cause. It's also wonderful training. You will be going on the real block soon enough, and I thought you might as well get a sense of what it will be like and how you will react to it. Marc may never see those auction blocks. But he should be able to understand more what will be going on if he's had at least this experience.

"Of course, you'll both need more of a...costume to carry it off. But Sam and Joseph have agreed to help provide one for each of you. We're going to the store after dinner tomorrow night. They'll be waiting, and we'll get what we need then. Later, I'll get to present the two of you to the audience and see how well you can do at raising a good bid from the crowd."

"But this isn't The Network," Tim objected. He was right. I wasn't going to argue with him. This was, in a very real way, a desecration of The Network and all it stood for. It was making fun of the serious intentions that he had. But it was something they were going to do, I had decided that.

"Consider it an exercise in humiliation," I told him. I reached out and took one of his nipples in my hand. "You can never have too much of that, after all."

"It's cruel," he said.

I pinched the tit as hard as I could between my nails. "There are many things that are cruel." When I let go, he was still glaring at me. "Go take a swim," I said. "If your swimsuits are wet the other men will have a better look at your cocks. I want to study them while they watch you."

They moved more slowly than they ever had while they followed my instructions. But they did do it. They dove into the water and did laps up and down the cement pool. Around the edge there were dozens of eyes following as they made their trip back and forth. There was hunger in those eyes, and there was enormous envy. I wanted to go up to the men who were doing nothing but watch and tell them they were the ones who were keeping themselves from knowing what was going on in life. They were the only reasons that they were on the sidelines. These boys might not be available to them, but there were so many who were. If you would only dare to do what Marc and Tim had finally done, each in his own way: Take the chance, risk, ask for help in releasing whatever is inside. But instead, there was only the crowd of people who would always be the onlookers and never the actors.

An Interlude

The three of us swam and sunbathed for the rest of the afternoon. Marc and Tim got over their anxiety and reverted to their playful selves. They were freed by being here in the resort so far from home. Marc had been right, he was much more able to ease into the roles here than he would have been in New England.

Tim was reacting to it all as though it were a vacation. Yes, of course I would do things like tie that rawhide around his cock and balls and then leave it on while the heat of the sun shrank it and made the grip on his genitals even more tightly painful. But this was nothing compared to the highly ritualized life he had grown experienced to at home. There wasn't the constant labor, and there wasn't the omnipresent possibility of some elaborate new form of sexual pleasure that I might devise for myself.

They were also renewing their own relationship. Tim liked nothing more than to have another slave to play with. It made him feel infinitely better to have someone to share the pleasure and the pain. He rose to the occasion whenever Marc was within hearing, just as he had whenever Sven had been close by.

That wasn't a terribly unique form of slave mentality. It was a device that many used to turn their experiences into something of a bonding ritual with another bottom. *We can make it — together; I can do this if you help me…* . Those were only some of the ways that the motivation showed itself in Tim and in others.

There was just the fact that they had been close at one time and had been separated. They had both had adventures that I know they were talking about together in ways they would rather not with me. There would be silly things that had happened to Marc in his trips to the city that he wouldn't want me to hear. And Tim would have his secret moments that he'd want to tell Marc about.

They would go into the pool, get money from me to buy a drink, sit just far enough away from me to be able to claim they were within distance to hear any request, but they would actually be beyond my ability to hear their whispers.

Through the whole afternoon their cocks were clear in their briefs and their balls pressed against the fabric. I entertained myself and the onlookers by having them occasionally come and rub lotion on my body. The guest house was gay, and I could take certain liberties here without any possible problem. My hand could rest on one of my young men's thighs, pinch a nipple, or feel a hard stomach.

I eventually took them back up to the room. My ideas for the slave auction and the sight of their near-naked bodies by the pool had gotten to me. With the slippery suntan lotion on our bodies. I had them climb on the bed. I dragged off their briefs and undid the rawhide. I was anxious for some play with them now; they'd had enough time with one another.

They were giggling and were more than willing to have something happen. I sent Tim off to get the condoms and lubricants from my bag.

"A nice start on a tan," I told Marc as I ran a hand on the white stripe around his middle. He was smiling at me with more than simply a hint of seduction.

I had taken off my own suit and stood in front of him with my half-hard cock near his face. He made a move toward it, expecting that the light manner I was using gave him that kind of permission. He might have been right, actually. That was certainly the signal I had given him. But I had better things in mind.

"Whoa!" I grabbed his head and kept him away from my cock. "A little more discipline here."

Before he understood what I was doing, I had taken a seat on the edge of the bed and was dragging his wonderful body across my lap. "Spread those legs!" I commanded. He stopped resisting then; the tone of my voice told him that I was getting more serious than he had realized. I reached over him and wrapped an arm around his midsection so I could grab hold of his cock and balls with it. His legs had obediently parted. I could see the whole inside of the crevice between his buttocks now with the small brown hole that had been shaved again that morning.

Tim was standing beside us with the things I had told him to get. "I think this one needs to remember his place better," I said to Tim. A broad smile came, and his fine white teeth showed.

I ran a palm over both of Marc's asscheeks. The young flesh was so rubbery and resilient. It was cool from the recent swim in the pool. "Do you expect me to be satisfied with a cold fuck?" I was using a prankish tone of voice. Tim only smiled more; Marc tightened his buttock muscles. He knew perfectly well what was coming.

I lifted up my hand and brought it down hard onto the waiting ass. The room echoed the loud slap. I hit again, on the other side this time. "Just a little warm-up," I said jovially. My hand went back in the air and slammed home again.

Marc was trying not to show the effect this was having on him, but he couldn't help but move his ass. He was only trying to find some way to avoid the full brunt of the spanking that he knew was going to continue, but the effect was the opposite. He looked as though he was rotating his bottom like a happy hustler, actually asking for the next one.

Tim laughed at that. I simply enjoyed looking at it for a moment and then went on, finding more and more tender little spots on Marc's fine ass to leave a good, red imprint. By the end of it he was gripping hold of my legs and hiding his face in the covers. I could see from the movements of his shoulders that he was beginning to cry. My hand was stinging from the use, and the surface of his buttocks was a uniform scarlet.

"Now, that's better," I said. I pushed him forward further on to the bed. He immediately separated his legs. The movement lifted up his midsection and the hairless anus was in perfect view again.

I crawled up between his thighs. My cock was hard. His own had been trapped by his upward motion and was pointing down, pressing from above by the mattress. Both his fine balls were stuck between his half erect cock and his body. I let my erection feel its way up and down his cleft. He shuddered when the tip of my shaft would run around his hole. But he certainly wasn't trying to escape it, not even a little bit.

"Get me ready," I told Tim.

The other young man moved over beside us. He reached in and took a careful hold of my cock. He unwrapped one of the condoms and used it to sheath my erection. He took the lubricant then and smeared the rubber with it.

I took my prepared cock and aimed it at Marc's ass. "This belongs to me now," I said, only half-aloud. "This is mine." I lunged forward, and my cock was quickly ensnared in the smooth and hot inner flesh. Marc lifted up his back as the intrusion was being completed.

I pumped easily and joyfully at the fine ass, its hairless surface was my personal aphrodisiac. I could see it as its muscles were pumped up by his resisting position. It was such a fine ass. To think that I was going to be able to have it whenever I wanted…how I wanted…the way I wanted.

Tim had moved closer. I looked at him as he studied my fucking movements. He put his head down near us. He had been the receiver of this cock often in the past few months, but it still seemed to amaze him as he watched. He'd done the same thing when I used to fuck Sven.

He reached over and put a hand on top of Marc's buttocks. He could graze my erection as it moved in and out of Marc. He moved it only slightly, just enough to be able to feel the fall of my balls when I would dive into Marc's anus. When I lifted up, my testicles would also lift up away from his touch.

He moved a little and studied my face then. He was staring deeply into my eyes, as though he wanted the answer to a puzzle. Why did I want to do this to Marc? And why would other men want to do it to him? I somehow understood the question, but there was only one answer that I could conceive of giving him. I leaned down and kissed him on the lips.

I fought against letting myself go. I wanted to continue the fucking for the entire night. But the pressures were building up. I lifted up away from Tim's mouth, but then leaned back again in a slightly different way. He understood what I wanted and his lips came up and sucked in the closer nipple. One of his hands moved to the other. I closed my eyes in something close to ecstasy and threw my head back as I felt my cock gripped by Marc and my chest being manipulated by Tim. I pumped more quickly and even more violently, letting my belly slam against Marc's upturned buttocks.

Finally I yelled out, and my cock seemed to send all of my body's fluids pulsing out of me and into the young man I had wanted for so long.

I collapsed on top of Marc. Tim moved to rub my back then. I let my erection subside. When it had, I pulled back my hips to let my cock escape from the hot hold of Marc's ass. I rolled off him to the edge of the bed.

Tim's cock was hard now. It was pointing straight up in the air. That was one of the things about it that I liked the most. It sometimes seemed as though it were flat against his belly when he was hard, even when he was standing.

I dragged him over to me. He seemed to expect that I was going to use my hand on him now. He went to assume the position to let me have that pleasure. But, instead, I stopped him. I sat him up on one of my knees. I took a nipple in my mouth and began to chew on it, just slightly. I took hold of his hard cock and began to pump it. He understood now what I was doing. I was simply going to masturbate him.

He responded by holding on to me tightly and pulling me against his neck. I could feel him kissing the top of my head. My one hand moved up and down the shaft and felt the drops of liquid that were escaping from the tip.

I have never been able to understand or communicate how much I adore men's cocks — that hard yet vulnerable flesh and the feel of the blood filling it up, the way their heads become so smooth-skinned when they're erect. I have always enjoyed the opportunity of having a young man climb up and let my hand grab his erection.

My ear was against Tim's chest, and I could hear the building rhythm of his breathing. I let go of his nipple just long enough to say, "Yes," giving him encouragement and permission to orgasm. The cadence increased, the quickness of the expansion and contraction of his lungs picked up, and then, in a moment that's always been miraculous to me, I felt the small geyser of come spill out onto my hand.

I looked up. His eyes were closed in his moment of relief. I kissed him. His eyes opened, and he smiled, then kissed me back on the forehead. "You're not nearly as terrible as you want to make us think you are."

"No," I said, "I'm worse. And I'll prove it." I was full of mock severity now. "Marc, get over here. It's time you had the same treatment." I tossed Tim aside with a playful move and dragged Marc on to my lap. He was stiff from the show we had put on and from his body's memory of the recent fucking. There was still heat coming from his abused buttocks. I could feel it when I had him sitting on my thigh. But that seemed a distant memory now. I took his cock and smiled at him. "I'm going to show you how terrible I am." Then I bit lightly on his chest and started to pump his cock just as I had Tim's.

The Unexpected

Marc and Tim had hated the second visit to the leather store the next day. Sam and Joseph had been unrelenting in the attention they had paid the two younger men. Their hands had explored with even more audacity than they had the other day; after all, this time they had my explicit permission, and it was also clearer just how much Marc and Tim had agreed to this sexual slavery.

The smiles that I'd gotten after the small bout of fucking and masturbation the previous afternoon were gone. So were the memories of Marc sliding against my body that night and being allowed to rub himself to orgasm on my side while we shared the double bed. I had been affectionate to Tim the next morning and had not only shaved his ass for him myself after his shower, but had taken the opportunity to explore that opening with my fingers and let him jerk off into the shower stall.

All those kindnesses were faint recollections in just a few hours. Instead I only had pouts and hurt looks. I decided to let them have their moment. I looked at the pile of purchases and borrowed merchandise we had gotten from the store and thought that the result would much more than adequately compensate for an afternoon by the side of the pool spent with sullen slave boys.

They hated the idea of the auction, and the things that we'd gotten only made them loathe it more. As the hour approached, they retreated further and further into their individual minds. Too bad, I realized, because if they would have talked about it and if Tim had found that strength he always found when he shared an

ordeal with another slave, they would have had a much easier time
of it. If they wanted to forget all those learnings, it was not my
problem.

Their petulance was almost amusing in the afternoon. In our
room, while we were showering away the lotions and the heat of
the sun, it became slightly annoying. I felt, at one point, like taking
a belt to them and clearing the air. But I should never have underestimated the minds of slaves. They solved the problem in their own
way, and they did it without even being aware of how it happened.

I had dressed for dinner and was sitting with a cigarette and a
cold drink while they were moving through the room. They
weren't under the strictest discipline, and I was allowing them to
have small conversations. They would ask one another where a
piece of clothing was, could Marc borrow a shirt of Tim's? That
kind of roommate inquiry was flying around the small suite.

The auction wasn't until midnight. We were going to a fine
restaurant that Joseph had recommended for dinner first. They
were being allowed to leave the leather chaps and the SLAVE shirts
behind. The chance to wear "civilian" clothing was a treat, and
they were reacting to it just that way.

In the course of it all, the items in the black paper bags began
to be discussed. I hadn't gotten perfectly matched sets; there were
some discrepancies in the uniforms. Somehow their talk moved
from the color polo shirt each was wearing to which jockstrap
would suit whom better later in the evening.

"Don't you want the belt with those diamond shaped studs?"
Marc asked Tim at a certain point.

"I think it'd look better with that collar you wanted to wear."

I nearly missed the change in their attitude and almost broke in
to point out the simple reality that I would be choosing their outfits for the auction. But I barely caught hold of myself in time to
listen to the metamorphosis they were going through.

"Where can we put some of those chains? There are so many
of them." Marc was going through one of the bags.

"Around our boots, like Sam does?" Tim wondered.

"That'd be good."

They bantered on like that for a few minutes. It was time to go.
The three of us left the room and walked down the main street to
dinner. I ordered for us and listened as the conversation moved
even more into the evening's future events.

"I wonder how much money they're going to raise?" Tim asked. But he was really wondering how much he would bring at auction; it's the omnipresent concern of the slave to be sold. Who thinks he's worth how much?

"I know you'll get more than I will," Marc answered. He knew perfectly well what Tim was really saying.

"No, no," Tim responded. "I don't have your looks."

"But look at your body, they'll think you've been in a gym full-time for the whole past year."

Tim flexed an arm and studied it. "Gym? God, they should try just spending a week working at the house, and they could save a fortune in expenses." They both thought that was humorous.

The whole tone changed. I tried to bring them back to their anger and concern. "What if Sam or Joseph buys you?"

Tim looked down at his plate. "I figure you're probably going to give me to them anyway, the way you've become so friendly." He didn't like the idea, but the firmly disciplined Tim was in control now, the one who understood that he was going to be sold into The Network. I saw, then, the Tim who might even be looking forward to the experience of being handed over to a master who was not his choice. This was one of the adventures he had been looking forward to, after all. Wasn't it?

Marc seemed to expect the same fate. "You're going to be doing it to me often enough, I guess. I should get accustomed to it." There was my first real indication that he was assuming that this vacation was going to work as much as I was.

"I just wish you'd... I just understand more things now," Tim said.

"Like what?"

He was playing with his dinner now. Finally he answered, "This is so much...less than what happened between Sven and you and me, isn't it? It's...common. This is the stuff that regular people do. I don't like it, all the clothes, it's so much less exciting than wearing Sven's gifts. I know now that it's one of the things you've been trying to teach us.

"Sven made that stuff for me. They're a special gift from a man who is as much my teacher in a way as you are. They're like a graduation gift. I hated them at first, you know that. They're so small, and their whole purpose is to leave me looking good for you — for my master — and to make me more...sensual.

"Isn't that the big part of it? It's what you're always saying that so much of this is for us to learn how to be attractive for a master, to make our bodies more accessible to him?

"Instead, all the leather and chains and studs that we have to wear tonight make us look hard. It's different when we see those things on you. It turns me on — a lot. But it's armor, it's stuff to keep your body from someone else.

"I wasn't so sure about this trip. I knew it was really for Marc. But now I'm glad I'm doing it too." He looked at Marc then. "This was what you got at the leather bars, wasn't it? All the bottoms dressed up in their metal and being hard-assed and throwing attitude?"

Marc nodded agreement. "It was one of the problems I had. The ones who looked the best were the ones who didn't really want what I did. They were the ones who sent out some kind of signal of strength and promised more than anyone else. But they turned the whole thing into a match.

"I'd seen signs for slave auctions in the city bars, too. I never got to one, but I understood they'd be like tonight. The other most common event I saw advertised was wrestling matches. Why! I mean, that's fine, if people want to do that. But why were they such a regular fantasy for so many people?

"I asked around a bit and I learned that it was really just this whole big system that was an excuse for the bottoms. 'If I lose a match, then he can do anything he wants with me.' That's still all right, if someone wants it. But I kept running into the attitude that it was all there was. That was all those people could think of doing. It didn't make a whole lot of sense to me. Submitting to a man you choose makes much more." He looked at me and blushed.

Yes, yes, this was all going to work.

* * *

The bar was packed when we arrived. There was a Mardi Gras feel to the place. The patrons filled the entire spectrum of a gay bar: Leather and denim were expected, but the charity event had brought in men in suits, others in pressed cotton slacks, and the younger ones who would be spending most of the season on the dance floor.

Marc and Tim looked around at the crowd and had a touch of nervousness about them. I led them to the back of the room and into the dressing area. Most of the other participants were already there. About a dozen men were drinking beer and a couple of them smoking joints. We were introduced around, and then my two young men began to change.

As it was all going on, I could only wish that these other men's costumes were honest indications of their desires. There was one redhead with truly spectacular muscles who was wearing only a leather jockstrap and his boots. He would have been such a fine specimen on the real auction block, a real prize for his buyer in The Network. Here, he was only playing a game. The "good cause" had given him an excuse to show off his hard-earned body. But his banter made it clear that he was more interested in the current voguish movies, than in casting himself in a supporting role.

There were also a pair of quite young men — no more than eighteen — who were going to present themselves in their underwear. They were clad only in bright white briefs and athletic stockings that covered their entire calves. They would have brought so much joy to a master who could have appreciated them. But they would be offered only to the ones in this common audience. I sighed, not really wanting to deny their purchasers the pleasures they would get tonight, but thinking of the unused potential the transactions would represent.

Not one of the men here really inspired me — other than my own two, who were quite something. They stripped down and began to get out the items that had been chosen and transported in duffle bags. They were much more at ease when they were naked than the other men expected. They made no move to either hide or expose themselves, but went about their work easily.

Marc pulled on a leather jock first. There were lines of small metal studs along the seams. Then he zipped on a pair of chaps. From the front, the effect was as though he had on a pair of leather pants, and the lines of white flesh that would show as he moved were small moments of personal pornography to me — and I'm sure the rest of the people who were watching him as well. It seemed that those glimpses of his bare thighs between the leather pieces were much more intimate than his total nudity had been.

His hairless torso was gleaming in the red light that came from the backstage fixtures. It was a fine body, smooth and hard, with more than enough definition to satisfy even the most discerning onlooker. He took out the plain white T-shirt that he had so carefully torn earlier. When he dragged it down over his head the natural-looking holes left both of his nipples bare. There was a tear down the side, as well, that left a swatch of his stomach exposed.

He put his boots on over his thick socks next. The final touches were the chains. The two had decided that Marc should wear most of the pieces that had been accumulated. A particularly heavy length was looped around and around his right ankle. It wasn't the subtle signal of a masochist who would have a single strand on his boot at most. Marc's looked as though it had a substantial weight to it; he looked like a real slave, not a playmate. Another, shorter piece of chain went around his right biceps. Then a third was put through a belt loop on his right waist. It went underneath his crotch and back up his ass to the same section of his belt; finally the ends were allowed to hang from the waistband of the chaps.

Tim was also wearing chaps. But his jockstrap was the more usual white elastic material. It didn't cover up the lines of his genitals the way Marc's heavy leather codpiece did. On the contrary, the shape of his cock and balls would be apparent to every eye. He also wore a pair of heavy black boots. But there was no shirt. Instead, he wore only a leather vest. Tim's hairy chest would be an attraction in and of itself. There was no reason to hide the thick rug that covered the two big pectorals and then dove into a neat and thin line as it fell down his belly into the athletic supporter.

Rather than chains from his side, we snapped a pair of handcuffs to the belt loop. His right ankle was adorned with a pair of tit clamps and their metal chain. It was a subtle little message, I thought, and I hoped that someone in the audience would pick it up.

I was changing as well. The role of bar performer is hardly one to which I aspire. I almost never enter the places anymore. But the evening's activities were all in fun and I had decided to join. I had older, much more worn clothes than Marc and Tim. I already had on my black leather pants and my boots. They weren't the new and unused footwear that so many of the others had on, but Tim had polished them to a remarkably high sheen earlier in the day. He had really accomplished a great feat in his labor. Of course, he had done it with a riding crop in his mouth, a little hint as to the payment he'd make if the work hadn't been satisfactory.

I decided that I wouldn't wear a shirt either. I wore only my heavy leather jacket. I also had on my leather cap — the other two were to go hatless. On our way to the bar Marc had stopped at a store and seen something that he insisted I had to have a part of my gear: a pair of reflector sunglasses. In the spirit of the evening, I had gone in and bought them. I put them on now and the effect seemed to be quite impressive — at least from what I could see of the way my redheaded friend was reacting to me. A pair of leather gloves finished off the outfit, and I felt ready for the event.

Outside this dressing area the sounds of the night's entertainment were getting louder. The two youngsters in the jockey shorts had already gone onstage and had been greeted with yells and screams of delight. I could hear the voice of the master of ceremonies as he made rude and embarrassing comments on the pair. A sudden surge of sound indicated that the sale had been completed and the prizes were being delivered.

Marc and Tim were ready; they were dressed; they were waiting. I could only guess what was going through their minds. Tim had to be imagining the scene at The Network. This is what it would be. I would have to convince him that it wasn't so, this wasn't even a hint of it. The fear he might be feeling now about walking out onto that stage was nothing compared to what would surge through his body when he was presented in the chambers of The Network. The slight anxiety of being humiliated in front of a crowd of strangers and then being sent off with one unknown person and being expected to perform a few sexual favors was meaningless compared to the sudden realization that years of his life were going to be decided for him in the hour or two of The Network auction. Still, I knew I could use tonight to help him get ready for the real thing.

Marc was just as shocked. These were the things he had thought about and dreamed of for so long. These were the acts that he had gone to cities to search out and had been so disappointed in. He stared at me quickly, as though he understood now just how much we were going to be doing together and how much we would mean to one another. He was here with me and his friend and he was doing these things. How could he? How could he have even crossed the line when it was cushioned by the thousands of miles of distance from his home? And what did it mean to him? Would he go backward? Could he? Did he want to? Those questions must have been coursing through his thoughts.

More men left the dressing room and went on to the stage as their names were called. We were to be the last. The organizer had been so taken with the possibilities that we represented that we were to be the stars of his little event. The redhead was the only other one left. I watched as he studied each of the three of us. His tongue would come out and wet his lips. Who did he want? I wondered. But the way he would look at my gloved hands while I smoked a cigarette gave away his desires.

"Let's get ready," I said to Marc and Tim. They moved toward me cautiously. The sounds of the full house of the bar were getting louder. They knelt in front of me. I reached into the closer of the two duffle bags and found the two leather collars that I had put there. I pulled them out and attached one to each young man's neck. I got out the leashes that matched the collars and attached them.

The redhead was entranced with all of it. He was studying the two young men, and I swore he was debating joining them on their knees. I looked at him and wondered if he'd dare ask. But someone came and beckoned him on to the stage. He'd be next. I pulled at my leashes, and Tim and Marc fell to their hands and knees and followed me to the edge of the stage so we could watch.

My interested and anxious redhead was clowning now, he'd left behind those hints of submission when he'd walked out in front of the crowd. His hands were thrown up in the air, as though he were a victor and not someone being sold. The image he presented now was much, much less interesting than what I had seen earlier. The small picture of his tiny tongue moving over his lips had been a hint of something that might have intrigued me. This was the usual boorishly macho image of the gay bar.

The men in the audience made lewd comments to him as the master of ceremonies theatrically pinched one of his tits, and he recoiled from the slight contact. "Fine slave," someone joked with a demeaning intent. I agreed. What a sham of decent manhood that he would react to such a little thing as fingers on his nipples? He had clearly been dreaming of so much more in our moments of silent communication.

Then he turned around and showed off his ass. It was not bad, not bad at all. The master of ceremonies gave it a good slap, and the redhead at least didn't recoil this time. The crowd laughed again. The redhead played to them a bit, mimicking one weightlifter's pose to display his considerable biceps and then another to show off his substantial chest.

The bidding began. I hadn't actually seen it before, and I was interested. Even though they were on their knees beside me, I knew that Marc and Tim were also studying it. It was in straight cash sums; all of it would go to the charity. The bids began at very small amounts. But that seemed to be on purpose, to allow many different men a sense that they were really taking part in the activities. The final offers were quite generous and seemed to be coming from only a few individuals. The lights were so bright that I couldn't make out any of their features. Only a few people right at the edge of the stage could be easily seen from where I stood.

Then the master of ceremonies was announcing the final opportunities to bid. "Going, going…" Something seemed to grip my chest. I hadn't expected that. I drew in a deep breath.

There was one final yell from the crowd, and then the redhead disappeared into the mass of men. We were next. The master of ceremonies made an introduction. Two men were going to be presented next, he said. These were the ones he expected the highest bids on. There was little, he implied, that couldn't be done to these "real" slaves so long as the purchaser stayed within the confines of health. Tim was startled to hear those words spoken. He knew I had had to have given permission. He must have been shocked to understand that any stranger was being told that he and Marc were even more available for even more acts than the rest of the men had been. But it was too late to object or protest — neither of which would have done him any good.

I tugged at their leashes and led the two crawling men onto the stage. A roar went up from the crowd even louder than any before. There was a round of applause. They were getting more from the three of us than they had from any of the others. We weren't awkward, and we weren't acting stupidly in response to this auction. They were two of the best-looking males in the room, their asses naked in the frame of their chaps. My hold on their leads was more than an act, and that must have been apparent to at least some of them.

I took the two young men to the center of the stage and then pulled up on the leashes sharply enough that Marc actually let his hands fly to his neck to protect it. He sheepishly caught himself and, to the enjoyment of many of the onlookers, dropped his hands back to his side. They thought they were ready for the sale, but I had made other arrangements. I reached into my pockets and took out two sets of tit clamps. The audience roared again as they saw me place one of the devices on each of the male's bodies.

Now we were ready. The master of ceremony began with Marc. He was petrified by the whole thing. He looked out into the crowd with a wild expression on his face that left his fear naked to anyone who would look at him. The sums bid for him began to climb quickly. I walked behind him, never letting up on my grip on his leash or on Tim's. I reached down and took hold of the torn T-shirt and pulled hard to rip away almost all of it. Only a few strips hung onto the neck. The crowd went wild, and a new wave of bids came in.

I knelt and reached in front of him. I whispered an obscenity into his ear, a promise of something I planned to do to him. He rubbed the side of the face against mine. I was playing with the cup of his codpiece, and the combination of the erotic words and the physical touch was too much. It overcame his stage fright. His cock was lengthening, and the tip crept up over the top of the leather. Someone in the crowd saw it and yelled to the rest of them to see what was going on. The size of his erection proved to be still another selling point. There was a further wave of offers.

I stood up and moved so that my leather-covered crotch was resting on the top of his head. There were more jeers and even more bids. Then, finally, the master of ceremonies announced the close of the auction. "Going, going…"

A hammer hit the lectern he was standing behind, and there was a round of applause for the lucky winner. I undid the leash to Marc's collar and stood him up. I gave him a kiss and slapped his bare ass to send him running off the stage and into the arms of his transient master.

Then I went to Tim. I knelt beside him, just as I had with Marc. I whispered into his ear too, but my message was different. "So you want to be sold to The Network," I said, my voice dripping with sarcasm. "And you want to have your contract bought. Then you might was well get used to it and take advantage of the practice. Let's see you show them some good reason to put out good money for you. What are you going to offer in exchange? These men are only after a good time for an evening. Can you show them you're worth it? If you can't, how do you expect to have someone in The Network believe that you are going to be worth any considerable sum?"

My lecture enraged him. He knew perfectly well that I didn't even believe it all myself. This wasn't The Network. This was a gay bar full of men, almost all of whom were just acting silly. But I had given him a challenge, and he was going to meet it.

He threw out his chest, pushing aside the vest and making sure that everyone could see the rubber-tipped clamps that were attached to his flesh. His arms went behind his back. He moved from side to side to make sure that they all got a good look at him. He did it all quite well, I thought. But the best moment came while the master of ceremonies was introducing him and making a jest about his "good training." As soon as it had been said, Tim leaned over and kissed each of my boots with a delicate and grace-ful gesture that didn't bring a yell from the crowd, but a moment of embarrassed silence. A lot of them suddenly understood that Tim and I meant these things to be serious.

The master of ceremonies broke into the awkwardness and began the auction. It went just as quickly as Marc's had. There were some men here who obviously were taken with Tim's body hair and with the very simple fact of the tit clamps. I heard remarks that proved that. I helped them along by lifting up the chain between the two clamps and pulling it enough that they could all see pieces of Tim's flesh pulled away from his torso.

The bidding war picked up even more. Tim seemed to want to put in his part as well. Or else he was trying to say something to me. He moved over and ran his tongue up and down the leg of my leather pants. The crowd went wild one more time.

When the master of ceremonies was making his final state-ments, "Going, going…" the price was the highest it had been for any sale all evening. I joined in the applause this time and sent Tim on his way to the buyer. The lights had kept any of us from seeing those faces back in the crowd. He couldn't possibly have known what the man would be like. I could only imagine the terror in his mind as he ran through the bodies that were pushing him to the goal they knew, even if he didn't.

The master of ceremonies and I shook hands and started to walk off the stage. The event was over. But then there was cry from the crowd. "*Sell the master!*" I took it as a joke and waved back as we kept on moving. "Yes, sell the master," another man yelled. The idea was infectious. Even before we could leave the stage, it seemed as though the whole audience had taken it up.

The master of ceremonies grabbed my arm and said, "Why not?" I stared at him. I had no intention of allowing this to go on. I tried to take my arm out of his grip, but he kept on talking, "It's for a good cause, and you're what they want right now. Come on, your friends did it."

The audience took our hesitation as agreement, and the applause was thundering. I gave in. It was only a joke, I reminded myself. I was being sold as a "master" and while that might offend me, this was simply a resort community. This was — as I had told Marc and Tim — a break in the intensity of our lives in the mountains. Why not…

Why not, indeed. I stood in the center of the stage. I refused to posture, but my natural stance with my hands on my belt was more than satisfactory for the crowd. There was a continual flow of lewd remarks about the shape of my genitals in my pants, questions about the worth of a bid for the sake of getting hold of the prize inside. The master of ceremonies began with a lecture, reminding the men that this was a different sale altogether. He teased them by saying that they should remember that they needed to question more than whether they could afford the cost, they had to wonder if they could afford the consequences of winning the auction.

There were loud guffaws and more clapping. And then it started. The lights were what set it off in my mind. They blinded me the moment I took off my dark glasses. I couldn't see the faces of the crowd. They were all anonymous. That was the beginning. Then the jokes, the crude remarks — this wasn't the closed world of The Network; this wasn't a study in elegance; there was no safety in its ritual.

I was there — in The Network. I could only vaguely bring myself back to this place and realize that the master of ceremonies had begun the bidding on me. *They are bidding on a master,* I reminded myself. But the memories were too powerful, they were too intense. I looked down at the lights that shone up from the edge of the stage to blind me. Instead I saw a mirrored surface. It was years ago. I wasn't dressed leather, and I didn't have on any glasses to hide the expression of my eyes. I was naked, kneeling on a mirrored table...

Now — in my mind — the faces came into focus, and they filled me with fear. I saw them — the men and the women of all races. There were Asians whose long nails clawed delicately at my chest and Africans whose intentions were as primeval as the forests they came from. Then there was a woman, a gorgeous woman with a full skirt and fine make-up who lingered so long in front of my table that I was sure that she would be the one.

But she wasn't. I knew who it would be when he was standing there. He was tall and substantial looking. He put a hand on my cheek and lifted my head up to look at me more closely. There was nothing to hide behind on that day. That day was so long ago, but this act of being here on this stage made me remember all the little details.

The master of ceremonies was shouting out to repeat the bids that came from the audience. I looked at him and barely comprehended what he was doing. It was so insignificant compared to that day so many years ago when a much more august auctioneer had held my fate in his hands. His sale had been silent, communicated only with the hand motions of the guests who sat in regal and silent comfort while the proceedings went on. When they were over, I was the one who was taken from the stage — but not in leather finery to make me look more like a fantasy of one of these men in a crowded bar. Oh, no, I was taken naked and totally, utterly vulnerable to that man, that one man who...

"Going, going, gone!" The hammer went down on the lectern, and I was standing there, sold. I was dripping perspiration. It was gluing my body hair to the lining of the leather jacket. I couldn't quite get myself back together. The memories were still coming so strongly that I wasn't back here in the bar yet.

I was stunned. How could memories be forced so far back in one's consciousness and then be so suddenly released? I hadn't really thought of that evening where I'd been introduced to The Network with that much detail in years. Now, on the stage, it had forced itself to the forefront of my mind. I had to get away from it and return...

"So you're my master," the man said. He had climbed up on the stage to claim his prize. Joseph. I smiled at him. He put an arm around my shoulders, and we climbed down off the stage.

Unwritten Chapters

Tim got back to the room before Marc. I was glad, I wanted some time alone with him. He smiled when he saw me in the bed. "Come here," I said. He walked over to me. I reached up and gently drew him onto the mattress. I wrapped my arms around him and kissed him. He was startled at first, but soon his arms came up and embraced me.

"Get undressed," I whispered into his ear. He jumped off the mattress and took off the leather clothing from last night's auction. I stripped too. Now we both climbed under the covers. I carefully rolled him onto his back and then climbed on him. He obediently spread his legs to accommodate my hardening cock. I kissed him more, enjoying the sensation of having my whole torso laid out on his hairy flesh. I lifted myself up on my elbows so I could look down onto his face. He was staring back, a little puzzled, but obviously pleased.

I reached over to the nightstand and got out a condom and lubricant. He started to reach for them, but I stopped him and unraveled the latex onto my erection and greased it up myself. Then I once again pressed my weight onto him. His legs moved up and around my waist to give me easy access. I took advantage of the position and let my cock move against the ring of muscle that guarded his anus.

I slipped past into the warm insides. I moved my hips carefully and luxuriously. I let myself — and him — enjoy a slow, casual fuck. My whole length would slide back and forth, drawing the most intense reactions from him. There was no assault in this; this was lovemaking, and he seemed to understand that from the very beginning.

I kept on kissing him, letting my lips move from his forehead to his mouth, then over his cheeks and down to his neck. I still had my elbows supporting me, and I could run my hands through his thick hair. I played with his beard, never pulling it or tugging it the way I might have another time, but letting my fingers weave their way through its strands, even sucking on the wiry hair at one point.

He wasn't in control of his reactions to the strong, deliberate fucking I was giving him. His legs would move with quick jerks, then they'd pull me into him like the arms of a vise. His hands tried to simply rest on my shoulders, but the constant pumping of my hips made him clutch hold of me at times. After a number of minutes, he was kissing me wildly. I kept back my orgasm and simply kept it up. I wanted him to remember this. There wasn't going to be another one like it in a long time.

I rolled him onto his side so I could reach my head down and suck in one of his nipples. He froze, preparing for my teeth to attack his delicate tits. But I only played with them with my lips. My tongue was all that ran over the sensitive surface. The new contact made him even more frenzied.

My hands were on the sides of his buttocks. I began to move them. One came around to wedge itself between our bellies and find his hard cock. I played with it gently. All the time that I kept up that insistent fucking, I ran my fingertips over the surface of his erection. I started to grip his cock harder and make my manipulations more intense only when I knew that I couldn't hold either one of us back much longer.

I picked up the tempo of my fucking then. I moved more quickly, and my actions let him know I was close to coming. I kissed him full on the mouth, and our tongues played with each other. My hand was driving him further and further while our bellies slapped against each other. When we came it was as close to perfectly timed orgasms as I think I've ever known. Just as my cock was pulsing against the walls of his ass, his own was sending waves of hot fluid out of its slit onto both our stomachs.

It was over. A whole lot of things were over. I gently pulled out of him. He was sprawled on his back on the mattress, one arm was over his head. He was clearly exhausted. He was also impressed. His eyes had a slight glaze to them. We hadn't had that kind of sex before — ever.

I didn't say anything. I got out of the bed and went into the bathroom and showered. He joined me in a very short time. He must have expected more of the same affection. But I ignored him. He began to soap up my body as he had so often in the past. He moved languidly over my chest and shoulders. Then, with a move he clearly didn't expect, I pushed him onto his knees. The stream of water from the showerhead was raining down on him. He looked up at me, almost shocked. But the intent was obvious. He lathered my genitals and then his hands washed my thighs, my calves and finally my feet.

I turned around, and he went over the whole bottom half of my body from the rear. I could feel him washing my ass and the backs of my knees. When he was done I rinsed off and stepped out of the stall.

He came right after me. His eyes were red from having been in the path of the shower for so long. But I didn't say a thing. I stood there, and he realized I expected him to dry me off. He took one of the big bath towels and went about his work silently. There was an obvious expression of anger mixed with confusion on his face. He didn't understand the sudden transformation I'd gone through.

Then I went into the bedroom and got dressed. He came out after he'd wiped himself dry and stood there awkwardly. "Get some clothes on," I said. He nodded and got out a pair of jeans and a T-shirt. When he had them on I sent him down to the lobby to fetch a cup of coffee for me. He came back with two; one was obviously supposed to be for him. I took one of the cups and poured it out the window He stared at me in disbelief. But I think he understood at that moment that we'd come to an important milestone in his training. It was time for us to prepare for the end.

I took one of the comfortable chairs, and he knelt by my side while we waited. Marc wasn't much longer. I had just finished drinking my coffee when he came through the door. I stood up and met him, giving him a kiss and a strong hug to welcome him.

"You smell good. Have you already showered?"

"Yes," he said.

"Fine. Just jump into some street clothes, and we'll go out. I don't think the villagers are ready for your bare ass in the morning."

"Okay." He turned and said something in greeting to Tim who was still kneeling by the chair. The other young man didn't answer but only stared at the floor. Marc didn't seem to notice or else didn't take it seriously. Perhaps he thought that he'd walked into one of our discipline sessions. He simply pulled off the auction clothes and got into an outfit much like Tim's — jeans and a T-shirt and running shoes.

The three of us left the room and walked onto the main street. "What was your night like?" I asked Marc.

"It was fine. Very uneventful. The guy wasn't unattractive, but he wasn't into much either. He was more intrigued than anything else, I think. He liked the leather and asked me to keep it on when we got back to his house. He didn't really want to do much of anything. I think he was embarrassed about the circumstances. It had all seemed pretty hot to him at the bar, but when he was faced with a stranger he couldn't follow through. We talked for a long time, and we went to bed. He did ask me to sleep with just the chaps on — I thought that was hot. When I was almost asleep he reached over and began to play with me and with himself. He ended up jerking us both off.

"This morning — like so many of the tricks I've had before — he couldn't even talk about it. He made me breakfast and got very worried about me walking through town with nothing over my behind. He made me promise I'd take some back streets to get home." He laughed. He liked the story.

"You? I saw you and Joseph go off together. What happened?"

"A lot of things — not that much sexual. We talked a great deal. I had a chance to think through what I'm doing and what's happening between us."

"That sounds heavy."

I had to admit that I'd spoken with a very portentous tone. Before Marc had a chance to say anything else — and before he could notice that Tim hadn't taken any part in our conversation — I led them into one of the fine gift shops.

The clerks were helpful as we walked through the store. I kept asking Marc what he thought of various potential purchases. Did he think this clock would look good in my study? What about these candlesticks in the living room? I wasn't terribly surprised when he fell right into the conversations. I had even — after last night's introspection — expected him to.

We ended up with a pile of boxes. The pleased shopkeeper took my credit card and processed the sale while one of his helpers put our things in two large bags. When it was all completed, the clerk passed the bags over the counter. Marc went to take one of them. I stopped him. "Tim will carry them."

He was startled, but wasn't going to argue with me. We kept on with our shopping. After that time in the first shop, I watched carefully to see what assumptions both young men would make. It was uncanny. I had predicted everything perfectly. Tim never spoke a single word for the next two hours. He glowered for a while, but then seemed to fall into his role of porter, quickly and efficiently taking the parcels. At one point I told him to run back to the guest house and unload the armful he had accumulated. He did it, and, when he caught up with us again, he was out of breath — he had actually run the whole distance.

One of the last stops was a menswear shop, one of the most stylish in the South. We passed the underwear section and I stopped at one display. Marc came up and stood beside me. There was a whole collection of silk garments. "We should buy some for you. It'll make you feel more erotic. The fabric will cling to you and caress you. You still have a lot to learn about becoming more voluptuous. This could help you."

"You just want to feel it on me," he joked.

"Of course I do," I answered. "You should know that by now. Which styles should we buy? Which colors?" We went through the selection and I ended up taking a half-dozen assorted pair to the counter.

"But you've only bought one of each," Marc said. "What about Tim?"

Over lunch I explained that this was our last day. I'd already booked our passage back to New England. That was the reason for the spree. I hadn't expected either one to argue, and neither did. When we got back to the room, they went about packing. We ate our dinner — one of those packaged abominations — on the jet as it flew north.

I drove the car from the Boston airport in complete silence. They didn't speak either — as much from fatigue as anything else, I think, though they both had to have questions and thoughts about my actions.

When we got to the house in the mountains, I walked in first. I had left the heat on very low, only high enough to keep the pipes from freezing. It was cold inside. I went to the fireplace where wood was already laid out and took a match to start the flame going.

Marc and Tim came in soon after, each with his arms loaded with luggage and other packages. I stood up and told Marc to stay with me. Tim was to get the rest of our things out of the car. I took a seat on the couch, and Marc came and sat beside me. I put an arm around his shoulder, and he leaned into me. There were occasional noises as Tim came in and out of the doorway.

"I have it all," he finally said. He was standing in the doorway looking at the homey scene that Marc and I must have composed.

"Why are you in those clothes?" was my only response.

"It's cold." I could tell from the petulant sound of his voice that he knew he'd made a mistake.

"First of all, strip. Then go and unpack all of our things. When you're done, bring a leather paddle downstairs so I can punish you for your insolence."

"Yes, sir."

Marc started to get up. He already had a hand on his top shirt button. He obviously expected that the order referred to him as well.

"Stop," I said.

"Aren't I just a slave too?" He was angry, and there was a hint of defiance in the way he sat.

"No. Actually, you're not. You agreed to take a vacation and to try certain things. That was the limit to what we had decided. The trip is over and so are your obligations."

I went over to the bar and poured each of us a drink. I brought them back to the couch and handed him his.

"Then what happens now?" he asked.

"We can make an arrangement, or we can end it all."

"Just like that," he said.

"There aren't a great number of options now."

"What are you offering me?"

I turned and looked at him, wondering just what he meant.

He seemed to understand my confusion. "You've always said that The Network contracts gave the slaves some things — money, at least."

"That's true," I said. "I'm prepared to put you through college. I'll cover all the expenses. In addition, I'll deposit money in a savings account for you every month that you remain here in this house." I mentioned a specific sum that seemed more than adequate. "In return, you'll agree to provide any and all sexual services I request…"

"Including the sadistic ones?"

"Yes. Including the sadistic ones in all ways. I expect you to dress as I tell you to, spend your time only as I approve of it, travel with me when I desire."

"And if there's a… 'friend' who wants me, you'll expect me to go with him, just as I did at the resort after the auction?"

"Yes. I could add that it will happen very, very infrequently. But that would have to be a part of the agreement."

"How long will this last?"

"Quite possibly for the rest of our lives."

"Just like that? We're going to be lovers?"

"We've started falling in love already, haven't we?"

"Probably a long time ago — at least we started a long time ago."

"I'm only asking you to admit that it's happening."

"And you think that it will happen more easily and more effectively if we structure everything this way?"

"I underestimated you, Marc. I wasn't sure you understood that part of it. But, yes, I think we'll fall in love more easily if we start this way."

"How can we? You aren't falling in love with Tim."

"Aren't I? I think I am. But in a totally different way."

"Then, this…relationship of ours could change? It might not stay this way?"

"I strongly doubt we'll ever put a white picket fence around the house, if that's what you're asking. For now, you're young and inexperienced. You've proven that you are perfectly capable of not facing many things in your life and of messing up many others. For the next few years you're going to put your life in my hands, and I'm going to see if I can't do a decent job of getting you going in certain directions. In return, you're going to give me a kind of sexuality that I want.

"When this chapter is over, then we'll have to renegotiate."

"But you do admit there's a time when that will happen?"

"Yes. I know it will. There are going to be a lot of things that will happen in the time to come."

"Is this the stuff that you learned while we were away?"

"Some of it." I didn't want to discuss too much of that. There were still parts of my conversation with Joseph that were painful to recall. "I was remembering all that's happened to me over the years and all the alterations my life has gone through." That was as much as I wanted to admit now.

"I don't understand," he pressed. "What could happen to change how you want me?"

"How you want to be." That was the key. I turned and looked at him carefully. "You're young. This might not be the place you'll stay. You're going to pay for the education you're going to receive in the next few years — trust me, you're going to pay. And I don't mean the college diploma that you're going to receive from it. That's one of the most minor points, in fact.

"Your education is a series of lessons in sexuality that hardly any people ever receive in this world. Living in this house is going to expose you to options of erotic life that you've never dreamt about. You can't know how you'll react to them all now. It may take years for you to understand the many attractions. But you're going to have the opportunity to explore.

"I'm going to be your guide. That's why you're going to have to put so much faith in all of my decisions. I'm going to take you on a tour of the senses that you couldn't even map out for yourself. When it's done? Well, if we're both honest and we're both intent on the learning that you have to do, we'll undoubtedly be in love. But it might not mean that you'll be here with me when it's over — at least not in the way we're going to start."

"You're going to be my Network."

"No. In fact, that's one of the things I've realized. The Network is totally different. Anyone who enters it does it all alone. There is the constant threat that other forces will intrude and change the location, the cast of characters, the action — all of it. There is no control, and there is no constant in The Network. That's why what's going to happen to you and to Tim will be totally different.

"I'm offering you a life with me where the outcome isn't settled. It could go in many different directions. Tim won't have your security, and he won't have your options. He can hope for companionship on his road, but there's no assurance he's going to get it.

"I allowed him to have Sven. I even allowed him to have you while you were being introduced to so many things. But this is the end of your friendship with him. It's the beginning of your life with me — if you want it — and the start of the final phase of his education."

At that moment, Tim appeared in the doorway. He was naked. The leather paddle was in his hand. He looked at me and then at Marc with a slight sense of fear. That same fear had made his cock half hard. It hung heavily down from his body. He was going to do very well in The Network.

The furnace had been turned on, but it hadn't really warmed up the house yet. There were bumps on Tim's skin, visible even through the thick body hair.

"Kneel down facing the fire," I said calmly. "Put your forehead on the floor, spread your legs and lift up your ass."

He moved quickly to do what I said. The paddle was left on the floor beside him. It wasn't fear that was making him shiver now, it was the anticipation.

"Marc, pick up the paddle."

Marc looked at me for a brief moment and seemed to hesitate. But then he stood up and went and got the paddle. He was standing beside the naked, kneeling figure.

"Beat him."

Marc looked at the leather in his hand and then down at the young man who only a few months ago was his roommate. I wondered if he remembered just how intensely important it had been to Tim that other slaves and he not be separated. But now these two were being divided into starkly different classes.

Marc gripped the leather handle and then let it fall on Tim's waiting buttocks. "Harder! It's not a sign of affection. He failed his duties."

The leather went through the air again and this time it landed with a resounding slam. "That's more like it," I said. He lifted up the paddle again and delivered another blow. Then another.

It took about six before he made Tim cry out. Then another half dozen before he was in tears. I wouldn't let Marc stop until I could hear the sobs.

"Tim, get a sleeping bag out of the closet. From now on, you're to stay at the foot of the bed at night. Only Marc will be sleeping with me. You're to consider him a master over you and fulfill every one of his requests quickly — if not, you'll be punished.

"You," I said to Marc, "are to use him as you want. Take advantage of the next couple of months. It may be a long time before you're able to have his chance with another man. He's going into The Network. He's no longer another guy who's going to have his sexuality with a partner in privacy, and he's no longer the man who you knew for years. He's different — he's chosen to be different. If you spare that paddle, if you let him forget what his mouth and ass are for, if you let him think that life can be some little game, you'll only do him a disservice.

"He's committed himself to a certain path and anything that lets him forget that is not kindness. Not at all."

*   *   *

It took them a month, really, to accept what had happened and how it all changed their relationship. Marc was like the unsophisticated customer who can't accept the gracious attention of a waiter in a fine restaurant at first. He'd apologize for making requests. He'd put his desire in the most ambiguous language. He wouldn't really be able to pull back far enough to make himself comfortable with the idea of someone serving him.

It was especially difficult because he was having to have to learn my desires at the same time. He was caught between the two roles — both of them my demands. He was to learn his place in relation to me, and at the same time he was to take part in Tim's training.

They were so uncomfortable at the start that they would occasionally break into smiles. I took care of that soon enough. It wasn't fair to punish Marc when it happened. It also invited him to take an escape route that would make him feel better: He could take the abuse and think he was being noble by doing that rather than disciplining Tim himself. I solved it by declaring that Tim would always have to assume the responsibility for any falling short they did.

It only took one session with Tim under a lash to convince Marc that he was doing his old friend no good by not demanding service.

But Marc didn't really have to do that much. Tim, it turned out, was the one who understood that this was the time he had to use to prepare himself. He had his last contact with the "real world" taken away from him — Marc. And to make it all the more emphatic, he had to live in my house with that same person constantly reminding him that a line had been crossed.

His passage wasn't yet irrevocable, but it was getting very close to that and he knew it. It was — finally — the most important lesson I had to give him. Here was his old friend, now being groomed to take over the duties of running the household. Tim had no choice but to accept this new ruler in addition to myself.

He threw himself into it. I would pass by a doorway and overhear a conversation: "No, you should make me do that." Or: "Just tell me, please, don't ask."

The final proof came sexually. They had permission — even orders — to have sex. I came across the bedroom one day and could spy on them inside it without their knowledge. I watched as Marc asked for sex. He didn't make the request with any sense of power at all. But, as I watched, Tim walked over to him and knelt down with a movement of astonishing grace.

I recognized it as one that he'd seen Sven accomplish many times. On his knees, before he even moved to put on Marc's condom, Tim's hands went to the side of his loincloth and untied it so it fell to the floor. He did it in a way that seemed to show that he shouldn't have any clothing on when he was about to serve a master.

Marc saw the action and put a hand on Tim's head. It seemed as though he was really trying to comfort him. But Tim took the action in a manner that a slave would, as a gesture of great kindness from a lord. He moved into the hand as it stayed by his face, and I could see him kiss it.

Only after all of these fine gestures did Tim take a condom and carefully — almost reverently — put it on Marc's now hard cock. When it was stretched over the erect flesh, Tim moved forward and kissed it gently. Only then did he open his mouth and let the whole of it slide in.

I watched them while they went through the entire sex act together. I saw the way that Tim's throat struggled to keep all of Marc inside. I carefully looked at the wonderful way that Marc's hip muscles worked as they pumped at Tim. They were quite beautiful with one another.

I watched to see if there was any sign that Marc would have the indications, the inclinations...

But I didn't see them — yet. I wondered. I wondered what would happen to him. In the years ahead it might be that he and I would go together to an auction to find some slave who would have to satisfy us both. Or it might be that I would have to take Marc there, myself, and leave him.

The thought hurt. It was foolish of me. Those were things in the far, far future. He had so much to learn, and I had so much to learn about him.

I wondered how this next stage of my life would work. I now had Marc. There was so much that would happen to us. I had little idea what it would be. If I had bought a slave at auction, I would have known — I would have been certain what the outcome would be. But that hadn't happened. I had insisted on having my own story.

Now, I would have to wait to have it unfold. I had done this before — when I had climbed on a mirrored glass table years ago and hadn't known what could possibly come next.

So, all three of us were waiting for our chapters to be written. Marc and I here, in my house in the mountains. And Tim, who would soon know what it felt like to be naked on a leash, being led on hands and knees, toward a line of glass tables...

Alyson publishes a wide variety of books for
gay men, lesbians, and their children. To receive
our mailings, please send your request to

Alyson Publications Inc.
P.O. Box 4371
Los Angeles, California 90078-4371
or E-mail: Alyson@advocate.com